MAY

Yngve's hand was shaking slightly as he finely tuned in the proper digital sequence, and his hopes for success were high when the door to the radio room burst open and Otto Brauer, the rough-looking, brown-haired man who had initially greeted him from the bow of the first Zodiac, quickly entered the compartment. His heavily lined, beard-stubbled face was flushed, and a look of pure contempt emanated from his blue eyes when he spotted Yngve at the radio console.

"You stupid Norwegian bastard!" he cursed as he lifted up the barrel of his Uzi, adding with finality, "*Auf Wiedersehen*, Viking."

Yngve knew that his luck had run out. His final thoughts before the Uzi's bullets ripped into his body were of his beloved bride and the baby that he'd never live to see.

Also by Richard P. Henrick

ECOWAR

Available from HarperPaperbacks

ICE WOLF

RICHARD P. HENRICK

HarperPaperbacks
A Division of HarperCollins*Publishers*

HarperPaperbacks   *A Division of* HarperCollins*Publishers*
10 East 53rd Street, New York, N.Y. 10022

Copyright © 1994 by Richard P. Henrick
All rights reserved. No part of this book may be used or
reproduced in any manner whatsoever without written
permission of the publisher, except in the case of brief
quotations embodied in critical articles and reviews. For
information address HarperCollins*Publishers,*
10 East 53rd Street, New York, N.Y. 10022.

Cover illustration by John Berkey

First printing: August 1994

Printed in the United States of America

HarperPaperbacks and colophon are trademarks of
HarperCollins*Publishers*

❖ 10 9 8 7 6 5 4 3 2 1

To the seekers of the Grail—strength to lift
the veil on this holiest of eternal quests.

ICE WOLF

How you are fallen from heaven, O Day Star, son of Dawn!

How you are cut down to the ground, you who laid the nations low!

You said in your heart, "I will ascend to heaven; above the stars of God. I will set my throne on high. I will sit on the mount of assembly in the far south. I will ascend above the heights of the clouds, and will make myself like the Most High."

But you are instead brought down to Sheol, imprisoned in the icy, black depths of the Pit.

—ISAIAH 14:12–15

PART I

FIRE AND ICE

Follow Hitler! But always remember, he is only the puppet, and I am the one who pulls the strings. For I have initiated him into the Sacred Doctrines, opened his centres of vision, and given him the means to communicate with the Powers beyond.

—DIETRICH ECKHART, DECEMBER 1923

I move like a sleepwalker, where Providence dictates.

—ADOLF HITLER

1

Judean Wilderness—the Present

A slight flicker of movement diverted Shai Weinberg's glance to the downward sloping trail lying immediately before him. He halted instinctively, his pulse quickening in dread as he caught sight of the sand-colored, three-foot-long serpent that blocked his way. Another stride and Shai would have stepped on the slithering reptile, whose triangular-shaped head hinted at its deadliness.

But Shai was no stranger to this particular species of poisonous viper, whose nickname was "twenty paces" in honor of the limited distance a doomed man supposedly traveled after being bitten by one, and his fear quickly turned to loathing. He unstrapped his M16, and after double-checking that the safety was engaged, he smashed the snake's head with the rifle's flat butt. Only last month, a snake like this one had bitten his pet Labrador retriever near the Qumran site just north of here. Shai was nearby at the time and could only look on in horror as his faithful companion of three years managed but a single pained whimper before succumbing to the venom.

It took another rifle blow to finish smashing the snake's head. While its body wildly writhed in its death throes, Shai wiped clean the butt of the rifle in a patch of white sand, then reslung it over his shoulder and continued on his way.

The confrontation was all but forgotten by the time he rounded the next switchback and spotted a familiar collection of canvas tents on the valley floor. A spiraling plume of gray smoke rose from a central campfire, beside which squatted a single white-robed figure. Shai recognized Gamal, their bedouin cook.

The trail steepened, and Shai increased his pace, anxious to reach the campsite and complete the chore his father had sent him on. The climb down from the dig site had so far taken him more than a quarter of an hour. When he had started off, the sun was just showing itself on the eastern horizon, yet already the air had been thick and hot.

As a Sabra, Shai was accustomed to the desert heat. He had practically been raised in the Negev, and had long since learned to respect the harsh climate of his native land. A wiry eighteen-year-old, he had grown even tougher during his recently concluded basic training in the Israeli Defense Force, and now proudly wore his uniform of black paratrooper boots, khaki shorts, and short-sleeve mesh shirt, whose shoulder epaulets displayed the winged insignia of his airborne regiment.

Ignoring the sweat that constantly dripped down his forehead, Shai crossed over the boulder-strewn remains of a dry wadi and began to descend a series of steep rock steps. This rough stone stairway, which led directly to the edge of their campsite, had originally been placed on this hillside over two millennia ago.

"Uncle Jake!" he yelled toward the collection of pointed roof tents.

"The professor has yet to show himself this morning," Gamal informed him from the campfire. "His light was on well into the night."

Shai moved to join the bedouin and watched him reach out and carefully remove a dented, fire-scarred saucepan from the red-hot crackling embers. The light of the fire clearly illuminated the Arab's wrinkled, beard-stubbled face, the skin of which resembled nothing so much as sun-dried brown leather.

"Here, he'll need this," Gamal said as he poured the muddied contents of the pan into a chipped, white porcelain mug.

Shai took the now scaldingly hot cup and winced in pain. Not about to give the Arab the satisfaction of displaying any weakness, he gripped the mug's handle and proceeded through the closed flaps of the nearest tent.

It was dark inside, and it took several seconds for his eyes to adjust. The hoarse sounds of snoring drew him to the structure's sole cot, where the shirtless figure of the man he was to return to the dig site lay asleep on his back.

For as long as Shai could remember, Jacob Litvak had been a close family friend. Though he was not related to the Weinbergs by blood, Shai fondly called the forty-three-year-old professor of archaeology Uncle Jake, and looked up to him as a role model. A Russian by birth, Jacob Litvak grew up in the dark days of the Cold War. Against all odds, he managed to escape the Soviet Union and get a Western education at Harvard University. Then, with two degrees in hand, he returned to his homeland, where he diligently worked his way up to the top of his field, becoming one of the world's leading archaeologists. Litvak's research was world-renowned and often publicized by the media, his face appearing on the covers of newspapers, magazines, and professional journals around the world, but it was hard to reconcile this fact with the figure snoring away before Shai's proud eyes—in rumpled khaki trousers, with holes in his threadbare socks and a well-worn faded green bush hat covering his face.

Feeling guilty to disturb his slumber, Shai took a moment to examine the contents of the drafting table set up beside the cot. Assembled here was a battery-powered lamp, several pairs of long, tapered tweezers, and a large, vise-mounted magnifying glass, beneath which he saw a dozen jagged, postage-stamp-size strips of brittle yellow parchment, etched with faded, black Hebrew characters. Several of these fragments had already been pieced together, revealing some sort of document. Shai assumed that the assembling of this ancient jigsaw puzzle had kept the archaeologist busy until the wee hours of the morning.

"Uncle Jake," he whispered, finally summoning up the courage to carry out his task.

When this halfhearted attempt failed to produce results, Shai cleared his throat and called out, *"Uncle Jake, you've got to wake up!"*

Again the archaeologist failed to stir, prompting Shai to reach out with his free hand and shake Litvak's shoulder. At his touch, the rhythmic pattern of Litvak's snores was momentarily interrupted. Shai shook him again.

"Come on, Uncle Jake. Rise and shine!"

With the slowness of a zombie rising from the dead, Jacob Litvak stirred groggily. "What the hell time is it?" he mumbled hoarsely.

"Sorry for the early wake-up call, Uncle Jake," Shai answered. "But there's been an important find in the cave, and Father wanted you up there for a firsthand look."

All but ignoring the young man's revelation, the archaeologist lazily stretched his arms overhead, yawned, and pushed aside his bush hat, revealing a square, beard-stubbled jaw, aquiline nose that had been broken in a fall and never properly set, sharp angular cheekbones, and bloodshot blue eyes, which covetously locked on the mug that Shai timidly held out like a peace offering.

Shai noted his interest and nodded. "This coffee's for you, Uncle Jake."

Litvak sat up stiffly and reached for the mug. While he took his first tentative sip, Shai seated himself on the long-legged stool beside the drafting table.

"Gamal must have learned how to prepare this swill he passes for coffee from a Muscovite," Jacob observed bitterly after gulping down a mouthful of the scalded brew. He spat out some coffee grounds, then asked, "Now, what's this about a new find?"

"One of the bedouin diggers found a previously sealed alcove in the rear of the cave earlier this morning," Shai readily replied. Father feels that its integrity was compromised during yesterday's earthquake."

"And this alcove's contents?" Jacob's curiosity was piqued.

"Father has already uncovered several coins originating from the time of Herod. He's also found a large cache of incense and, most importantly, what appears to be an intact, three-foot-tall clay scroll jar."

This last detail aroused Litvak's complete attention. "Intact, you say?"

"So it appears," Shai answered, watching the archaeologist gulp down the rest of his coffee and then reach out for a wrinkled blue cotton shirt that had been balled up at the foot of the cot.

"Then perhaps the diary was correct after all," Jacob muttered while hastily dressing.

Shai sensed Litvak's excitement and returned his attention to the contents of the drafting table. He switched on the battery-powered light and peered through the magnifying lens at the pieced-together scroll fragments. Though the penmanship of the scribe who had written the faded Hebrew letters left much to be desired, Shai was to translate the document.

"'How you are fallen from heaven, O Day Star, son of Dawn!'" he said aloud. "'How you are cut down to the ground, you who laid the nations low!' Isn't this from Isaiah, Uncle Jake?"

"Isaiah fourteen, verse twelve, to be exact," Jacob

answered as he laced up his boots. "Interestingly enough, the fallen angel called the Day Star is in fact Lucifer, making this the only place in the Old Testament where the devil is directly referred to by name."

"I wonder how this particular version compares with our modern-day translation?" Shai asked as he continued his study of the remaining fragments.

"The two are remarkably similar," Jacob answered. "The translation retains the power of the original."

Using the tweezers, Shai carefully inserted one of the loose scroll fragments into the bottom portion of the document, turning it several times before it fit properly. Once he was satisfied with its placement, he was able to piece together several more missing fragments, revealing, in the process, another verse.

"'But you are instead brought down to Sheol, imprisoned in the icy, black depths of the Pit,'" Jacob translated, now fully dressed and standing directly behind Shai, massaging the tight muscles of the young man's shoulders. "Shall we see what great mysteries await us in the black depths of our own dig site?"

Needing no more prompting, Shai put down the tweezers, switched off the lamp, and followed Jacob out of the tent. A sunny cloudless blue sky greeted them. After taking a moment to stretch his slim, six-foot three-inch frame, Jacob picked up a cypress walking stick that lay beside the tent flap and gazed up at the heavens, where a single vulture lazily circled.

"Good morning, effendi," Gamal's accented voice called out from the nearby campfire.

Jacob addressed the cook without taking his eyes off the soaring vulture. "Looks like we've got some hungry company up there, Gamal. I just hope that he's not waiting for victims of your infamous coffee."

Gamal's leathery face lit up with a grin as Jacob met his glance then hid his eyes behind a pair of aviator-style sunglasses, smoothed back his full mop of black hair, and covered it with his bush hat.

As Shai began to walk up the sloping trail, Jacob gazed at the twisting path that led up the marbled hillside. No plant life of any sort was visible here, only bleached rock for as far as the eye could see. Gripping the smooth handle of his walking stick, Jacob crossed the dusty clearing and began to climb.

It didn't take him long to work up a sweat, and by the time he stepped over the smashed corpse of a desert viper, his forehead and upper torso were soaked. No matter how long he stayed in this godforsaken region, he could never get used to the stifling heat. Here it was well into autumn, and afternoon temperatures were still approaching the one-hundred-degree mark. He wondered how the religious zealots who settled in these hills two thousand years ago had been able to survive it.

As he negotiated a narrow switchback Jacob saw Shai climbing a particularly steep portion of the trail a good seventy feet above him, and he readied himself for the most difficult portion of the ascent. With a minimum of switchbacks, the trail here led to a plateau over 550 feet above the campsite. Here, their current dig was located.

The muscles of his legs were cramping, his clothes were soaked, and his heart was pounding in his chest by the time he reached the summit, where he gratefully joined Shai, who was also recovering from the ascent. Gradually his heartbeat slowed, and after wiping his forehead dry, he focused on the magnificent vista that lay before him beyond the edge of the plateau.

Filling the eastern horizon were the dark blue waters of the Dead Sea, the gray hills of Jordan visible beyond the distant shoreline. The valley here was the lowest point on the earth's surface, thirteen hundred feet below sea level. What with the blistering heat of the sun making the air feel like the inside of a hot oven, Jacob knew that he presently stood closer to the eternal fires of Hades than anywhere else on the planet.

To the immediate north lay a seemingly endless expanse of limestone. It was in this direction that the famous Qumran site lay, with Jericho and the lush Jordan River valley visible in the far distance.

Hearing a muted roaring sound coming from the south, toward the isolated, sunbaked wilderness of the Negev, Jacob turned. As the roar intensified Shai pointed out a sleek jet aircraft, and seconds later they watched a tight triangular formation of three metallic-gray F-16 fighters zoom overhead. The planes, which carried a full load of bombs and missiles, were so close that their pilots were visible as well as the dark red Star of David insignias on their wing tips. Jacob's hands shot up to cover his ears as the pilots simultaneously engaged their afterburners, and moments later he heard a deep, resonant sonic boom as the planes sped off to the north, leaving a smoke-filled contrail.

Shai and Jacob were so busy watching the planes that neither of them noticed the heavyset, bearded man who emerged from a cave cut into the westernmost edge of the jagged hillside.

"I hope to God that those planes were ours," the man called out.

Shai quickly turned toward the cave and responded, "That they were, Father. And from the direction they were headed, I'd say they're bound for the Bekka Valley."

As Jacob set his eyes on the burly figure of Shai's father, he smiled warmly. "I hope you didn't get me out of bed just to enjoy this breathtaking view, Uri."

Uri Weinberg stepped forward, his eyes aglow with excitement. "I guarantee you won't be disappointed, old friend. The secret alcove was back there, just like your father's diary hinted. It's a miracle that yesterday's earthquake exposed it, and if that scroll jar we found inside is indeed intact, there's no telling what treasures are locked inside."

"And here I was all set to abandon this site," Jacob admitted. "Thank goodness you convinced me to extend our stay."

"Patience is an archaeologist's best friend," said Uri, who pivoted and led the way back to the cave's narrow mouth.

Shai followed close on his father's heels, and Jacob watched the two Israelis disappear into the dark recesses of the cavern. As he did so he became aware of a new band of sweat forming on his forehead and knew that it had not been caused by the heat, but instead by his fear of confined spaces. For as long as he could remember, this phobia had been his Achilles heel. Afraid to admit its existence, Jacob had always managed to live with the dread as best he could, and this occasion proved to be no different. He summoned his self-control with a series of deep breaths, then quickly ducked inside the cave's mouth.

It was cool inside. The hollow echo of voices led him into a fairly large room, where he could stand fully upright without fear of banging his head. Shai handed him a powerful halogen flashlight and led the way into a narrow rock corridor. A projecting rock shelf forced them onto their knees for a portion of this transit. Daring not to hesitate at this point, Jacob scurried forward.

Fortunately, he didn't have to travel far. A small, hollow nook was exposed in the solid rock wall at the end of the corridor. Uri Weinberg waited for them here. The bearded Israeli squatted expectantly, the beam of his own flashlight focused on the bottom portion of the alcove.

As Shai and Jacob joined him, Uri proudly displayed his find. Partially buried in the sandy soil at the base of the nook was a tapering, three-foot-long earthenware container. Both of its rust-colored ends appeared to be sealed. At the sight of it, any fears that Jacob might have had regarding the constricting space of their current environment were instantly forgotten.

"It appears to be an exact twin of the container that housed the copper scrolls at the Qumran site!" he exclaimed.

"I thought the very same thing when I first laid eyes on it," Uri concurred. "Jacob, why don't you brush away the debris at the base while I work on the neck. That will leave the bulk of the work in Shai's capable hands. I think it's best to free it completely before we try to determine its contents."

The others agreed and began diligently sweeping away two millennia worth of debris. As instructed, Jacob concentrated on the container's base. He did most of his work with a stiff wire whisk broom and a picklike dental tool. These implements allowed him to remove the maximum amount of sediment with minimum damage to the delicate object he desired to free.

After uncovering three quarters of the base, he stopped briefly for a close-up examination of the earthenware seal and noticed a circular hairline fracture. The extent of the fracture became evident as he resumed the excavation and began removing the debris immediately beneath the base. No sooner was the sediment brushed away than the container's clay end cap unceremoniously snapped off. Fearing the worst, he angled the beam of his flashlight into the exposed hole.

"It's empty, comrades," Jacob announced, his disappointment obvious. "It appears that someone has beaten us to it."

"But that's impossible!" Uri protested. "This alcove's been sealed for over two thousand years."

"I seriously doubt that," Jacob said as he picked up the circular end cap and studied its smoothly cut edges. "Because whoever broke this seal did so with a piece of modern excavating equipment, most likely a diamond-bit saw."

Shai scooted over to the now open base of the clay container and peered inside with his flashlight. "It's empty all right," he confirmed dejectedly.

"I'm beginning to wonder if there was anything in there in the first place," said Uri.

"Take a look at this end cap yourself," Jacob suggested. "It doesn't require much imagination to see that it's been surgically cut. And you know as well as I do just who it was who did it."

Shai examined the cap before handing it to his father. Just as he was about to ask Jacob to explain his words, a low, guttural rumbling sound diverted his attention. At first he thought that the F-16s had returned. But then he realized that not even a wide-open afterburner could account for the way the ground on which he knelt began to shake wildly. When the rumbling intensified to a deafening roar, he knew the exact nature of the phenomenon that had befallen them.

"Earthquake!" he screamed.

His words hit Jacob with the force of a punch to the gut, and suddenly all the self-control he had managed to summon up instantly dissipated, to be replaced by the terrifying claustrophobic dread he had experienced upon entering the cave.

Like a flood through a broken dam, panic-induced sweat poured off his forehead. He felt his limbs turn to lead, and with his pulse beating madly, mere breathing became a struggle.

As the quake continued small chunks of the rock ceiling began breaking off. Thick dust veiled the air like fog, and Jacob suddenly thought, Oh my God, I'm going to be buried alive!

In the background, he heard a familiar voice, echoing as if it were coming from another dimension. "Come on, Shai. We've got to get out of here!" Uri urged. "Jacob!" he added. "Jacob, are you coming?"

Mute with terror, the Russian found himself unable to move a muscle, as if oblivious to the chunks of falling rock that were bruising his back. A nightmare that had been with him for as long as he could remember was about to come true, and there was absolutely nothing he could do about it.

Yet destiny had its own say in the matter as a firm hand grabbed the Russian's upper arm.

"Uncle Jake?" It was Shai, his voice filled with concern. "Are you hurt?"

Somehow Jacob managed to meet the young Israeli's gaze. Unable to hide his distress, he fought to speak, and as he was overcome with frustration he felt the impact of the severest tremor so far.

It struck with a gyrating, rumbling jolt. To the sickening crunch of falling debris was added the violence of vibrating ground, as if the very earth beneath his feet were undulating like waves in a storm at sea rather than being rigid rock. Beyond hope, Jacob rode out this furious convulsion, which was the result of a shifting of the same fault line that had once destroyed the ancient city of Jericho.

As abruptly as it arrived, the quake disappeared. The deep tectonic rumbling faded, to be replaced by a deathly silence. Jacob remained on the ground, curled up in a fetal ball, his eyes tightly shut. Slowly, as his pulse was returning to normal, he heard himself called back to the land of the living by a voice filled with both wonder and amazement.

"That last tremor uncovered another alcove," Shai exclaimed. "And there appears to be a scroll jar inside."

Jacob's eyes snapped open, and his intellectual curiosity quickly replaced his fears. A bright beam of light cut through the blackness, illuminating the partially collapsed wall immediately to his right. Without bothering to brush himself off, he rose to his knees and peered inside the exposed nook.

In the exact center of the alcove was a three-foot-long earthenware container that looked to be a twin of the one they had just excavated. Yet this piece's midsection was broken by a jagged fracture that exposed a tantalizing copper-colored object inside. This unexpected sight, miraculously restored Jacob's powers of speech.

"This one's still got a scroll inside!" he cried triumphantly, and reached out to retrieve the container's contents.

"Uncle Jake, no!" Shai screamed as he grabbed the Russian archaeologist's arm and yanked him back out of the alcove.

Before Jacob could question the young man's motives, Shai explained his action. "Scorpions, Uncle Jake—there are scorpions in there!"

Shai readjusted the angle of his flashlight to include the nook's floor, and Jacob spotted dozens of the scurrying two-inch-long insects with bleached, elongated bodies and narrow, segmented tails, where their venomous stingers were situated.

Just then, the occupants of the cave became aware of the distinctive sound of shifting rock, and a large portion of the alcove's roof collapsed, just missing the fractured container. Fearful that their discovery, not to mention themselves, would be buried for all eternity, Jacob considered his alternatives. The logical thing to do was to return with a long probe and remove the object without having to put his hands on it. But, as Shai Weinberg reminded them, they hardly had the time to do this in their current plight.

"What's the matter with the two of you?" Uri called out from the passageway leading to the cave's exit. "You'd better get the hell out of here this instant, or this entire roof will collapse and bury the both of you."

Not about to abandon the treasure so readily, Jacob decided to take a risk. Without even bothering to explain their predicament to Uri, the Russian crawled up to the very edge of the alcove and precipitately shoved his arm inside its uninviting recesses. Blind luck directed his hand through the container's fracture. His fingers made contact with a rounded metallic object, approximately twelve inches long, that felt cool to his touch. He had no doubt about what it was as he grasped the tightly wrapped scroll and yanked it free.

Unbeknownst to Jacob, a single scorpion stubbornly gripped the scroll's copper edge. Shai spotted the creature the moment Jacob's hand emerged from the alcove.

Its deadly stinger was only inches away from the Russian's exposed palm when the young Israeli grabbed a wire whisk broom and, with a lightning-quick movement, smashed the scorpion.

Seeing the copper scroll, Uri realized why Jacob was endangering their lives, yet he allowed them no time to celebrate. "Move it, the two of you!" he ordered. "If the roof of this cave collapses, we'll be buried in here for all eternity!"

The true nature of their find became evident under the direct light of the midmorning sun. The cylindrical scroll appeared to be composed of pure copper, which over the centuries had oxidized and become extremely brittle. Faint Mishnaic Hebrew script was visible on the outer skin, and Jacob estimated the entire strip to be about three feet long. Yet the question remained as to how to unroll it so as to cause the least amount of damage.

It was Uri who recommended that the scroll be immediately transferred to his lab at Hebrew University. Shai and Jacob disagreed, feeling that this was too time-consuming a luxury, and instead proposed opening the scroll right there in camp. After much discussion, they reached a compromise over lunch: Shai and Jacob would have their way if a proper saw could be jury-rigged.

With Gamal's able assistance, they created a crude one-and-three-quarter-inch circular saw, then carefully skewered the scroll lengthwise on a wooden spindle, which they fitted onto a movable cradle, allowing the spindle to do all the moving while the blade remained stationary. A vise-mounted magnifying glass they set up allowed them to maintain strict control of the depth of the cut. To prevent the brittle material from shattering the moment the blade touched it, they coated the outside skin with adhesive.

The preparation of the saw took the rest of the

afternoon and kept all of them busy well into the night. Thus it was decided to make the first cut the following morning.

Uri was not really surprised to awake to the buzzing sound of a saw biting into metal. A quick check of his watch showed it to be just after 6:00 A.M., and he hurried from his cot, barely taking the time to throw on a pair of shorts and a T-shirt.

Outside his tent, the dawn sky was a cloudless powdery-blue canopy: only a thin trickle of smoke rose from the campfire. Heading directly to Jacob Litvak's tent, where the saw had been set up, Uri found the Russian in midcut, studiously peering through the magnifying glass, his hands firmly on the wooden spindle. Not wishing to take him by surprise, he waited until the completion of the procedure before announcing himself.

"So you couldn't wait for the rest of us, old friend," he said, only slightly annoyed at his friend's impatience. "I gather that our improvised saw is working properly."

Jacob held back his response until he had carefully removed a four-inch-wide rectangular section of scroll, which he gingerly laid on the drafting table beside seven similarly shaped segments. "It's working splendidly, comrade. As you can see for yourself, the copper did not shatter. I've made the cuts between the margins wherever possible, and should be able to complete the job with this next cut."

"Any idea of the scroll's contents?" Shai wanted to know.

"From what little I've managed to translate, I'd say that we've stumbled upon a religious commentary of some sort," Jacob answered. "Why don't you get on with the task of cleaning the segments to make them more legible while I finish this final cut."

As Jacob returned his attention to the spindle Uri eagerly donned a pair of surgical gloves and selected a stiff nylon brush from the toolbox. He located the first cutting and began gently sweeping the copper surface with the brush. The cave dust was removed with a minimum of effort, revealing four columns of engraved Hebrew lettering. Though it was clear to him that the scribe's penmanship wasn't of the highest quality, Uri was able to skim the segment and try his luck at a tentative translation.

With the saw whining in the background, he confirmed that the language was indeed Mishnaic Hebrew, a form of the language dating back to the year 200 A.D. and characterized by a sparse use of vowels. Faced as he was, however, with a conundrum of consonants, a hasty deciphering would be most difficult.

Frustrated, Uri decided to stick to cleaning. By the time he completed brushing the dust off all seven of the segments, Jacob had laid the final two portions on the table. He dutifully brushed these clean and watched as the Russian organized them in chronological order, beginning with the last segment to leave the spindle.

"So the ancients have once more left us with a puzzle to complete," Jacob commented while skimming the text. "It looks like this poor Mishnaic scribe was writing in great haste. Let's begin our game of fill-in-the-blank, and see what he had to say."

The document was entitled, *The Time of the End of the Days,* and proved to be fascinating beyond their wildest expectations. It told the tale of the Nephilim, divine creatures who descended to earth, where they fell from grace through the sins of pride and lust. Together with their leader, Belial the deceiver, these fallen angels cohabited with mortal women. Thus were born the Children of Darkness.

To counter this evil bloodline, the One Father sent the archangel Michael into the southern desert to do battle. Michael assembled the Children of Light, and armed with the Spear of Destiny, he led his troops into combat.

Belial feared this spear more than any other weapon, and attempted to negate its great powers by consuming a substance cryptically described as "Lucifer's Flesh." Only then was he ready to meet Michael's onslaught.

A good portion of the scroll was dedicated to a detailed description of this battle. It was a bloody, prolonged struggle that only ended when Michael successfully summoned the magical powers of the holy spear he carried. He did so by means of a powerful ritual, a secret ceremonial rite originally taught to him by the One Father, and supposedly described in detail in a sister scroll. In such a way were the Children of Darkness defeated, their leader condemned to eternal imprisonment in a distant land of fire and ice.

Uri's impression, after he and Jacob had finished their initial effort at translation, was that this tale was a work of pure fantasy, a fictional retelling of the Book of Enoch. His coworker was less quick to dismiss the wild story, however. Jacob was particularly interested in the references to the so-called Nephilim, divine beings that were actually described in Genesis 6:2. He also found great symbolic meaning in the story of their leader, wondering aloud if Belial could be another name for Lucifer, and if the story of his fall from grace was a parable about the origin of earthly evil.

The one element that particularly captivated the Russian was the scroll's mention of a magical ritual that was used to tap the powers of the Spear of Destiny. Jacob was already familiar with such a secret rite, having learned about it from his father. Since his reading of his father's diary had led him to the cave in which he had discovered the scroll, he could not help but be struck by the coincidence.

"I tell you, comrade, it's this mention of a sister scroll that truly bothers me," Jacob said to Uri over their second cup of coffee of the morning. "I'm sure it's referring to the contents of the empty scroll jar in the first alcove."

Uri slowly turned away from the draft table where the copper plates were displayed. "That's pure speculation, Jacob, and you know it. The container could have held all sorts of things, and could even have been placed there empty."

"Impossible," Jacob countered. "The Essenes would not have gone to the trouble of preparing a secret storage nook for an empty vessel. No, it held a copper scroll, all right, possibly the most important of all, and I know who got to it before us."

Uri shook his head in exasperation as Jacob continued. "Have you already forgotten our reason for excavating in this region in the first place? There's no way you can ignore the warnings in my father's diary. Make no mistake—the hand of divine providence guided us to that secret alcove."

"Believe me, it was no miracle that brought us this scroll, Jacob. Unless you see something miraculous in long hours of tedious, backbreaking fieldwork and a bit of good luck in the guise of that earthquake."

"I wish that I could concur with your rather naive and skeptical viewpoint, comrade, but my gut tells me that there was much more than luck and hard work involved in bringing us this incredible document. Six decades ago, my father came to these very same hills in search of the lost treasures of the Temple. Instead of gold and silver, he uncovered an even greater mystery, a mystery that concerned nothing less than the essential grounds of good and evil.

"For three years he remained here on the western shores of the Dead Sea, where he met a young German archaeologist who was on a remarkably similar quest. The object they both sought was a symbolic key to tapping the powers that run the universe. According to King Solomon, this key involved some kind of solemn rite, a magical combination of symbolic objects and divine utterances, designed to allow mortal man direct access to the Holy of Holies."

Becoming more excited as he spoke, Jacob continued. "Our incredible discovery confirms this ritual's existence. It also validates my father's greatest fear. For before he could complete his excavation of the cave in which we found our scroll, the Nazi invasion of our motherland called him back to the Soviet Union. In the dark days that followed, when pure evil was once more loosed upon the planet, he warned all who would listen that the Nazis' extraordinarily swift rise to power had its origins in the occult. I know that it sounds crazy and farfetched to you, but to his dying day, Father insisted that it was from a cave on the shores of the Dead Sea that this monstrous evil originated."

Uri, who patiently listened to his friend although he had heard this story before, remained skeptical, and this despite their recent discovery. Realizing that it would be a waste of breath to voice his opinion, he thoughtfully sipped his coffee. As he did so he began to hear a distant, hollow, clattering noise that sounded as if it were coming from a helicopter. As its volume intensified he looked up to see his son poking his head through the closed tent flap.

"Father, we've got an IDF Huey coming in to land," Shai announced excitedly.

By now, the sides of the canvas tent were rippling in the chopper's downdraft, and the clattering noise rose to an almost deafening level.

"I wonder what in the world this is all about?" Uri practically had to shout to be heard. His question was addressed to Jacob, who looked unusually glum as he stood and pulled on his bush hat. The morning's activities had emotionally drained him, and he found himself unable to shake a feeling of impending doom.

Once more the canvas walls shook as the tent was caught by a violent, rotor-created gust, and for a moment Jacob feared that he would lose his tent altogether, but soon the roar of the helicopter's engine began to die down.

"She's landed," Uri observed, and followed his son out of the tent.

Jacob took a second to solemnly glance over to the

table where the nine copper scroll segments were laid out before exiting the tent himself. The helicopter had landed at the very center of the clearing. It was painted a drab olive green, with the blue-and-white, six-pointed star decal of the Israeli Defense Force on its tail strut.

The door to the main cabin opened, and a tall, straight-shouldered individual in a one-piece, green flight suit climbed out. A blue beret covered his skull, and when Jacob viewed the black patch that covered his right eye, he instantly knew his identity.

He had been introduced to Colonel Simon Bar-Adon over a decade ago, shortly after arriving in Israel for an official dig. Though Bar-Adon was only a junior officer at that time, he had a powerful presence, displaying the type of forceful leadership men liked to serve under.

His job was to provide the archaeologists security at their excavation site. He performed his duties with great attention to detail, and made it a point to get to know each member of the dig team personally.

During Jacob's first one-on-one encounter with Bar-Adon, the Israeli opened his eyes to the many dangers involved in working in the Holy Land. A virtual war zone perpetually existed inside Israel's narrow borders, with the enemy randomly choosing its victims regardless of their political convictions or nationality.

Jacob was surprised to learn that Bar-Adon knew of his father's earlier work in Israel. Even though Soviet-Israeli relations were strained at the time, Bar-Adon revealed his country's sincere desire to establish closer political ties. The controversial area in which he proposed to open a dialogue was cooperation in hunting down Nazi fugitives.

In the closing days of World War II, Jacob's father had been ordered to Berlin to assist in the arrest of German scientists. At the war's conclusion, he was given the additional responsibility of bringing to justice any Nazi scientists who might have escaped the Soviet snare.

Upon his father's death, Jacob inherited the open files

of the criminals still rumored to be at large. As a representative of the Mossad, Israel's Intelligence service, Simon Bar-Adon knew all about Jacob's expertise in this field. And it was ten years ago, shortly after their first meeting, that Bar-Adon offered Jacob a rare glimpse at the Mossad's intelligence reports on these fugitive Germans. Of course, this opportunity did not come without a price, and Jacob had to fight to receive KGB permission to share the contents of the Soviet files with the Israelis. A mutual understanding was eventually reached, which had advantages for both sides, who after all shared a common goal.

During the years that followed, this shared intelligence resulted in several successful apprehensions, most of which took place in South America. The passage of time was also responsible for the rapidly dwindling number of open files. Those few individuals still on the loose were old men now, close to the end of their lives. And with their deaths, Jacob had more and more time to devote his attention to that other great passion that his father had passed on to him—archaeology.

Jacob had last seen Bar-Adon three weeks ago, at the Jerusalem Hilton. For the most part this was a social get-together. They traded tidbits about their family lives, with Bar-Adon donning his official hat as he warned Jacob about continued isolated acts of Arab violence in the area of their proposed dig. To ensure their safety, he personally signed the orders assigning Shai Weinberg to their security detail.

Jacob thus wasn't all that surprised to see that it was Shai who was the first to greet Bar-Adon as he stepped from the helicopter. The young Israeli stood ramrod straight and crisply saluted his superior. Bar-Adon returned the greeting, then exchanged a warm handshake with Shai's father. All three of the Israelis were soon involved in a spirited conversation. Curious as to the nature of this discussion, Jacob crossed the clearing to join them.

"Jacob," Bar-Adon greeted, a hint of concern in his deep bass voice. "Uri was just telling me about your brush with disaster during yesterday's quake. Thank God none of you were injured or worse."

Jacob accepted a viselike handshake from the senior officer. "Yes, comrade, we were extremely fortunate to escape with barely a scratch."

"That you were," Bar-Adon added. "I just flew in from the Fuller excavation at Qumran, and must sadly report that not all of your associates shared such good luck. A cave-in there was responsible for not only the loss of an entire month's work, but a broken leg for the expedition's leader."

Uri Weinberg shook his head. "I'm sorry to hear that. I guess we really should count our blessings, because if it wasn't for that tremor, we might never have found a fascinating copper scroll that looks to date from the time of the Essenes. Wait until you hear the wild tale it tells!"

"I'm looking forward to that." Bar-Adon looked at Jacob and added, "But before you share the contents with me, I'd like to have a few private words with Jacob."

"But of course," Uri replied. "Take all the time you need. Come on, Shai. Let's give these two some space."

As father and son turned back to the tent holding the scroll segments, Simon Bar-Adon led Jacob over to the deserted southern edge of the clearing. Here, beside a dry ravine, the Israeli met Jacob's inquisitive gaze.

"I thought that you'd be interested to know that there's been a confirmed Wolf sighting, Jacob," he began solemnly. "Our agents report that less than twenty-four hours ago, a heavily armed convoy of four-wheeled vehicles left the compound heading north toward the Brazilian border. Eckhardt was positively spotted in the lead truck, and from the manner in which the convoy was outfitted, it appears to be another one of his field expeditions.

"It's been decided to use this opportunity to capture our old friend once and for all. And knowing full well your personal interest in this case, I'd like to invite you to be there when we spring the trap."

Jacob was momentarily taken aback by this surprising revelation, and a full minute of shocked silence passed as at long last he realized the reason for the feeling of impending dread he'd had all morning. Somehow he had intuitively sensed the imminent news of a tangible evil, an evil he had spent an entire lifetime tracking down.

How very fitting that this news came so soon after their discovery in the hills. For Jacob had actually sensed the presence of his nemesis when he first set eyes upon the empty scroll jar in the first alcove.

Wolfram Eckhardt, who at twenty-two years of age had become the head of the fabled SS Occult Bureau. Wolfram Eckhardt, who had explored these same hills in the 1930s, on the heels of Jacob's father. Both men had been on the trail of similar treasure, a treasure whose nature Jacob was only just beginning to comprehend.

Surely, as he had told Shai, it was the hand of divine providence that had led Jacob to the incredible copper scroll he had just deciphered. But just as his father had warned, Eckhardt had beaten them to the sister scroll, on whose length was recorded the words of the sacred, all-powerful ritual composed at the very dawn of time.

Jacob also sensed that Simon Bar-Adon's presence was no mere coincidence. His revelation was an integral part of a complex divine prophecy, whose potentially apocalyptic conclusion was rapidly approaching.

Thus there was no doubt in his mind as he returned the Israeli's penetrating stare and accepted his invitation. The challenge had been issued. Now he could only pray for the strength needed to prevail in the infernal conflict that would inevitably follow.

2

Yngve Rakke had sailed many a lonely sea before, yet the portion of the South Atlantic where he currently found himself was the most desolate stretch of water that the thirty-seven-year-old Norwegian had ever laid eyes on. Since leaving the island of Tristan da Cunha two days ago, they hadn't sighted a single surface vessel. Even the gray skies here were empty, eerily devoid of jet contrails.

From his perch at the forward rail of the *Seaway Condor*'s bow helideck, Yngve could barely glimpse the surrounding sea. The fog had been with them since early dawn, and not even the noon sun was able to burn it off. There was a damp chill in the air, which vaguely reminded him of another portion of the Atlantic far to the north.

The North Sea was the *Condor*'s normal stomping grounds. The ship was based in Haugesund, Yngve's hometown, where their present journey had begun. After making stops in Lisbon and Dakar, they were now a very long way from the North Sea oil fields they normally serviced, and a journey of another six hundred nautical miles remained before they reached their final destination. Even smaller and more isolated than Tristan da Cunha, Bouvetoya Island would be their home for the next five months. Located approximately sixteen hundred miles southwest of Capetown, Bouvetoya's nearest neighbor was Antarctica, with the Falklands and South America lying well to the west.

The exclusive property of Norway, Bouvetoya was formerly used as a seal and whaling station, and the *Condor*'s current mission was to establish a permanent base camp there. From this strategic location, the vessel would be free to begin the first extensive exploration of Antarctic waters for crude oil. Previous surveys of these virgin seas had been most promising, with the majority of scientists projecting the existence of oil deposits as vast as those of the Arabian peninsula.

From the elevated bridge of the *Condor,* the ship's foghorn sounded mournfully. Yngve looked on as a powerful spotlight vainly probed the wall of fog that lay ahead. As the deck rolled with a rising swell the senior diver was forced to grab onto the rail to keep his balance.

He knew that the *Condor* was superbly engineered to meet the challenge of the rough seas. One hundred meters in length, the ship displaced well over five thousand tons. Its twin stacks, lying amidships, bracketed the navigation bridge, allowing a clear view of the bow helideck where Yngve was standing.

The aft portion of the ship was dominated by a large crane, with two working moonpools cut into the hull. The diesel electric plants of the two fully equipped engine rooms belowdeck powered three tunnel thrusters in the foreship and two Azimuth thrusters aft. A dynamic positioning system with dual redundancy controlled all of these state-of-the-art systems.

Yngve had generally enjoyed his past cruises aboard the

ship. The mere idea of going to sea made his Viking blood pound, and it was in the spirit of adventure that he initially picked this line of work. Yet, though he knew he should be thrilled to have the opportunity to explore these relatively uncharted waters, he couldn't ignore the feeling of unease that possessed him soon after leaving Haugesund.

As he vacantly stared out into the fog he supposed this anxiety had a lot to do with the new bride he had left back home. The summer just passed had been glorious and exciting. Though he had met Ashild only a few months ago, he had no doubt that she was the girl he had been waiting for. They had been married barely a week when he was offered his current position, and Yngve had been all set to turn the offer down, since he and Ashild hadn't even moved into their own apartment, but Ashild wouldn't hear of it—the salary was just too tempting. Yngve knew she was right: five months of work would earn enough money for an entire year, and give him the luxury to be more choosy about his next job.

Ashild also liked the idea of having him around the house next spring, when their first child was due. When she revealed the news of her pregnancy only ten days before the *Condor* set sail, he was thrilled with the idea of being a father for the first time, yet saddened by the thought of leaving the mother-to-be behind.

The foghorn's forlorn cry perfectly fit his present mood, and he was startled when a voice snapped him from his melancholy reverie.

"Keep a sharp lookout there, mate. I just learned from the captain that our radar's down for maintenance."

Yngve looked on as a short, blond-haired figure joined him at the railing. Thor Sperre was the *Condor*'s helicopter pilot and a longtime friend from Haugesund. They had sailed together on many previous occasions, and Thor had been the best man at Yngve's wedding.

"I seriously doubt that the loss of our radar will affect us in the least," Yngve replied. "There's nothing out there to hit in this godforsaken sea but a whale or two."

"Isn't that the truth," said Thor. "We're certainly a long way from the nearest shipping lane, with even more isolated waters to come."

Thor pulled a battered briar pipe from his orange flight jacket and placed its scarred bit between his lips. Cupping his hand around the bowl, he used a well-worn Zippo to light the tobacco. As a fragrant cloud of rum-and-vanilla-scented smoke escaped his nostrils, he turned around to inspect the bright red Bell-212 helicopter strapped to the deck behind them.

"It sure would be nice to get airborne and see some blue sky for a change," he said. "Though from the looks of this pea soup, who knows if I'd ever be able to find the *Condor* again to land." Taking another puff of his pipe and returning his gaze to the fog-enshrouded sea, Thor watched another large swell rock the *Condor,* managing to remain calmly balanced without grabbing the rail.

"This weather and the unknown waters we sail makes me think of our forefathers, Yngve. How brave they were to take on unexplored seas in their fragile longboats."

When this comment failed to elicit a response from his preoccupied mate, Thor added, "Something tells me that you're far removed from the Viking spirit on this invigorating afternoon. By chance, are your thoughts back in Haugesund, with a certain beautiful lady with child that we both happen to know."

The barest of grins cracked Yngve's lips and Thor grunted. "I thought that could be the reason for your lousy mood of late. So listen up to what I'm about to say and get rid of your homesickness. Otherwise, the next five months will be murder."

Yngve knew his blond friend was right, yet before he could answer him, he was distracted by the sudden appearance of a flashing light amid the fog.

"Jesus Christ, Thor!" he exclaimed. "There's another ship out there, and we're headed straight toward it."

Thor saw the same mysterious light and wasted no time snapping into action. "Grab a torch out of the chopper's cockpit, Yngve, and try to make contact with them. I'll run to the bridge and warn the captain."

The aviator turned and sprinted across the helideck for the nearest ladder as Yngve headed for the helicopter. He found a flashlight strapped onto its interior Plexiglas doorframe, hurriedly removed it, and returned to the bow railing. For a confusing moment he was unable to relocate the mysterious light. He switched on his own torch and desperately swept the beam along a wide horizontal swath. The thick fog bent the beam at odd angles, and just as he was about to give up all hope of making contact, a light began urgently blinking several degrees off the *Condor*'s starboard bow. It seemed to be a good deal closer than before, and Yngve found himself praying that a collision could still be avoided.

His silent petitions continued even as the Condor's air horn sounded three deafening blasts. Surely this meant that Thor had reached the helm, and that the next order would be directed to the engine room to cut their forward speed drastically. Unlike many ships its size, the *Condor,* with its full array of sophisticated thrusters, could come to a full halt and hold its position in a matter of seconds. A sudden lurching movement of the deck below illustrated this capability, and Yngve redirected his attention to the waters off their bow with a renewed sense of hope.

This time his search was assisted by the *Condor*'s powerful bridge spotlight. Fully expecting the sharpened bow of another ship to slice out of the fog, Yngve was surprised to see a vessel of a much less threatening nature materialize. Much to his relief, the mysterious craft turned out to be nothing more than a rubber Zodiac life raft. Two men in bright yellow survival suits manned the craft, one of them perched on the blunt bow holding the torch that had caught Yngve's attention. As his fear dissipated Yngve proceeded to the deck below. He arrived at the amidships boarding ramp just as the raft drifted out of the fog.

"Greetings, comrade!" cried the occupant of the raft's bow.

He was a rough-looking, middle-aged man, with spikey brown hair and a weathered face sporting a heavy growth of reddish stubble. The figure at the Zodiac's aft wore an officer's hat and had a much more dignified appearance, with a black, neatly trimmed Vandyke. Courteously saluting Yngve, he began to speak in English with a slight German accent.

"I certainly thank my lucky stars that our paths crossed this afternoon, my friend. We've been adrift for almost forty-eight hours, ever since our trawler went down with all hands. May we tie up?"

"Of course," Yngve replied, leaning over the rail and adroitly catching the raft's nylon bowline.

As he tied the line to a deck cleat, Thor Sperre and Jon Skogstad, the *Condor*'s captain, breathlessly arrived. A veteran of the sea, Skogstad's portly figure, glowing red cheeks, amiable disposition, and full gray beard had earned him the nickname of Father Christmas. The two castaways scrutinized him as if he were indeed the mythical Santa.

"Hello, gentlemen. I'm Jon Skogstad, the *Condor*'s commanding officer. What in the name of heaven are you two doing out here in the middle of nowhere?"

"We're the only survivors of a horrible shipwreck," the tall figure at the raft's stern answered. "May we come aboard to tell our tragic story, Captain? Both of us have been exposed to the elements for almost two days now."

Captain Skogstad hesitated briefly before replying, "By all means, gentlemen. The *Condor* is at your service. Thor, Yngve, help them transfer over."

The two Norwegians alertly lowered the amidships gangway, and Yngve climbed down the narrow loading ramp to secure the Zodiac's stern line. Once this was accomplished, he offered his hand to the castaways, who grabbed it to steady themselves while stepping up onto the raft's rounded, rubberized gunwales and then climbing onto the *Condor*'s gangway. Yngve thought it odd that neither of them wore gloves of any sort, and that their hands were not as cold as he would have expected after two days' exposure to the chilling temperatures of this latitude.

"Welcome aboard the *Seaway Condor*," Captain Skogstad said politely. "Do either of you require medical attention?"

"Thankfully, we don't," answered the castaway with the Vandyke, appraising the layout of the *Condor*'s deck. "We are doubly lucky, first to have been plucked from the sea, and second to have been saved by a ship such as this one. You Norwegians certainly know how to build a solid, seaworthy vessel."

This comment struck the *Condor*'s captain as strange. "You say that your own ship went down. What caused such a disaster?"

The bearded castaway caught the glance of his companion before answering. "We believe it was an explosion in the engine room. It happened so quickly that we barely had time to abandon ship before she went down."

"May I ask the destination of your vessel, and its reason for being in this seldom-traveled portion of the South Atlantic?" Captain Skogstad wanted to know.

"We were bound for Port Stanley in the Falklands with a load of diesel fuel, which we originally took on in Capetown," the bearded castaway matter-of-factly replied.

The *Condor*'s commanding officer sounded skeptical as he replied, "That's a long way to go merely to deliver diesel fuel. I would have thought that the British could get a South American supplier and save substantially on the transportation charge."

The bearded castaway reacted to this with a strained grin. His cheek muscles flinched as he slowly reached into the deep pocket of his survival suit and, with a lightning-quick movement, yanked out a blue-gray Glock pistol. His grin instantly turned to a sneer as he aimed this weapon at the *Condor*'s captain.

"Enough of this charade," he spat. "Otto, make certain that we don't have any Viking heroes here."

"Yes, sir," returned his brown-haired associate, who proceeded to unzip the top portion of his survival suit, pull out an Uzi, and load a live round into its compact chamber. Flicking off the safety, he used the stubby barrel to signal the stunned Norwegians to form a tight group.

As they complied with this order Jon Skogstad angrily asked, "What in the hell is the meaning of this outrage?"

"Please be so good as to keep your voice down, Captain," the pistol-toting castaway instructed. "And do calm yourself, comrade. I guarantee you that no one will be harmed as long as you do as ordered."

Then he calmly pulled a flare gun from his left pocket, aimed it skyward, and squeezed off a single round. A bright red starburst shell exploded overhead with a resounding crack. Soon afterward the buzz-saw whine of powerful outboard engines could be heard in the fog-shrouded distance.

Three Zodiacs wasted no time racing over to the *Condor*'s lowered gangway, each raft holding two men in matching yellow oilskins. All of them wore sidearms, and appeared to be led by the tall, lanky, smooth-shaven man who stood at the bow of the lead raft. With straight blond hair slicked back off his forehead and tied in a short ponytail, he anxiously called out, "Is everything all right, Captain?"

From the *Condor*'s amidship railing, Gunther Hartmann smoothed his Vandyke with his free hand and answered, "That it is, Karl. You may begin transferring the men as planned, and we can get on with it."

"I demand to know what this act of brazen piracy is all about!" the *Condor*'s commanding officer exploded.

At this moment several curious Norwegian sailors appeared on the foredeck. As they did so Gunther Hartmann coolly rammed a bullet into his Glock's chamber and aimed the barrel squarely at Skogstad's flushed forehead.

"Captain, I did warn you about keeping your voice down," he firmly reminded. "My men and I are merely here to requisition several badly needed items from your well-stocked storerooms. I assure you that our intentions are honorable, and that no one will be hurt as long as you and your crew cooperate."

"So you're pirates with honor," Jon Skogstad spat back. "That's a contradiction of terms if I ever heard one. And regardless of the fact that our lives might be spared, all of you will hang for this."

Gunther Hartmann laughed. "Your protest is duly noted, Captain. Now, if you'll be so good as to accompany me to the bridge, I feel that an announcement to your crew is in order. So that none of them get any brave ideas, I want the *Condor*'s entire complement sequestered in the ship's mess." Flicking off the pistol's safety at this point, he added, "Do I make myself perfectly clear, Captain, or must I make you an example of what will happen if my orders are contradicted?"

Jon Skogstad peered at the barrel of the pistol and opted for the prudent approach. "I hear you loud and clear, sir. The lives of my crew are of paramount importance to me, and I'll do whatever you say to ensure their safety."

"That's more like it," Hartmann said as he reengaged the pistol's safety and lowered the barrel.

Standing immediately beside their captain, Yngve and Thor watched this confrontation with disbelieving eyes. The *Condor*'s senior diver was particularly affected by the takeover of their ship, and couldn't help but feel responsible for it. After all, he had been the one to spot the castaways' distress signal, and to give them permission to tie up beside the gangway. He, too, had naively swallowed their fictitious tale of distress and practically invited them aboard.

Having been fooled once, he didn't really believe that they were only after the *Condor*'s stores. With no mother vessel of any sort in view, Yngve feared that their true motive was to hijack the *Condor*. And since it was evident that these were truly desperate men, what was to keep them from breaking their promise and killing the ship's crew to remove all witnesses? With such thoughts, Yngve vowed that it was up to him to rectify his mistake and save the *Condor*.

The ship's diving locker contained several high-powered rifles, which were used to scare off sharks. Yngve's plan was to get his hands on these weapons and take back the ship. But first he thought it wise to get a signal off to warn the authorities of their plight. And this meant somehow slipping away to the radio room.

His opportunity to begin implementing his plan came sooner than expected. While the rest of the pirates tied up their Zodiacs and boarded the ship, their bearded leader ordered Yngve and Thor to lead the way to the bridge. With Captain Skogstad in tow, the head pirate pocketed his pistol and followed them up a ladder to the deck, where a hatchway led into the main superstructure, with the bridge situated inside along the forward bulkhead.

As they entered the interior corridor a trio of curious officers, led by the *Condor*'s executive officer, intercepted them from an adjoining passageway. The pirate quickly pulled out his pistol and actually shot a round into the ceiling when the officers disobeyed his commands and tried to rush him.

Though the pirate eventually prevailed, he was distracted enough for Yngve to slip away unseen. The diver could hardly believe his good fortune when he found himself alone in the passageway to the radio room. Luck was again with him when he found the door to the compartment unlocked. He switched on the overhead light and hastened to the transmitter.

As a former communications officer in the Norwegian navy, Yngve had no trouble operating the unit, whose digital frequency dial he hurriedly turned to the international distress band.

He broadcasted both vocally and with the backup Morse system, all the while inwardly praying that there was another ship or aircraft in the immediate area that could assist them. Not yet able to determine his effectiveness, he decided to inform the home office of their plight as well. To do so, he retuned the transmitter's frequency dial in order to make contact with an orbiting communications satellite, his hand shaking slightly all the while.

His hopes for success were high when the door to the radio room burst open, and Otto Brauer, the rough-looking, brown-haired man who had initially greeted him from the bow of the first Zodiac, quickly entered the compartment. His heavily lined, beard-stubbled face was flushed, and a look of pure contempt emanated from his blue eyes when he spotted Yngve at the radio console.

"You stupid Norwegian bastard!" he cursed as he lifted the barrel of his Uzi, adding with finality, *"Auf Wiedersehen,* Viking."

Yngve knew that his luck had run out. His final thoughts before the Uzi's bullets ripped into his body were of his beloved bride and the baby that he'd never live to see.

3

A soft electronic buzzing noise rang in the distance, calling like an alien entity from another dimension. Commander Philip Michaels groggily awakened, his pleasant dream of home already fading by the time he reached for the telephone handset mounted to the bulkhead at the head of his bunk.

"Captain," he mumbled into the transmitter.

"Skipper," replied the familiar gruff voice of his XO. "Sorry to disturb you, but it looks like we've got a submerged sonar contact. After seven hours of sniffin' around, this could be them."

"Very good, XO," Michaels replied. "I'm on my way."

He yawned, and it took him two tries before he secured the handset in its vertical cradle. His weary eyes opened wide, and took comfort in the pitch blackness that prevailed in the stateroom. Not looking forward to switching on the lights, he rolled over onto his back and gazed up at the red gas-plasma display mounted to the bulkhead above his feet. A quick glance was all that was needed to check the boat's status, and after determining their current speed, heading, and depth, he reluctantly sat up and swung his bare feet onto the cool linoleum floor.

His night vision still intact, he scanned the ten-by-eight-foot compartment that was his exclusive domain. A small table covered with paperwork and a pair of seats set against the outside bulkhead were the extent of the furnishings. Though many outsiders might have considered such tight quarters unbearable, he knew he was privileged to have them.

He stood and stretched. The joints of his shoulders, neck, and knees ached dully, the aftereffects of a brief college football career. Michaels had long ago learned to live with the almost constant pain, and he stiffly shuffled toward the adjoining bathroom he shared with his XO. ·

As he flicked on the head's fluorescent light he shielded his eyes, then rinsed his face with cold water in the stainless-steel washbasin. He allowed himself a brief glance at the mirror, and though he could use a shave, he took only the time to comb down his thick black mustache and brush back his crewcut.

After a quick stop at the urinal, he returned to his stateroom, where he dressed in clean blue coveralls. Also known as a poopy suit, this comfortable, practical uniform was worn by officers and enlisted men alike. He then slipped on a pair of soft leather running shoes and took a moment to walk over to a nearby shelf, where a single football sat wedged between several stacks of technical manuals. The side of this pigskin was dated "11/7/71" in faded black Magic Marker. Beneath this date was printed NAVY 24–ARMY 21. Michaels had kicked this very ball through the goalposts from army's forty-yard line with only seven seconds left in the game, a field goal that turned out to be the longest and most important of his abbreviated career. He touched the brown leather for luck before turning for the cabin's exit.

His emergence into the brightly lit passageway outside his stateroom commenced his official return to duty. With quick, brisk strides, he headed up to the deck above, with a renewed sense of urgency and purpose.

Command of a nuclear-powered attack submarine had been his dream from the first day he entered the naval academy. And though it had taken him two decades of hard work and study to realize the goal, he knew that the sacrifice had been well worth it.

The USS *Springfield* was one of the most advanced warships ever to sail beneath the seas. A much-improved version of the ever-capable 688/Los Angeles class, Michaels's current command was equipped with state-of-the-art submarine technology.

In addition to a new high-output reactor core, the *Springfield* was one of the first U.S. submarines to be equipped with the BSY-1 combat system. The "busy one," as it was called, effectively integrated the boat's sensor, fire control, and weapons systems. A new passive "thin line" towed sonar array was specifically designed to detect very low-frequency noises at very long ranges. A strengthened fairwater sail and retractable hull-mounted forward dive planes made under-ice operations possible. The *Springfield* also carried a wide variety of weapons, including the Mk-48 ADCAP torpedo, several types of mines, and missiles such as Harpoon and Tomahawk. Finally, the boat's basic design was enhanced, making it almost ten times quieter than early-model 688s.

Well aware of his vast responsibilities to both the taxpayers who funded this incredible warship and the families of the 127 men who made up its crew, Philip Michaels confidently strode into the *Springfield*'s control room. This all-important portion of the boat was an equipment-packed, brightly lit space, approximately the size of a two-car garage.

He entered by way of the forward port passageway, passing the diving control console on his right. Seated here were two young sailors, their hands tightly gripping

the airplanelike steering yokes that controlled the boat's
dive planes and horizontal stabilizers. Perched between
them was Master Chief Ellwood Crick, the *Springfield*'s
senior enlisted man and current chief of the boat, or
COB. At forty-seven, Crick was also the oldest sailor
aboard, his twenty-nine years of navy experience making
him an invaluable asset.

"Afternoon, Cap," he said, without taking his eyes off
the multitude of instruments on the bulkhead immediately in front of the planesmen.

"How's she running, COB?" Michaels asked while
scanning these same instruments himself.

"Like a dream, sir," Crick answered. "Except for that
continued problem with our TB-23, all systems remain
fully operational."

Michaels determined with a single glance that the
Springfield was 585 feet below the sea's surface, traveling
on a northeasterly bearing at a speed of twenty-one
knots.

"Do you think we finally tagged 'em, Cap?" Crick
hopefully queried.

"Hang in there just a little bit longer, COB, and I'll
give you a definite answer," Michaels said while looking
over to Crick's immediate left, where the diving officer
controlled the sub's ballast and trim.

"Conn, sonar," came a clear voice over the intercom.
"Sierra Seven remains on bearing three-two-five, signature ID incomplete."

Michaels turned toward the control room's central
periscope pedestal, where Lieutenant Art Noonan currently occupied the officer-of-the-deck watch station.
Noonan was the weapons officer, better known as Weaps.
He was also a newcomer aboard the *Springfield,* and a born
optimist, as his initial comment to Michaels displayed.

"Looks like we can finally even the score, Captain."

Michaels grunted. "Don't pop the champagne just yet,
Weaps. We still have a hell of a lot of work ahead of us,
including the all-important job of getting that definite sig-

nature ID." A quick scan of the group of sailors gathered around the aft navigation plot and the starboard weapons control consoles prompted Michaels to add, "Where's the XO?"

"In the sound shack, sir," Weaps answered. "Shall I call him in?"

"That won't be necessary," Michaels replied, proceeding to the forward starboard passageway and a closed accordian-style partition that was labeled with a decal reading HOUSE OF PAIN.

Michaels slid back the doorway and entered the dimly lit, hushed confines of the sonar room. Four technicians with headphones covering their ears were seated before their consoles, their eyes locked on their dual, green-tinted CRT screens. Standing behind the forwardmost console was the stocky figure of his XO, Lieutenant Commander Gerardo Perez. The XO's wire-rimmed glasses shone in the light of the CRT screen he was intently studying.

"What's so interesting, XO?" Michaels asked, joining him at the console.

"Unfortunately, it's not quite the movie of the week," Perez retorted without shifting his glance. "This empty waterfall display says it all, Skipper. One minute Sierra Seven was there as clear as day, and the next thing we know it's nowhere to be seen."

"I say it's gone and popped back up through the thermocline," offered Petty Officer First-Class Mark Bodzin, the sailor whose console they stood behind. "From what I understand, that layer out there is unbelievably thick, and this would account not only for Sierra Seven's sudden appearance, but for its disappearance as well."

"What's the status of our thin-line array?" Michaels wanted to know.

As the current sonar watch supervisor, Bodzin answered, "We've finally tracked down the malfunction to a shorted signal processor, sir. My boys are replacing the component even as we speak."

"I say that we should go up over the layer and take a peek," the XO offered. "Our remaining towed array is more than adequate for the job."

Michaels replied while thoughtfully studying the multitude of vertical white lines visible on the waterfall display. "Though I agree that the TB-16 could do the job in most instances, I'd feel better having our TB-23 on-line before breaking that layer."

"Just give my boys a couple of more minutes and that thin-line array will be as good as new," Bodzin promised.

The captain looked at his watch. "You're on, Mr. Bodzin."

At this moment a young, pimply-faced seaman entered the compartment by way of the aft passageway and somewhat nervously addressed the XO. "Lieutenant Commander Perez, sir, Lieutenant Carr instructed me to inform you that he's got the results of the latest bathythermograph probe."

Michaels appeared excited with this news. "That should give us a pretty good picture of the exact nature of that layer. Come on, XO, let's see what we're up against."

Perez followed Michaels back into the control room, where they found Lieutenant Ronald Carr in the aft portion of the compartment, bent over one of the two plotting tables. The navigator, who was penciling in their latest course update, didn't appear the least bit surprised when the two senior officers appeared at his side.

Spread out on the table before them was a detailed bathymetric chart, showing a portion of the South Atlantic just north of the South Sandwich Island chain. Carr's latest mark showed them transiting a banana-shaped subterranean feature labeled, THE ORCADAS RISE.

"I still find myself simply amazed every time I update our position," he said. "I never dreamed that one day I'd actually be working such a chart."

"I share your amazement," Michaels admitted. "As the first American submarine ever sent to actively patrol the waters south of the Antarctic convergence zone, the *Springfield* is indeed making history."

"Wait until you hear the results of our latest probe," Carr said. "It shows an incredibly dense layer up there, which starts at five hundred and twenty feet and extends another fifty feet upward, with a fifteen-degree temperature variation. Now, that's a real thermocline!"

"It also explains why sonar is having trouble tracking our latest contact," Michaels put in. "To escape detection, all Sierra Seven has to do is return to the warmer side of the layer, with the colder water of our present depth shielding it as effectively as a solid barrier."

"That's why I say that even without the benefit of our thin-line array, the most expedient way to tag them is to go up there and flush 'em out," the XO repeated.

"I agree," interjected a deep, hoarse voice from the adjoining aft passageway.

The three officers looked up in unison to identify the speaker of these words. Casually leaning against the nearby bulkhead, a mug of coffee in hand, was a solidly built man in green fatigues. Lieutenant Steven Collier was one of four nonregular crew members aboard the *Springfield*. Not a submariner by trade, Collier was the leader of a four-man SEAL team that had boarded the boat during a recent stop at Port Stanley in the Falkland Islands. Since then, he had for the most part kept himself and his men segregated in the torpedo room.

"Since it's evident that you know where your target is, why the hell wait any longer?" he now asked bluntly.

Michaels had disliked this man instantly. Not only was he physically intimidating, but there was an aggravating roughness to his personality and a corresponding darkness to his soul. The captain had to struggle to respond to the SEAL's question politely.

"Hunting down another submarine is a complex, time-consuming process, requiring great amounts of patience. I'll make my move soon enough, but only after I've carefully considered all the variables."

"From what little action I've seen on this pigboat, I'd say you guys are a little too cautious," the SEAL observed. "In my book, success in battle depends on taking the initiative. And since this is a warship, after all, I think it's time for you to stop acting like engineers and begin thinking like warriors."

"Conn, sonar!" the amplified voice of Mark Bodzin interrupted over the intercom. "Sierra Seven is back on the screen. Bearing three-three-zero, relative rough range fourteen thousand yards and closing."

Though Michaels hated to give the SEAL the impression of agreeing with his presumptuous comments, he knew that it was time to alert the crew.

"Battle stations!" he ordered.

A self-satisfied sneer appeared on Collier's face as a loud electronic gong began sounding in the background. Michaels did his best to ignore the SEAL as he turned to the diving control station, his XO close behind him.

Michaels arrived at his destination in time to see the COB pull his customary cigar from his breast pocket and clamp it firmly between his lips. This was a sure sign that the boat was ready for action, and Michaels positioned himself beside the chief as the various members of the battle staff took up positions around them.

"It appears that we've got us a real live nibble, Cap," COB excitedly observed. "Of course, now comes the hard part of settin' the hook. Damn, those bastards are good!"

True to form, Michaels remained pessimistic. "Don't count your fish just yet, COB. Let's put the pedal to the metal and take a closer peek. Take us around to course three-two-zero, at one third speed."

"All ahead one third on course three-two-zero, aye, Cap," COB repeated as he watched the helmsmen carry out this order.

As they turned their yokes to the left the *Springfield* canted. Michaels reached up to grab an iron handhold to keep from losing his balance and noted the tense anticipation that seemed to fill the air.

"What about our depth, Cap?" COB questioned, his own body kept in place by a tight seat belt.

"Hold her steady, COB," Michaels instructed. "I don't want to go up near that layer until I know just what it is we're up against."

Once more Bodzin's voice emanated from the intercom, this time with a bit of uncertainty. "Conn, sonar. We've lost 'em in the layer. Sierra Seven is off the screen."

"Skipper, we've got to go up into that layer and flush them out," the XO urged from his position on Michaels's left.

The captain impatiently looked at his watch, then reached overhead and pulled the nearest intercom handset to his lips. "Mr. Bodzin, I want that thin-line array up, and I want it now!"

Mark Bodzin winced as he listened to the captain's frustrated outburst. This was about as angry as he had ever heard his CO, and Bodzin didn't dare incur the captain's further wrath, or he'd end up peeling potatoes for the duration of the patrol.

With the slim hope that the TB-23 had been repaired within the last couple of minutes, he readdressed his keyboard to access the system. As he feared, the computer would not accept his command, and he knew that there was only one thing left for him to do.

Bodzin yanked off his headphones, stood, and told the sailor seated to his right to take over the watch. Then, without further explanation, he hurried forward to the adjacent compartment, where much of the busy one's hardware was maintained.

Sprawled out on the deck of this compartment between a virtual canyon of computers was a trio of sailors. Amid a mess of spare parts and empty storage boxes, two of them were aiming their flashlights into the cavernous recesses of an open access panel. Only the legs and lower torso of their associate was visible, the rest of his body hidden deep inside the panel itself.

"What in the blazes is keeping you guys?" Bodzin asked. "The captain just read me the riot act. And if that TB-23's not up pronto, I'm dead meat."

"I don't understand it," said a muffled voice from inside the access panel. "I've got the right replacement part, but the component just won't fit."

Bodzin raised his arms and eyes in mock frustration before kneeling down to join his shipmates on the deck. "Bubba," he said as he peered into the open panel, "get the hell out of there and let me give it a try."

The technician needed the assistance of his colleagues to fulfill this request. When he was finally pulled free, his bewilderment was most obvious.

"I don't understand it, Chief. This replacement circuit's supposed to just slide on in."

Bodzin grabbed the thin, four-by-six-inch circuit board. "So this is the sucker that's responsible for putting my chosen career path in jeopardy," he observed to no one in particular. "By any chance is there a lubricant of any kind in all this mess?"

"I'm afraid not, Chief," answered the technician who handed him the part.

"I've got some Vaseline lip balm on me," reported the freckle-faced sailor on Bodzin's right.

Bodzin's free hand shot out toward the sailor and he snapped his fingers. "Then that's just gonna have to do. Hand it over, Bubba."

The sailor pulled a small plastic tube from the breast pocket of his poopy suit and dropped it in Bodzin's palm. Bodzin wasted no time unscrewing the cap and smearing a minute amount of the translucent jell on the edges of the circuit board.

Satisfied with his effort, Bodzin grinned. "Now, with a little luck on our side, this problem's history. So get those flashlights up guys, 'cause I'm goin' in."

He had to awkwardly scoot himself forward to squeeze his upper frame into the open panel, but with the assistance of the combined illumination of the flashlights, he quickly located the vacant slot where the circuit board supposedly belonged. With the delicate touch of a surgeon, he managed to align the board properly. But even with the additional lubrication, it slid in barely a third of the way before getting hung up.

"Are you absolutely certain that this is the proper part?" he asked, the sweat forming on his forehead.

"The manual says it is," answered a strained voice that didn't sound all that sure of itself.

"Ah, just great," Bodzin whispered in disgust.

Not looking forward to the tedious task of accessing the manual, Bodzin allowed his growing desperation to determine his next course of action. He ever so slightly slid back the stuck circuit board, then regripped its rigid plastic edge and shoved it forward, yelling, "Damn it sucker, fit!"

This time the board slid firmly into place with a loud click, and Bodzin was one big grin as he scooted free of the panel and addressed his shipmates. "So much for a delicate touch in servicing high technology. Now all of us better pray that this does the trick, because I sure don't want to be the one who has to tell the captain that we still have a problem back here."

All three of the technicians anxiously followed him back into the sonar room to gather behind his console. Their collective eyes didn't leave his hands as he expertly addressed the keyboard. Only after he completed accessing the proper validation sequence did they expectantly turn their glances to the flickering monitor screen to await the verdict of their efforts.

"Conn, sonar, the TB-23 is back on-line and fully deployed!" the relieved voice of Mark Bodzin from the control room's overhead speakers reported. "We're initiating a broad-band full-spectrum scan."

Philip Michaels's own relief was apparent as he stood on the forward portion of the periscope pedestal and issued a long-anticipated order to the sailors gathered to his left.

"Helm, make our new depth four-five-zero feet, on continued course three-two-zero at one third bell."

"Four-five-zero feet, on bearing three-two-zero at one third bell, aye, Cap," the COB repeated, chomping down on his cigar as the planesmen pulled back on their steering yokes.

With the bow and stern planes now engaged, the angle of the deck noticeably increased. COB's glance shifted to the digital depth gauge, and he began to read out the rapidly descending numbers.

"Five hundred and seventy-five feet . . . five hundred and seventy . . ."

Behind the seat-belt-constrained members of the diving party, the control room's battle staff found themselves having to seek out secure handholds to keep from falling. The captain and the XO both grabbed specially designed steel rungs suspended from the ceiling above the pedestal on which they stood.

As the *Springfield*'s bow continued angling sharply upward, a coffee mug slipped from its restraint beside the forward weapons control console and went clattering to the deck. This sudden racket caused Michaels to turn. He saw the fallen mug sliding backward, but before it crashed into the aft bulkhead, a hand shot out of the shadows and grabbed it.

Before turning his attention back to the helm, Michaels met the glance of the individual with the quick reflexes. Lieutenant Steven Collier was holding the mug like it was a precious piece of war booty, and Michaels sensed that the contemptuous sneer that continued to paint the SEAL's face was meant just for him.

"Five hundred and fifty feet," COB continued in a monotone.

Michaels's gaze went to the digital depth gauge. As it clicked past the 530-foot mark the XO anxiously addressed him.

"We're entering the bottom portion of that layer, Skipper. Our TB-23 should tag our target anytime now."

Michaels grunted. Without removing his eyes from the depth gauge, he imagined the newly deployed thin-line array, a passive sonar system unique to the BSY-1. It allowed them to trail a 1.1-inch cable, stored on a reel on the port horizontal stabilizer, to which was attached a 960-foot-long hydrophone array, which was currently being towed over three thousand feet behind them, far from any noises that the *Springfield* might be generating. This hydrophone was specially designed to detect very low-frequency noises at extremely long distances. It was the most sophisticated sensor device in their inventory.

"Five hundred and twenty feet and continuing to ascend," COB reported.

The temperature of the outside sea would be gradually rising now, and the cold, dense Antarctic waters they were leaving would protect them no longer as they sliced through the thermal layer. Of course, this would also signal their arrival into a radically new sonic environment, where sonar was deflected off the denser bottom layer, just as if it was a solid wall.

"Approaching the five-hundred-foot mark," COB observed to all those unable to see the flashing depth gauge.

The moment of truth was almost upon them. For the second they popped up over the layer, their commitment would be complete, and the *Springfield* would no longer be veiled from any potential adversary patrolling these upper reaches of the sea.

"Conn, sonar!" Bodzin's amplified voice called from the intercom. "We've got a new unidentified submerged contact, bearing one-three-five, designate Sierra Eight, possible hostile."

Michaels reacted forcefully to this news. "Helm, take us back down to six hundred feet, full angle on the dive planes!"

"Six-zero-zero feet, full angle on the dive planes, aye, Cap," COB shot back as he watched the planesmen push forward on their control yokes until their arms were fully extended.

They lost another ten precious feet of depth before the abrupt reversal of plane position finally showed results in the form of a slowly stabilizing depth gauge. Michaels readjusted his grip on the overhead handhold as the deck momentarily evened out before angling forward steeply by the bow. A ruler slid off the navigation plot behind him, and a sailor at the weapons console cursed when he lost his balance and smacked into a chair beside the BSY-1 panel.

Ignoring these distractions, Michaels listened as COB announced the new depth reading: "Five hundred and five feet . . . five hundred and ten . . . five-fifteen . . ."

Only when he was fully satisfied that their course reversal was complete did Michaels address his XO. "That sly son of a bitch. He was up there all along, silently hovering, waiting for us to pop up through the layer and show ourselves."

"But what about Sierra Seven?" Perez asked.

"That was nothing but a decoy, designed to lure us up through the layer," Michaels explained. "And if it wasn't for our ever-lovin' thin-line array, we'd be a sitting duck right now."

"These guys are going to be impossible to tag," the frustrated XO said.

"I don't know about that," Michaels countered. "Since they still don't know that we're onto them, let's turn the tables and give them a dose of their own medicine. Load up a MOSS in tube number two and program a preset course straight for Sierra Seven."

"I've got ya', Skipper," the now grinning XO said. "They'll think that our decoy is the real thing, and when Sierra Eight moves in to tag it, we'll be there to spoil their day."

Barely ten minutes passed between the plan's formulation and its implementation. As the mobile submarine simulator shot out of the torpedo tube and rocketed up through the thermocline, the *Springfield* silently hovered, veiled in a cloak of ultra quiet.

In the control room, the focus now shifted to the five weapons control consoles. Here the men of fire control alley prepared to initiate the localization/tracking process. Expectations were high as the MOSS decoy broke through the layer at a depth of 470 feet. Shortly thereafter, Bodzin's amplified voice spurred them into further action.

"Conn, sonar, Sierra Eight is on the move, bearing three-two-zero, range ten thousand yards and closing."

"Fire control tracking party," Michaels ordered from the periscope pedestal, "initiate your TMAs."

The hunt was now on in earnest, and as the tracking team addressed their keyboards Steven Collier curiously approached the periscope pedestal.

"Excuse me," the SEAL said to the boat's two senior officers. "But exactly what's going on here?"

Michaels glanced at his XO and sarcastically answered, "This is the part that you've been waiting for, Lieutenant. XO, why don't you explain what our fire control team is attempting."

"Lieutenant Collier, what you're seeing here is a target motion analysis," the XO began. "Besides positively identifying our target, the TMA will provide a usable fire control solution showing course, speed, and a reliable range."

"And I bet that's when you can launch torpedoes," the SEAL assumed.

Perez shook his head. "Not quite, Lieutenant. The technicians still have to go through a process known as 'stacking the dots.' If you take a close look at their monitor screens, you'll see a series of dots corresponding to the targets bearing over an extended period of time. The solution must be fine-tuned by adjusting the estimates of the target's range, course, and speed, until the dots are aligned in a straight column. Only then will it be time for a torpedo release."

"What kind of weapon will we be launching today?" the SEAL asked.

"Hang on and see for yourself, Lieutenant," Michaels answered, looking at Perez. "Come on, XO. It's time for the *Springfield* to do what it does best."

The somewhat confused SEAL remained at fire control while the sub's two senior officers proceeded to the aft portion of the pedestal, which gave them a clear view of the men gathered around the two navigation plotting tables.

"Mr. Carr," Michaels said to the navigator. "I need you to plot the shortest course that will take us smack into Sierra Eight's baffles. It's time to get up close and personal."

Carr appeared to relish this assignment, and he answered without having to look back down at his chart. "I've been waiting for that request, Captain, and a course of three-three-zero should do us just fine."

"Three-three-zero it is," Michaels repeated, continuing forward with his XO to the diving console, where COB anxiously awaited them.

"Is this it, Cap?" Crick asked, his cigar now chewed down to a bare stump.

Michaels nodded. "It's all yours, COB. Have your boys bring us up hard to four hundred and fifty feet, on bearing three-three-zero."

This time when the Springfield shot up through the layer, there was a confident, enthusiastic gleam in its commanding officer's eyes. This feeling reached its peak after the weapons officer revealed that the TMA was complete and the dots stacked.

"Sonar, conn," Michaels barked into the intercom handset. "Prepare to go active on target coordinates, three-quarter volume."

As Bodzin repeated these orders Michaels put down the handset and addressed the control room's battle staff. "We've successfully maneuvered into our target's baffles, and now we're going to even the score for last week's sonic lashing by delivering one of our own."

"Captain," a sailor from the forward passageway interrupted. "Excuse me, sir, but we just received a flash VLF page from COMSUBLANT."

Immediately sobered by this news, Michaels accepted a copy of this dispatch and hastily read it. "Damn!" he muttered as he handed the dispatch to his XO.

Michaels was well aware that his crew was still wound up for battle. Though he hated to disappoint them, he waited until the XO had read the document before disclosing its contents to all.

"Gentlemen, I'm afraid this exercise is officially over as of this moment. We've just been ordered to investigate a supposed act of international piracy that took place on the high seas east of here. Lieutenant Carr, I need you to draw up the most direct course to Bouvetoya Island, where our investigation will begin."

"Skipper," said the XO, "what about the *Turbulent?*"

Almost as an afterthought, Michaels reached for the nearest intercom handset and spoke into its transmitter. "Mr. Bodzin, instead of going active on our target, I need you to open a direct underwater comm line with them."

"Excuse me, sir," came the confused voice of the sonar officer. "What about our payback for last week's lashing?"

"That's just going to have to wait a bit longer," Michaels replied. "Now, if you'd be so good as to open that underwater line, Mr. Bodzin . . ."

As upsetting as it was to cut the exercise short, Michaels was even more distressed by the conversation that followed. With the telephone held tightly to his ear, he firmly addressed the transmitter.

"HMS *Turbulent*, HMS *Turbulent*, this is the USS *Springfield*. Do you read me, *Turbulent*?"

The scratchy voice that answered had a definite British accent. "This is the HMS *Turbulent*. Go ahead, USS *Springfield*."

Almost reluctantly, Michaels continued. "HMS *Turbulent*, this is Captain Philip Michaels. We are breaking off our exercise to establish a SATCOM link with command to confirm new orders."

"I'm sorry to hear that, old chap," replied yet another British voice, which had a clipped way of speaking. "Does this mean that you're once more capitulating?"

"Captain Hartwell," the exasperated American sub driver answered, "I'm making this call from a position smack in your baffles. Don't you Brits ever give up?"

4

The view from 23,000 feet was awe-inspiring. Dr. Laurie Anderson peered out the LC-130's circular porthole and took in a seemingly endless expanse of sparkling water, on whose surface dozens of icebergs floated. This was the first time the thirty-two-year-old geologist had ever seen an actual iceberg, and it was an exciting sight.

She found it hard to believe that less than a week ago she was on Oahu, packing her bags for this long-anticipated trip. Seeing the icebergs was a reminder of how very far from home she really was.

Any further thoughts of home were interrupted when the fuselage of the LC-130 momentarily shook as it passed through a pocket of turbulence. The pitch of the aircraft's four turboprop engines deepened in response to this rough air, and Laurie leaned back from the window to tighten her seat belt.

A quick glance at the other passengers showed that

few of them gave the unexpected turbulence so much as a second thought. About half the plane's sixty-three occupants were scientists like herself. The other half were civilian contractors and military personnel, who amazed Laurie with how readily they made themselves comfortable.

The aircraft was far from the luxurious 747 that conveyed her from Hawaii to New Zealand. The seats had hard nylon webbing and the cabin's walls were covered in a thin quilted, grayish fabric from which hoses and pipes protruded. The sole bathroom was little more than a portable toilet, with a flimsy curtain strung over its doorless entryway for the benefit of the women on board.

Shortly after takeoff from Christchurch, the sailors and airmen left their seats. Most headed for the rear of the cabin, where they sprawled out on huge flat, cargo-filled pallets. Others climbed up into the flimsy hammocks that hung overhead, where they slept soundly, oblivious to the turbulence and the constant whine of the airplane's engines.

Laurie felt a cold draft on her neck, and she zipped up the red nylon parka she had put on soon after they reached cruising altitude. A distinctive garment with a fur-lined hood, it was standard civilian issue, compliments of the United States Antarctic Research Program.

She was just wishing for something hot to drink when a U.S. Navy helicopter pilot, who had been seated beside her during takeoff, approached from the cockpit. He was dressed in a form-fitting, green flight suit and carried a silver thermos. From what little conversation they had already shared, she found him a friendly, inquisitive young man, with a markedly devil-may-care attitude toward life.

"I thought you'd might like some hot joe," he said as he took the vacant seat to her left.

"Actually, I was just wondering if there was something hot to drink on board," she replied.

With a steady hand, he unscrewed the thermos and poured a stream of coal black coffee into its plastic cup.

"Sorry," he said as he handed her the steaming brew, "but there's no sweetener or cream."

"No problem," she replied, gratefully warming her hands on the cup's sides.

Again the cabin shook, and Laurie just managed to keep from spilling the coffee. The pilot noted her unease and eyed her sympathetically.

"I'm afraid we're in for a little more rough air as we approach the ice. It shouldn't be too bad, though."

Laurie nodded and took a sip of the piping-hot, strong coffee. It did the job of warming her up, and she watched as the pilot pulled out an envelope-size, sealed silver packet from his zippered breast pocket.

"I also managed to rustle up a couple of MREs," he said as he tore off a corner of the packet and sniffed the contents. "Ah, I believe this one's turkey pot pie."

"No thanks," Laurie said quickly. "To tell you the truth, I've been feeling a little queasy ever since we left Christchurch, and this coffee's more than sufficient."

"I assume that you don't fly much," he commented after hungrily swallowing down a mouthful of his "Meal Ready to Eat."

"As a geologist based in Hawaii, I've made my share of interisland hops and flights to the mainland U.S.," Laurie said. "But never in a plane like this one."

As if in response to her comment, the cabin rattled noisily, which caused a wide grin to turn the corners of the pilot's mouth. "I hear ya', Doc. A CH-130 certainly wasn't built for comfort. It's meant for long-distance cargo handling to some of the harshest, most desolate corners of this planet, which our current destination certainly is. Say, what draws a warm-weather wahine like yourself down to the ice? It surely isn't the weather."

Laurie took a long sip of coffee before replying. "Actually, I've been hoping to visit Antarctica ever since graduate school. My current National Science Foundation grant will allow me access to one of the earth's largest and least explored areas of volcanic activity."

"Sounds like someone's gonna be visitin' Marie Byrd Land," he observed.

Laurie's eyes opened wide at the mere mention of this region. "Do you know the volcanic mountains of West Antarctica?"

"Do I know the volcanic mountains of West Antarctica? Say, Doc, who do you think's gonna most likely fly you out there?"

"I'm sorry, I forgot that this was your third consecutive season flying in Antarctica," Laurie said. "Are those mountain ranges really as magnificent as they appear in the photos?"

"Doc," the chopper pilot answered, "believe me when I tell ya that pictures can't do justice to the unbelievable landscapes that are waitin' for you on the ice. Once you spend a season there, you'll know what I'm talkin' about, and even Hawaii will start lookin' shabby to ya."

Laurie looked pleased by his sincere observation, and she excitedly continued: "I also hope to spend some time at the Mount Erebus Observatory. Much like the volcanoes on the big island of Hawaii, Erebus has been in a continuous eruptive state for most of this century. If all goes as planned, I'll be monitoring the release of sulfur dioxide from the volcano, and analyzing the other gases that its vents are constantly releasing into the atmosphere."

"Sounds like you're gonna have a full plate this season," the pilot observed. "And if you ever manage a day off, please feel free to look me up at the naval barracks. I'd be honored to show you around Mac Town."

"Mac Town?" Laurie repeated.

"That's what we call McMurdo," he explained. "And hey, I'm serious about that tour offer. Just ask anyone in the barracks for A.J., and they'll know where to find me. By the way, is there a significant other in your life?"

Laurie had been anticipating this question, yet she still found herself blushing. "I'm one of those boring souls who are married to their work, A.J."

Her companion seemed pleased with this news and waited until she finished her coffee to ask, "How would you like to visit the flight deck of this old rust bucket?"

"I didn't think unauthorized civilians would be allowed up there," she replied.

"Normally, they're not. But in your instance, I believe the flight crew would be willing to take the chance that you won't turn out to be a security risk. Besides, the aircraft commander just happened to be my roommate at the naval academy, and I've got so much dirty laundry on him that he wouldn't dare turn you away."

Having been unable to concentrate on the geophysics textbook she had brought along to read during the eight-hour flight, Laurie decided to accept. She unbuckled her seat belt and followed her handsome escort down the aisle to the forwardmost section of the cabin. Here a ladder led them up to the flight deck.

They emerged into the aft portion of the cockpit. Though cramped with both men and equipment, it was warm, well lit, and cozy. The two pilots were seated in their leather command chairs contentedly sipping coffee, a gorgeous patch of bright blue, cloudless sky visible through the large windshield that partially surrounded them. The flight engineer sat directly behind them, his attention fully focused on a stripped-down electrical switch he was repairing.

The navigator spotted the two newcomers first. He had just completed verifying their position and was stowing the retractable periscope sextant back into its ceiling mount when he caught a glimpse of them and smiled.

"Well, well," he greeted. "You returned just in time to fork over that twenty bucks you owe us. Read it and weep, A.J.," he added as he handed the helicopter pilot the log into which he had just made an entry.

A.J. skimmed the log, grimaced, and then unzipped one of his many pockets to remove a wad of bills. He peeled off a twenty and reluctantly handed it to the navigator, then turned to the pilots.

"This must be a conspiracy. I could have sworn that we wouldn't hit our PSR for another quarter of an hour yet."

"At least you're running true to form, A.J.," the pilot on the left-hand side of the cockpit said. "Your math's just as bad today as it was back at the academy." Turning to Laurie, he couldn't help but break out into a smile as he introduced himself.

"Hello, ma'am. Lieutenant Commander Vince Adams at your service. And please, don't think that we're running a gambling house up here. We always put together a little pool to see who's farthest away from guessing the exact time we reach our point of safe return—PSR for short. That's the part of our flight when the weather and our fuel state forces us to either commit to a landing at McMurdo or return to New Zealand."

"I still think this game's rigged," A.J. mumbled, then broke into a smile. "Gentlemen, I have the distinct honor of presenting one of the bright stars of this season's NSF research program. From the Aloha State, volcano maven Dr. Laurie Anderson."

The scientist shyly blushed at this dramatic introduction and accepted a warm round of winks, grins, and nods from the flight crew. Lieutenant Commander Adams seemed particularly pleased with her presence, and he quickly made her feel right at home.

"I bet you're on the U of H staff. Do you live in Honolulu?"

"Actually, when I'm not in the field, I keep an apartment in Waimea," Laurie replied.

"No kidding," Adams said. "Why, I grew up practically right next door, on Sunset Beach. Unfortunately, I haven't been back since college. Don't tell me that they paved over the Fern Grotto and built condos there?"

Laurie laughed. "No, Lieutenant Commander. I can reliably report that as of last week, the Fern Grotto and most of North Beach was as pristine and beautiful as ever."

"Thank God for that," said Adams, "because I under-

stand that the developers really did a number to Waikiki.
And by the way, what's with this Lieutenant Commander
stuff? My friends call me Vince. Now, in addition to
being a North Beach resident, you wouldn't happen to be
a navy brat, would you?"

Laurie nodded. "As it so happens, my father spent
thirty-three years as a submariner. When it came time to
finally retire, his choices were either New London or
Pearl Harbor. Mother loved the sun, and that's how we
ended up in Hawaii."

"My pop was a Lieutenant JG on the USS *Arizona*,"
Adams revealed. "Luckily for me and my mom, he wasn't
on duty the morning of December seventh, 1941, though
most of his closest friends were. And after the war, he
decided to retire on Oahu, where many of his best bud-
dies died."

A moment of silence was broken by the voice of the
copilot, who spoke while tapping the speaker of his headphones. "We've got a weather special comin' in from Mac
Town."

Vince Adams quickly activated the cabin's external
radio receiver in time for everyone inside the cockpit to
hear a scratchy female voice emanate from the overhead
speakers.

"Alpha-Charlie-Foxtrot, this is Mac Center with a special
weather advisory. Do you read me, Alpha-Charlie-Foxtrot?"

The copilot spoke into his chin-mounted transmitter.
"We copy you loud and clear, Mac Center."

"Alpha-Charlie-Foxtrot," the amplified voice went on,
"please be advised that blizzard conditions prevail. Sky
obscured, visibility less than one eighth of a mile in blowing snow."

"Roger, Mac Center," replied the copilot, who broke
the connection to a chorus of groans from his coworkers.

"Damn!" said the navigator. "Fifteen minutes ago Mac
reported high overcast and forty miles visibility."

"So much for weather forecasting in Antarctica," the
disgusted flight engineer put in.

"The entire continent only has thirty weather report-ing stations," A.J. explained to Laurie. "Even then, storm fronts on the ice can develop with incredible swiftness. In Mac Town we call these storms a Herbie. They seem to come out of nowhere, sweeping down off Minna Bluff and heading straight toward McMurdo. That's why the best forecasters always keep an eye on the bluffs, because when they disappear, you can start stringin' the rope between the buildings. In another five minutes, you won't be able to walk outside without them."

It was evident that the weather update had soured the mood of the flight crew, and Laurie thought it best to excuse herself and return to the main cabin. As she pro-ceeded toward the ladder Vince Adams spoke again.

"Doc, you needn't worry about the weather, since these storms tend to die out as quickly as they form. Besides, we can land this baby even in the worst whiteout. So if you'd like, please join us up here in a coupla hours, and we can show you how we really earn our paychecks. There's a pair of jumpseats behind you that I guarantee will afford the best view of Antarctica in town."

Laurie didn't know how to refuse this offer, and she returned to the main cabin wishing that she had the nerve to express her real feelings. She had never been a real fan of flying in the best of circumstances. And she would have been very happy to remain in the main cabin and try her best to sleep through the entire landing process.

She spent the next hour in a vain effort to make some headway in her textbook. But it was hard to focus her attention, and she found herself eavesdropping on a spir-ited conversation between the two bearded scientists seated behind her. Sometime during their talk about the spectroscopic and interferometric studies of airglow and auroral processes in the upper atmosphere over the Amundsen-Scott South Pole Station, she drifted off into a deep sleep.

She dreamed of a pine forest, a vision no doubt inspired by her recent four-day stopover in New Zealand

and her outing to the foothills of Mount Cook in that country's southern Alps. Yet this idyllic setting soon shifted into the dark realms of nightmare, when the snows began to fall in thick windblown drifts. In a heartbeat, day turned to blackest night, and Laurie was terrified when she heard a piercing howl fill the woods. Her bare legs now weighed down by blocks of solid ice, she dared to look to the tree line, where dozens of menacing red eyes met her own. As she vainly screamed for help several wolves appeared and charged at her with jaws wide, their eyes filled with hunger.

"Doc," a voice called from the outer realms of consciousness. "Doc, wake up! It's me, A.J."

A gentle hand on her shoulder pulled her from sleep, and she looked up into the concerned eyes of her new friend.

"I'm sorry to have to wake you, Doc. But the way you were twisting and turning, I thought you might pop right out of your seat belt. Was it a nightmare?"

"I guess you could call it that," Laurie managed, the horrific vision still fresh in her mind's eye.

The cabin shook, the roar of the turboprops dropping an octave, and Laurie turned her gaze to the porthole. A wall of pure white filled the sky, and she turned back to A.J.

"Is everything all right out there?"

"Of course it is, Doc," the helicopter pilot reassured her. "We're just losing altitude in preparation for our landing on the ice. Come on, the experience of a lifetime awaits you in the cockpit."

Suddenly remembering her commitment, she reluctantly unsnapped her seat belt, shakily stood, and followed her escort forward.

They reached the flight deck just as violent turbulence shook the 175,000-pound aircraft like it was a mere toy. With A.J.'s assistance, Laurie was able to keep from falling over, and she gratefully crawled into the jumpseat and tightly buckled the shoulder and waist restraints. A.J.

settled in beside her, and together they watched the crew fight to control the shaking plane.

Through the cockpit's wraparound windshield, all that was visible was a blindingly bright white wall of clouds and blowing snow. Laurie felt herself being violently jerked from side to side, then slammed into the hard nylon seat again and again. The whine of the engines constantly changed pitch, and it was most evident that it was taking a supreme effort on the part of Vince Adams and his crew to keep them in one piece.

The intercom filled with a constant jumble of complex landing directions. Laurie nervously watched as Adams did his best to compensate for the turbulence and manipulate the throttle with his right hand, all the while keeping a firm grip on the vibrating steering wheel with his left.

"Airspeed one hundred and fifteen knots, rate of descent two hundred," the copilot reported.

"Altitude three hundred and fifty feet," the engineer added.

"Drift eight," noted the engineer.

Laurie took some comfort in the predictability of these updates. There was no trace of uncertainty or panic in the crew's voices. To them, this was merely another day at the job.

"Hey, you okay?" whispered A.J., seated to Laurie's immediate right.

Laurie nodded tensely, struggling to flash him her bravest smile.

"Don't be embarrassed to ask for an airsick bag if you need it," he said, after a particularly violent series of jolts. "And hey, off the record, I'm as nervous as you are."

When he reached over to grab her hand, she didn't pull away. There was a warm protective innocence to his touch, and she felt better just knowing that he was close by.

A.J.'s grip tightened when the plane reached one hundred feet and they commenced their final approach. Even at this lower altitude, the turbulence continued, the wall of white unbroken.

Vince Adams leaned forward and peered out the window. "It's no good," he commented. "Let's break the pattern and try again."

There was a sinking feeling in Laurie's stomach as the pilot yanked back on the throttle and the plane regained altitude. She wondered if she was going to need that airsick bag, and was thankful that she hadn't eaten since leaving New Zealand, a virtual lifetime ago.

Much to her dismay, the next approach also had to be broken off at the last moment. And this time when they gained altitude to repeat the pattern, the engineer made them aware of one additional complication—a rapidly dwindling fuel supply.

"Enough of this horsin' around," Adams said with a tone of finality. "This time we're puttin' this baby down on the ice. Prepare for whiteout approach."

In a bare whisper, A.J. explained Adams's strategy. "Since we can't sight the airfield's ice runway, we're gonna land on the snow beyond. And for your information, Vince Adams is the best there is in whiteout landing technique."

"I heard that, A.J.," the pilot interjected without turning his head from his cockpit controls. "And even with the compliment, you're not gettin' your twenty bucks back. How are you doin', Doc?"

"I'll make it," Laurie croaked.

"Sorry about the rough ride," Adams said. "And to make up for it, drinks are on me tonight at the officers' club."

"All right!" A.J. exclaimed.

"One hundred and five knots, down five," the copilot reported.

"One hundred feet," added the engineer.

Vince Adams began a running commentary while continuing to manipulate the steering wheel and throttle. "This is where it gets real interesting. Below one hundred feet in whiteout conditions, you tend to lose your sink rate and experience ground effect. It seems only natural at this point to cut power. But if you fall for the illusion, you and the ice will become one real quick. That's why you've got to think the power back, and meet the ice on your terms."

"Fifty feet," said the engineer with a hint of excitement.

The copilot was not to be denied. "One hundred and ten knots, down two."

"Drift ten," the navigator added.

There was a deep thunderous sound as the plane's skis made sudden contact with the snow below. The unexpected impact caught Laurie by complete surprise. She unconsciously squeezed her companion's hand and listened as Vince Adams broke the tension with a spirited, "*Yes!*"

Though loud, the landing was smooth, and the pilot sounded relieved as he recommenced his running commentary. "To keep from pushing the nose over at this point, you've got to fight the impulse to pull back on the yoke, and hold this altitude just like you're still flying. All I've got to do is keep the heading and artificial horizon indicators straight and level, and let the snow do the braking for me."

Less than a minute later the plane lurched to an unceremonious stop. There was no applause inside the cockpit, only a shared realization that the tension had finally broken.

A strong wind buffeted the fuselage. Ice pellets clattered on the windshield, which displayed the very same veil of white that had accompanied them in the air.

"Welcome to Antarctica, Doc!" said A.J.

Laurie tried her best to smile. She summoned the nerve to finally let go of A.J.'s hand, yet found her gaze glued to the swirling gusts of snow that engulfed and blinded them like a cloud. Strangely enough, her apprehensions had not dissipated with the landing. They had merely refocused on the frightening, alien world that waited outside.

As it turned out, the blizzard raged unabated. Unable to find their way back to the airfield, the flight crew faced a new crisis, knowing they would freeze to death the moment their fuel-starved engines died and the heaters stopped operating.

A fuel truck was blindly dispatched from the airfield to save them, a desperate act that nevertheless succeeded thanks to a newly installed radar unit and the heroic efforts of the truck's driver and his assistant. The plane's tanks were topped off, and the decision was made for the passengers and crew to remain on board until the white-out was over.

Eight hours passed before the plane was able to taxi back to the airfield. Laurie spent most of this time down in the main cabin, huddled within her parka. A.J. awoke her shortly after they reached their final destination.

Her first real view of Antarctica came as she climbed out of the plane and walked over to the van that would carry them the five miles into McMurdo. The first thing she noticed was a brilliant blue sky, and then the cold hit her like a stinging slap in the face. The numbing chill penetrated deep into her bones, rendering the mere act of breathing painful.

Yet her discomfort was all but forgotten the moment she set her eyes on the familiar profile of a distant mountain range. Dominating the range was a single snow-capped peak, a plume of smoke spiraling up from its cinder cone. She knew in an instant that this was the legendary Mount Erebus, and knew as well that the great risks she had run to get here had been well worth it, if only for this single magnificent sight.

With renewed enthusiasm, she climbed up into the van. The driver was a personable young woman, who checked her name off a list on a clipboard and informed her that the van would be dropping her off at her prese-lected residence, the Hotel California. The vehicle soon filled with the other new arrivals, and they got on their way, with a marked absence of conversational chatter among the nervous but stoically calm passengers.

The road to McMurdo was little more than a flat, snow-covered expanse of ice, its broad lanes outlined by a series of bamboo stakes sporting red-and-green flags. They passed by the airfield, where a pair of LC-130s were parked beside a large Quonset hut. Men driving forklifts could be seen removing pallets from these planes, and Laurie looked on with interest when a trio of Sno-Cats whizzed past them.

Minutes later McMurdo Station finally came into view. The outpost affectionately called Mac Town was larger and more sprawling than Laurie had anticipated, a small city, in fact, complete with its own power and water desalination plant, administrative building, dormitories, firehouse, mess hall, gym, laboratories, garages, and warehouses. The buildings themselves were mostly of modern construction and no taller than three stories. Insulated water and sewer lines were clearly visible aboveground, in deference to the permafrost. Seeing them, Laurie sensed that a definite frontier spirit prevailed here.

After a brief delay caused by a polar traffic jam of bulldozers, four-wheel-drive utility vehicles, and snowmobiles, the van pulled to a halt at its first stop.

"All off for the Salmon River Inn!" the driver called out.

Several passengers exited and made their way to a beige, multistory building that stood on concrete blocks. It had the boxy, nondescript look of several Monopoly hotels placed side by side and proved to be an exact twin of the dormitory to which Laurie had been assigned, which, as it turned out, was the next stop.

She chuckled to herself upon noting the saying stenciled above her dormitory's doorway. YOU CAN CHECK OUT ANYTIME YOU LIKE, it said, alluding to the lyrics of the song from which the building took its name. It was warm and cozy inside, and Laurie found the small reception desk unoccupied, though a manila envelope with her name was lying on it. She opened it, and removed a key marked "108," a thick orientation booklet complete with a foldout map of the compound, and a smaller business envelope that was sealed, which she decided to open in the privacy of her room.

Room 108 turned out to be a spotlessly clean, private chamber at the very end of the hallway. It was simply furnished with a metal cot and a government-issue desk and chair. Two large posters of Malibu Beach hung on the walls. It reminded Laurie of her first college dormitory room.

The sealed envelope held a letter of welcome from Dr. William Levering, the on-site director of the National Science Foundation. He expressed his regrets for being unable to greet Laurie personally and invited her to make herself at home. Their first meeting together would take place at 2:00 P.M., at his office in the NSF chalet.

A quick check of her watch showed that she had two and a half hours to prepare and she quickly decided her first priority was to unpack her two nylon duffel bags then find the shower facilities. She located the women's rest room halfway down the hall. It held several prefab shower stalls and a warning that their use was to be limited to a pair of two-minute showers per week. She did her best to shower as quickly as possible and returned to her room feeling like a new person.

She spent the next hour sprawled out on her cot reading the orientation booklet. Hunger pangs inspired her to check the mess-hall schedule. She realized that if she wanted a hot lunch she'd have to get it within the next quarter of an hour. Her last complete meal had been back in Christchurch, and she decided to get dressed and see if she could find the mess hall in time.

With the assistance of her map, she located the sprawling building with a whole five minutes to spare. It contained a cavernous, well-lit room, only partially filled because of the late hour. Food was served cafeteria style, and Laurie was pleasantly surprised by both its variety and the quality. As she was soon to learn, this was a U.S. Navy–operated mess, and the chow lived up to this service's superb food service reputation.

She selected a coleslaw-and-beet salad, and the blue plate special of meat loaf, mashed potatoes, and corn. A fluffy sesame roll, hot apple cobbler, and coffee completed her feast, and she was barely able to carry her fully loaded tray to the nearest table.

Her dining companions proved to be two bearded glaciologists from the University of Nebraska. They politely introduced themselves and, while Laurie dug into her meal, explained the project that had brought them to Antarctica. By studying ice-transported microfossils, they hoped to further document the continent's glacial and climatic history, concentrating on the Cenozoic, or most recent geological era.

She soon found herself listening to a complicated discourse on the use of diatoms to interpret past sea-level change, sea-ice cover, and paleotemperatures. By the time she finished her cobbler, she knew all she ever wanted to know about identifying marine biogenic productivity in former Antarctic seas and embayments to determine the hidden stratigraphy of the region's subglacial basins.

The mess hall was nearly empty by the time her dinner companions finally excused themselves, leaving her with an open invitation to visit their laboratory. Laurie was impressed with their scholarly ardor, and once more felt as if she was back on a college campus. Anxious to get on with her own project, she had time for one more mug of hot coffee before going to her two o'clock appointment.

A well-trodden, snow-covered path led her up to the headquarters of the National Science Foundation. Occupying two sides of this chalet-style structure were sixteen poles displaying the flags of the Antarctic Treaty nations. The colorful pennants flapped in a stiff breeze, and

Laurie stopped beside a bust of Admiral Richard Byrd, the first man ever to fly over the South Pole, in 1929, a remarkable achievement, in the days when aviation was still in its infancy. The difficulties that modern aircraft continued to experience in this harsh environment made it all the more extraordinary.

Her speculations about aviation were interrupted when a frigid gust of wind hit her full in the face. Yet before ducking indoors, she took the time to survey the surrounding area and was able to identify her dormitory and the mess hall among the collection of buildings below her. Beyond these, she was afforded a breathtaking view of the sea of ice that stretched to the blue horizon in a glistening, unbroken sheet. She remembered from the orientation booklet that this was the world's southernmost portion of solid ground accessible by ship, and she wondered when the first icebreaker would be paying them a visit.

A bright red helicopter roared overhead, and as Laurie looked upward she spotted a single bird soaring high in the blue heavens. It was a huge, white-feathered creature, either an albatross or a giant snow petrel, she supposed. Exhilarated by her surroundings, she turned toward the shelter of the nearby chalet.

Dr. William Levering turned out to be a warm, personable host. He could easily have passed for a college dean, with his full head of white hair, kindly green eyes, bow tie, soft chinos, and worn leather patches on the elbows of his cardigan. His office was lined with shelves filled with pictures, books, and other mementos gathered during a decade spent in Antarctica.

Laurie was surprised to hear that he was a geologist by trade, and that during an earlier stint with the U.S. Geological Survey he had participated in a drilling operation off the coast of Kauai. This led to an extended discussion of Laurie's Hawaiian upbringing, which was interrupted by the arrival of a uniformed U.S. Navy officer.

Commander Bruce Evans was a serious, doleful-looking

individual, who seemed to bring his somberness into the room with him. Carrying a rolled-up chart at his side, he introduced himself to Laurie and then pinned a poster-size, computer-enhanced aerial photograph to a cork-board.

William Levering appeared uneasy as he nervously cleared his throat and met Laurie's confused gaze. "Dr. Anderson, we're fully aware of the nature of the projects that have brought you to Antarctica. Your survey of the volcanoes of Marie Byrd Land has been eagerly antici-pated, and we're extremely fortunate to have a scientist of your caliber working with us this season. Yet before you get started on your actual fieldwork, we were won-dering if you could help us with an altogether different matter. It came to our attention only recently, and I'm certain that you're well qualified to attend to it. Com-mander, why don't you take it from here?"

The dour naval officer pointed to the photograph he stood beside and began speaking with all the seriousness of an official military briefing. "The National Oceanic and Atmospheric Administration has just completed the first high-resolution satellite image map of the entire Antarctic continent. This map was made possible by com-bining twenty-six separate satellite scans, with each pass focused on a different portion of landmass. The photo-graph I've brought with me today is a thermal infrared image of one of these twenty-six mosaics.

"This particular mosaic represents the region known as New Schwabenland, and is roughly due south of South Africa's Cape of Good Hope. The distinguishing geologi-cal feature of New Schwabenland is the Mühlig-Hofmann mountain range. It was while scanning this range that the thermal imager detected an unusually intense heat source. This heat source corresponds to the reddish por-tion of the mosaic, with the cooler areas colored in blue.

"Though the United States has no bases in this sector, several other nations do, including Germany, India, and Russia. And since it's our fear that this heat source could correspond to a potential volcanic eruption, we thought it prudent to investigate further before releasing a formal warning."

Evans hesitated at this point, and William Levering was quick to take over. "Dr. Anderson, we were counting on you to handle this initial investigation for us. I realize that you already spent countless hours preparing for your project in Marie Byrd Land, and I know it's asking a lot of you to put your plans on temporary hold. But we can't ignore the hundreds of lives that could be at risk if a volcano were to erupt out there. And since all the other qualified NSF geologists are already in the field, you're our last hope. Will you do it for us, Doctor? Will you go up there and see just what it is that we're up against?"

Laurie was unable to ignore the emotion with which his request was uttered. As she walked over to the thermal image photograph to take a closer look, she asked, "Are there any active volcanoes in the Mühlig-Hofmann range?"

Levering's answer was terse. "None that we know of. In fact, I have no record of any volcanic activity in all of New Schwabenland."

Laurie traced the deepest red portion of the photograph. "If this thermal image is accurate, we could be facing a newly risen lava tube. Such a formation would precede the actual fissuring process, which could take place hours, days, or even years from now."

Sensing her rising interest, Levering walked over to the photograph to join her. "The exact depth of that tube is just what I need you to find out, Doctor. And believe me, I'd do it myself if these old bones would allow it."

Laurie grinned. "This actually sounds more intriguing than my project in Marie Byrd Land."

"Which, I promise you, will be waiting for you upon your return," Levering reminded her.

"If we don't have a base up there, where will I stay and how will I get there?" she asked.

Levering nodded at Evans, who immediately began:

"The largest base in New Schwabenland is Novolaza-revskaya. It's run by the Russians, and has a fully operational, all-weather ice runway. We've worked with them before and found the folks at Novo base, as they call it, to be an accommodating, well-trained, safety-minded bunch."

"Will language be a problem?" Laurie wondered aloud. "My Russian's limited to *da* and *nyet.*"

This time Levering replied. "As in McMurdo, most of the occupants of Novo base are scientists. They're generally well traveled, many of them trained at American schools. I personally know one member of Novo's current staff who speaks English as well as you or I. She'd also make the perfect companion to accompany you into the field. Her name's Dr. Anna Litvak. She's a Harvard-educated geologist, and one of the world's foremost seismologists. I'll write you a letter of introduction, and Anna will take it from there."

Unable to think of any other objections, Laurie shrugged. "I guess you've got yourselves the services of a vulcanologist," she said with a smile. "When do I leave?"

"I'll contact Dr. Alexandrov, the director of Novo base, and let him know that you're coming," Levering replied. "Commander, how's tomorrow?"

"No problem," Evans said. "We can ship Dr. Anderson out on the morning supply flight to the Pole. From there, it's a short hop of a thousand miles or so to New Schwabenland."

Only then did Laurie realize how very far away she'd be from McMurdo. To get there, she'd have to travel by way of the South Pole, and endure a flight almost as long as the one from Christchurch. With her eyes still focused on the thermal image photograph, she wondered if she hadn't been a bit hasty in accepting this new assignment, which would literally take her to the ends of the earth in the company of strangers.

5

The Dourados River, on the border of Paraguay, deep in the heart of the Brazilian state of Mato Grosso . . . if anyone had predicted to Jacob Litvak twenty-four hours ago that he'd be in such a place, he would have thought them insane. Yet here he was, standing on the prow of the battered, twenty-five-foot wooden launch called the *Piranha*, breathing in the steamy, humid air and watching the green-forested shores steadily pass by.

Beyond the thumping growl of the *Piranha*'s ancient diesel engine rose the distinctive sound of Hebrew, emanating from the vessel's open amidships' cabin. Jacob recognized the voice of Colonel Simon Bar-Adon, the senior Israeli paratrooper, who was deep in conversation with the trio of Mossad agents they had rendezvoused with in Asunción, Paraguay.

To make this meeting, both Jacob and Bar-Adon had had to travel nearly halfway around the world. The first major leg of their trip took them from Tel Aviv to Cape Town. An equally long commercial flight brought them to Buenos Aires, where they were provided an Argentine military C-130. This noisy means of transport carried them to Asunción.

Bar-Adon seemed to be well acquainted with the trio of rugged Mossad agents, who introduced themselves to Jacob by first name alone as Lev, David, and Elie. It was Lev who piloted their unmarked, jungle-green Bell JetRanger helicopter to the obscure, border town of Pedro Juan Caballero. The sixth member of the party awaited them here. Macari, as he turned out to be named, was a small, wiry native with a full head of curly gray hair and a deeply furrowed forehead that showed him to be well past middle age. The fast-talking native, who was clearly on the Mossad payroll, immediately took the four Israelis aside and gave them a long, animated briefing in broken English. Bar-Adon communicated this briefing's contents to Jacob while the helicopter was being refueled.

Three Land Rovers had recently arrived in Pedro Juan Caballero from the direction of Concepción. They briefly stopped for gas, then proceeded northeast over an infrequently traveled, narrow dirt roadway to the banks of the Dourados River, where their occupants were transferred to a trio of Zodiacs that continued upstream. Back in Pedro Juan Caballero, the helicopter was once more utilized to whisk Jacob and his associates to an isolated jungle clearing beside a ramshackle frontier trading post on the banks of the Dourados. Macari was well-known here, and the sinewy, bare-chested native led the way down to a rickety pier, where they boarded their current means of transport.

Less than an hour ago, the *Piranha* passed the trio of mud-speckled Land Rovers, parked on the riverbank among thick vegetation. The mere sight of these vehicles was cause for celebration for the *Piranha*'s six occupants, since it was their first actual proof that they were indeed on the correct trail of their quarry.

The sighting of the Land Rovers was of particular significance to Jacob Litvak. Until this point, his long journey had almost seemed unreal. Yet here was the convoy of vehicles that he had been told about barely twenty-four hours ago, on the distant shores of the Dead Sea.

How very strange it had been to leave Uri and Shai Weinberg behind, so abruptly and with barely a word of explanation. The dig site had been Jacob's exclusive home for well over a month, during which time he had thought of little else but archaeology. The harsh world of reality greeted him the moment he climbed into Bar-Adon's IDF Huey, and it took the Rover sighting for the events of the past day and night to come finally into true perspective.

From a pursuer of buried ancient artifacts, Jacob had become a hunter of man. He had played this role before, and though he found it distasteful each time, it was a sworn duty that he could not refuse.

As the *Piranha* began transiting a series of terraced rapids, Jacob was forced to reach out and grab the splintered wooden railing of the launch. He had watched the bubbling expanse of white water take form in the distance ever since arriving at the prow several minutes ago. Even then, he found himself momentarily caught off balance by a sharp, bobbing motion that began soon after the *Piranha*'s bow bit into the first of the turbulent white water.

The vessel seemed to pick up speed in the swift-moving current, and this increase in velocity, and corresponding increase in wind gusts, provided Jacob a blessed moment of relief from the saunalike atmosphere. With his right hand still gripping the rail, he dared to free his left hand and reach into the pocket of his shorts to remove a wrinkled red bandanna. Already damp, the cotton fabric was completely soaked by the time he finished blotting his forehead, face, and neck.

The stifling tropical temperatures had engulfed him the moment they arrived in Pedro Juan Caballero.

Compared with the dry heat of the Judean wilderness, the great humidity of the surrounding rain forest generated a draining, incessant warmth, that brought forth torrents of sweat from his pores. Along with the heat came the all-encompassing smell of decomposition, the air ripe with the fetid stench of mildew and rot. This was an alien climate, and an alien world that he had entered.

Macari showed himself to be a competent skipper as the *Piranha* negotiated the rapids and entered a wide stretch of calm, brown water, where Jacob was able to let go of the rail altogether. With this slack water came the loss of a knot or two in speed, and the subsequent dissipation of the breeze. Not even the tight cotton rim of Jacob's rumpled bush hat could keep the sweat from pouring down his forehead and dripping onto the dark green lenses of his aviator-style, wire-rim sunglasses, and he finally gave up wiping off this annoying moisture. He soon found his gaze drawn to the right bank of the river, from where a series of high-pitched cries were coming. The source of this scratchy commotion proved to be a group of colorful toucans. The birds sat on the limbs of a massive tree, seeming to watching the *Piranha* pass by, their bright orange, blue, and green feathers and distinctive, banana-shaped beaks making them readily identifiable.

The sound of slapping water diverted Jacob's gaze to the muddied waters of the opposite bank. The surface here was unusually agitated, a roiling, bubbling disturbance filling a ten-foot-wide circular area.

"Piranha!" Macari shouted from the open wheelhouse. "There are piranha feeding over there!"

This was Jacob's first sighting of the infamous carnivorous fish for which their launch was named, and he hurried to join Macari in the wheelhouse.

"That frothing circle of water only hints at the ferocious nature of the creatures responsible for it. The caribe, as my people call the piranha, is a dangerous, bloodthirsty breed. I have personally seen such a swarm cleanly pick the flesh off a full-grown man who had the misfortune of falling into their hungry midst. The feeding frenzy that followed was something I'll never forget."

"I once took on a shark in the Red Sea," Simon Bar-Adon put in. "A punch on his blunt, leathery snout eventually sent him scurrying, though my greatest fear was getting attacked from behind in my blind spot. I imagine that since the piranha feed in a group, repelling them would be almost impossible."

"That's something I hope to never have to experience," Macari said solemnly.

This prompted Lev, the youngest of the Mossad agents, to chime in. "I'd still rather take my chances with a pack of piranha than with our current prey. At least with the piranha you know what you're up against."

"Man has certainly done a good job of distorting nature and putting his own unique stamp on the character of evil," Bar-Adon reflected, adjusting his eye patch. "And I agree with Lev that the odds of surviving a hungry swarm of piranha, or even a shark, are far greater than they are in tangling with the unpredictable beast we currently hunt. What do you say, Jacob?"

Jacob grunted, withholding his answer until the swarming piranhas were well in their wake. "The evil man mistakes in nature's harsh ways is in fact nothing but the primal law of survival of the fittest in its most basic application. The piranha's sole motive to kill is to satisfy its hunger. Real evil takes the shape of a man such as Wolfram Eckhardt, who was indirectly responsible for the slaughter of millions of human beings, all for the sake of a warped political doctrine. Yes, comrade, I, too, would rather take my chances with the piranha."

"Thank God that this source of blackness will shortly be standing before the hand of justice," Bar-Adon said passionately. "For with his apprehension, the souls of untold millions will finally be laid to rest."

Jacob's thoughts remained on the complex nature of earthly evil as he briefly met Bar-Adon's determined gaze, then redirected his eyes to the still waters of the river. It was evil that was drawing them deeper and deeper into this desolate wilderness, a place where death was a constant companion.

How fitting a backdrop it was for the confrontation that would, he hoped, follow soon, a battle as old as time itself, and one documented by the ancients in manuscripts such as the copper scroll Jacob had recently exhumed. He knew from the moment he dared the dangers of the earthquake and the sting of the scorpion to take possession of this scroll that no mere coincidence had led him to the treasure. As far as he was concerned, Simon Bar-Adon's arrival soon afterward was nothing more than another piece of the unfolding puzzle.

A sudden change in the pitch of the *Piranha*'s engine interrupted his thoughts, and caused Jacob to look in the wheelhouse as the launch abruptly veered to the right. Macari's eyes were open wide with excitement as he sharply turned the boat's wheel.

"Aquí, señores!" he screamed, pointing a finger toward the shoreline.

Jacob immediately turned his glance in this direction. A stream, little more than a trickle really, could be seen entering the main channel of the river. But in this insignificant channel was the trio of gray rubber Zodiac rafts.

"Excellent work, Macari!" Bar-Adon stood expectantly beside his three countrymen on the *Piranha*'s transom.

Jacob joined them at the stern, after making certain that the Zodiacs were vacant and that no ambush awaited them, just as Macari was cutting back on the boat's throttle. The incessantly growling engine faded to a purr then ceased as they neared a semicircular wedge of open land where the Zodiacs were moored. Human footprints could be seen in the clearing's mud floor. Jacob was certain that these sharply etched prints were fresh, and he eagerly accepted a leather holster with a canvas gun belt wrapped around it from one of the Israelis.

"Jacob, we've given you a standard-issue, U.S. military forty-five-caliber pistol," Bar-Adon informed him. "It's a semiautomatic with a seven-round clip."

Jacob wrapped the belt around his waist and then carefully removed the heavy black pistol from its holster. He had shot such a weapon before at the practice range and had no trouble ramming a bullet into the chamber and engaging the safety on the gun's grip.

Meanwhile, Simon Bar-Adon and his men prepared their own armaments. Their arsenal included Uzis, combat shotguns, ultralight rifles complete with sniper scopes, various sidearms, grenades, and razor-sharp, Rambo-style survival knives.

Macari led the way onto the clearing, after tying the *Piranha* to an overhead branch. One by one, the Israelis followed. Jacob brought up the rear, with his trusty cypress walking stick in hand. With the security of solid land beneath his booted feet, he watched Macari disappear into the thick vegetation that masked the way inland.

From this new vantage point, the call of the distant river was all but inaudible. In its place was a cacophony of strange new sounds. Like the rhythm section of an orchestra, the undulating buzzing cry of a cicada provided the beat for a chorus of constantly croaking tree frogs and a variety of singing tropical birds. One of the latter's song was particularly haunting, sounding to Jacob like a melancholy *tin-tin-amou*.

Macari returned silently and with a flurry of hand signals indicated that he wanted them to follow him into the thick underbrush. Ever curious as to what lay beyond the tangle of branches and vines, Jacob was the first in line, with Simon Bar-Adon and his three associates bringing up the rear.

Jacob had to hunch over to fit his tall frame through the narrow passageway that penetrated the thick hedge-like tunnel. Only the barest of trails was visible, and with each step further into this vine-covered burrow, he felt his claustrophobia stirring.

His anxiety was eased by the distant sight of a softly glowing, diffused light that indicated the tunnel's end. He increased his cramped stride as best he could and, ignoring the brambles that tore into his back and shoulders, proceeded toward this welcoming light.

He was soon standing fully upright, his awestruck gaze taking in one of the most memorable sights in a lifetime of travel. As far as he could see, the rain forest stretched out before him. It was almost as if he had just entered an immense, tree-covered hothouse. With the thick scent of humid rot full in his nostrils, he sensed a cathedral-like solemnity here. Only this church had a hundred-foot-high ceiling of branches and leaves, a canopy that effectively blocked out the direct sunlight and helped form this self-contained paradise.

An exotic variety of singing birds and humming insects filled the steamy air, their soothing sounds amplified by the thick, overhead foliage, which also produced a constant shower of dripping water.

"Ah, to be back in the rain forest," Simon Bar-Adon observed from behind. "There's truly no more beautiful place on all the planet."

"I can't help feeling that I've just entered a church or temple of some sort," added Jacob.

Bar-Adon concurred. "It's indeed a shrine to the diversity of life, my friend, and is in its own way a holy place."

Ahead, the barest of trails led into the forest. Macari halted just as he was about to disappear into the tree line and waved his arm for them to join him. They briefly waited for the three Mossad agents to emerge from the hedge before doing so.

"There are six individuals in the party we trail," the native whispered, pointing to the footprints impressed in the soft mud floor. "All wear Western-style boots and weigh at least one hundred and sixty pounds. From the freshness of these tracks, I'd say they passed here within the last few hours."

"Where does this trail lead?" Bar-Adon questioned.

Macari was quick to answer. "From this point, all paths lead only further into the heart of the Mato Grosso."

Macari's answer prompted a question from Lev. "I wonder what they're doing out here?"

"There's only one way to find out," Bar-Adon said as he peered farther into the deep woods. "We must proceed most cautiously now. Macari, as you take the point, you must be on the lookout for possible booby traps. And all of you, always remember that our prey is one of the most dangerous creatures to ever walk this planet!"

"We are also entering the realm of the deadly fer-de-lance, gentlemen," Macari added. "This is a snake that you won't be encountering on the ground. It lives in the overhead branches and vines, and prefers to strike man on the neck."

With this chilling warning, Macari led the way into the forest. Jacob allowed the Israelis to precede him and was content to take up the team's rear. Their pace was quick, and Jacob had little time to take in the diverse array of tropical flora and fauna. At one portion of the trail, he was forced to step over an army of swiftly crawling ants with three-inch-long bright red bodies. Crossing the trail in a tight column like a single entity, they seemed to have a definite purpose in mind.

Shortly afterward, a bloodcurdling screech overhead led to Jacob's discovery of a large family of monkeys. The small gray-skinned, dark-eyed primates were incredibly boisterous and, between quick bites of fruit, appeared to be discussing the passage of their human cousins down below.

Jacob made good use of his walking stick to brush away any threatening limbs. He needed a full stride to keep up with his party, who maintained a blistering pace for the better part of an hour. They finally rested at a spot where the trail was bisected by a swift-moving stream.

A deep boom of thunder resonated in the distance, and Macari ominously pointed toward the stream's opposite bank, where the trail split into two branches. "It appears that our party could have gone in either direction," he whispered. "There are tracks present on both of those trails."

Simon Bar-Adon knelt down beside the stream, cupped his hands into the rippling waters, and splashed his sweat-covered face. "Macari, you take David and Elie and proceed on the trail to the right. The rest of us will take the left-hand path, with all of us meeting back here in another hour."

The native nodded that he understood and without a second's hesitation leaped over the stream and swiftly began to march down his assigned trail. David and Elie had to scramble to keep up with him, and the rain forest soon engulfed all three of them. Jacob, Simon Bar-Adon, and Lev stood alone beside the stream.

"He's close, my friends," the one-eyed Israeli whispered. "I tell you, he's very, very close."

"How very symbolic it was for you to save us the left-hand path," Jacob mused. "If the evil stays true to form, surely that's the direction our quarry chose to travel."

"All this mumbo-jumbo talk of evil is starting to get on my nerves," Lev commented. "The prey we're hunting is just a man like you or me, and this talk of supernatural powers is nonsense."

Before responding to this outburst, Bar-Adon caught Jacob's glance and grinned. "Yes, Lev, you're right. Wolfram Eckhardt is just a mortal, whose skin will not prove impervious to the bullets we carry. So please feel free to ignore this evil we speak of, and let us proceed with the very real chore that brought us here. Jacob, would you like to take point?"

The Russian shrugged. "That's fine with me, comrade," he said while stepping over the brook.

As lead man, Jacob was now able to set their pace. He maintained a moderate stride that allowed him just enough time to brush back the encroaching vegetation with his walking stick.

Jacob momentarily froze when a noisy flock of surprised parrots was flushed from the nearby brush. Their raucous cries caused his pulse to quicken. As the birds shot overhead he laughed at his silliness and continued down the trail.

For the briefest of moments he diverted his glance from the meandering path to admire the brightly colored feathers of the last of the fleeing parrots. This was all the time that was needed for him to stumble into the sticky threads of a huge spiderweb. Jacob cursed in disgust as he wildly brushed away the web, which covered his head and most of his upper torso. The spider that built this trap must have been a monstrous brute, and Jacob hurriedly checked for its presence on his soaked clothing. He even pulled off his hat and shook it, then used the hat to slap clear any insects that might be lurking on his back and shoulders.

"Easy, my friend," Bar-Adon cautioned as he caught up with Jacob and helped him remove the last of the cobweb. "You weren't bitten, were you?"

Jacob couldn't help but be embarrassed. "I'm fine," he shakily responded.

Soon afterward, Lev arrived. It was the young Israeli who pointed out yet another intersecting pathway, only a few feet beyond the dangling remnants of the torn spiderweb. This trail further complicated matters and prompted Bar-Adon to make the reluctant decision to thin their party even more.

"Jacob, why don't you and Lev continue on down the main trail? I'll see where this one leads and meet you back here in another half hour."

Still flustered by his encounter with the web, Jacob shook his head in protest. "If it's all right with you, Simon, I'd like some time to myself. You two go ahead down the main trail. I'll be fine on my own."

"Are you positive of that, my friend?" Bar-Adon queried.

Jacob's only answer was a determined stare that the Israeli didn't dare challenge. "Very well, Jacob. You take this new trail, but be careful not to get lost. Every fifty feet or so, bend the stem of a piece of vegetation. This will prove as good as a map should you get confused on your way back."

Jacob nodded that he understood and accepted a crisp good-bye salute from the senior paratrooper. Without further ado, Bar-Adon pivoted and beckoned Lev to lead the way. It didn't take long for the jungle to swallow them. Jacob could now afford the luxury of fully regaining his composure. He stood at the juncture of the new trail and inhaled a series of deep, calming breaths. He then leaned his walking stick up against a tree trunk and pulled out his bandanna. This time after wiping his face and neck, he wrung dry the rectangular piece of cloth, causing a sizable amount of moisture to fall onto the ground.

It was as he bent over to regrip his walking stick that he had the distinct impression that there was someone behind him. The hairs on the back of his neck bristled, and he quickly turned. A wall of solid trees festooned with twisting vines and lianas met his glance. Once again he had the sensation of being watched, and was actually thinking about pulling out his pistol when a slight movement caught his attention.

Turning just in time to see a group of naked Indians materialize out of the forest and surround him, Jacob was instantly captivated by both the fantastic designs painted on their thin, sinewy five-foot-tall bodies and the many spears and bows and arrows that were now aimed at him.

Before he had a chance to introduce himself and express his peaceful intentions, one of the Indians darted forward and yanked his pistol from its holster. At the same time two Indians grabbed him from behind and tied up his hands. It was all done so quickly that Jacob had no chance to resist. And with the odds at least fifteen to one, what good would a struggle do anyway?

He tried to address them with every language in his inventory, but to no avail. They merely stood there, silently studying him with their big, dark eyes, appearing more curious than belligerent.

Still having no idea what their intentions were, Jacob dumbly listened as one of the Indians animatedly addressed him in an unknown language. Jacob pointed to his lips and ears and shook his head that he couldn't understand. The Indian, who was apparently the leader, lifted up his spear and angled its sharpened tip toward the trail that Jacob was preparing to traverse.

Then, without further warning, the rest of the pack formed a single line with Jacob in the middle. The leader positioned himself immediately behind Jacob and prodded his prisoner forward with the sharpened point of his spear.

The Indians seemed to glide through the forest without effort. With his hands tightly tied, Jacob often found himself caught off balance. Vines and thorns were constantly tearing at him, and whenever his step faltered, his captors' spears were always there to urge him on.

As best as he could tell, they were traveling to the southwest, as the sun was consistently over his left shoulder. At first he tried his best to keep track of the small streams they crossed for use as future landmarks. But as his captors' brisk pace kept on, he became less and less aware of his surroundings. Soon it was an effort just to keep walking.

Bathed in sweat and his muscles aching, he stumbled over an exposed root and went crashing to the ground. The resulting blow caused a trickle of blood to flow from his nostrils, and the Indians finally halted to allow him to catch his breath. One of them handed him a water-filled gourd, and Jacob greedily drained it. Another began rubbing the crushed leaves of a plant on Jacob's many cuts and scratches, which greatly relieved the pain and itching and also stopped his nose from bleeding.

After a brief rest, they were again on their way, this

time at a much more moderate pace. With each painful stride, Jacob's anxieties intensified. He all but forgot his reason for being in this rain forest. Fear clouded his mind, his every thought focused on sheer survival. Were these Indians representatives of the infamous cannibals of this region? Was he to be condemned to a lifetime of slavery? His only hope was to escape.

The shadows lengthened, and as the tree frogs began their evening chorus, Jacob wondered where they'd be spending the night. With the arrival of dusk, the trail was increasingly difficult to follow. Yet instead of slowing, the Indians increased their strides. Jacob knew that it would be impossible to keep up with them much longer. He was exhausted, confused, and scared. His loss of hope was leading to despair, and he just wanted to drop to the ground and take his chances with the leader's spear.

It proved to be the distinctive yelp of a barking dog of all things that kept him upright. This familiar sound was coming from nearby, and he tapped his last reservoirs of strength to see its source firsthand. He stumbled across a wide stream and soon found himself entering a broad jungle clearing, filled with primitive wooden lean-tos and a blazing communal bonfire as centerpiece.

The dozens of naked Indians encircling this bonfire were performing a primitive, ritualistic dance of some sort. To the hypnotizing accompaniment of beating drums and an irritating chorus of high-pitched reed instruments, the celebrants danced around the blazing embers with an ever-quickening orgiastic frenzy. Jacob could clearly hear their monotonous, indecipherable chants. With the nightmarish realization that he was witnessing a scene right out of a Hieronymus Bosch painting, the Russian swayed back dizzily and collapsed to the ground, unconscious.

When he finally came to, he was greeted by utter silence. It took several confusing seconds to reorient himself, and he was somewhat surprised to find the clearing completely empty of other humans. From his current vantage point, flat on his back on the hard mud ground, he peered straight up into the night sky. Never had he seen such an expanse of crystal-clear heavens, that took on additional beauty as a shooting star streaked overhead.

It was the hollow sound of a flute playing that redirected his attention to more earthly matters. He stiffly rolled on his side, and as he scanned the darkness he spotted a single individual seated before the barely flickering flames of the once great bonfire, holding a simple wooden flute to his lips and oblivious to Jacob's presence.

Jacob managed to get to his hands and knees, and only then realized that his bonds had been cut. New hope gave him the strength to stand fully, and he decided that now was the ideal opportunity to escape. Yet no sooner did he turn for the shelter of the black woods than a deep bass voice addressed him from the campfire.

"Comrade Litvak, must you go so soon?"

An icy chill ran up Jacob's spine, and he halted and turned to identify the speaker of these words. The flute player remained the only person visible, and Jacob watched as this individual put down his instrument and spoke once more.

"That's more like it, comrade. After all, why be in such a rush to leave, when I'm the one you came all these thousands of miles to track down."

This shocking revelation caused the hairs on the back of Jacob's neck to stiffen, and he found his limbs trembling. Could it really be him? Was this innocent-looking flute player indeed the man he had dedicated a major part of his life to bringing to justice? Having come too far to run away now, Jacob summoned the nerve to face his greatest challenge, and he solemnly took one tentative step after the other toward the crackling fire circle.

The dimly flickering flames illuminated a bald-headed, smooth-shaven old man seated on a small wooden stool. He was immaculately dressed in safari clothing and seemed totally at ease with Jacob's continued approach.

"So at long last we finally meet," said the elder. "My, but you do favor your illustrious father."

Jacob found himself unable to speak, his attention focused on this stranger's somewhat familiar face. He certainly looked old enough to be his adversary. Deep lines wrinkled his forehead, and the skin on his cheeks and neck was unnaturally taut, as if the result of a recent face-lift. It was apparent from his well-formed features that this old-timer had once been extremely handsome, and Jacob found himself captivated by the man's eyes. His clear, powdery-blue irises were the vibrant color of a spring sky and had an almost mesmerizing effect.

"Yes, Jacob Litvak, your long search is really over, for I am Wolfram Eckhardt."

The sincerity of this curt introduction hit home, and Jacob instantly accepted the words as truth. Yet now that he had found his nemesis, what was he to do with him?

"It's too bad that Colonel Bar-Adon and his Mossad cronies couldn't be here to share this historic moment," Wolfram continued. "But fate willed it otherwise. Do you believe in destiny, Jacob Litvak?"

The Russian nervously cleared his throat. "I believe in destiny only to the degree that it is man who ultimately controls the future."

Wolfram Eckhardt grinned. "So you share your father's pragmatism as well. No doubt it's a by-product of your socialist upbringing. Practicality certainly has its place on one shallow level of our existence. But how can you explain why our paths crossed on this fated day? Was it mere chance, or are there greater, unseen forces at work here—the alignment of the heavens or the phase of the moon, for example?"

Jacob had sensed these same powers at work much earlier, on the shores of the Dead Sea. And though part of his being believed in such occult forces, he had another rational side that remained skeptical of them.

Wolfram Eckhardt seemed to sense Jacob's confusion. "Your spiritual quandary is not a new one, comrade. It is as old as time, and one that I, too, faced at your age. For you see, you and I are really not that different. We both share a passion for archaeology and are dedicated students of history. The gulf that separates us is a matter finally of mere semantics, and can be bridged by a proper understanding on your part of the true meaning of the terms *good* and *evil.*"

Jacob could feel the powerful pull of Eckhardt's will, and he firmly resisted. "Did you ever think that you might be the one with the improper understanding? After all, you're the one who supported the Nazi death camps, the greatest manifestation of pure evil this planet's ever witnessed."

Eckhardt laughed. "It's just like a Jew to associate all earthly evil with the concentration-camp program. You put far too much importance on a nonevent, which will have little significance to future historians. Dare to look beyond the lies and contemplate the true essence of good and evil. Take a lesson from the Cathars, who successfully lifted the veil and saw that true evil manifested itself in the form of the Catholic Church, blinded by materialism and a lust to dominate. And even though the pope and his minions sent the First Crusade into the Languedoc to wipe out this heresy, the Cathar secret prevailed, hidden in the Albigensian hills, in the shadow of the ruined castle of Montsegur.

"Did you know that it was at Montsegur that I first met your father, Jacob? Of course that was many years ago. I was but a young man at the time, fresh out of the university, and excited to be on my first real archaeological expedition beyond the borders of my native Germany. As it turned out, both of us were seeking the very same thing, the legendary treasure of the Cathars. This priceless collection was previously stored in the Cathar stronghold of Montsegur, and was said to include such legendary items as the Holy Grail, the spear that pierced Christ's side, and other relics belonging to the First Temple.

"The Crusaders subsequently laid siege to Montsegur. And on the night before twenty thousand Cathars succumbed to mass suicide rather than surrender, a portion of this treasure was lowered over the castle's walls and hidden in a nearby grotto.

"I can proudly report that it was my expedition that recovered it from oblivion. And as we were soon to learn, its incredible value was far beyond the monetary. Thus it was destiny that brought the Cathar secret to Germany and delivered into our worthy hands the means to communicate with the powers beyond."

"My only regret is that you picked the wrong path," Jacob dared to say with rising emotion. "My father learned of your discovery, and tried to warn the world about the black powers that you were unleashing. Not even twenty-five million dead could convince the judges at Nuremberg of the true evil that Nazism was based upon. They instead explained it away in psychoanalytical terms, calling it a mere mental aberration. But you and I know differently, don't we, Comrade Eckhardt?"

Wolfram's thin lips turned up in a satisfied smirk. "So, you're a believer after all, Jacob Litvak. Only it's you who has the true meaning of good and evil reversed. I would have thought you would better understand this, especially after your recent discovery in the Judean wilderness."

Jacob was unable to hide the shock this unexpected revelation generated, and he desperately tried to regain control of the moment. "What discovery are you talking about, comrade?"

"Oh, come now, Herr Litvak. Must we continue on with these childish games? Do you think that I didn't know the moment you and Uri Weinberg first set foot into that cave on the dry shores of the Dead Sea? You forget that you were following in my footsteps! And now that fate has willed you here, it's time for me to lift the veil that has blinded you from the truth. Prepare yourself to become an initiate on this oldest of quests, Jacob

Litvak. For I am about to share with you the secret of the Holy Grail!"

Eckhardt reached down and pulled a leather pouch from his breast pocket. His eyes gleaming with demonic intensity, he delicately removed two large mushrooms from the pouch. Their silver-dollar-sized caps were a brilliant bright red, with white speckles studded in their solid flesh.

"This is the unique life-form that has drawn me to this jungle," Eckhardt revealed, while solemnly cradling the mushrooms in his palm.

"The natives call these beauties *carne de diablo,*" he added with a snicker. "How very fitting it is that they associate the devil's flesh with the great powers this particular fungus can release in man. Didn't you ever wonder why mushrooms such as these have been revered by such diverse ancient civilizations as the Aztec and the Aryan? To tell you the truth, I never gave the subject much thought, until our discovery of the Cathar treasure opened my eyes to a secret hidden since the time of Adam's fall from grace. For mushrooms such as this Amanita muscaria are the true representatives of the forbidden fruit that Adam and Eve first plucked from the tree of good and evil in the Garden of Eden. They dared consume its fiery flesh and were greeted with a vision of heaven so grand that they were driven from the Garden for all eternity.

"Now I give you this once-in-a-lifetime opportunity to lift the veil. Dare join me in the partaking of this rare life-form's flesh. Together we shall experience colorful vistas of worlds beyond and travel from the blackest abyss to the loftiest of heights, where a vision of heaven awaits us. And if the truths you learn on this journey fail to convince you of the purity of my motives, I'll humbly surrender to your judgment. With the dawn, you can do with me as you like."

"And if I don't consume the mushroom with you?" Jacob interjected.

Eckhardt somberly shook his head. "Refuse this offer, and I must sadly hand you over to my Indian hosts. It seems that they have designs on making you the main course of tomorrow evening's feast. And since I've already gone and shared too many a forbidden secret with you, your refusal will indicate unworthiness on your part, and I'll have no choice but to condemn you to such an untimely, horrific death."

Almost to underscore Jacob's lack of options, the Indians began pouring from their huts. Like lifeless zombies, they silently encircled the compound, effectively ending any hope Jacob might have had of escape. With a grudging respect for Wolfram Eckhardt's strange powers, Jacob reluctantly reached out and grabbed one of the mushrooms.

"That's a wise decision, Herr Litvak," Eckhardt said triumphantly. "Now join me in a wondrous trip to the land of the Grail."

Jacob watched Eckhardt lift up the remaining mushroom, reverently holding it before him with all the reverence of a priest performing the Eucharist. The German's eyes momentarily closed, and his lips began moving in what appeared to be a silent prayer.

Jacob found himself mumbling his own prayer of protection, to a god he was only just now rediscovering. Having absolutely no idea how this mushroom might affect him, he looked on as Eckhardt's eyes snapped open. His powdery-blue eyes were strangely vacant, and like a man possessed, he conveyed the mushroom to his lips and took a bite of the bright red cap.

Fear stirred the hair on the back of Jacob's neck as Eckhardt turned his cold, evil glance his way. No words were needed to convince the Russian that it was in his best interest to take a bite from the cap of his own mushroom.

He unwillingly did so, and found the spongy flesh extremely bitter, leaving an acrid, fiery taste in his mouth that remained even after swallowing. Following his host's lead, he needed to force down three more mouthfuls of the mushroom before the cap was completely consumed.

It was shortly after Jacob swallowed the final bite that a drum began beating nearby. The monotonous rhythm had a soothing effect on him, and he surrendered to his fatigue and knelt on the ground. His glance was inexplicably drawn to the remnants of the once great bonfire. The remaining flames danced before his weary eyes with a bright, golden glow that proved captivating beyond his wildest expectations.

Beyond the constant bass pounding of the drum rose the deep hum of the jungle night creatures, a cacophony of buzzing cicadas, croaking tree frogs, and chirping crickets. In the distance, the haunting cry of a single tropical partridge could be heard, its melody evoking feelings of isolation and loneliness.

With his gaze still locked on the glowing orange embers, Jacob's thoughts flashed back in time. He remembered that magical moment—it seemed an eternity ago—when he first set his eyes on the rain forest. Suddenly he no longer minded the dank, humid dampness, nor feared the variety of strange creatures that made this unique place their home.

Without having to leave the fire circle, he allowed the flames to convey him deep into the surrounding woods. In a mushroom-induced hallucination, he became a slinking jaguar, silently stalking the shadows for the prey that would fill his empty belly. The satisfaction of this gnawing hunger was the reason for his existence, and became the focal point for his every contemplation.

It was a deep, resonating clap of thunder that transferred him high into the forest canopy. He was an eagle, adrift on the warm thermals, surveying his lordly domain. From this lofty vantage point, the rain forest appeared like a single entity, a wave tip of life in an otherwise cold, lonely universe.

Another clap of thunder sent him spiraling down, and he became a small deer, vainly struggling to free itself from the viselike grasp of a huge, green anaconda. Jacob's wonder turned to fear as he felt the snake's coils tighten around him. A dark wave of claustrophobic dread conveyed him to a terrifying realm of snapping, frenzied piranha, huge black spiders, and immense, fanged bats. To the eerie, bloodcurdling cries of a howling wolf, the snake cemented its grip on him, and began the long-drawn-out process of squeezing the breath of life from him.

An unbearable, overwhelming weight made each breath painful. Suffocating from the lack of air, he valiantly attempted to break free from a sealed coffin, whose walls were composed of hundreds of cold, stiff human corpses. Vainly he tried to push away the heavy limbs, to reach the surface of this sea of death. With a final desperate motion, he pushed himself free. And it was while filling his heaving lungs with blessed fresh air that he looked up into the cold, powder-blue eyes of a familiar bald-headed man, dressed in the black, swastika-bedecked uniform of a Nazi SS officer.

"Welcome to Ravensbruck!" said Wolfram Eckhardt, a sardonic sneer turning the corners of his thin, cruel lips.

This chilling greeting awakened a feeling of uncontrollable rage within Jacob. He climbed out of the corpse-filled pit and vented his anger with a deafening, earsplitting howl that easily rivaled the wolf's in both volume and primal fury. For Jacob was actually reliving the horrifying plight of his own mother, who as a young girl miraculously escaped a concentration-camp mass execution by being accidentally buried beneath the bodies of her friends and relatives.

With this horrible realization, Jacob's hallucinatory vision safely returned him to the edge of the fire circle. A new sense of purpose and a firm resolve allowed him to refocus his gaze on the glowing embers. The drum no longer pounded in the distance, and the incessant hum of the night creatures had given way to the utter silence of dawn.

Following, a deep, dreamless, trancelike sleep, which was broken by the sound of men softly conversing, he awoke feeling heavy and groggy. Unable to move, he barely managed to open his eyes and was surprised to find himself lying on his belly near the smoldering remains of last night's bonfire. The dawn had just broken, and he could clearly see Wolfram Eckhardt conversing with a younger, blond-haired associate. Jacob willingly closed his eyes and concentrated on their muffled words.

"This news is most disturbing, Hans," spoke the deep voice of Eckhardt.

"I knew the importance of the radio message the moment the facility was mentioned," his associate explained. "And when the dispatch went on to explain that the Ice Lair had been threatened, I knew that I had to awaken you at once."

"And it's a good thing that you did," Eckhardt added. "There's much to prepare, now that they've sent the helicopter. Come, Hans, let's begin crating the specimens."

The voices faded, and Jacob lapsed back into sleep, paying little heed to the meaning of this perplexing conversation. Once again his slumber was deep and dream free. Yet this time it wasn't the sound of voices that awoke him but the explosive, ear-splitting crack of gunfire.

Jacob's eyes snapped open in time to see the tall distinctive figure of Simon Bar-Adon emerge from the tree line, his twin Uzis blazing. With his three associates providing cover fire, the Israeli sprinted straight for Jacob. A long staccato burst of gunfire sounded from the direction of the compound's dozen or so huts. Jacob found himself caught in the middle of this frightening cross fire. With bullets whirring overhead, he rolled over into a shallow pit, pressing his trembling flesh as close to the protective contours of the earth as possible. Seemingly oblivious to this barrage of lead, Simon Bar-Adon completed his mad dash across the clearing and dove headfirst into the pit beside Jacob.

"Are you all right, my friend?" the breathless Israeli asked.

Nodding that he was, Jacob winced when a trio of deafening grenade blasts split the air. Thick columns of spiraling white smoke followed these bursts and soon veiled the clearing as effectively as a thick fog.

"Can you make it back to the jungle?" Bar-Adon wanted to know. "Because that smoke screen is for our benefit."

"I believe I can," said Jacob, who managed to shakily get to his knees and then stand with Bar-Adon's assistance.

A whining series of bullets overhead provided all the incentive Jacob needed to crouch over and run for the cover of the closest portion of rain forest. By the time the Israeli joined him behind a fallen lupuna trunk, yet another sound merged with the crackling gunshots and exploding grenades. It was the deep, resonating roar of an approaching helicopter.

"We didn't know if we'd ever see you again," Bar-Adon said between breaths. "Is he in there?"

Still groggy from the aftereffects of his mushroom trip, Jacob weakly nodded. "Eckhardt's there all right, and I'm afraid that helicopter's one of his."

"We're not about to let him get away so easily, my friend," Bar-Adon informed him. "So you just wait right here while me and my men see what we can do about closing the snare."

Though Jacob wished that he had the strength to help in this brave effort, he could only watch as the Israeli sprinted off to join his countrymen. The roaring sound of the helicopter intensified, and it was soon visible hovering over the far side of the clearing. Its sleek fuselage was expertly camouflaged, and Jacob could barely pick it out from the tree-lined backdrop.

A new series of explosions rose from a portion of the rain forest to his immediate right. A screen of thick white smoke veiled the brush here, and Jacob watched the

Israelis appear from behind it. As they defiantly dashed onto the clearing a human wave of naked Indians armed with spears and bow and arrows emerged from the compound's interior. Interspersed with the brown-skinned mob were several khaki-clad Caucasians who carried a full assortment of modern firearms.

To counter this massive attack, the Israelis were forced to take up a defensive position behind a waist-high earthen berm. From here, they unleashed a wall of lethal gunfire that mowed down dozens of the madly screaming Indians.

Meanwhile, Jacob could see that this costly diversion was succeeding. On the far side of the clearing, a single, harness-clad, bald-headed figure was being winched upward into the helicopter's main cabin. Seeing this, Jacob pounded the rough surface of the tree trunk that protected him. All he could do was sit there and watch the helicopter holding his nemesis gain altitude and roar off to the southeast.

6

"There she is on bearing zero-nine-five, Skipper," said Lieutenant Commander Gerardo Perez, peering through the eyepiece of the *Springfield*'s Type-2 periscope. "Bouvetoya, the most isolated island on the planet."

Philip Michaels was bent over the more sophisticated Mk-18 search periscope beside his XO. His current line of sight was due south, where a row of icebergs was visible. The floating islands of ice glistened under a partly cloudy, blue sky. The sea was calm, and with his XO's observation in mind, Michaels swung the scope to the east.

Seeing a tiny gray speck of land, Michaels increased the lens magnification tenfold. The landmass abruptly increased in size, and Michaels's eyepiece filled with a snow-covered, mountainous landscape.

"It sure doesn't look very inviting," Perez said. "But I guess to the early Antarctic explorers, after being trapped in the ice for months on end, this place must have looked like paradise."

"I don't know if I'd go that far," Michaels added. "The atlas shows Bouvetoya to be barely twenty-two square miles, most of it uninhabitable ice-covered rock that rises over three thousand feet out of the ocean."

"Sounds like the perfect spot to take the family on our next vacation," quipped the XO. "LuAnn and the kids have been complaining that they're getting bored with always visitin' her folks back in Arizona."

Michaels chuckled, his gaze still locked to the eyepiece. "Yeah, I could just see your travel agent trying to arrange your transport. Hell, it's already taken us the better part of a day and a half to reach this position from the nearest land off the South Sandwich Islands."

"Not if you count Antarctica," the XO returned. "And besides, if we were to vacation down here, think of all the frequent-flier points we'd accumulate!"

A wave slapped up against the lens and momentarily obstructed Michaels's view. As the glass cleared he spotted a large white bird in the sky halfway between the *Springfield* and the distant land.

"Looks like we've got some airborne company, XO. From its size, I'd say it's a giant petrel."

Perez also spotted the bird. "Man, look at the size of that sucker! It must have a ten-foot wingspan."

"All the better to survive in this harsh climate," said Michaels. "As a scavenger, those sturdy birds eat everything from unwary penguin chicks to seal and whale carcasses."

"I don't know about you, Skipper, but just the idea of being so close to Antarctica excites the hell out of me. It's like there's an entire new world to discover down here."

"I hear ya loud and clear, XO. This is a great opportunity for all of us. As the first American submarine ever to operate in these waters, the *Springfield* definitely has an all but virgin underwater realm to explore. We can all be very proud to have been picked for this patrol, which is taking an interesting new turn with our current orders. It sure was a stroke of good fortune for that Norwegian ship that was attacked that we were close by."

"That report of piracy still sounds a little bit fishy to me, Skipper. You know as well as me how desolate these waters are. Why, there's not even an inhabitable island nearby for these supposed pirates to use as a base."

Michaels backed away from the scope and stretched his arms overhead. "We'll know what befell our Norwegian friends soon enough, XO. Let's just keep an open mind and head over to navigation and see what kind of course Mr. Carr has come up with for our approach."

They found the navigator in the aft portion of the control room, huddled over the auxiliary plotting table. Lieutenant Ronald Carr was intently studying a chart marked BOUVETOYA ISLAND and didn't even bother to look up as his CO addressed him.

"How does it look, Mr. Carr?"

The navigator pointed to a small cove on the island's northern shore. "This appears to be the only accessible harbor. The chart indicates that this is where the abandoned Norwegian whaling station is situated. There's a wooden access pier, with plenty of deep water in the channel."

"Are we going to moor alongside that pier, Skipper?" the XO asked.

"Though the deep water inside that cove looks inviting, I'm a bit hesitant to trust this chart's accuracy," Michaels admitted. "Mr. Carr, what do you think?"

The navigator highlighted an area of open sea immediately outside of the harbor's access channel. "I agree, Captain. And that's why I think it's best to play it safe and anchor out here. That headland should keep the swells down, and *Springfield* should be able to ride out just about anything other than a full-fledged gale."

"We'd better make certain to leave plenty of room between our anchorage site and that promontory for the

Turbulent," Michaels suggested. "And let's just hope that the Norwegians still have a serviceable launch to pick up our shore party."

"Who are you taking along, Skipper?" the XO asked.

"Until I know just what it is that we're facing out there, I think it's best to keep the shore detail to a minimum. Mr. Carr, I'd like you to accompany me, along with Weaps and Petty Officer Bodzin. And just in case things get rough, I'd better invite Lieutenant Collier."

The XO grimaced. "Do you really think it's wise to include him? He's not exactly what I call a team player."

"I realize that," said Michaels. "But his SEAL training should come in handy if we're indeed faced with an act of piracy. XO, I'd like you to handle our getting settled into the anchorage. Of course, *Springfield* will be yours while I'm gone."

"Make sure to keep me posted with frequent radio updates," Perez reminded.

"Don't worry, XO. You'll know the facts of this mystery as soon as I do," Michaels promised as he backed away from the plotting table. "Now I'd better get down to the forward torpedo room and inform Lieutenant Collier to ready his gear. Then I'm going to need some time to pull out my own long johns."

As Michaels turned for the control room's forward port accessway, he stopped momentarily beside the helm. Ellwood Crick was seated between the two planesmen, giving the young seamen a lesson in the arcane art of submarine driving.

"Excuse me, COB," Michaels interrupted, "but I just wanted to pass on a job well done. This thirty-six-hour sprint run we're just completing certainly shows that *Springfield*'s got the right stuff."

"Thank you, Cap," the COB replied. "It sure is a joy to let this little lady stretch her legs. Damn, thirty-six hours, and not once did our knot indicator drop below thirty."

"She's a wonder, all right," Michaels agreed. "And it's

not only because of superb engineering. You've done a first-rate job with the men, COB."

Not the type who relished the spotlight, the master chief humbly grinned. "I guess someone's gotta be around to keep this bunch of scalawags in line. And I'm just glad that someone's me. Say, Cap, is it okay if I go topside and throw a fishing line in the water once we reach that island?"

"Permission granted, COB." Michaels smiled. "Although Lord only knows what type of fish you'll find in these waters."

"Thanks, Cap. Whatever I catch, you'll get the first one for dinner."

Michaels left the master chief with a thumbs-up and continued down the forward passageway. Two flights of stairs conveyed him deep into the bowels of the *Springfield*. He turned forward and followed the corridor straight into the torpedo room.

The compartment was dominated by three two-tiered stowage racks. A lethal combination of Mark-48 torpedoes, encapsulated Harpoon rockets, and Tomahawk missiles were strapped to these steel pallets, which were positioned just aft of the boat's four bow-angled torpedo tubes. Twenty-two separate reloads could be stored here, though the *Springfield*'s current load was significantly less than this.

Michaels soon enough saw why. In place of torpedoes, the top tier of the port rack was covered with mattresses and was currently home for the four members of SEAL Team Bravo.

The commandos were sprawled out on their racks, fieldstripping their weapons as Michaels approached the side of their pallet. Steven Collier was the first to spot him, and the SEAL sat up ramrod straight and crisply saluted.

"Attention!" he barked to his colleagues.

The three SEALs instantly followed Collier's lead. Michaels somewhat halfheartedly returned their salutes.

"As I said before," he reminded them, "saluting is not necessary aboard the *Springfield*."

"Sorry, sir," said Collier as he lowered his right arm. "But some habits are just hard to break."

Michaels surveyed the jumbled assortment of weapons parts on the mattress. "Looks like you've got yourselves quite an arsenal there. What exactly are you outfitted with?"

Steven Collier, whose handle was Ice Man, lovingly stroked the smooth black stock of his weapon of choice as he answered. "I've got an M16 A2 assault rifle. It holds a thirty-round clip of 5.56-millimeter ammunition and has an effective range of five hundred and fifty yards."

The wiry, dark-haired commando called Hawkeye spoke next. "I brought along a Heckler and Koch PSG1 sniper rifle. She fires a 7.62-millimeter cartridge that's carried in a twenty-round magazine. And with the addition of a Hensoldt six-by-forty-two scope with LED-enhanced manual reticle, any target within eight hundred yards you can consider eliminated."

"None of that fancy stuff for me," said the hefty, big-shouldered commando appropriately called Bear. "I do my turkey shootin' with an old-fashioned 7.62-millimeter M60 machine gun. She might be a little heavy at thirty-nine pounds, but give me a target within a thousand yards, and I'll soon enough pepper it with two hundred rounds per minute."

"Who needs two hundred rounds per minute when one well-placed 5.56-millimeter shell will do the trick just as effectively," said the baby-faced, smooth-talking SEAL known as Tenderfoot. "You can keep your machine gun, Bear. My weapon of choice is this Colt Commando. It's got a shorter barrel than the M16, and because of its reduced muzzle velocity, it's a tiger at closer range."

"I sure wouldn't want to mess with you guys in a dark alley," said Michaels, looking at Collier. "Can I have a word with you in private over by the launch control console?"

Without waiting for an answer, Michaels proceeded forward to the centrally located console, with the ever-curious SEAL close on his heels.

"Lieutenant, we'll be reaching our destination shortly, and I'd like you to be part of the shore detail."

"Any reason to get off this pigboat is fine with me, sir," Collier replied. "What will my responsibilities be?"

Michaels hesitated. "Since I still don't know what we're facing out there, I can't really say, Lieutenant. I'm sure you remember the moment we received our new orders, which have yet to be updated in any way."

"I remember all right," Collier said. "And I still say that we should have gone and finished the exercise we were in the midst of. Especially since we were so close to success. It seemed a damn shame to waste all that effort."

"Who says that it was wasted, mister? As far as I'm concerned, the *Springfield* passed that exercise with flying colors."

Collier shook his head in disagreement. "Your opponent sure wouldn't agree to that. You should never have let that limey bastard off the hook."

"Don't think that it was easy for me to break off that pursuit, Lieutenant." Michaels was trying his best to keep from losing his temper. "Sure, I was looking forward to going active and paying back the Brits, just like the rest of you. But one thing that you still have to learn is that with command comes responsibility. And when that priority dispatch arrived, I had no choice but to abandon all selfish concerns and break off the exercise, regardless of how much I wanted to continue."

Any further explanation was interrupted by the ringing of a nearby telephone. Michaels picked up the closest handset and barked into its transmitter.

"Captain, here."

"Skipper," said the XO, "I think you'd better get up to the conn on the double. Because you'll never believe what's waitin' for us on the other side of the harbor's headland."

"I'm on my way." Michaels hung up the handset, still flustered by the SEAL's presumptuousness. "I'll see you topside, Mr. Collier, in full cold-weather gear and with an appropriate sidearm."

This said, he stormed out of the torpedo room. His exchange with the cocksure commando was all but forgotten by the time he strode into control and proceeded to the periscope pedestal.

"What have you got, XO?" he asked his second in command, who was intently draped over the eyepiece of the Mk-18 search scope.

"Skipper, you'll never believe it!" Perez exclaimed as he backed away from the periscope. "We were in the process of rounding the point, and just as I was surveying our anchorage site with the scope, look what was waiting for us out there."

Not having the slightest idea what the XO was referring to, Michaels took his place at the eyepiece. After the slightest of adjustments, the lens came into focus and a truly perplexing scene took form on the surface of the waters directly before him. At anchor here, with a red, white, and blue Union Jack innocently flapping from its sail, was the sleek, distinctive black hull of the HMS *Turbulent*.

"What?" Michaels's astonishment was apparent.

"Tell me about it, Skipper," said Perez. "Because it just doesn't add up. There's no way they could have beat us here."

His gaze glued to the eyepiece, Michaels shook his head in wonder. "Damn, those guys must have been averaging over thirty-three knots. I honestly didn't think that their PWR-1 reactor was capable of such sustained speeds."

Having seen enough, Michaels stepped back from the scope and added, "It appears that Captain Hartwell and his gang of buccaneers are just full of surprises. Prepare to surface the boat, XO. It's time to find out what's so damn important to warrant traveling at such a speed."

• • •

Not even the magnificent view through the Bell 212's Plexiglas windshield could lighten Thor Sperre's somber mood. With the stirring strains of Grieg's *Peer Gynt* suite flowing from the chopper's cockpit CD system, Thor took off from the *Condor*'s helideck a half hour ago. This was to be the first aerial survey of their new island home for the next five months. Before Yngve Rakke's untimely death he had been looking forward to this flight, but this morning he could barely drag himself from his bunk.

With last evening's painful radio telephone call to Yngve's young widow still fresh in his mind, Thor made a slight adjustment to the helicopter's altitude. He had already circled Bouvetoya's twenty-two square miles and found the island little more than a snow-covered, inhospitable mountain range.

To get a better idea of the seas they had been sent to explore, he swung the helicopter south. It didn't take long to encounter a multitude of icebergs, and ten miles offshore, he reached the northernmost extent of the Antarctic ice pack. Only a few weeks ago this solid sheet of ice had encircled Bouvetoya, but with the arrival of spring, it was rapidly receding.

Thor studiously scanned the ice and picked out the fracture faults, which showed the thinnest portions of the ice sheet. In a couple of days, he'd be relaying their position to the *Condor* as it smashed its way southward to the shores of the frozen continent.

The sight of several polynyas—areas of open water in the ice—showed that it was hardly as impenetrable as it initially appeared. It was beside one of these polynyas that he spotted his first penguins, a flock several hundred strong, and when Thor descended and hovered directly above them, he got a clear view of their distinctive black-and-white-feathered bodies.

Surprised that the noisy helicopter didn't drive them into the water, Thor soon enough found out why: a trio of large seals were patrolling the open water, and the penguins had apparently decided that the helicopter was definitely the lesser of two evils.

A lowering cloud deck and a stiffening wind signaled the end of this brief exploratory flight. As Thor headed back for the *Condor* he found himself once again thinking of last night's telephone conversation. Ashild had been totally unprepared for his call, and at first the excitement in her voice when she recognized him was unmistakable.

Thor had decided on a direct approach, and with his mention of an accident, Ashild went instantly silent. On Captain Skogstad's firm instructions, all he could tell her was that Yngve had been the victim of an unfortunate occurrence that had resulted in his death. A moment of stunned silence was followed by an agonizing scream of disbelief from Ashild. As she sobbed uncontrollably Thor struggled to express his own grief. It was one of the darkest moments of his young life when he had to end the transmission with a promise that his prayers would be with her.

The deep clatter of the helicopter's rotors merged with the solemn strains of Grieg's music, providing an appropriate backdrop for his somber recollections. With Bouvetoya's rugged southern shoreline rapidly taking form on the northern horizon, he allowed his thoughts to focus on his friendship with Yngve.

Thor had first met him seven years before, when both were assigned to the same North Sea oil rig. They became instant friends, sharing as they did a love of the sea and a craving for adventure. Soon they formed their own dive club, NUEX, the Norwegian Underwater Explorers. In the spirit of their Viking ancestors, they spent their free time diving in the vicinity of local wrecks. They documented their expeditions on film, and soon attracted the attention of the local media.

Subsequent dives took NUEX to Norway's Telemark region, where they explored Lake Tinn. It was on the bottom of this lake that the ferry *Hydro* rested, sunk by Allied saboteurs with a load of heavy water for Germany's atomic-bomb project in its hold. With the assistance of an ROV—(a remotely operated vehicle)—that Yngve cleverly designed, they found the *Hydro* in 450 meters of water. Future plans were for NUEX to attempt to salvage the wreckage.

Another adventure conveyed NUEX to an Oslo fjord and the wreckage of the German heavy cruiser *Blücher,* while one of Thor's favorite projects took them to the Bay of Sande, where they searched the seabed for a legendary German U-boat that supposedly sank in these waters with ten tons of precious Russian gold. Though they never found this fabled treasure, they had plans to return to try again.

Yngve's death put an end to these dreams. Without him, NUEX lost not only its project manager, but also its major inspiration. Thor couldn't help but feel that a part of his own self had died with his friend.

As Thor pulled back on the steering yoke, in preparation for the passage over the island's mountainous spine, he pondered the mysterious circumstances that led up to Yngve's death. The crew of the *Condor* still had no idea as to the actual identities of the pirates. And though it was obvious that Yngve died a hero's death at the radio console trying to inform the authorities, it was a shame that he had to lose his life for a measly load of food and spare parts. This was the ultimate tragedy, and it only increased Thor's desire for revenge. He would not rest until the men responsible were tracked down and forced to pay for this act of cold-blooded murder.

Retribution was heavy on Thor's mind as he guided the helicopter up over the final ridge overlooking the island's sole harbor. From this lofty vantage point, he had a superb view of the group of dilapidated structures belonging to the abandoned whaling station. The *Condor* was moored nearby, its bright yellow hull tied to the remains of the station's wooden pier.

The ship's launch was approaching the pier from the open sea, but Thor's attention was drawn not to it but to a pair of newly arrived vessels, the cigar-shaped, black hulls of which showed them to be submarines. He rarely got a chance to view such vessels from the air, since they were usually submerged, so he circled them for a closer look.

They were formidable-looking warships, appearing at first to be some kind of deadly sea creatures. The smaller of the boats displayed a Union Jack on its sail, while the larger sub flew the Stars and Stripes of the United States. Interestingly enough, Thor made out a sailor on the deck of the American sub, in the process of throwing a fishing line into the water. The Norwegian received a friendly wave from this hearty individual before turning the helicopter back toward the *Condor*'s helipad to find out for himself just what this unusual visit was all about.

From the foredeck of the wooden launch, Philip Michaels looked up at the red Bell helicopter roaring overhead. The chopper was evidently headed toward the same yellow-hulled ship as they were, and he watched as it smoothly swung around to land on the *Condor*'s helipad.

"Damn, it's cold out here!" observed Petty Officer Bodzin, one of the three members of the *Springfield*'s crew to accompany Michaels.

"You call this cold, sailor?" retorted the gruff voice of Steven Collier. "Buddy, today's air is balmy compared to the normal temperature around here."

The sub's navigator was quick to agree. "The temperature really isn't that bad this afternoon. In fact, I'm finding the fresh air invigorating."

Michaels remained silent as he watched the helicopter hover over the *Condor*'s foredeck and gently touch down. With the launch's continued approach he took a moment to admire the Norwegian ship's unusual lines.

A rugged-looking vessel, the *Condor* had been built with practicality in mind, with its twin stacks positioned on either side of the elevated bridge. The helipad was cleverly placed forward of the bridge, with a large crane dominating the aft deck, where the twin moonpools were situated. This unique feature, which was utilized to lower ROVs and diving bells into the water, allowed the *Condor*'s crew direct access to the sea.

As the launch approached the *Condor*'s amidships boarding ramp, Michaels spotted a familiar figure at the rail. It was none other than Captain Robert Hartwell, commanding officer of the HMS *Turbulent*. With a certain cool detachment, the bearded Englishman watched the launch pull up to the ramp.

While the Norwegian sailors busily secured the boat's nylon mooring lines, Hartwell saluted Michaels, and said, "Afternoon, old chap. So good that you could join us."

Michaels returned the salute and made certain to be the first one up the boarding ramp. The Englishman was waiting for him with a warm handshake as he stepped down onto the *Condor*'s main deck.

"It's good to see you, Robert," said Michaels. "You certainly made excellent time."

"So we did, Philip," Hartwell replied. "The Admiralty hasn't allowed us to operate the kettle wide-open like that since the Falklands war."

"I guess I didn't realize the high priority of your current orders."

"Actually, Northwood is taking this entire incident most seriously," Hartwell admitted. "Because of our joint petrol interests in the North Sea, the Norwegians are a valued ally, and we've been instructed to provide whatever assistance we can in resolving this rather nasty incident."

"Was this ship really the victim of an act of piracy?" Michaels asked.

Hartwell nodded. "So it appears, old chap. And not only robbery on the high seas was involved, but murder as well. The captain of the *Condor* is presently in the ship's wardroom, where a full briefing awaits us."

With his three crewmen in tow, Michaels followed Hartwell to the *Condor*'s wardroom, where Jon Skogstad, the ship's portly captain, waited for them. As introductions were made they were joined by a short, blond-haired Norwegian in an orange flight jacket, who introduced himself as Thor Sperre, the *Condor*'s senior helicopter pilot. Coffee and pastries were served, and Captain Skogstad graciously thanked the governments of the United Kingdom and the United States for responding to their call for assistance so rapidly. He then began the briefing by requesting the helicopter pilot to describe his role in the incident.

Thor Sperre looked uncomfortable at having to speak, making certain that his pipe was well packed and lit before shyly saying, "I guess you could say it all started three days ago, when I joined Yngve on the *Condor*'s prow for a smoke. Yngve Rakke was the ship's senior diver and a longtime friend. We were approximately halfway between Tristan da Cunha and Bouvetoya at the time and encountering some very heavy fog. In fact, we were talking about the fog when Yngve spotted a flashing light somewhere in the water dead ahead of us. I saw the light, too, and, fearing a collision with another surface vessel, ran to the bridge to inform the captain."

"That's when I got involved in the matter," Skogstad interjected between sips of his coffee. "With the ship's radar temporarily down for maintenance, we sounded a collision alarm with the ship's air horn and quickly cut the engines. Then Thor and I joined Yngve at the amidships boarding ramp. That's when the pirates first showed themselves in a Zodiac. There were two of them in that first raft. One was a tough-looking, middle-aged brute, with spiky brown hair. The other one sported a Vandyke and had a certain worldly air. There's no doubt in my mind that he was the leader, for his shipmate called him Captain. Both had slight German accents, and made up some cock-and-bull story about being the victims of a shipwreck. I saw through their story at once, but foolishly gave them the benefit of the doubt. Then the next thing I knew, they had weapons trained on us. The shooting of a starburst shell overhead caused three more Zodiacs to materialize out of the fog, and soon we had six more armed intruders to deal with."

"These Zodiacs," the Englishman interrupted. "Where did they originate? Was there any sign of a mother ship?"

Skogstad shook his head. "None that we ever saw. And that's the really strange part. Because what followed just didn't make any sense. With a pistol held to my head, I was instructed to call together the ship's entire complement here in this wardroom. All but one of my crew obliged. That was poor Yngve, who snuck into the radio room to issue an SOS. While we sat here with our tails between our legs, he was discovered and shot to death right there at the radio console.

"An hour later our armed guard left us with a warning to stay put at the cost of our lives. When fifteen minutes passed without sight or sound of the pirates, I left the wardroom. Lo and behold, the pirates and their Zodiacs were nowhere to be seen. We searched the *Condor* from stem to stern and that's when we found poor Yngve's bullet-riddled body. I know you're wondering what these pirates were after. Believe it or not, all that we found missing was a sizable amount of food, liquor, and tobacco from our hold, and a few spare parts from engineering. Other than that, nothing was touched."

"Tell them about the radar, Captain," the helicopter pilot put in.

"Ah, yes, the radar." Skogstad scanned the faces of his rapt audience. "With the hopes of tracking the mother ship responsible for this pillage, I had our radar unit made operational once more. Strange as it may seem, a mere twenty minutes later a fifty-mile-wide scan of the waters surrounding the *Condor* showed absolutely nothing. The Zodiacs, their loot, and the ones responsible for killing one of our best crew members had completely disappeared."

A burst of excited chatter followed the captain's revelation. Thor Sperre, recovering from his shyness, invited all those present to join him in the ship's radio room to see for themselves the bullet holes that the murderer's weapon had made.

Robert Hartwell used this opportunity to request a private audience with Michaels and their portly Norwegian host in the secure confines of Jon Skogstad's stateroom. No sooner was the door shut than the Englishman began to speak.

"What I'm about to share with you is said in the strictest confidence. It concerns an incident that took place in these same waters fourteen years ago, during the Falklands war. I was a first lieutenant at the time, assigned to the nuclear-powered attack sub HMS *Spartan*. We were escorting a troop convoy bound for South Georgia Island. As the *Spartan* took up a defensive position well forward of the convoy, we made contact with an unidentified submerged source. We tracked the contact on and off for over forty-eight hours but lost it before we could make a positive signature ID. We thought we had seen the last of it when two of the ships in the convoy reported that they were under torpedo attack. By the grace of God, one of the torpedoes just missed striking a fully loaded fleet oiler. The other torpedo hit on the hull of our amphibious command ship, but lucky for us failed to detonate. Unfortunately, the torpedo sank before we could retrieve it and identify its owner."

"Surely it was Argentina," Jon Skogstad suggested.

"That's just what we thought," Hartwell replied. "So you can imagine our surprise when we learned that on the day those torpedoes were fired, Argentina's entire fleet of submarines was securely tied up at port."

"Then who in the hell launched those torpedoes?" Michaels asked.

A sardonic grin filled the Englishman's bearded face

as he leaned forward and replied in a hushed, conspiratorial tone. "To answer that question, I'm going to have to take you back to the days immediately following the end of World War Two. In late July of 1945, more than two months after Germany's surrender, U-530 sailed into Puerto Plata, Argentina, with a white flag flapping from its sail. A week later U-977 surrendered at the same port. Both submarines had set sail from Bergen, Norway, in early May and were well beyond their operational ranges. They would have had to refuel to reach Puerto Plata, yet no record of any such refueling stop exists.

"Inspection by Argentine authorities turned up no papers of any sort aboard the submarines—no money, logbooks, magazines, or letters. Since normal transit time from Bergen to Puerto Plata was thirty days, the question arose as to where these subs had spent the extra month and a half. Also, why did both U-boats surrender in the same small, isolated port?

"Now, you ask, what does this tale have to do with the identity of the vessel that attacked our convoy, or the act of piracy aboard the *Condor,* for that matter? The answers have to do with the fact that reliable witnesses in Norway reported that yet another submarine accompanied U-530 and U-977 on the trip south. No trace of this vessel, an advanced Type XXI, was ever found. This leads one to speculate whether this last submarine could have been the same rogue vessel first sighted as early as February 1960. It was at that time that a phantom submarine was spotted by the citizens of Puerto Madryn, Argentina. You can only imagine the shock of these same citizens when, after watching their own navy carry out an extensive depth charge attack on this vessel, the wreckage was never located.

"Ten years later our phantom submarine made another appearance off the southern coast of Brazil. This time it participated in a blatant act of piracy against a Brazilian container ship. I'm certain that Captain Skogstad will find it of particular interest to learn that the pirates' loot was limited to food, liquor, tobacco, and selective machine parts."

"Hold on a minute," interrupted Michaels, ever the skeptic. "Are you actually implying that a rogue German U-boat is responsible for this incident aboard the *Condor?*"

"Why not?" Hartwell retorted. "A submarine would be the ideal mother ship for this band of raft-borne pirates. It would explain how they got out there on the high seas, and why the *Condor*'s radar was unable to make contact with them afterward."

Jon Skogstad looked convinced. "Don't forget their accents. They were German all right. I'll bet my pension on that."

"And don't forget the nature of the articles stolen from the *Condor,*" Hartwell added. "You know as well as I, Philip, that a submarine's greatest need at sea is to replenish its food stocks. This would especially be the case on a vessel the size of a Type XXI, where storage space is extremely limited."

"But it's been nearly fifty years since the end of the war," Michaels countered. "Do you really think an operational U-boat still exists after all that time? Besides, where's its base? Where did the crew come from, and what could their ultimate mission possibly be?"

The Englishman stroked his full beard before replying. "The answers to those questions lie somewhere in the surrounding seas. And to see if my conjecture is correct, I propose the following. Per my current orders, the *Turbulent* will remain in this immediate sector and escort the *Condor* south to the shores of Antarctica. Philip, that gives you the South Sandwich Islands, the nearest inhabitable landmass, to patrol. If there's a secret base in the area, that's where it's most likely to be situated."

7

Dr. Laurie Anderson was starting to feel like a veteran polar aviator. The clear afternoon made it a perfect day to fly, with none of the rough weather that delayed their takeoff from the Amundsen-Scott South Pole Station.

From her familiar jumpseat perch in the rear of the CH-130's flight deck, the vulcanologist peered out the windshield. A cloudless, blue sky stretched for as far as her eye could see, and she completely relaxed knowing that she was in the expert hands of Vince Adams and his crack crew.

If all went as scheduled, they'd be landing shortly. Not really certain what would be waiting for her, she allowed the deep, constant drone of the airplane's four engines to redirect her thoughts. And with her gaze still locked on the blue horizon, she mentally recreated the amazing place that they had taken off from much earlier in the day.

It was over forty-eight hours ago that they left McMurdo, for what was to be but a brief stop at the Amundsen-Scott Station. For most of the flight, the weather had been splendid, and Laurie was afforded a spectacular view of an unbroken expanse of white. The snowpack was over two miles thick here, effectively veiling the frozen continent beneath it.

The weather began deteriorating shortly after they began their final approach to the South Pole station. Yet this time, they were able to land before the blizzard enveloped them in a thick veil of white.

An enclosed Sno-Cat transferred them from the airfield to the station. As she emerged from the plane Laurie was engulfed in a frigid blast of air that left her feeling both dizzy and nauseated, and during the short ride to the station's geodesic dome, she learned the reason for her discomfort. The temperature was a "balmy" forty-three degrees below zero Fahrenheit outside. This, combined with their current altitude of 9,300 feet above sea level, would adversely affect even the heartiest of souls.

The Sno-Cat arrived at the station just as whiteout conditions began to prevail. A ramp led them straight into the dome by way of a large square door, above which was a sign that read UNITED STATES WELCOMES YOU TO THE SOUTH POLE. As Laurie exited the Sno-Cat she found herself standing on the snow-covered floor of an incredible structure, an immense, 53-foot-high, 165-foot-wide rounded aluminum shelter containing several orange modular buildings, living quarters for a staff of eighty people. The dome also held an assortment of fuel bladders and heating, snow-melting, and research equipment.

Vince Adams led the way up the stairs to one of these long orange buildings, which reminded Laurie of a cargo container. They stepped through an air lock and entered a warm, brightly lit room that turned out to be the station's library. Set amid the shelves of books was a big-screen television monitor hooked up to a videocassette recorder. Several of the residents were immersed in a movie that Laurie recognized as *Pretty Woman*. It seemed strange to be watching the adult fairy-tale antics of Julia Roberts and Richard Gere from one of the most isolated outposts on the planet while a full-fledged blizzard raged outside.

Laurie was equally surprised by the excellent, full-course gourmet meal that was served after the film's conclusion. The cooks were graduates of the Culinary Institute of America, and they turned out a superb Chinese dinner, complete with egg rolls, wonton soup, stir-fried chicken, fried rice, and vegetable lo mein. Over green tea and fortune cookies, Laurie got to talk with several of the local scientists. She learned even more about the research that had brought them to Antarctica when the continuing bad weather forced Vince Adams to postpone their flight indefinitely.

Late yesterday afternoon, however, the weather cleared enough to permit Laurie to leave the dome, under the ever-vigilant eye of her handsome aviator escort. She made certain to pay close attention to Vince Adams, and she bundled up in almost every piece of warm clothing she had brought along before following him out the dome's exit ramp.

Even with her extra clothing, the bitter, numbing cold took her breath away as she plodded over the frozen ground. Ten long minutes later they stopped in front of a simple bamboo pole, from which flew a dark blue flag bearing the crossed hammer-and-pick insignia of the U.S. Geological Survey. Laurie momentarily forgot about her discomfort when she was told that this was the exact position of the South Pole.

After deciding to spend another night inside the dome, they awoke this morning to see a brilliant blue sky, and knew it was time to pack up and say their good-byes.

Now that Laurie was on the final leg of her long journey, she couldn't help but feel somewhat apprehensive. Not for the first time she thought of how her current assignment was taking her to a distant, alien place, where she'd be in the company of strangers. Wishing she had given this assignment a bit more thought before accepting it, she found herself having to reach down and grab the bottom edges of the jumpseat as the flight deck began violently vibrating.

"Hang on, Doc," Vince Adams warned from his customary seat on the left side of the cockpit. "It appears that there's gonna be a little rough air as we leave our cruisin' altitude and initiate our descent into Novo base."

This "little rough air" turned out to be a pocket of powerful turbulence that smacked into the lumbering aircraft with the force of a storm front. Laurie's newfound confidence was tested as she found herself jerked from side to side, then pounded into her hard, nylon-webbed seat. The flight crew seemed oblivious to this pounding, their attention focused on the static-filled, Slavic-accented voice that unexpectedly boomed from the cockpit's overhead radio speakers.

"Alpha-Charlie-Foxtrot, this is Novolazarevskaya Station calling. Do you read me, Alpha-Charlie-Foxtrot?"

With his left hand gripped on the steering yoke, Vince Adams flipped down his chin-mounted microphone and answered, "That's a roger, Novo base. This is Alpha-Charlie-Foxtrot, and we read you loud and clear. Request current weather conditions."

"Alpha-Charlie-Foxtrot, I'm most happy to report clear skies with unlimited visibility. The winds are from the north at eighteen kilometers per hour, with the temperature of minus-six degrees Celsius. Do have a safe landing, comrade."

"Thank you, Novo base. This is Alpha-Charlie-Foxtrot, over and out."

Vince Adams brushed aside the microphone and used both hands to push forward on the steering yoke. As the CH-130 quickly lost altitude the rough air blessedly passed, and Laurie was able to let go of the edges of her jumpseat.

"There she is," said Adams, referring to the sprawling complex of buildings now visible on the hilly, snow-covered ground.

As Laurie took her first look at her new home through the wraparound windshield, she was relieved at its size, which appeared almost as large as McMurdo. She made out a dozen or so large, three-story buildings as well as the usual circular oil storage tanks and various support facilities on the outer edges of the compound.

The snow-covered airfield was several miles away from the base. A bright red smoke flare at the end of the runway allowed the flight crew to have a better idea of the wind's actual strength and direction. With a minimum of difficulty, Vince Adams swung the plane into the wind and initiated his final approach. The landing that followed was flawlessly executed, resulting in the barest of jolts as the CH-130's skis made contact with the slick, snow-paved runway.

They wasted no time taxiing over to an awaiting fuel truck. As they slid to a halt Vince Adams switched off the engines and turned to address his only passenger.

"This is it, Doc. You know, I'm gonna miss seein' that pretty face of yours. Take care of yourself out there, and hopefully I'll be the one picked to fly you back to Mac Town when your job here is over. Aloha," he added with a wink.

"Aloha," she repeated sadly while taking a last fond look at the man who was becoming more than a mere colleague. Feeling tears gathering in her eyes, she quickly unbuckled her harness, said her good-byes to the rest of the flight crew, and climbed down the ladder to the main cabin.

The finality of the moment sank in as the crew chief beckoned toward a partially open hatch near the cabin's tail. "Good luck to you, miss," he said.

Laurie nodded bravely and, with her nylon duffel bag in tow, climbed out. Any misgivings that she might have had about her reception were temporarily eased by the kind eyes and warm smile of her one-person welcoming committee. Waiting for her beside an idling snowmobile was a tall, broad-shouldered, red-cheeked gentleman, whose immense stature was augmented by a full-length white fur coat. His thick bushy eyebrows arched upward as his face lit up in greeting.

"Ah, Dr. Anderson," he said in excellent English, "how very exciting it is to personally welcome you to Novolazarevskaya Station or, as we call it around here, Novo base. I am Viktor Alexandrov, the director of this settlement. Dr. Levering told me all about you, and I can't tell you how privileged we are to have such a talented scientist visit us."

Genuinely flattered, Laurie accepted a fatherly hug and a brief kiss to each cheek. It felt more like a homecoming than a visit with strangers.

"It's a pleasure to make your acquaintance, sir. To tell you the truth, I was afraid that we'd have to make these introductions in sign language, since my Russian is nonexistent."

"We'll soon enough fix that, my dear," Alexandrov said while gesturing to the snowmobile. "Come now, it's time to get out of this cold and put some food and drink in that belly of yours."

Laurie climbed onto the back end of the snowmobile and clasped the broad waist of her host as he put the tracked vehicle into gear and it noisily lurched forward. Even with this friendly reception, there was a forlorn look in her eyes as she peered up to the CH-130's cockpit. Vince Adams was clearly visible, and the last she saw of him as they shot off toward the settlement was a determined thumbs-up.

The growling whine of the snowmobile's engine made conversation all but impossible. Viktor Alexandrov proved to be an excellent driver, and he guided them past the airfield's storage sheds and up an adjoining icy incline with a minimum of bumps.

Laurie was startled when they rounded a broad curve

and sped past a curious flock of penguins. They were much larger than she had anticipated, over three feet tall and weighing a good seventy pounds. Their coloring was striking, with a jet-black cap, blue-gray neck, bright orange ear patches, and breasts of a light lemon yellow that merged to pure white.

"This is our very own flock of emperor penguins," Viktor explained practically screaming to be heard. "You'll get to know these rascals well if you stay with us long enough."

Since this was her first penguin sighting, Laurie looked forward to spending some time studying them. As the last black-winged straggler waddled by she noted how very close they lived to the realm of man, for the compound began beyond the next rise.

Unlike those at McMurdo, the structures they were soon whizzing by seemed substantial, made mostly of dark brick and connected by shoveled walkways that made them look like the kind of apartments that might be found in a small town. This impression of homeyness increased as they passed a shared common space and Laurie spotted a group of small children playing in the snow. It appeared that the settlement was not composed entirely of visiting groups of scientists, but that families actually made this isolated place their home.

The snowmobile finally halted beside an elongated, three-story building in the central portion of the settlement. As she climbed off the benchlike seat Laurie found herself looking up at a bronze bust of Lenin on a granite pillar.

"Poor Vladimir Ilyich," her host said as he climbed off the snowmobile. "I realize that such busts are an anachronism in these new enlightened times. But so much effort was applied to ship this statue all the way from the Rodina that we decided to keep it here as a reminder of our checkered past. But enough of such maudlin sentiments. It's time to look to the future, and what better way to do so than to celebrate a young couple's wedding day."

With great gusto, Víktor led her inside the adjoining building. Since it was pleasantly warm inside, Laurie slipped off her parka and gloves as she followed her host up a twisting flight of stairs to the top floor. The joyful sounds of a party in full swing drew them to a large communal hall. Dozens of happy party goers were congregated alongside a long table filled with a delectable assortment of food and drink.

"Comrades!" Viktor shouted. "Please, comrades, may I have your attention?"

Within seconds, the music stopped and the conversation died to a whisper. With the flair of a born actor, Viktor took his time scanning the faces of those gathered around him before gesturing to Laurie. "My dear comrades, I have the distinct honor of introducing Dr. Laurie Anderson, the esteemed American vulcanologist, who will be our guest these next few days. Welcome her into your hearts and homes, comrades, and let's show her the proper way to party. Sasha, Andrei, please grace us with your presence, dear ones."

From out of the crowd, a rosy-cheek young man and woman emerged, shyly holding hands. They were dressed in their Sunday best, and it was soon apparent that this party was being held in their honor.

"Sasha and Andrei Korsakov," Viktor joyously announced, "may your days together be many, and your nights filled with . . . well, I'm sure you'll soon enough figure out what to fill those nights with."

As the crowd roared with laughter Viktor continued. "It's time for champagne and caviar! Mikhail Sergeivich, ready your balalaika, and let's have the wedding dance!"

A tall, lanky fellow dressed in jeans and a tight-fitting tunic appeared from the direction of the bar. He held a glass filled with clear liquid in one hand and a triangular bodied, three-stringed instrument in the other. He took a second to bow tipsily to the newlyweds before downing the drink in a single gulp and smashing the empty glass to the floor. Only then were both hands free to cradle his colorfully painted balalaika.

Laurie was amazed at the rich variety of sounds the instrument was capable of producing. After a slow, drawn-out series of melancholy chords, he broke into a rousing jig that the audience accompanied with spirited clapping. Laurie joined the chorus and watched with delight as the newlyweds seized each other's hands and began dancing.

The rhythm steadily quickened, and the young dancers had to increase the pace of their steps to keep up with the frenzied beat. A heavyset woman with an accordian strapped around her plump torso began playing, a signal for members of the audience to join the newlyweds on the dance floor.

Before Laurie realized what was happening, a tall, good-looking young man with long blond hair took her in his arms. Awkwardly at first, she struggled to follow his lead. She hadn't danced like this since high school. But the happy, carefree atmosphere was contagious, and she soon relaxed enough to allow the spirited rhythm to guide her.

When the song merged into another fast-paced tune, Laurie was surprised to find herself in the tight embrace of Viktor Alexandrov. For a large man, he moved gracefully, and dancing with him proved to be no problem at all.

It wasn't until the musicians began a slow ballad that her host guided her off the dance floor and over to the food table. "Here you go, my dear," he said, handing her an empty china plate. "And don't be bashful."

Laurie surveyed the table, which was filled with appetizers, salads, main courses, and desserts. She decided to follow her host's lead and helped herself to black caviar, sour cream, chopped egg, onion, herring, beets, and what appeared to be coleslaw. A thick slice of fresh black bread perfectly complemented this feast, and Laurie ate with gusto.

She cleared off her plate in time to witness the cutting of the wedding cake. A serious-faced photographer documented this event, and before the cake was distributed to the guests, a champagne toast was made. Right after this, the newlyweds kissed passionately, then, to a chorus of boisterous screams and whistles, the groom swept his bride into his arms and carried her off to the private cottage that had been reserved for their honeymoon.

With their exit, the atmosphere turned a bit more subdued, and several smartly dressed men and women, several of whom were fellow geologists and other specialists in the earth sciences, took the opportunity to introduce themselves to Laurie, but few spoke English as well as Viktor Alexandrov.

Over piping hot, heavily sweetened tea, her host took her into a side room, where they seated themselves on a well-worn corduroy couch. The soulful sounds of soft folk music emanated from the party, and Laurie laid back her head and stretched languorously.

"I can't tell you how long it's been since I've had such a good time," she admitted. "You've got a wonderful group of people here, and I already feel right at home among them."

"It's stimulating to get a visitor from the outside, my dear, especially one as attractive and talented as you are. We live a very isolated life here at Novo base, and your presence is like a breath of fresh air. Now tell me more about this important project that brings you here."

"I'd be glad to," Laurie said. "But first, you must tell me where you learned to speak such excellent English."

Viktor grinned. "My father was a Foreign Service official, and he wisely looked beyond the dark days of the Cold War to the time when our two countries would be close allies. To prepare us for that day, he hired an English tutor, and I began my first lessons when I was but a primary-school student. Of course, this only gave me the rudiments of your difficult language, but I got the ideal opportunity to perfect my skills during a fascinating year spent in Los Angeles, where I was an exchange student at the University of California."

"What did you study?" Laurie asked.

"Though most of my attention was focused on a better understanding of American culture, my official course of study was mycology, the branch of botany that deals with fungi. And I eventually returned to Moscow with not only a genuine respect for the American way of life, but also a firm decision to become a full-time mycologist."

"Is that the official course of your work here in Antarctica?" Laurie asked. "I would think that a botanist would have little to study on this frozen wasteland."

"You'd be surprised, my dear. Did you know that some two percent of Antarctica's fourteen million square miles is completely free of ice? And living in these dry valleys is a variety of higher vascular plants, mosses, lichens, algae, and as I'm currently learning, fungi as well. Wait until you see the two species of mushrooms I recently found just west of here. That such advanced life-forms could exist in this harsh climate is simply amazing. But enough of my selfish interests. Tell me more about the project that brings you to Novo base."

Between sips of her tea, Laurie explained the recent results of NOAA's thermal infrared imaging satellite scan. As she described the location of greatest heat activity and passed on Dr. Levering's fear of a possible volcanic eruption at this location, her host's expression turned solemn.

"I know these relatively unexplored mountains that you speak of," he revealed. "The Mühlig-Hofmann range is directly downwind from us, and a major eruption there could have disastrous effects on Novo base. How can we help you with your investigation?"

Laurie sensed his genuine concern and got right to the point. "My number-one priority is just getting to the mountain range, and then having the support necessary to remain in the field until my initial observations are completed. I believe, weather permitting, a week should give me plenty of time to track down the area of greatest heat emission and determine its source."

"And a week's worth of support you shall have," Viktor promised. "As far as your means of transport, you need not worry, my dear. With much of our motherland's landmass well north of the Arctic Circle, we Russians have decades' worth of experience working in cold-weather conditions. Our tracked transporters can cross the roughest terrain, and I'll make our crack alpine team available for your guide. Is there any additional scientific equipment that would make your search easier?"

Laurie thought a moment before answering. "A portable seismograph would be welcome. Also, do you happen to have any infrared thermal imager detection equipment?"

The Russian nodded. "As it so happens, this is the first season that we've been equipped with just such a device. I believe it was originally developed by our navy to be used to locate downed personnel in the heavy smoke generated by a fire onboard ship. And since fire is also one of our main concerns here at Novo base, the battery-powered thermal imager is a real boon."

"As you put together my support team, Dr. Levering mentioned that one of your staff geologists could be of invaluable assistance to me. I believe that her name is Anna Litvak."

"Of course, Anna Litvak," Viktor repeated. "She's the one occupant of Novo base who speaks English better than I. You two would get along splendidly. Unfortunately, Anna is out in the field herself at the moment. She's visiting the Indian research station of Dakshan Gangotri, which is situated in the foothills of the Mühlig-Hoffmann range. I'll contact her by radiotelephone at once. And you can even pick her up at the Indian facility on your way into the hinterland."

Jacob Litvak lay on his back, his weary gaze locked on the spinning wooden arms of the overhead fan. The comfortable mattress did little to ease his anxieties. Even though he was now safe, in the Russian embassy in Buenos Aires, Argentina, his recently experience would not stop haunting him.

Less than forty-eight hours ago, he was in a far different world, deep in the rain forest of that jungle hell called Mato Grosso. Could he ever erase from his mind that frustrating moment when he watched the helicopter carrying Wolfram Eckhardt fly off to God knows where? Mentally and physically drained from his mushroom "trip," Jacob felt powerless and confused.

Vulnerable to the alien dangers that surrounded him, he could easily have died had it not been for the intervention of the brave Israelis. Somehow they had prevailed in their struggle with the Indians, and though two of the Mossad agents had been wounded, they managed to retreat to the tree line and gather beside Jacob. After a grueling journey through the rain forest, they reached the banks of the Dourados River, then traveled by launch to the isolated outpost of Pedro Juan Caballero, where the helicopter waited to bring them back to Asunción.

Before leaving that city, Jacob said good-bye to Simon Bar-Adon and his brave countrymen. The one-eyed Israeli would be remaining in the Paraguayan capital, where his men's wounds would be attended to, and plans made to resume their stakeout of Eckhardt's compound. Though Jacob expressed his desire to stay with them as they began their surveillance, Bar-Adon would not hear of it. Genuinely worried about Jacob's fragile state of mind and body, he personally made the arrangements for his flight to Buenos Aires.

It took the valued opinion of Ambassador Nikolai Kalinin for Jacob finally to comprehend the seriousness of his condition. The veteran statesman was an old acquaintance as well as a personal friend of Jacob's father. He had practically watched Jacob grow into manhood, and there could be no hiding his horror as Jacob walked into his embassy office. Noting his haggard appearance and dark-circled, bloodshot eyes, the ambassador insisted that he stay in a private apartment at the embassy to recuperate. A team of physicians was called in, and only after Jacob's physical ailments were attended to did Kalinin reveal his true concerns. A survivor of Stalin's purges as well as an expert on South American culture and politics, Kalinin was the official point of contact for the Nazi-hunting, KGB/Mossad investigatory teams. He was thus well aware of the identity of the notorious war criminal whom these groups were currently pursuing.

Nikolai Kalinin's greatest fear was that Jacob was becoming obsessed with the capture of Wolfram Eckhardt. Thus, with fatherly concern, he warned Jacob of the dangers of such a preoccupation and to assist in turning his mind into other channels, invited him to accompany a group of local archaeologists on a dig in Patagonia, where the remains of an obscure, pre-Incan civilization awaited their shovels. Though Jacob had yet to complete his own work on the shores of the Dead Sea, he found Kalinan's invitation tempting, especially after a couple of nights of sound sleep and the embassy's excellent cuisine had restored his physical vigor.

Of course, he also had an ulterior motive for remaining in South America, one that he couldn't even admit to the ambassador: as long as Simon Bar-Adon and his men were nearby, there was always a hope that Wolfram Eckhardt would again show himself. With this possibility in mind, Jacob made his first tentative contact with the team of local archaeologists. They reacted to his offer to join them in Patagonia with great enthusiasm. If all went as scheduled, he would be with them in three days.

In the meantime, he had planned to immerse himself in a study of the Incas and the civilizations that preceded them. He began his research in the embassy's well-stocked library, where he found several excellent volumes, one of which, the subject of this morning's study, lay open at his bedside. Though he tried hard to focus on the material, he finally gave up and laid the book aside, surrendering his gaze to the spinning overhead fan.

He knew that he was only fooling himself if he thought he could exorcise the events of the past week from his mind. The discovery and translation of the copper scroll, Simon Bar-Adon's unexpected arrival at the dig site, and his confrontation with Wolfram Eckhardt deep in the rain forest—all these experiences could not be so readily forgotten.

Superimposed on the spinning blades of the fan were the flickering flames of a once great bonfire. He could almost hear the pulsating hum of the jungle creatures and smell the fetid, humid stench of the heavy air. And then there was the enigmatic figure of the flute player, and Jacob's initial inability to accept this individual's identity.

The true test of Jacob's convictions had come when Wolfram Eckhardt pulled out the mushrooms and challenged him to consume one. The colorful hallucinogenic journey turned into a nightmarish trip that forever changed Jacob—as both Simon Bar-Adon and Nikolai Kalinin had sensed when they peered into his weary gaze—bringing him to the brink of insanity. How terrifying it had been to look directly into the abyss and relive the horror his own mother had experienced in that hellhole called Ravensbruck. The image of the corpse-filled pit from which she valiantly crawled never left his waking thoughts. Regardless of the personal dangers involved, Jacob could not rest until the beast most responsible for this crime was brought to justice. This was the dilemma that weighed on his soul, and he could only pray for the strength to persevere.

The shrill ringing of the bedside telephone called him back to the external world. With a halfhearted effort, he reached for the telephone and knocked the book he had been reading to the floor.

"Hello," he mumbled into the black plastic handset.

"Jacob," said the worried voice of Nikolai Kalinin, "I must see you in my office, at once!"

With this enigmatic command, the phone line went dead, and Jacob hung up the handset and sat up. The anxiety in the ambassador's voice was obvious, and Jacob rose quickly to comply with his request.

He breathlessly arrived at the ambassador's office and found him standing beside a large picture window, vacantly staring out to the tree-filled courtyard below. He seemed to be deep in thought, and Jacob had to speak out to get his attention.

"Whatever's the matter, comrade?"

Kalinin's face was ashen as he turned to answer. "Jacob, it's Anna!"

"Has something happened to my sister?" Jacob's personal problems instantly fled from his mind.

"That's just it, Jacob," the stunned diplomat said. "I can't really say. All I can tell you is that I just got off the telephone with Dr. Viktor Alexandrov, the director of Novolazarevskaya Station, where your sister was based. It seems that in the course of her official duties, she was visiting a nearby installation run by the Indian government. When Alexandrov called this facility to contact her, the station's radio was inexplicably inoperable, and has remained that way for almost twenty-four hours now."

"Is such a thing really that unusual?" Jacob asked. "Maybe they're only having equipment problems."

Kalinin shook his head. "I wish that were the case, comrade. But in Antarctica, a radiotelephone is a station's lifeline. They must rely on it for all their contact with the outside world. I wish I could say otherwise, Jacob, but if it was just an equipment problem, they would have made their way over to our base by now to repair it."

Sensing that the ambassador was holding something back, Jacob felt the stirrings of frustration and fear. "What's keeping our people from going over to the Indian facility and checking it out themselves?"

"Alexandrov was in the process of doing that very thing," Kalinin said. "Yet a contaminant in their fuel supply fouled the engines of their tracked vehicles. The engines can be repaired, though he's relying on me to send them the replacement carburetors."

"Are they available here?" Jacob hopefully asked.

"Not only are they available, but I've already got a more than sufficient load on its way to the Buenos Aires airport, where an Antonov An-22 transport plane is being prepared to transfer the parts to Antarctica."

Jacob's eyes lit up with this news. "When is the aircraft leaving?"

Kalinin looked at his watch. "It should be ready for takeoff sometime within the next three hours."

"Then I must be on it!" Jacob exclaimed. "For the sake of my only living relative, I must be on that airplane."

PART II

SHADOW OF THE WOLF

In Berlin, I learned that the National Socialist leaders proposed to utilize the supernatural powers of Medieval black magic and Faustian pentagram incantations to pinpoint the position of enemy convoys at sea, so that German submarine flotillas could be certain of sinking them.

—WILHELM WULFF, HIMMLER'S ASTROLOGIST

Magic exists only when we lose the way.

—HERMANN HESSE

8

Gunther Hartmann never dreamed there'd come a day when he'd be taking a fifty-year-old warship out on sea trials. Yet here he was, on a vessel whose keel had been laid a full year before he was even born! Of course, great human effort and expense were needed to make this remarkable patrol possible. Hartmann had personally sacrificed several years of his life to the refitting and preparation of his current command. And then there were the selfless efforts of dozens of others, who dedicated thousands of hours of their time for this cause.

The true results of their toil only became evident after Hartmann had begun these sea trials. *Ice Wolf*'s performance had so far been nearly flawless, something all the more remarkable considering the unprecedented mix of old and new technologies within its hull.

Ice Wolf originally began its long life at the Deschimag AG Weser shipyard in Bremen, Germany.

At the time of its launching in January 1945, it was the most sophisticated submarine afloat. As a representative of the Type XXI U-boat, it was the first of the true *Undersee* boats, designed to spend the majority of its time submerged, running on electrical power from its huge batteries. To recharge these batteries, the Type XXIs merely had to proceed to snorkel depth and activate their diesel engines.

The ability to run submerged for prolonged periods of time was, of course, a great breakthrough, but in addition, *Ice Wolf* was outfitted with a full array of revolutionary new sensor and weapons control systems, making it the most formidable submarine of its time. Unfortunately, it came into the German fleet too late to affect the war's outcome, though surviving platforms did provide the navies of the world with the prototype for the next generation of submarines.

As Hartmann proudly began his customary morning walk through *Ice Wolf,* he was well aware of its remarkable history. There was the long voyage south from Bremen in the closing days of the war, when the boat survived barrages from both bombs and depth charges to reach its secret anchorage. There, the work of modernizing began.

In many senses, the result contained the best of both worlds. Hartmann had learned during his twenty years in the postwar Federal German Navy that new technology was not always the most practical, especially in the case of many of the resilient, low-tech, manually operated systems used during the war. He preferred such old standbys as their ballast-and-trim mechanisms and dependable Maybach Daimler-Benz MB-820-S1 diesel engines, which were simply designed to take a beating during the harshest of operational conditions. These proved capable of perfectly coexisting with many of the modern systems added to *Ice Wolf,* including a state-of-the-art Krupp-Atlas CSU-83 integrated sonar system, and the replacement of the bulky batteries with smaller, more efficient fuel cells.

Nowhere was this marriage of low and high tech more noticeable than in the compartment that Hartmann was currently entering. As he ducked into the forward torpedo room he saw six stainless-steel racks, stacked three to a side on each of the outer bulkheads. Secured in these racks were a half-dozen, twenty-three-foot-long, twenty-one-inch-in-diameter, G7e torpedoes, their streamlined, encapsulated bodies painted dark green. These "fish," though originally designed during the war, could still pack a lethal punch.

Currently gathered around one of the boat's four torpedo tubes was Senior Weapons Chief Fritz Cremer and three junior seamen. Cremer was also a twenty-year veteran of the Kriegsmarine, and Hartmann had gone to sea with him aboard a Type-206 FRG coastal submarine over a decade ago. Hartmann knew that they were very fortunate to get Cremer's services, for not only was he a resourceful, dependable sailor, but a first-class teacher as well.

"Ah, Captain," said the heavyset, personable chief, "please join us."

Hartmann moved forward and joined his men beside the open door of the lower port tube.

"I was just showing this gang of sea dogs how to properly hook up a wire," Cremer continued. "And you've arrived just in time to settle an argument. Seaman Voss here can't seem to believe that this wire-guided system is part of *Ice Wolf*'s original equipment. Do share your doubts with the captain, Herr Voss."

A young, freckle-faced sailor with short red hair cleared his throat and nervously addressed Hartmann. "Sir, it's not that I was doubting the chief's word. It's just that during my three years of service with the Kriegsmarine, we learned that wire-guided torpedoes had only just been recently incorporated into the fleet. How could this possibly have been done during the Second World War?"

Before responding, Hartmann winked at the chief.

"You'd be surprised how advanced the technology of our grandfathers was, Seaman Voss. Unbelievable as it might sound, the torpedoes we carry today are no different than those carried during this vessel's first war patrol. Of course, they were right off the designer's drawing board at that time, and were one of the best-kept secrets of the war. Like the G7e torpedoes we carry today, they were available in two models—the acoustic homing variety code-named Geier, and a wire-guided variety code-named Lerche."

"It's too bad that we can't show the lads the deadliness of these fish, Captain," the chief said, grinning. "That Norwegian ship would have made a perfect target."

"That it would have, Chief," Hartmann hesitantly replied. "Yet it served its purpose all the same. Maybe next time our orders will read differently."

Cremer sensed his commanding officer's unease with this subject and turned his attention back to his men. "Speaking of old but still-effective technology, I bet you lads didn't realize that it was a World War Two–vintage Mark-8 torpedo that the British submarine HMS *Conqueror* used to sink the Argentine heavy cruiser *General Belgrano* during the Falklands war. Not only were the Mark 8s much less expensive than the modern Tigerfish torpedoes that they also carried, but their warheads had over four times as much explosive power. Captain, would you like to help me open up the warhead of one of our fish and show the lads what makes it tick?"

"I wish that I had the time, Chief," said Hartmann. "But I must get on with the rest of my walk-through."

This said, the captain turned for the aft accessway, which brought him directly into the forward crew accommodations. Instead of torpedoes, the outer bulkheads of this portion of the boat were filled with three levels of bunks. The coffin-sized racks were six feet long, three feet wide, and two feet tall. Each one had a comfortable foam mattress, a reading light, a fresh-air blower, and a curtain for privacy. A stowage bin for personal gear lay beneath the mattresses. Because of the tight space confines aboard *Ice Wolf*, "hot bunking" was a common practice. This meant that two men often shared the same rack, with one sailor using the mattress while the other was on duty.

Hartmann found several of the curtains drawn tight and noted the presence of a familiar, Scivvies-clad figure sprawled on his stomach on the aftmost bottom bunk. He walked over to this bunk, knelt down, and addressed its curly-haired occupant, who was in the process of sorting through a thick stack of photographs.

"Good morning, Herr Schiffer. Looks like someone's got home on his mind."

"Good morning, Captain," Klaus Schiffer whispered. "I hope you don't mind, but I like to start my day off with my photos. That way my family's with me for the rest of the day."

"Of course I don't mind." Hartmann took a peek at the topmost snapshot. "May I?" he asked.

The young sailor readily handed it to him. It showed a shapely woman in her early twenties, with long braided blond hair, a warm smile, and sparkling blue eyes. She was casually dressed in lederhosen and carried a backpack and walking stick at her side.

"My, this one's a real heartbreaker," Hartmann observed.

There was definite pride in the young sailor's voice as he said, "That's my fiancée, Lottie, sir. I took that picture last summer, during an excursion to Berchtesgaden."

Hartmann handed the snapshot back. "You are a very lucky fellow to have a beauty like that one waiting for you back home."

"That I am, sir. Though it can be awfully hard sometimes being separated by so many thousands of miles. Who knows when I'll be able to return home and get married."

Hartmann sensed his frustration and replied most carefully. "There will be plenty of time for marriage,

Herr Schiffer. First, we have the new Germany to prepare. Never forget the reason for our sacrifice, lad. We endure these hours of loneliness and endless work for a single all-important goal. Only after its attainment will it be time for you and your Lottie to take your rightful places in the glorious new Reich. Now, if I remember correctly, wasn't Lottie's father the unfortunate fellow who was shot to death on the streets of Munich?"

The sailor nodded and Hartmann continued. "Your dossier mentioned that this murder was one of the prime factors in your decision to join us. Did they ever catch the killer?"

"It was a Turk, sir," Schiffer reported, disgust in his voice. "He shot poor Mr. Sanger for a lousy fifty marks. Not only was he an illegal immigrant, but the gun he used was bought with German Republic welfare money. And on top of all that, the authorities had the nerve to let the bastard go because of a judicial technicality!"

"This pitiful story is not an isolated one," Hartmann said. "It is endlessly repeated every day in cities all over Germany. When will our people wake up? It's time to clean the scum from our streets and drive the illegals from our borders. Only then will Germany provide the proper environment for you and your fiancée to marry and raise that Aryan family."

"So I understand, sir. But do you really see a time in the near future when such a lofty goal will be attained?"

"Herr Schiffer, that glorious day is rapidly approaching, on that you have my solemn word. *Ice Wolf* is only one small part of a complex movement designed to wrest the powers of government from the unworthy and guide Germany back to the right path. The first skirmishes signaling our ascension have already been fought. Ultimately, the minds and souls of our fellow countrymen will be ours. So have faith, lad, and know that the day of reckoning is almost upon us."

Hoping that his pep talk had served its purpose, Hartmann excused himself to continue his tour. As he passed through the aft hatchway, the sound of recorded music met his ears. He recognized the lilting female voice of the legendary chanteuse Lili Marlene singing "Lied Eines Jungen Wachtpostens," one of his very favorite old tunes.

Several members of the crew were gathered around the communal table, eating. Hartmann could tell from their beard-stubbled faces and greasy overalls that they had just gotten off watch, and he directed his initial comments to Otto Brauer, the table's seniormost petty officer.

"Good morning, Otto. I compliment you on your selection of music."

His mouth filled with the remains of a chicken leg, Brauer replied, "That Lili Marlene was a sweetheart all right, and we can all thank Jürgen for providing the CD. It contains songs originally recorded in 1939."

Hartmann found his foot tapping to the slow martial beat and surveyed the bountiful selection of food his men were tearing into. Most of their attention was centered on a large ceramic tureen filled with a fragrant chicken-and-vegetable stew. Other platters held a fresh green salad and plenty of fruit, including bananas, apples, and oranges. The drink of choice was milk, and plenty of it.

"Captain, can I get you a plate?" offered Jürgen Stoltz, the beer-bellied cook.

"No thanks, Jürgen," Hartmann said. "It's still a bit early in the day for such a heavy meal, though I must admit it looks very appetizing."

"Early, late, what screwy hours us submariners keep, with some of us eating dinner, and others just ready for breakfast." Otto Brauer capped this remark with a hearty belch.

"There will be plenty more stew when you're ready for it, Captain," said Jürgen. "What a delight it is to have our food larders overflowing with fresh provisions for a change."

"We can thank our Norwegian friends for that," Hartmann commented.

Otto Brauer wiped the grease from his face with the back of his hand and began to dig into a chicken breast. "You know, these Viking chickens are just like their women—plump, moist, and tasty. If we only had a little schnapps and tobacco, this feast would be complete. What do ya say, Captain, can we get into those other provisions that we brought over?"

"Content yourself with the fresh food, Otto, because there'll be no alcohol or cigarettes until this sea trial is over."

Before Hartmann could explain his reasoning, a sailor ducked through the aft hatch, saying, "Captain, we've got a communiqué coming in."

That was all Hartmann had to hear; he followed the sailor aft into the radio room that was little more than an equipment-packed cubbyhole. The captain had to squeeze himself between the consoles to reach the seated, headphone-clad radio operator.

"Well, Hans, what's this about a communiqué?" Hartmann anxiously asked.

The operator briefly held up a finger for a moment of quiet, then returned to transcribing the coded dispatch being conveyed through his headphones. Less than a minute later he pushed off the headphones, tore off the top page of the pad, and handed it to Hartmann.

"This is the extent of the message, sir," he said. "It's been confirmed and verified."

Hartmann glanced down at the dispatch. It read: ICE WOLF—DISCONTINUE SEA TRIALS—RETURN TO THULE—WOLF.

"I should have expected as much," Hartmann mumbled, and folded up the note, slipped it into his breast pocket, and proceeded at once to the adjoining control room.

He found his second in command bent over the navigation plot, immersed in a chart of the waters they were currently transiting. Of all those on board, Oberleutnant Karl Kromer was his closest ally, and Hartmann excitedly pulled out the dispatch and spread it out on the chart. Without looking up, Kromer read the communiqué and grunted.

"So, the wolf finally calls home his cubs," he reflected. "Do you think this time he'll give us the go-ahead, Gunther?"

"Your guess is as good as mine, Number One. At least we return home knowing that *Ice Wolf* is ready." Hartmann fondly patted the overhead bulkhead, adding, "This old lady has met my every expectation, my friend. If only the men who originally designed her were still around to see this momentous day. How very proud and amazed they would be."

His expression rapt, Gunther surveyed the control room as if he were seeing it for the very first time. His eyes passed over the two seated planesmen, who looked more like computer technicians than sailors, their own gazes locked on the newly installed digital speed, course, and depth displays. Beside them, the chief of the watch monitored the complicated, old-fashioned valves and levers of his station, applying a technology developed long before personal computers were even dreamed of.

"Yes, Karl," Gunther said with a sigh, "the original designers of this boat would be impressed. Though I can't help but wonder how many of the high-tech systems we've added they, too, envisioned."

Hartmann patted Kromer on the back, then pointed toward the navigation chart. "Is there a chance that we can make it home for cocktails?"

Kromer returned his glance to the chart. Using a ruler and red grease pencil, he traced a line from their current position just west of Candlemass Island, almost due south, to the southern end of the South Sandwich Island chain. He then measured this line with a set of calipers and, after a quick mental calculation, reported his findings.

"At our current speed, our ETA at Thule should be somewhere around seventeen hundred hours. I believe that should give you just enough time for a quick schnapps before dinner, Gunther."

Hartmann's face lit up in a smile. "All that remains is for the Shadow to keep up his miracle work inside the engine room. I'll encourage him while you inform the helm of our new course."

To get to the engine room, Hartmann continued aft, having first to pass through the hushed compartment containing their sonar gear. A pair of alert technicians sat before their modern, green-tinted cathode-ray display screens. This setup was no different than those which graced the Kriegsmarine's latest warships.

Addressing the senior operator, Hartmann asked, "Peter, how goes it?"

The heavily bearded operator looked up from his console as if he had just been abruptly awakened from a deep trance. "Except for a boisterous group of humpbacks, the waters around us remain clear of any traffic, Captain."

"Pray that it remains that way," said Hartmann, "because we're headed back to Thule now, and we surely wouldn't want to compromise the location of our secret home."

"Of course not, sir." The technician suddenly reached up to press his right headphone closer to his ear. At the same time his glance returned to the display screen, where he analyzed the sound analysis curves visible there. "Damn those whales!" he cursed. "They're singing a friggin' undersea operetta out there!"

Hartmann left the technician to his problems and proceeded farther aft, to a sealed hatchway. As he undogged the hatch and yanked it open, the deep, clattering roar of the boat's twin twelve-cylinder, six-hundred-horsepower diesel engines greeted him. The heavy machinery here was spotlessly clean, and Hartmann noticed the man responsible for their maintenance on the far port side.

A six-foot-tall skeleton of a person who always wore grease-stained coveralls, Chief Willi Schwedler was known as the Shadow. The hollow-eyed, sunken-cheeked engineer seemed never to sleep, and when he did nod off, it was usually for only a short catnap right here beside his beloved engines. He was the kind of dedicated sailor every commanding officer dreamed of, and Hartmann knew that the Shadow was one of the best in the business.

The Shadow was currently working on their air purification system. Hartmann waited until he completed the installation of a fresh potash container, used to scrub carbon dioxide from the air, before saying, "Hello, Willi," and ducking beneath the suction duct for the air-cooling system.

Looking every bit the eccentric genius that he was, the Shadow turned to see who it was that dared trespass in his exclusive domain. Seeing the captain, his grease-smudged face lit up.

"Hi, Captain. Is there a problem that I could help you with?"

"It's not a problem that brings me here, Willi. I just wanted to see how you're making out, and get a report on the engines."

The Shadow made a dramatic sweeping gesture with his large hands. "Listen for yourself, Captain. That sweet sound says it all. My diesels are purring like kittens, and should you need Alberich, I'm showing a ninety-seven-percent fuel-cell availability."

"Splendid," Hartmann complimented. "Willi, you and your men are doing an excellent job back here. I'm proud to tell you that you've passed this sea trial with flying colors. So prepare to celebrate, because new orders have just been received, directing us back to Thule—"

"Captain!" a frantic voice from the forward hatchway interrupted.

Hartmann turned and saw the anxious face of their senior sonar technician. Sensing trouble, he quickly followed the man back into sonar.

"I believe that there could be another submarine out there on bearing zero-two-zero," the shaken technician said as he seated himself behind his console and pointed to the thick white line visible on the display screen. "That flutter on the narrow band is either an anomaly, an off-key whale, or trouble."

Hartmann's hand shot out for the nearest intercom handset.

"Number One!" he barked into the transmitter. "We've got an unidentified submerged contact, bearing zero-two-zero. Engage Alberich! Take her deep! Ultra quiet!"

No sooner did he hang up the handset than a piercing electronic tone began sounding throughout the boat. As the crew went scrambling to their battle stations, Gunther Hartmann knew that this alert could be the ultimate test of *Ice Wolf*'s state of readiness.

Breakfast was an important event inside the USS *Springfield*'s wardroom. It reflected the long-standing belief of its commanding officer that the best way to start off a new day was with a substantial, hearty meal. The early-morning gathering of the boat's officers also provided a relaxed, informal atmosphere for them to plan the day's activities.

On this particular morning, Philip Michaels woke up with a ravenous appetite. He quickly washed and dressed, then headed straight for the wardroom, where he found three members of the crew already assembled. As he took his customary seat at the head of the table, he exchanged greetings with his XO, seated to his right. The sub's navigator sat opposite Perez, while Lieutenant Steven Collier was seated at the far end of the rectangular table.

An alert mess steward served Michaels a half grapefruit, five prunes, and a glass of orange juice, followed by a bowl of oatmeal, flavored with brown sugar and raisins, three thick slices of French toast, hash-brown potatoes, and an order of crisp turkey bacon.

With a bare minimum of conversation, Michaels polished off his meal. Only after the steward brought him his first mug of coffee of the day did he get down to business.

"Gentlemen, by now you've had plenty of time to think about yesterday's visit to Bouvetoya Island, and I'd like to know your conclusions. What do you think happened aboard the *Condor?* And what's the best way for *Springfield* to assist in solving this mystery?"

After a thoughtful pause, the navigator was the first to comment. "From what little that I saw during our tour of the *Condor,* I'd say that the Norwegians were the victims of an isolated, random act of robbery. It was most likely committed by a desperate group of individuals, whose main motivation was hunger."

"And the murder?" Michaels probed.

"I find it hard to believe that homicide was part of their plan," Carr concluded. "Otherwise, why would they leave so many other witnesses? No, it's my contention that the shooting was an unfortunate afterthought, prompted by the victim's rash decision to send that SOS."

"I disagree," the SEAL interjected. "If these desperate, hungry individuals, as you call them, really exist, what kind of vessel were they traveling in? Surely they didn't reach that isolated portion of ocean via those Zodiacs. That's why I smell an internal cover-up. If you ask me, that pirate story was a bunch of hokum, to cover the ass of the Norwegian responsible for blowing away that poor diver."

"That's certainly an interesting theory," Michaels reflected between sips of his coffee. "I realize that you didn't get to visit the *Condor,* but what do you think, XO?"

"Lieutenant Carr's story makes the best sense to me, Skipper," Perez answered, "though that lack of a solid radar return on the fleeing pirate vessel still bothers me.

You did say that the *Condor* was able to get its radar unit operational shortly after the pirates left them."

"That's what the Norwegian captain told us," said Michaels, who decided not to reveal, for the moment, Robert Hartwell's wild supposition that a phantom, World War II–era U-boat was the pirate vessel.

"Even with a radar scan, a small trawler could have easily escaped detection," the navigator offered. "From what I understand, the visibility was nil, and a quick-moving trawler would have had little trouble remaining unseen."

Michaels grunted. "I appreciate your thoughts, gentlemen, and realize we've drawn a difficult assignment. Right now it's imperative that we keep an open mind and go about our business with all the circumspection of a detective."

"Then we're going to be continuing our patrol of the South Sandwich Island chain?" Perez asked.

"That's affirmative, XO," Michaels replied. "Since the chain offers the nearest land to the scene of the incident, other than Bouvetoya itself, the South Sandwich Islands would make the most practical home for our pirates, if they really exist. So I want to continue our extensive recon until all of the islands have been covered."

The XO looked at his watch. "Which island will we examine this morning?"

"Candlemass," Carr replied, and looked to his own watch just as the wardroom door swung open.

All eyes were on Chief Warrant Officer Frank Cunetto, who entered the compartment carrying a large white sheet cake with two lit candles on it. A group of officers and enlisted men followed him. Philip Michaels looked puzzled as the ship's supply officer placed the cake in front of him.

"Hey, you guys, my birthday's not for another three months!" he exclaimed.

Only then did he take a closer look at the cake and see that it was decorated with a football gridiron in red icing, with candy canes forming the goalposts. His face lit up with a surprised smile as he read the score and date inscribed in black icing on the fifty-yard line:

NAVY 24—ARMY 21
11/7/71

"I realize that it's a little early in the morning for cake, Captain," announced Cunetto, who was among other things the overseer of the sub's galley. "But we decided that now's the proper time to celebrate this all-important anniversary. And speaking for the rest of the crew, sir, I'd like to say that we'll never forget your last-minute field goal. Because as far as we're concerned, only one thing really matters, and that's to beat Army!"

As it turned out, beating Army was the farthest thing from the minds of Petty Officer First Class Mark Bodzin and the three other members of the *Springfield*'s current sonar watch. Instead of football, their attention was focused on the extremely noisy sonic environment in which the *Springfield* currently found itself.

Bodzin was monitoring the broad-band scan, and no matter what frequency he chose, a frustratingly familiar racket was conveyed through his headphones. The sounds ranged from long-drawn-out, high-pitched squeals to low, resonating bass bellows, and often had an almost eerie quality. The senior sonar technician was well aware of their source.

"These damn humpbacks are all over the place!" he observed disgustedly.

"How do you know that these whales are humpbacks?" asked the sonarman seated on his right.

"Bubba," Bodzin replied, "there's only one whale species on the planet that's as boisterous as these guys, and that's the humpback. Not only do they vocalize in an incredibly broad range, but they can actually repeat their elaborate, rhythmic sequences note for note."

"Mr. Bodzin," interrupted the sailor responsible for monitoring the TB-23 thin-line towed array. "Sierra Seven just went off the screen, sir."

"What?" Bodzin wasted no time addressing his keyboard to tap into the towed array's data link. As his display screen filled with this new request, he scratched his head in confusion. "Damn, where in the hell did Sierra Seven go?"

"Maybe Sierra Seven is a whaler, and they've gone and switched off their diesels to begin the hunt," offered the sonarman on Bodzin's immediate right. "And then there's always the possibility that they're experiencing engine problems."

"Or perhaps Sierra Seven isn't a merchant after all," Bodzin surmised. "Maybe it's a diesel-electric submarine that was at periscope depth, and we just tagged it switchin' over to battery power."

"Even then, the TB-23 should be able to pick up some kind of signature on it," the towed array operator countered.

"Shit, these damn whales aren't makin' our jobs any easier," Bodzin said as he cautiously turned up the array's volume gain another notch. "Hell, maybe Sierra Seven is nothin' but a whaler goin' in for the kill. But just to make certain, I'm gonna run a duplicate tape to put through the acoustic spectrum analyzer."

In an adjoining portion of the sea, another sonar watch team was also anxiously huddled over their consoles. From a position directly behind the seated operators, Gunther Hartmann pressed his headphones closer to his ears in a vain attempt to better hear the sounds being conveyed by *Ice Wolf*'s own towed sonar array.

"It's quiet," he intently whispered. "Oh, so very quiet."

"What class of submarine do you think it is?" the heavily bearded senior technician asked.

"My best guess is that it's either a British Trafalgar or an American 688," Hartmann answered.

"But what would the Americans be doing in these waters?" queried the technician.

Hartmann answered while reaching out and tenderly massaging the sonarman's shoulders. "Come now, Peter, have you already forgotten about the geopolitical realities of the new world order? With the Russians now out of the picture, the Americans have vast new portions of the planet's oceans to turn their attention to. Though with Alberich on our side, even the ever-capable 688 will have to earn its pay to track down *Ice Wolf.*"

9

The path led out of the compound and up into the windswept, treeless hills. Oblivious to the frigid chilling air, Wolfram Eckhardt set a brisk pace. Since his arrival on Thule, this was his first real outdoors excursion, and his first exposure to the harsh polar climate. Yet for an individual who was born and raised in the Bavarian Alps, it was more like a homecoming than an endurance test. The damp, humid air of his adopted home in South America was alien to his blood. The crisp, clean polar winds were like a tonic, and he felt instantly invigorated.

As the footpath began to slope gently upward he passed a trio of tall, rusted-out storage tanks. Though they had been long since drained of their contents, the sickly-sweet smell of whale oil was particularly notice-able. In 1904, the Norwegians founded Thule Station as a whale processing center. By 1940, overharvesting and the resulting reduction of the local whale population had led to its closing. Five years later the island was sold to a Paraguayan businessman, who was in fact a front for Wolfram and a German consortium, Thule's real owners.

Finding it hard to believe that five decades had already passed since the fated day that Thule became theirs, Wolfram continued up the sloping incline. He was winded by the time he reached the level ground of the ridge, but barely noticed the cold as he halted to catch his breath.

He turned around to survey the ground that he had just covered. The footpath was clearly visible from this height, and he followed it down to a motley collection of dilapidated wooden structures. These dozen or so weather-scarred buildings were the remains of the abandoned station, which was situated on the shores of a broad inlet, the deep, calm waters of which gave the place its strategic importance. It allowed direct access to the sea, and the whaling ships merely had to tie up to a sturdy wooden pier, where a massive rectangular processing shed was conveniently located.

Wolfram surveyed the remnants of this pier and the rusted, tin-roofed processing shed. When they first inspected the site for possible purchase, this was the feature that most excited them. It turned out to meet their every expectation.

A partially sunk whale catcher ship on the distant shoreline was an additional reminder of the site's past. Even Wolfram found it hard to believe that a modern, modular city was buried beneath the ground here. Yet proof of the city's existence soon became evident with the sudden appearance of a dark green utility vehicle in the deserted compound below. It appeared to have magically materialized from the interior of the white clapboard, tin-roofed building that once housed the site's church. As the four-wheeled truck turned toward the ridge on which Wolfram stood, he continued on to a nearby promontory that gave him an unobstructed view of the snow-covered mountain range that made up the island's desolate interior.

A huge albatross soared overhead and beyond the sound of the constantly gusting wind rose the distinctive, deep barking cries of the seals that lived on the beach below. How very different this world was from the one he had recently left. The rain forest seemed to belong to a different planet, yet was barely one thousand miles distant.

With his gaze on the soaring body of the immense, white-feathered seabird, Wolfram tried his best to visualize the thick jungle. As he did so a flood of suppressed memories filled his consciousness. The Mato Grosso—his magical quest for the sacred mushroom—all these thoughts formed a colorful tapestry that received its crowning touch the moment Jacob Litvak walked out of the rain forest and joined him beside the bonfire. Like a ghost from the past, the determined Jew had traveled halfway around the world for this meeting. And even though Wolfram knew that the Russian archaeologist was his eternal enemy, he found himself pitying the poor fool. Like his stubborn father before him, Jacob Litvak was wasting his life in a blind quest for revenge.

Their confrontation proved beyond a shadow of a doubt that Litvak had no comprehension of the eternal struggle to which Wolfram had dedicated his life. To lift this veil of unawareness and test the true strength of his convictions, Wolfram dared to share with him the flesh of the sacred Amanita. When he last saw his young pursuer before destiny called him here to Thule, the man was on the brink of insanity, the fate of those pilgrims who dared lift the veil without proper preparation. Sensing that he was no longer alone on the promontory, Wolfram pivoted and set his eyes on a tall, sloop-shouldered old-timer, whose full head of shocking white hair was visible beneath the hood of his down-filled parka.

Heinrich Westheim was his oldest living friend. They had fought together in World War II, during which Heinrich gained notoriety as the founder of the Ahnenerbe, the Nazi Occult Bureau. A valued adviser to

SS Reichsführer Himmler, Heinrich had been a loyal soldier to the very end. He would have willingly given up his life in the defense of the Reich Chancellery during the last days of the war if it wasn't for a serious wound caused by an exploding Russian shell. Because of this wound, he escaped certain death and, with the assistance of the Werewolf program, was eventually reunited with Wolfram in South America.

Wolfram raised his voice in greeting. "Heinrich, old friend, whatever are you doing out here? I thought that you were going to take a nap."

"To tell you the truth, that was my intention. But the moment I laid my head on the pillow, I realized that I was much too excited to sleep. I can't tell you how wonderful it is to have you here, Wolfram. It's just like the old days again, when there never seemed to be enough hours in the day."

"I know what you're saying, Heinrich, because I'm feeling the very same way." Wolfram pointed toward the deserted whaling station. "I was just admiring the unbelievably splendid job you did with the camouflage, old friend. I doubt that even the most sophisticated of reconnaissance satellites could crack our secret."

"You flatter me," said Heinrich as he peered down into the valley. "I was only one of a long list of talented, hardworking individuals responsible for our little masquerade here."

"Nonsense," Wolfram replied. "As Thule's senior administrator from the very beginning, you deserve more credit than you think. I remember those all-important early days when the project went from the design stage to implementation. If it wasn't for your selfless efforts then, Thule might have never become a reality."

A numbing gust of wind blew in from the sea, and Heinrich turned his back to its penetrating cold. "Brrr," he said, his teeth chattering. "My blood is getting much too thin for this bitter climate. Come, Wolfram, let's return to the compound. This is no time for you to risk pneumonia. Besides, dinner will be ready shortly. Afterward, I have a marvelous surprise for you."

Though Wolfram was sufficiently dressed to ward off the nastiest of chills, he agreed. "A surprise, you say? I've always had a soft spot in my heart for surprises. And I guess I could do with a spot of dinner. What's on the menu?"

Heinrich beamed. "In your honor, I had my Heidi fix up a special Bavarian feast. How long has it been since you had authentic potato pancakes?"

This was all Wolfram had to hear to break out into a broad smile. "Enough said, Heinrich. Lead the way!"

A short drive brought them back into the valley and to a white clapboard church. The dirt road they were traveling on appeared to merge right into the building's back wall. A good fifty yards before what appeared to be a certain collision, Heinrich casually reached up to the truck's visor and depressed a remote-control switch. An entire section of the wall moved upward, revealing a well-lit interior ramp.

In this manner they entered the subterranean realms of Thule base. A paved tunnel led them further underground, and they passed by intersecting tunnels leading to the modules reserved for the base's main dormitory, which was capable of holding up to one hundred individuals, a fully equipped kitchen, dining room/lounge, library, surgery, and a well-equipped radio room. It was beside an accessway marked MACHINE SHOP that the vehicle parked.

"I still have trouble adjusting to the quiet and lack of activity," Heinrich said as he led the way out of the truck and down a tiled corridor.

They entered the cavernous, well-lit machine shop. Of the dozen work stations situated here, only one was currently occupied by three workers dressed in coveralls and hard hats. Wolfram briefly stopped when a glaringly bright welder's torch momentarily blinded him.

"It seems like only yesterday that this shop was a hub of activity," Heinrich reflected. "One afternoon, during the height of *Ice Wolf*'s renovations, I counted over fifty men and women at work."

His sight now restored, Wolfram grunted. "I imagine that those workers were only too glad to return to Germany once their jobs here were completed."

"That they were, Wolfram. I'm afraid Thule doesn't offer much in the way of nightlife."

"Who had the energy for nightlife after the full day's work that you squeezed out of them?" Wolfram commented lightly.

Heinrich laughed. "I guess I did demand quite a lot from them, although it was nothing in comparison with the twenty-hour days we put in during the war."

"It's comforting to know that the same workers that toiled here at Thule are waiting for us back home, their vows of loyalty and secrecy intact," said Wolfram. "When the time comes for our return, they'll be in an ideal position to spread the word to their fellow workers."

"My limbs tremble with excitement just knowing that the glorious day of our return is at long last almost upon us," Heinrich said, leading the way into an adjoining corridor.

The wide asphalt passageway led to a pair of tunnels at its end. The tunnel on the right-hand side had a golden swastika encirled by a gilded laurel wreath mounted above it.

As they passed by it on their way to the adjoining tunnel, Wolfram said, "If all goes as scheduled, in only a couple of more hours, we'll be transiting that tunnel to welcome back our gang of underwater marauders."

"And don't forget that soon afterward, we'll be boarding *Ice Wolf* ourselves for the long trip back home!" Heinrich triumphantly added.

This thought put new purpose in the white-haired veteran's stride, and he quickly ducked into the adjoining accessway. With the assistance of a hard plastic keycard, he opened a locked door at the end of this corridor and led the way into his private quarters.

This suite of rooms was one of Wolfram's very favorite portions of Thule base. With exacting detail, Heinrich had recreated the intimate warmth of a Bavarian hunting lodge. There was plenty of dark wood paneling, simple, comfortable furniture, and an abundance of pictures, all of which showed scenes from the fatherland. There were even several working cuckoo clocks, a display case holding a superb collection of Hummel porcelain, and to make the atmosphere complete, a full-grown German shepherd named Blondi.

The dog made her presence known as they entered the living room. She had been asleep on the hearth, in front of a crackling fire, and with the entrance of her master, her head shot up and she sprinted to Heinrich's side. Wolfram felt honored when Blondi allowed him to stroke the soft fur on her neck, though this scene was cut short by the arrival of Heidi, Heinrich's longtime cook.

"Take off those outer garments and wash up," the hefty, fifty-four-year-old Heidelberg native commanded. "Dinner will be served in ten minutes sharp."

Without waiting for a reply, she pivoted with military exactness and marched back to the kitchen, with Blondi close behind her. Heinrich mockingly clicked his heels together, then caught his guest's glance and winked.

"Come on, Wolfram. We'd better do as ordered, or there'll be no strudel for us this evening."

Precisely ten minutes later the first course of piping hot lentil soup arrived at the dinner table. For as long as he could remember, Wolfram had never had a bad meal at Heinrich's table, and this evening proved no different. Wiener schnitzel à la Holstein was the main course, and Wolfram found his white veal cutlet cooked to perfection, with the egg served over easy, just as he liked it. Tart, shredded red cabbage was served on the side. And when the promised platter of plump, potato pancakes with applesauce arrived, he ahhed in delight. The meal ended with a slice of hot apple strudel and a demitasse of rich Viennese coffee. Only after paying their sincere compliments to the cook did the two men excuse themselves for Heinrich's private study.

"Now, that was a meal fit for a kaiser," Wolfram said as he patted his bulging stomach and sat down in one of the study's two high-backed leather chairs. "If I had a cook like that, I'd be as fat as a goose."

"Believe me, that meal was in your honor," Heinrich said as he walked over to his desk. "Ordinarily, I'm content with a simple vegetarian diet."

Heinrich picked up a remote control device, depressed one of its many buttons, and the gas-powered fireplace popped alive, its flames providing instant warmth. Wolfram watched as his host removed two cigars from a dark, cherrywood humidor.

"I saved these Temple Hall cigars just for you, Wolfram. Please allow me to prepare one for you. Then I'll pour us some Armagnac, and I can get on with that surprise I promised you."

Heinrich expertly clipped the end of each cigar and placed them on a silver tray alongside two heavy crystal snifters partially filled with golden-colored brandy. He graciously served his guest and lit both their cigars with a thick wooden match. Only then was he free to lift up his snifter.

"*Es lieber Deutschland!*" he cried out passionately.

Wolfram raised his own glass and took a sip. The brandy went down like a jolt of fire and proved a perfect compliment to the heavy taste of the cigar.

"I'd like to issue a toast of my own, Heinrich. Here's to the old fighters, and to a movement that will never die. To the Fourth Reich, my friend!"

Heinrich took special pleasure in this toast, and a devilish gleam twinkled in his eyes as he walked over to the far wall, which was veiled by a thick, red velveteen drape. "This is the first part of your surprise," he said, reaching for the drawstring and yanking the drapes open.

Wolfram gasped as the drapes parted and he set his eyes on a huge, crimson-red Nazi flag. The black swastika and circular white border seemed to have an almost hypnotizing effect on him, and he couldn't help but stand and walk over to have a closer look.

"No, it can't be!" he exclaimed, spotting the flag's frayed, red-stained edges.

Heinrich had been waiting for this moment, and he took his time responding. "I thought that you of all people would find this relic of particular interest, Wolfram. Yes, it is the infamous Blood Flag of the abortive Munich putsch of November 1923. That fabric is stained with the blood of our martyred, National Socialist forefathers!"

Wolfram gingerly touched the tattered edge with the reverence of a disciple touching the hem of a garment worn by his Lord. "My God, Heinrich! Where did you ever get this priceless relic?"

Heinrich slyly grinned. "From the Führer's bunker, where else? While Axmann and his cronies were desperately trying their best to cremate the body of our brave leader and his new wife, I managed to gain entrance to the room where the fated suicide took place. The almond scent of cyanide was still heavy in the air as I pulled the flag from the depths of our beloved Führer's footlocker. Hell, the way I looked at it, the flag was better off with me than with the advancing Russians."

"My God, Heinrich!" Wolfram exclaimed, clearly in awe.

"As a student of history, I'm certain you'll appreciate the second part of my little surprise as well," Heinrich said, walking over to his desk to pick up the remote-control device. "Now, do return to your seat, and let's enjoy our cigars and brandy."

Wolfram did as instructed and was soon joined by his host, who settled himself into the other high-backed chair. Heinrich allowed himself another sip of brandy before pointing the remote control toward the wooden wall immediately above the fireplace. A large panel slid open, revealing a twenty-seven-inch television monitor.

Again Heinrich addressed the remote control, and this time the television set switched on.

The screen filled with a somewhat scratchy black-and-white film, whose first frame showed the imperial German eagle perched on a laurel wreath. Stirring martial music began in the background, and when the title of the film flashed onto the screen—TRIUMPH DES WILLENS—Wolfram's face flushed with excitement.

"Ah, Heinrich, *Triumph of the Will!* I haven't seen a copy of this in over thirty years. What a great surprise."

"I thought you would appreciate it, Wolfram. During the war, it seemed we watched this film at least once a week. Yet it wasn't until I received this print from our friends in Florida that I realized what an incredibly powerful propaganda tool it was."

A moment of intense silence followed as both viewers watched the opening sequence unfold. The date 1934 flashed on the screen, and from the cockpit of a Fokker trimotor airplane, the city of Nuremberg took shape below. The scene cut to an excited crowd gathered at an airfield. Wolfram finally broke his silence when Adolf Hitler emerged from the newly landed airplane, to the rousing cheers of thousands of adoring citizens.

"How young and vibrant the Führer appeared back then. These images are remarkable!"

"We can all be thankful that the Führer allowed Leni Riefenstahl and her film crew permission to record these events, Wolfram. In this way, the exciting days of the birth of the Third Reich can live forever."

A motorcade carried Hitler into the city. All along the route, he received an even more enthusiastic greeting than at the airfield.

"Look at the people's eyes as they raise their arms in the Nazi salute and watch their Führer pass," Wolfram said, with deep feeling. "There appears to be a love beyond comprehension in those adoring glances, almost as if they were mesmerized."

Heinrich's reply was made against a background of the

soundtrack's stirring martial music. "What we're witnessing is a people's hunger for greatness. Just look what can happen when the Aryan blood spirit is awakened. Just as they mobilized en masse six decades ago, so shall they unite again to bring in the new century!"

A scene flashed onto the screen showing an encampment of thousands of young army recruits. Wolfram fondly smiled as he watched these troops scrub themselves clean at their communal washbasins, line up for food at the outdoor mess, then playfully engage in such schoolboy antics as wrestling and a spirited blanket toss.

"How very innocent it all appeared," he observed. "To think that the majority of these handsome, energetic young men would soon lose their innocence on the battlefield."

The viewing of a solemn, torch-lit night march prompted Heinrich to comment soberly, "I remember well my first night rally. What an inspiring impression it left on me. To be assembled alongside tens of thousands of my fellow Aryan brothers, under the veil of darkness, with the stirring Germanic music calling us together as one! I pledged my blood to the cause that fated evening, and would have willingly walked through the gates of hell had my superiors asked it of me."

"As it turned out, you and I would pass through those gates together, not long after these pictures were taken," Wolfram said, then lapsed into silence as the screen filled with a scene showing Hitler delivering a speech.

Thousands of soldiers formed his rapt audience. They stood ramrod straight, their individual units in perfect alignment. Hitler started his address slowly, with a deceptive, almost fatherly calm. Yet it didn't take long for him to reach a feverish, inflamed pitch, emphasizing his main points with firm hand gestures. Hitler's eyes appeared to glaze over with demonic fury as he extolled the glories of a united Aryan Reich, pledged to blood purity.

"Sometimes I forget what an incredibly effective orator the Führer was," Wolfram said as the speech reached its climax with a spirited chorus of "Heil Hitler." "And I still find it unbelievable that the world never truly grasped the great forces that we were able to set into motion with the Führer's assistance."

"If that audience could have only seen their beloved Führer a few years earlier," Heinrich interjected, "I seriously doubt that they would have been impressed with the bumbling second-rate Austrian artist he then was, eking out his pitiful living selling landscapes on the street corners of Vienna. If the world only knew the true sequence of events that led to the most remarkable transformation in all of history."

Wolfram took a puff on his cigar. "Sometimes I wonder if the course of history would have turned out differently if my university studies hadn't led me to the tale of the legendary Dr. Faust. Because the moment I immersed myself in this fascinating subject, my own occult vision came into focus. Determining the exact nature of the ancient ritual that Faust used to call forth the devil took precedence over all else, and indirectly led me on that fated archaeological dig to Montsegur. I was about the same age as those soldiers on the screen at the time, and filled with a similar innocence and youthful zest for life."

Turning away from the television, Heinrich met the serious gaze of his guest. "I remember your tale well, my friend. And I'm certain that it was no mere coincidence that drew you to the long-buried Cathar treasure. You must have been thrilled when your excavation pick penetrated the rock of that sealed grotto for the first time. Who would ever have dreamed that among the great treasures you brought to light on that day would be one that would aid Hitler's incredibly swift ascension to power!"

All but forgetting about the movie, Wolfram continued. "Often in my old age, I find myself wondering if we were the ones who made the terrible mistake of choosing Hitler as our vessel."

"Nonsense!" Heinrich retorted. "Every movement needs its leader. Such an individual is a necessary evil, and the Austrian appeared to have all the qualities that we needed. He was the perfect patsy, an empty shell just waiting for possession by the cosmic doppelgänger. We couldn't dare let him slip through our hands.

"When you returned from the Judean wilderness with the secrets of the Grail, the masters took this as the sign that the time of the reawakening was upon us. When Hitler voluntarily stepped forth to lift the veil, how could we possibly refuse him? We had nothing to lose and everything to gain, and just look at the results."

Heinrich pointed to the screen, where Hitler was reviewing a large contingent of troops, who displayed unwavering loyalty as they goose-stepped past the reviewing stand, a disciplined, well-oiled fighting machine, sworn to defend the Reich to the last drop of their blood.

"The potential was definitely there, Wolfram," Heinrich said after a contemplative sip of brandy. "Your great discoveries set into motion a predestined chain of cosmic events, which we, as mere mortals, soon lost control of. And that's the ultimate source of the anxieties that vex you, old friend, for what power has man in the realm of the gods?"

"You're right, Heinrich. It's just that it's so very frustrating knowing how close we came to success. The passing years have made me take for granted the omnipotent powers we had at our disposal back then. Seeing this film again reminds me of our many achievements. You know, I've almost forgotten how blind the rest of the world was to our existence."

Heinrich grunted. "As if the masses could ever have understood the nature of the forces that made up National Socialism." Pausing for a moment to take a puff on his cigar, Heinrich added, "Of all our opponents, Churchill was the only one to take us seriously. Under Walter Stein's guidance, the Englishman became a firm believer in the power of the Holy Spear and the other relics you brought back to us from southern France.

"I've heard from several sources that Sir Winston had Stein instruct him in our magical techniques. In such a way, he hoped to tap his own psychic energies and focus his stubborn will on resisting us.

"They say that Churchill was particularly interested in the manner in which these techniques influenced Hitler's rapid rise to power. More than any other outsider, the Englishman wanted to know how an itinerant, unsuccessful painter and former private first class could suddenly develop such astonishing leadership qualities. Most of all, Churchill wanted to know the reason that rational, educated people would go to Hitler's speeches as skeptics and leave in a trance, almost like religious converts."

Wolfram briefly glanced at the television screen, where an adoring audience was in the process of saluting their Führer. "I still find it amazing that what we took for granted, the rest of the world was totally blind to," he said. "I'll never forget the infamous trials that took place at the same location that *Triumph of the Will* was shot only twelve years later. This so-called judgment at Nuremberg showed that the West refused to comprehend what Nazism really was. At the time I was just settling into my new home in South America and couldn't believe the Western newspaper accounts, which explained away twenty-five million dead in psychoanalytical terms, as a mere mental aberration. It was almost as if the West was denying the very existence of evil!"

"I heard stories of Allied security guards being totally blind to the black-mass last rites that our condemned were performing right there in their cells!" Heinrich exclaimed. "If only I could have brought a couple of those guards with me to Wewelsburg Castle, and let them witness one of Himmler's macabre loyalty ceremonies. I wonder what they'd have to say after watching the inner core of the SS take their irreversible vows of service to the Luciferic Oracle. That would soon enough have made believers out of them!"

Wolfram nodded in agreement and returned his attention to the film. Another spirited political rally was in process, this one indoors in an immense, cathedral-like meeting hall. The ever-faithful Rudolf Hess was at the podium, bushy eyebrows and all, introducing Hitler. As the camera scanned the assemblage of uniformed dignitaries on the stage, Wolfram recognized Goebbels, Himmler, Göring, and Bormann, among others.

"If you want to know the real reason behind the Third Reich's abrupt fall, you don't have to look any further than that group of vain, incompetent clowns gathered there behind the podium," Heinrich said bitterly, pointing at the same group. "Their selfish shortsightedness doomed the movement to failure, and not even the intervention of the cosmic Antichrist could make up for their inadequacies. What I wouldn't have given to trade the entire lot of them for a single man like Reichprotektor Reinhard Heydrich."

"The Black Prince was a capable one all right," Wolfram agreed. "When I first shared with him the initiation ceremony, he showed an immediate interest. Of all those who participated in the Rite of Awakening, he displayed the greatest promise. What a wasteful shame that he had to die from blood poisoning after that pitiful assassination attempt in Czechoslovakia. If he had outlived Hitler, Heydrich would have been the perfect person into which to transfer the entity."

On the screen, Hitler had taken the podium and passionately lectured his spellbound audience on Germany's desperate need for increased living space. Heinrich appeared to take genuine interest in the fiery discourse, and he waited until Hitler concluded his speech before speaking.

"The movement will be forever in your debt, Wolfram. You foresaw our Führer's insanity and convinced us to prepare for the transfer of the sacred relics. If it wasn't for your prescience, we would have absolutely no reason to be gathered here today.

"It was an act of sheer genius on your part to direct the Kriegsmarine to begin that survey of New Schwabenland. You displayed uncanny intuition when you ordered our brave Antarctic explorers to prepare the Ice Lair. With the successful transfer of the holy relics to the hold of *Ice Wolf* in May of 1945, what could have been the blackest day in German history became a time for renewed hope. How thrilling it is to know that the time of the reawakening is almost upon us, old friend, and that we are still alive to witness it!"

"That we are," Wolfram concurred, raising his glass for yet another toast. "I'd like to drink to the new generation, from whose enlightened roots the Fourth Reich shall spring."

Each of the veterans took a sip of brandy, then Wolfram anxiously sat forward and continued. "I first knew that the time was approaching when the Berlin Wall fell. This signaled Germany's reunification, after five long decades of bitter division. The collapse of the Soviet Union guaranteed the success of our country's rebirth, and helped sow the seeds of discontent that our movement needed. Just as it was during the 1920s and 1930s, the Germany of the 1990s is ripe for change. The undercurrents of discord and dissent can't be ignored, with unemployment and recession breeding further contempt and frustration.

"Further feeding the flames of discontent are the presence of unparalleled numbers of lazy, dishonest, social leeches. These blacks, Turks, Arabs, and Croats suck the lifeblood from our social institutions. They breed like flies, their numbers threatening to drive us from our own borders.

"Added to this sickening stew is a misguided German youth, poisoned by drugs, violence, and rock music. The decadent American mass media have taken over their souls and turned our best hopes for tomorrow into unimaginative, rock-video-addicted junkies.

"For the second time in this century, Europe finds itself threatened by war in the Balkans. This conflict has the potential to spread beyond the borders of the former Yugoslavia, with another world war almost certain to follow. With the so-called European Community weak, ineffective, and scared to act decisively, it's time for Germany to rise to the occasion and take matters into its own hands.

"To ensure our success, we have only one course of action open to us. With your invaluable assistance, we have already put this process into motion. The blood of the Reich, the by-products of the Lebensborn, patiently wait for our call. And we shall not disappoint them. The Luciferic Oracle shall once again be tapped, the cosmic powers summoned, and the Fourth Reich will rise from the ashes to take its rightful place as the leader of all nations."

"Well said, my friend!" Heinrich exclaimed as he raised his glass and drained its contents.

Wolfram did likewise, and as the fiery brandy coursed down his throat, he noted that the film was coming to a conclusion with a moving rendition of "Die Fahne Hoch," the Horst Wessel Song.

No sooner did the soundtrack fade than a knock sounded on the study's door. Without waiting for a response, Heidi entered. Blondi was beside her, and beat the cook to Heinrich's chair.

"This just arrived for you," she said as she handed her master a folded note.

Heinrich read its contents, and a wide smile touched his lips. "Excellent news, my friends!" he said. "The gatekeeper has spotted *Ice Wolf*'s running lights."

Heidi appeared not the least bit interested in this revelation. Her attention was instead focused on picking up their glasses and emptying the ashtray.

"I imagine that you'd like some coffee before going down to the pier," she said while heading for the door. "Do you want me to call Blondi?"

"She can stay with me," Heinrich answered, a bit distracted. "And yes, coffee would be most appreciated."

With Heidi's exit, Blondi settled in beside the hearth, and Heinrich's glance went back to the note he had just received.

"I can't wait to get the results of the sea trials, Wolfram. Only then will we know exactly how much work remains to be done on *Ice Wolf* before we can embark on our long journey."

"Hopefully, the turnaround will be a quick one. I won't be able to rest comfortably until I know for certain that the Ice Lair hasn't been compromised."

Heinrich seemed disturbed by this comment. "The report from Ritter said absolutely nothing about the lair's integrity actually being compromised, Wolfram."

"Then why did he go to the extreme of setting that fire at Dakshan Gangotri?" Wolfram asked.

"That was only a precautionary measure, and you know it, my friend. So relax, and have faith in the remarkable installation that you yourself helped design."

It was obvious that both men were under tremendous pressure, and Wolfram did his best to take his friend's advice. He sat back in his chair, focused his gaze on the flickering fire, and took several deep, relaxing breaths.

"I'm sorry, Heinrich. Fifty years is a long time to wait, and I guess I'm getting just a little bit overanxious."

"Apologies aren't necessary, my friend. To tell you the truth, I'm just as anxious as you to get on with it. But worrying won't get us on our path any sooner. Besides, weren't you always the one who advocated the power of positive thinking to manage even the worst of problems?"

With his hands cupped beneath his chin, Wolfram nodded, all the while fighting the urge to close his eyes and surrender to the great fatigue that had suddenly overtaken him. "So I did, Heinrich. So I did."

10

Jacob Litvak peered morosely out the double-paned, Plexiglas porthole where a cloudy white veil of blowing snow provided a suitable backdrop for his mood. Deep in thought, he was barely aware of the grinding roar of the Antonov's four Kuznetsov single-shaft turboprop engines and the constantly vibrating cabin around him. At the moment only one thing really mattered to him, and that was reaching his isolated destination as quickly as possible.

Ten minutes ago the cabin attendant had directed him to prepare for their final landing approach. Shortly afterward they began experiencing some of the worst turbulence of the entire eight-and-a-half-hour, nonstop flight from Buenos Aires.

Antarctica—the very name seemed alien to Jacob, the embodiment of remoteness and desolation. He had never given the South Pole much thought before, and his knowledge of this vast frozen continent was limited to the few books about the early polar explorers he had read as a youngster.

His sister, Anna, was a world-renowned expert on Antarctica's geological history. He first realized the extent of her interest in the South Pole during their last meeting, eleven months ago at a New Year's Eve party at Anna's Moscow apartment. Shortly afterward, she learned that the government had approved the funding for her third season's work at the pole.

Anna had been very excited and enthusiastic about this long-anticipated project. Over champagne and caviar, she took Jacob aside and gave him a brief overview of her project's goals. Jacob was genuinely surprised to learn that Russia had seven permanent winter bases and six summer stations in Antarctica. Anna's work would take her to the largest Russian installation, from which she planned to make field trips into the interior.

Except for an occasional phone call or letter, this New Year's visit was the last opportunity they'd had to spend time together. Though they parted with a promise to have another reunion in the summer, it never came to pass. Jacob had been preoccupied with a dig in Tashkent, while Anna found herself in the northern Urals, deep in a study of tectonics. For the last couple of years this always seemed to be the case, and they allowed their professional responsibilities to widen the gulf between them.

Now that Anna's life might be in danger, Jacob realized what a great mistake they had made. He couldn't help but blame himself for not taking the initiative and insisting that they get together more frequently. After all, they had no other family, neither of them was married, and their work was simply not a justifiable excuse for not seeing each other.

Jacob felt the pangs of guilt as the airplane was wildly shaken by a wind gust, and he absentmindedly tightened his grasp on his seat's worn leather armrests. What kind of brother had he really been? He and Anna had been so close as children, and he had promised himself that he would continue to keep a watchful eye over her after their parents' demise. Yet he had broken that promise, and now he was paying the price.

This was not the first time that his selfishness had embroiled him in such problems. Jacob thought of Ambassador Kalinin's warning about his unrelenting pursuit of Wolfram Eckhardt and its inevitable toll on his humanity. Just as he had wrapped himself up in his work, Jacob had devoted an enormous amount of energy to bringing the ex-Nazi to justice. Was this expenditure of precious time and effort indeed a waste, as the ambassador hinted?

The answer to this question seemed to come when he learned that the authorities were having problems contacting Anna. For the first time in years his single-minded pursuit of Eckhardt was ripped from his mind. Upon receiving permission to accompany this flight, he left the embassy in such a hurry that he hadn't even remembered to call Simon Bar-Adon to let him know his whereabouts. For once, the life of his sister took precedence over Eckhardt's capture.

The rumbling, groaning sound of the airplane's landing gear extending diverted his attention. He refocused his gaze on the porthole and the gusting snowstorm outside. He clenched the armrests as the Antonov made sudden jolting contact with the frozen ground. The deep roar of the engines seemed to intensify rather than decrease, and as he peered out at the constant wall of white, he wondered if they hadn't landed in the sky.

The amplified voice of the cabin attendant soon set him straight: "Welcome to Antarctica's Novolazarevskaya airfield, where the temperature outside is minus twenty-three degrees Celsius. Please remain in your seats with your seat belts fastened until we have come to a complete stop at the freight terminal. And thank you for flying Aeroflot."

Less than a dozen of the aircraft's twenty-nine passenger seats were occupied, and when the plane ground to a halt, Jacob was the only one to stand and depart. As he climbed down into the cavernous main cabin, he passed cargo pallets marked MOLODEZNAYA, BELLINGSHAUSEN, VOSTOK, and MIRNY, the names of the other Russian bases to which the transport airplane was bound.

It wasn't until he reached the tail end of the cabin that he spotted the pallet labeled NOVOLAZAREVSKAYA. An attractive, parka-clad attendant waited for him here.

"You'd better zip up that coat and put on those gloves," she warned. "And if I were you, I'd seriously think about getting a more practical hat than the one you're wearing. It's cold out there, comrade."

In response to her advice, Jacob stubbornly pulled down the rim of his crumpled green bush hat. "This old hat has seen me through many a Siberian winter. I'm sure it will do just as well in Antarctica."

The attendant flashed him her best "you'll be sorry" glance, and when she opened the Antonov's beaver-tail rear doors, Jacob was momentarily staggered as a blast of frigid, bone-chilling air enveloped him. He quickly zipped up his parka and slipped on his mittens.

As the massive rear doors opened completely pellets of icy snow blew into the cargo hold. From the veiled midsts of the raging blizzard, a tall figure suddenly emerged, dressed in full polar gear, including a woolen balaclava, on top of which was a fur-lined hood. This combined with a pair of dark sunglasses left his face completely covered, and when he climbed up the loading ramp to introduce himself, his voice was so muffled as to be barely comprehensible.

"Dr. Jacob Litvak?" he shouted to be heard over the gusting wind. "Lieutenant Mikhail Lopatin, at your service, comrade."

Even inside the cabin, he had to shout to be heard. "Director Alexandrov wished to express his sincere regrets for not being able to greet you personally, but his presence was urgently needed at the maintenance garage. I do hope that you have the replacement parts we requested."

Jacob pointed toward a compact wooden crate that sat on the very top of the rear pallet. "There they are, Lieutenant. Any word from my sister?"

"I'm afraid not, sir."

Any hopes that Jacob might have had for a quick resolution to this crisis were dashed by this news, and he somberly looked on as his escort quickly made his way to the rear pallet. The soldier deftly removed the crate from the restraining straps, grasped it in his arm, and turned for the exit.

"If you'll just follow me, comrade," he instructed as he strode past Jacob and walked down the ramp.

Jacob grabbed his duffel bag, pulled his walking stick from the interior, and followed his escort. As he stepped off the ramp onto the frozen ground, the wind knifed through his down-filled coat. The blinding glare of the constantly blowing snow impeded his progress, and he used his walking stick like a blind man did his cane, to "feel" for any obstacles on the ground in front of him.

Thankfully, he didn't have far to travel. Parked on the snow was a bright yellow, all-terrain transporter with a fully enclosed cab. Jacob spotted Lieutenant Lopatin loading the crate he carried into the vehicle's open-air cargo bed. This was where Jacob stowed his duffel bag, before gratefully climbing into the cab's passenger seat.

The heater vainly attempted to counter the intense cold. Yet without the wind to contend with, Jacob really didn't mind the chill.

"I thought it was supposed to be spring down here," he said to his escort, who was settling in behind the wheel.

"But it is, comrade," Mikhail replied. "If this were a full-fledged winter storm, the transporter's fluids would be frozen solid, and we'd have to be doing our traveling by foot or dogsled."

Mikhail engaged the vehicle's clutch, and it lurched

forward with a muffled roar. Although the dual wiper blades kept the windshield clear, Jacob wondered how his driver could see where they were going. The visibility was practically nil, and Jacob noted that Mikhail Lopatin kept a close eye on both the dashboard-mounted compass and the odometer.

"Where are we headed?" he asked.

"Straight to the garage," Mikhail answered.

A tall bamboo stake with a madly flapping, bright orange flag mounted on it passed on their right. They passed a dozen similar stakes placed at intervals of a quarter kilometer. With their route thus marked, the transporter soon came to a halt beside a large Quonset hut. Mikhail jumped from the cab to slide open the hut's large aluminum door.

From his vantage point, Jacob could see the structure's well-lit interior. Mikhail returned to the cab, and Jacob counted four bright yellow, all-terrain vehicles parked at their maintenance bays. The hood of each was wide-open, with a variety of coverall-clad mechanics huddled over the exposed engines.

Mikhail seemed genuinely excited as he guided their vehicle inside and switched it off. "The parts have arrived!" he reported as he swung open the door and climbed down onto the concrete pavement.

Jacob exited the cab and found that their transporter was now the focal point for all those gathered inside. The group's attention was on the crate he had brought from Buenos Aires.

A heavily bearded, grease-stained mechanic got the privilege of opening the crate. With an iron crowbar, he carefully wrenched free the nails that had kept the individual wooden slats in place.

Jacob was there as the mechanic brushed aside the straw packing material and pulled free one of the six carburetors that were stored here. There was a serious look in the senior technician's eyes as he studied the piece of machinery for a few moments, then shouted,

"It's the right one, all right! Come on, comrades, we have work to do!"

With the accompaniment of excited voices, two more carburetors were pulled out of the crate and distributed among the men, who divided themselves into three four-man teams to devote their attention to three of the transporters.

Jacob pulled out his duffel bag, and as he brushed the snow off of it, a deep, bass voice boomed out behind him.

"Ah, Dr. Litvak!"

The archaeologist turned around to see who was addressing him and saw a tall, barrel-chested bear of a man approaching him from the garage's office. He wore a green woolen shirt with black windproof trousers that were held up by rainbow-colored suspenders. When he spoke again, an expression of warm welcome lit up his face.

"Welcome to Novo base, Doctor. I'm Viktor Alexandrov."

Jacob replied while pulling off his right mitten and accepting a firm handshake. "Thank you, comrade. It looks like my arrival was anticipated."

"That it was, Doctor. How very frustrating it was for my mechanics to have to wait all these hours for parts from the mainland. But it appears that their patience has been rewarded. To tell you the truth, my greatest fear was that the bureaucrats would send us the wrong carburetors, and we'd have to wait even longer for replacements."

"I understand that you've yet to make contact with my sister. How long will it take us to get to the Indian installation once the repairs have been completed?"

Viktor heard Jacob's worry. "Normal ground transit time to Gangotri Station is eight hours. Yet the same storm that has grounded our helicopters will add several more hours to our drive."

"It's all so very frustrating," Jacob admitted, sounding dangerously close to his breaking point. "To know that my sister could be in trouble and there's absolutely nothing we can do about it."

"With your arrival, we are one all-important step closer to changing that, Doctor. My men will soon have the transporters operational. The rescue team has already assembled and is ready to go the minute the mechanics give me the all clear. So please, try not to worry yourself, my friend. Of course, I realize that's easy enough for me to say, as it's not my sister that we're off to rescue. But I must tell you that Anna is a dear, dear friend, and one of the most talented, devoted scientists I've ever had the pleasure to work with. You can rest assured that my concerns are as sincere as your own.

"So come now, my friend. May I be so bold as to call you Jacob? Let's go into the office and have some tea. Besides, there's another member of the rescue team there that I'd like you to meet. She's a delightful American geologist who recently came to us with the intention of working with your sister on an extremely important project."

Jacob couldn't help but respond to Viktor Alexandrov's friendly, sympathetic manner, and he followed him down a corridor lined with sealed barrels of lubricant and metal shelves filled with a variety of engine parts and machine tools.

The office turned out to be a small, cramped room, dominated by a paper-cluttered, wooden desk with a detailed topographic map tacked to the wall behind it. Jacob found his eyes drawn to the semicircle of chairs positioned in front of the desk. An attractive young woman, whom he guessed to be in her midthirties, sat here sipping tea. She was well dressed in a red turtleneck and floral ski sweater, with black, waterproof field trousers covering her long legs.

"Jacob," Viktor Alexandrov said rather eagerly, "this is the young lady I was telling you about. Dr. Laurie Anderson is a world-renowned volcano expert, from the exotic, distant American state of Hawaii."

The American alertly stood and politely offered her hand in greeting. Jacob sensed her shyness and did his best not to be too obvious as he appraised her simple, innocent beauty and tall, slim figure.

"I understand that you're here to work with my sister," he said to break the ice.

"That was the plan," she replied curtly.

"Laurie is a newcomer to Antarctica herself," Viktor revealed. "My dear, why don't you explain the nature of the project that brought you to us while I pour Jacob and myself some tea."

As Viktor turned to the nearby samovar Laurie spoke. "I'm here to investigate possible volcanic activity in the mountains west of here."

"Is this volcanic activity that you speak of a relatively new phenomenon?" Jacob asked, instantly interested.

"As a matter of fact, we believe it is," she returned. "It came to the attention of McMurdo's researchers only recently, during the first thermal infrared satellite scan of the Antarctic continent. I arrived at McMurdo shortly after the scan was completed and drew the assignment of determining whether or not this thermal heat source the satellite picked up is really a volcano."

"If it does turn out to be one, and in the process has since erupted, could this be the reason we lost contact with the base my sister was visiting?"

While Laurie took a moment to consider this question, Viktor returned with two tea-filled glasses. Handing one to Jacob, he caught Laurie's concerned gaze.

"That's an interesting theory, my dear," he said to Laurie. "And one that we've yet to give serious thought to. Perhaps it's the exploding debris from a newly erupted volcano that's responsible for disrupting communications with Gangotri."

"I guess it's possible," she admitted.

"I just hope that a communications breakdown is the only thing this eruption is responsible for," Jacob said somberly.

Noting the look of hopelessness on the newcomer's ruggedly handsome face, Laurie responded compassionately. "This entire line of thought is pure speculation. I can't even tell you whether there's a single active volcano within a thousand miles of here."

"Laurie's right," Viktor interjected. "Such an event is pure speculation, as are any number of possibilities. Maybe all we have to deal with here is a technical malfunction. Perhaps the Indians lost not only the use of their radio to a breakdown, but also their transporters. And with this horrible weather, who can blame them for not being able to hike out to inform us?"

Jacob seemed deaf to this optimistic explanation, and Viktor tried his best to give him hope. "Jacob, I can imagine how you must feel. You have every right to be worried. But believe me when I tell you that even in a worst-case scenario, your sister is able to cope on her own, if she has to. I personally attended polar survival school with Anna. For an entire grueling week, our crack alpine unit, under the able direction of Lieutenant Mikhail Lopatin, taught us just about everything there is to know about cold-weather survival. The course culminated in a brutally realistic exercise, during which we were forced to spend an entire night on the ice, without the protection of a warm dormitory room—or even a tent, for that matter. Though I had trouble with everything from cutting the snow blocks for our emergency shelter to sculpting the walls, Anna took to the training like a duck to water. When it was all over, she constructed an igloo that an Inuit would be proud of."

"Are you and your sister very close?" Laurie suddenly asked.

Jacob hesitated a moment before answering. "I guess we were as close as our diverse and demanding professions would allow us. You see, we have no family to speak of, other than each other. On those rare occasions when we were together, we got along splendidly. It was our work that kept us apart."

"I know what that's like," Laurie said. "I have a brother in the navy whom I hardly ever see anymore. What really hurts is that when we were growing up, we were the closest of friends, and you could barely pry us apart."

Her comment appeared to hit home, and Jacob nodded. "As children, Anna and I were playmates as well."

"By the way," Laurie said, feeling sorry for the sad-eyed Russian, "I'd like to compliment you on your excellent English. As I was telling Viktor earlier, when I first received this assignment to Novo base, I was afraid that I'd have to communicate by sign language. Were you also educated in America?"

Jacob's dark mood began to lighten as he answered. "I spent a couple of the best years of my life in Boston, where I did graduate work in archaeology. Since then, it seems I've spent more time out of Russia than in it, at various dig sites where English is the language of choice. Comrade Alexandrov, where did you hone your English skills?"

"While you were trudging through the snowdrifts of Boston Commons, I was enjoying my graduate studies in sunny Los Angeles," Viktor replied. "And please, Jacob, do call me Viktor."

Jacob raised his glass in a mock toast. "Very well, comrade, Viktor it is."

Viktor raised his own glass in response and took a sip of his tea. "I'm sincerely looking forward to working with both of you. And I'm not going to start our relationship off with any lies. The trip we face will be filled with peril. The journey is dangerous, even under the best of weather conditions. Yet with a bit of luck and plenty of hard work, we shall prevail."

He walked over to the wall-mounted topographic map and pointed to its surface. "Our route will take us to the Indian base by way of the Humboldt Glacier. The terrain here is relatively smooth, and we'll be able to steer by compass and dead reckoning. The one portion of our journey that will demand a good degree of visibility is the transit of Habermehl Pass. The ice here is unpredictable, with many fissures and eroded sastrugi—as the frozen seas are called. Fortunately, this crossing is not long, and smooth terrain awaits us during our journey up the Princess Astrid coast. Upon our arrival at the highland, we will again need some semblance of visibility to ascend the plateau on which Gangotri Station is situated."

Novo base's director couldn't help but notice the glum expressions of his audience, and he unexpectedly clapped his hands together and shouted, "Hey! I didn't mean to scare you to death with this briefing. I only wanted to give you a realistic picture of what we're up against. To ease your anxieties, you should know that I've made this trip dozens of times and have yet to lose a single coworker along the way. Besides, my old bones tell me that we're due for a change for the better in our weather."

As if to underscore Viktor's optimism, the deep, growling roar of a starting engine sounded outside the office.

"Now that's music to my ears!" said the grinning director as he led the way back into the garage.

Jacob was the last to leave the office, and as he passed down the shelf-lined corridor he heard the unmistakable sound of men celebrating. He entered the garage area to a chorus of hoots and whistles. Most of the noise was coming from the first service bay, where the tracked transporter's hood was now down and its engine puttering away with a healthy growl.

Another roar of celebration escaped the mechanic's lips when the engine of the second transporter turned over. And seconds later, when the third engine started up, even Jacob couldn't resist joining in the celebration by clapping his hands.

While the men got on with the job of fueling the vehicles, another group of support personnel appeared from a back room. Most of them pushed hand trucks stacked with a variety of different-sized wooden and metal storage containers. Viktor explained what these crates contained.

"There are our supplies for the trip. We've got enough food for two weeks in the field. We'll also be bringing along a full assortment of camping gear, spare engine parts, and other materials necessary to support an undertaking of this nature."

Jacob felt a sudden draft of cold air. As he turned to determine its source he saw someone entering the garage from an exterior doorway. This individual was heavily bundled in a thick, hooded parka and carried a pair of good-sized plastic cases at his side.

"Ah, there's Andrei," said Viktor as the newcomer put the cases down on the concrete floor and pulled back his hood, revealing the face of a blond-haired, rosy-cheeked young man.

"I see that your new bride finally let go of you, Andrei," said the grinning director. "Laurie, I'm sure you remember Andrei Korsakov from the party you attended upon your arrival at Novo base. It was his wedding that we were celebrating. I do hope that you had time to calibrate the equipment, comrade."

In Russian, Andrei replied shyly, "That I did, sir. I also placed a new battery pack in the seismograph and resealed the thermal imager's casing gasket."

Viktor patted the young man on the back and looked over at the American. "Laurie, Andrei here will be your assistant when it's time to do your fieldwork. Though his English is a bit limited, he's a smart lad, and has often worked with geologists."

The sound of clipped footsteps caused them to turn their gazes to the rear of the garage, where they saw a column of five, smartly dressed men in matching white snowsuits emerge from the back room. Each had a white plastic-stocked Kalashnikov assault rifle slung over his shoulder. Jacob could see that the column's leader was none other than his driver, Lieutenant Mikhail Lopatin.

"Ah, here's Mikhail Sergeivich and his squad of alpine rangers," Viktor said. "Again it was at Andrei's wedding, Laurie, that you first saw Mikhail. Although at that time he was wielding a balalaika not a Kalashnikov."

The soldiers lined up beside the first transporter for inspection. Viktor looked each of the tough-looking men square in the eye and made certain to check their equipment, which included matching white, fifty-pound backpacks.

"Alpha Squad is ready to deploy, Comrade Director," Mikhail Lopatin announced with rigid formality.

Viktor appeared to approve of what he saw, and he addressed the group as a whole. "Our mission of mercy and exploration is about to begin. Our transporters are fully operational, and all that remains to be done is to complete the loading of the equipment. As we commerce our transit of the Humboldt Glacier, I'll take the wheel of the lead vehicle, with our valued guests at my side. Mikhail Sergeivich, we'll leave the positioning of Comrade Korsakov and the rest of the men in your capable hands. But be forewarned. I have it straight from Sasha Korsakov's lips that if any misfortune befalls her new husband, you'll be the one to pay the consequences, Lieutenant!"

11

Petty Officer First-Class Mark Bodzin never had trouble sleeping at sea. This was especially the case now that his senior rank earned him his own rack, and he no longer had to endure hot bunking.

Though many landlubbers would consider his bunk space cramped, he saw it differently. The moment he crawled up onto his mattress and closed the curtains, this was his exclusive, private domain to do with as he liked. For the past six and a half hours, it had provided him a quiet, peaceful atmosphere, perfectly conducive to sound slumber. When he awoke several minutes ago, he found himself well rested and with plenty of time before his next watch.

To pass the time, he snapped on the overhead light and pulled out his Walkman. The tape it held was one he had recently made. He found that the whale songs that were soon emanating from his headphones had a more relaxing effect on him than the rap, rock, and country-music tapes his shipmates preferred. There was a certain eerie innocence to the whale songs, which ranged from a forlorn, mewing wail to a soothing, kittenlike purr. Altogether, this unique underwater symphony provided the perfect background music for him to reach up to the overhead bin and remove his latest familygram.

While on patrol, the familygram was the submariners' only contact with the outside world. The messages them-selves were limited to forty words, and arrived weekly when operational conditions permitted. Though heavily censored for security reasons and to limit the amount of potentially upsetting personal news, Bodzin and his wife had come up with a code of sorts. This allowed her to pass on the latest family gossip with the least amount of Command editing.

His most recent familygram was delivered soon after his last watch. He had anxiously waited until he was snug-gled behind the curtains of his rack before opening it, and as he read it again, he fondly visualized the remarkable woman who'd written it.

477. BODZIN 11/7: RECD BDAY FLOWERS + CARD— THANKS! GOOD NEWS. GOT PROMOTION TO SENIOR COUN-SELOR, WITH PAY RAISE TO FOLLOW! ERIN WON LEAD IN SCHOOL PLAY, REPORT CARD STRAIGHT A'S! BRAD ENJOYING PRESCHOOL + MISSES HIS PAPA, AS DO WE ALL. ILY. SANDY.

Bodzin knew he was one of the luckiest men on earth to have such a wonderful wife. Theirs was a classic love story. They had been high-school sweethearts, who were married only a week after graduation, and Sandy had been totally supportive of his decision to enlist in the navy. It was shortly after completing basic training and getting accepted into submarine school that their daugh-ter, Erin, was born.

In the years since, Sandy had adjusted to the difficult life of a submariner's wife. With her husband gone a good six months out of the year, she still managed to take care of their house in Plano, Texas, raise their two children, and even hold a full-time job as a school counselor. This was a lot to ask of any person, and the remarkable thing about Sandy was that she did it without a single word of complaint.

As Bodzin slowly reread the familygram his thoughts turned to the day he left Plano for this current patrol. His flight out of DFW was scheduled for late afternoon, and they spent the morning wrapping presents and writing cards for a Christmas he wouldn't be at home to celebrate. He had already made arrangements for Sandy's birthday flowers, and both of them tried their best not to get overly sentimental as his hour of departure approached. Sandy served him his favorite lunch of pizza and chocolate cake, then drove with him to the airport; it wasn't until he pulled the van up to the terminal building that the tears began falling.

Bodzin found himself choked with emotion at the memory. He couldn't think of a better accompaniment to these thoughts than the mournful cries of the singing humpbacks.

An abrupt change in this music broke him from his reverie. In place of the whale songs, he now heard a rumbling, throaty sound that was recorded during the same watch. His practiced ear had no trouble identifying it as a powerful diesel engine. In most instances, encountering such a signature would all be part of a routine sonar watch. What made the recording unique, however, was the abrupt manner in which it ended. One moment it was there as clear as day, and in the next, it had completely vanished.

His shipmates thought the source of this abrupt silence was a whaling ship that had cut its engines to begin its bloody harvest. Though this was possible, Bodzin's intuition told him otherwise, and he spent a good portion of the rest of the watch running the tape through the acoustic spectrum analyzer. He failed to come up with any conclusive evidence that this signature was of suspicious origin. Not about to be so readily thwarted, he decided that the tape warranted further investigation. If time permitted during his upcoming watch, he'd attempt to filter out any high-end interference with the analyzer's graphic equalizer. If this failed, he'd start eliminating the frequencies on the low end.

As he made this plan Bodzin was startled to see a head pop through his curtain.

"Morning, Chief," one of his junior technicians whispered. "We've got the watch in another quarter of an hour."

Bodzin peeled off his headphones. "I hear ya, Bubba. See ya in the mess in five."

As his freckle-faced shipmate left him Bodzin yawned and lazily stretched, then pulled back the curtain and climbed down to the deck. From the locker beneath his mattress, he removed his poopy suit, dressed quickly, and made certain to drop the cassette tape he had been listening to into the breast pocket of his coveralls before taking off for a stop at the head.

He was pleasantly surprised to find that his first meal of the day was pizza. Several hot pies were just being pulled from the oven as he joined the three members of his watch team at their table. His shipmates appeared to be engrossed in a football-game rerun that was playing on the overhead video monitor. Never having been a dedicated football fan, Bodzin concentrated on his meal. The pepperoni, onion, and green-pepper pizza was delicious, and he washed down the first slice with a sip of bug juice.

"I don't see how you guys can get into a game that you've already seen a half-dozen times before," he then said.

"But this game's a classic, Chief," explained the freckle-faced sailor who had delivered his wake-up call.

"The winner goes to the play-offs, and brother, are they hittin'."

Bodzin glanced up at the screen and shook his head. "I guess this is what I get for goin' to sea with a CO who's a certified football hero. Hell, I couldn't find a single basketball game in the entire video library. Now, there's a sport with some real strategy behind it."

This comment sparked a spirited debate over the athletic abilities of the average NBA player compared with those of his NFL counterpart. Long before any conclusion could be reached, their discussion came to an end with their transfer to the sonar compartment.

Bodzin settled in behind his console while listening to a condition update from the potbellied chief of the watch he was relieving.

"I hope you brought along some readin' material or playin' cards, Bodzin. 'Cause all we heard for the last six hours were a bunch of whales," the chief stated.

Bodzin pulled out the cassette tape from his breast pocket and set it beside his keyboard. "You know my love for whale songs, Bubba. I'm sure me and my boys will find something to keep us out of trouble. What are our environmentals?"

The portly chief seemed anxious to be on his way and responded from the forward accessway. "We've got pretty much of a flat calm topside. Skipper's gettin' ready to take us up to periscope depth to begin the next recon."

"So he's still at it," Bodzin said. "Maybe we'll be the ones to tag those pirates for him. Take care, Bubba, and save me a coupla slices of pizza."

"Pizza!" the excited chief exclaimed as he made a hasty exit.

By the time Bodzin clamped on his headphones, he noticed a definite upward angle of the *Springfield*'s bow. He all but forgot about the tape he hoped to analyze as he intently scanned the sonar display for any sonic signatures that might indicate a possible obstacle topside.

•   •   •

In the *Springfield*'s control room, Philip Michaels had similar concerns. As the sub began its ascent to periscope depth, a dangerous new environment awaited them. Collision and unwanted detection from above were his greatest fears, and he anxiously positioned himself on the periscope pedestal, close behind the Type-18 search scope. With his XO next to him at the Type-2 scope, he listened as the COB called out the boat's depth.

"Seventy-five feet . . . seventy feet . . . sixty-five feet . . . Periscope depth, Cap," Ellwood Crick revealed matter-of-factly.

Michaels immediately raised the scope, yanked down its arms, and bent over the eyepiece. It took several seconds for the lens to clear the water, and when it finally did, he made a rapid 360-degree scan of the surrounding sea. Only when he was completely satisfied that there were no surface obstacles did he turn the lens due east. The distinctive profile of a rugged, snow-covered mountain range could be seen in the distance. As he increased the lens magnification to its maximum amplification the range took on additional detail. Not a single tree was visible, with the desolate slopes dropping off precariously right into the sea.

"I've got Thule, XO, on bearing zero-nine-zero," Michaels observed.

Perez turned the basic optical scope in this direction and held back his response until he fine-tuned the lens focus. "I've got it, Skipper. It sure doesn't look very inviting."

A low-lying, gray cloud deck did little to aesthetically enhance the stark, lifeless scene.

"We're sure not going to be finding anyone living on those slopes," said Michaels.

"The chart notes indicate that the island has only one accessible harbor," the XO told him. "It's on Thule's northeastern shore and contains the remains of an abandoned whaling station, last utilized by the Norwegians in the forties."

Michaels grunted. "Sounds like it could have possibilities, XO."

"I sure hope so, Skipper. Thule is the last island in the chain left for us to recon. If it doesn't pan out, what are we gonna do?"

Michaels backed away from the scope and directly met his XO's inquisitive stare. "I thought we might move our search up north and take a closer look at South Georgia Island. Hell, even if it does turn out to be nothing but a wild-goose chase, this exercise is giving us an excellent opportunity to update our charts."

12

It was with the greatest of expectations that Gunther Hartmann left *Ice Wolf* and entered the tunnel inland. His footsteps echoed off the concrete walls, and it didn't take him long to leave the chilly, moist dampness of the pier area behind. He felt a bit uncomfortable, dressed as he was in his formal uniform—a well-tailored, black wool, double-breasted suit, with gold buttons, piping, and narrow shoulder epaulets. Instead of a white shirt and tie, he chose a black cotton turtleneck. And his black leather dress shoes were spit-shined, their hard rubber heels barely worn.

Though he had been stationed here for over a year, he was still amazed by the underground city's ingenious design. During the early phases of *Ice Wolf*'s refit, when he was brought here from Germany, he had made his home in Thule's dormitory. Throughout his stay, he could count on one hand the number of times he was allowed aboveground. This was fine with him. As a veteran sub-mariner, he found sunshine and blue sky alien.

When the tunnel he was following intersected with two others, he turned left. This tiled accessway was narrower than the one leading from the pier, and was designed so that nothing larger than a forklift truck could pass through. This route brought him to a closed door marked PRIVATE: NO ENTRY. Before knocking, he took a moment to straighten his lapel and pick off a piece of lint from his trousers.

There was a strange tightness in his stomach that he attributed to a slight case of nerves. He hadn't felt so anxious since he was a midshipman preparing for his first inspection. Such was the importance of the meeting he was about to attend.

He well knew that the prospect of working with such men as Heinrich Westheim and Wolfram Eckhardt was enough to make any sane man nervous. After all, they were both legendary figures, the last of the "old fighters," who actually knew the likes of Hitler, Himmler, and Gunther's favorite wartime hero, Grand Admiral Karl Donitz.

In addition, they were true survivors, who persevered and thrived in the difficult postwar world. Largely through their efforts, *Ice Wolf* had been preserved and Thule base contructed. It seemed that as long as the two old-timers remained alive, part of the magic of the Nazi heyday was alive as well. And today they brought with them an even greater dream, a vision of a modern Germany, a Fourth Reich, whose purpose was to lead a united Aryan people into the twenty-first century.

When Gunther first heard of their movement, he was a career officer in the West German navy. Through a Kriegsmarine social club reserved for submarine officers, his outspoken right-wing political views gained the attention of one of his superiors. As it turned out, the superior had already been recruited by the movement, and he cautiously probed to determine the sincerity of Gunther's convictions. Only when he was absolutely certain did he make any overtures, to which Gunther enthusiastically responded.

His previous life in West Germany, though comfortable, was never fulfilling. Each day at work was like a living lie, for he was protecting a system that he didn't believe in. As he saw it, the West Germany of the sixties, seventies, and eighties was nothing but a pitiful lackey of American, British, and French interests, a mere buffer zone between East and West. Corrupt to its core, with no social conscience, the government in Bonn was no better than a cheap whore, and Gunther felt dirty every time he donned his uniform.

The entire society, he felt, needed a radical overhaul. As far as Gunther was concerned, Germany still had the potential for greatness, if it only had the courage to act. Like the National Socialist party in the 1930s, he supported a thorough housecleaning, beginning with a purging of all non-Germans. Only when this stifling foreign burden was removed could the real work begin.

Gunther would never forget the day he learned that others existed who supported and encouraged such radical views. Not only were many of these people in the highest echelons of government, but their base was a powerful, stable movement, whose roots went back far into history.

The ultimate compliment arrived the day they invited him to Thule and informed him of the movement's strategy for attaining power. What they were asking of him was simple: to apply the leadership and technical skills he had developed during his two decades of military service in order to command *Ice Wolf* on a single all-important journey.

With assurances of a leadership role in the future Reich, Gunther accepted the challenge and began the task of putting together a crew from the same dissatisfied ranks from which he had come. Once this was achieved, he was able to focus all his energy on *Ice Wolf*'s redesign.

Germany's brightest technical minds were secretly tapped for this effort, and with their input, a seaworthy, sophisticated warship, fully capable of holding its own in today's modern underwater battlefield, had been born.

Today's meeting was the result of thousands of hours of hard work. But his goals had been worthy ones, and like the movement's veteran founders, he had managed to summon the strength to persevere despite hardships. Anxious to prove that they had picked the right man for this difficult job, Gunther inhaled a deep breath, smoothed down his beard, threw back his shoulders, and knocked on the door three times.

When it swung open, a stern-faced, matronly woman with a growling German shepherd close at her side greeted him.

"Good afternoon, Fräulein," Gunther said with his best diplomatic smile. "I am Captain Hartmann. Herrs Westheim and Eckhardt are expecting me."

"They are waiting for you in the study," she coldly replied. "It's this way."

Though this wasn't exactly the reception he had been anticipating, he entered the apartment and shut the door behind him. The German shepherd kept a close eye on him as he followed his apron-clad escort through the living room. The furnishings reminded him of home, and he wished he had the time to take a closer look at a glass display filled with Hummel figurines. He was halfway across the room when one of the many cuckoo clocks prematurely activated. As it began chiming loudly the dog forgot all about Gunther and turned its attention to the colorfully painted bird that was bobbing in and out of its clock home.

His escort waited for him to catch up with her before walking up to another closed doorway, upon which she lightly knocked a single time. Without waiting for a response, she pulled open the door. Gunther obediently entered, and she quickly shut it behind him.

He now found himself in a warm, comfortably furnished study. Seated behind the central desk, immersed in a stack of paperwork, was the white-haired, solidly built figure of Heinrich Westheim. Gunther identified the distinguished, bald-headed man seated beside the blazing fireplace as Wolfram Eckhardt; the legendary occultist was absorbed in a book. Neither man seemed to be aware of him.

A huge red Nazi flag caught his attention on the far wall. The flag's sinister black swastika provided instant inspiration, and Gunther again threw back his shoulders and cleared his throat loudly.

"Excuse me, sir," he said to Heinrich Westheim. "Captain Gunther Hartmann reporting as ordered."

A look of genuine surprise filled the old-timer's eyes as he looked up from his work, and Gunther realized that the old man had most likely not heard him enter.

"Captain Hartmann," Heinrich said with obvious delight. "How good it is to see you. Wolfram, our guest has arrived."

Wolfram Eckhardt had already closed his book and set it on his lap. As he looked up to inspect Gunther a pleased grin turned the corners of his lips.

"How very fitting it is to see you now, Captain," he said. "I was just reading Lothar-Gunther Bucheim's excellent *U-Boat War*. And now you appear, just like the ghost of one of the heroic sailors so vividly captured in Bucheim's photos."

Gunther politely nodded at the compliment, then turned back to Heinrich Westheim. "Herr Director," he said with a click of his heels, "I'd like to report that the repairs to *Ice Wolf* have been completed. As anticipated, the sea trials resulted in only the most minor of problems. Several gasket seals were replaced as well as an electrical switch that was shorted out due to condensation. Other than that, the boat's operational systems passed their first test successfully, and *Ice Wolf* is presently being refueled and reprovisioned.

"That's wonderful news, Captain," Heinrich replied. "Now tell me, how'd she handle?"

Gunther answered without a moment's hesitation. "Like a modern vessel, half her age."

"And Alberich?" Heinrich continued.

Gunther decided that now was the time to reveal the sensitive information he had previously kept to himself. "The combination of anechoic tiles, bubble-masking system and fuel cells allowed us to escape detection by another submarine that we encountered in the East Scotia Basin."

"Another submarine, you say?" Wolfram Eckhardt's concern was obvious. "Are you positive that this contact was a submarine?"

"That I am, sir," Gunther replied. "I heard it pass myself on our passive sonar array. From its ultraquiet signature, I'd say it was a nuclear-powered vessel, under the flag of either Britain or the United States."

Wolfram worriedly searched Gunther's eyes. "Captain, are you absolutely certain that this submarine was evaded and that it wasn't able to follow you to Thule without detection?"

"I stake my reputation on it, sir," Gunther firmly retorted.

"That's good enough for me." Heinrich sensed that it was time to redirect the conversation to more practical matters. "Captain Hartmann, did you get a chance to read your new order packet?"

"Yes, I did, sir. I've already had Oberleutnant Kromer draw up a course to the Princess Astrid coastline. If ice conditions allow, we foresee no problems in reaching the shores of Antarctica well within the forty-eight-hour envelope you specified."

"I do hope that the polar gear has arrived," Heinrich continued.

Gunther readily eased his anxieties. "The specialized ice transporters and survival gear have already been securely stowed aboard ship. A portion of this equipment has been placed in the aft torpedo room, where your quarters have been set up. To make the necessary room, all torpedo reloads and their storage racks have been removed. The only torpedoes that we'll be carrying aft will be those stored inside the two stern tubes."

"I realize that because of the cursory nature of the sea trials, you weren't able to work in the ice environment," Wolfram commented. "Do you have any reservations about taking your ship beneath the heavy polar ice pack, Captain?"

"None whatsoever," Gunther replied. "The upward scanning fathometer checked out perfectly. *Ice Wolf* should have little problem finding a suitable polynya in which to surface."

Westheim appeared most satisfied with what he was hearing. "Your concerns are noteworthy ones, Wolfram, but I'm sure that Captain Hartmann has considered every contingency."

"I'm not doubting the captain's competence, Heinrich," Wolfram said testily. "It's just that the mission we're about to undertake is a most complex, perilous one, and circumspection is a commodity we can never have enough of."

Heinrich nodded. "Prudence is a wise man's closest ally," he said thoughtfully. "And I commend the captain for his thoroughness. So I guess the one question that remains is, when will *Ice Wolf* be ready to put to sea?"

Gunther looked at his watch before answering. "The refueling should be complete within the half hour."

"And the tide?" Wolfram prompted.

"The next high tide will be upon us in approximately sixty minutes. With the next sailing opportunity in another twelve hours."

"Why waste another precious half a day when *Ice Wolf* is ready for action now?" Heinrich asked rhetorically. "Heidi!" he shouted. "We have bags to pack!"

Less than forty minutes later Heinrich and Wolfram walked down the concrete tunnel leading to Thule's central pier. Heidi accompanied them, with Blondi strapped to her wrist on a stout, nylon leash. Bringing up the rear were three blond-haired, khaki-uniformed orderlies. Each of these young men carried a large suitcase, with the lead figure also holding a wicker picnic basket.

With his brisk, long stride, Heinrich led the way out of the tunnel into a long, rectangular structure with a massive, fifty-foot-high enclosed roof. A narrow strip of seawater, which extended all the way to a set of large closed doors at the building's rear, cut the cavernous room in half.

The powerful ceiling-mounted halogen lights illuminated the structure's dominant feature. Tied to the concrete pier, with its crew smartly lined up on the forward deck, was a sleek, gray, 250-foot-long submarine. The streamlined sail of the vessel had an observation bridge cut into its roof. It also held a flagpole that displayed the red, white, and black ensign of the Kriegsmarine, with a black swastika in the center and an iron cross positioned in the upper left-hand corner.

Stopping briefly to take in this scene, Heinrich commented in a voice filled with emotion, "My, what an awe-inspiring sight!"

Wolfram also halted. "*Ice Wolf* looks every inch the lethal predator her name refers to."

Blondi suddenly began barking as if to confirm Wolfram's observation, and Heidi called out, "Blondi, stop that racket this instant!"

The dog immediately went silent and meekly sat down. Heinrich took a step backward to stroke her head, then spoke to Heidi.

"My dear, what do you think of our *Ice Wolf?*" he wished to know.

Heidi intently surveyed the moored vessel. "To tell you the truth, I think a person would have to be crazy to voluntarily travel beneath the seas in such a cramped, uncomfortable vessel. Surely the living conditions inside are squalid. And I'm afraid to even think what the cooking facilities are like."

Heinrich chuckled. "From what I've seen of the contents of that picnic basket you've packed me, I should have enough food to get me to Antarctica and halfway back to Germany before I need access the boat's galley. And as to the living conditions inside *Ice Wolf,* rest assured that Captain Hartmann and his crack crew keep a spotlessly clean boat."

Two figures dressed in black double-breasted uniforms broke from the ranks that were assembled on the submarine's deck and approached the vessel's amidships gangplank.

"Ah, I see that Captain Hartmann and his executive officer await us," Wolfram said. "Shall we get on with this momentous occasion, Heinrich?"

"Why, of course, my friend," Heinrich replied. "Lead on!"

With Wolfram now in the lead, the group proceeded down to the pier. As they passed by *Ice Wolf*'s rounded stern one of the officer's shouted, "Crew, attention!"

The line of blue, coverall-clad sailors simultaneously threw their shoulders back, clicked their heels together, and stood erect, arms at their sides and eyes to the front.

As Wolfram neared the two officers at the gangplank, he could just hear Heinrich softly addressing Heidi behind him.

"So you have nothing to worry about, my dear. I'll be in good hands. And before you know it, we'll be reunited again. Just think what a glorious day that will be. Because the next time I see you, we will be at the pier at Bremerhaven as we triumphantly celebrate the rebirth of our beloved fatherland!"

As the orderlies carried the baggage up onto *Ice Wolf,* Wolfram accepted a crisp salute from the vessel's bearded captain.

"I do hope that the tide is still in our favor," Wolfram commented.

Gunther replied while looking at his wristwatch. "The water level should be just approaching its highest level, Herr Eckhardt."

As Wolfram crossed over the gangplank and stepped onto the submarine's deck, he was greeted by the boat's tall, smooth-shaven executive officer.

"Welcome aboard, sir," said Karl Kromer.

Wolfram answered with a curt nod and turned to see what was keeping his white-haired associate. Heinrich appeared to be giving Heidi a list of last-minute instructions. Only after bending over to give his dog another fond pat on the head did Heinrich cross over the gangway.

A bosun's whistle sounded, and the crew stood down from attention and went scurrying belowdeck by way of the forward accessway. Meanwhile the three orderlies climbed out from the aft accessway and scrambled back onto the pier just as a group of longshoremen arrived to remove the gangplank.

"Gentlemen," said Gunther, "would you care to join me on *Ice Wolf*'s sail? The view from that vantage point as we head out to sea is most inspirational."

"Considering the fact that this will most likely be the last fresh air we breathe for the next forty-eight hours, I'd love to join you on the sail, Captain," Wolfram remarked.

Heinrich was waving a final good-bye to Heidi and seemed somewhat distracted. "The sail sounds fine to me. Please lead the way, Captain Hartmann."

They accessed the streamlined sail by way of a hatch set into its base. An interior ladder conveyed them up to the very top portion of the sail, where an exterior bridge was situated. Here they joined two parka-clad seamen, with binoculars expectantly held in their mittened hands. Though there was barely enough room for all five of them, *Ice Wolf*'s captain led his guests to the forward-most portion of the bridge, with the lookouts snugly positioned behind them.

Wolfram stood on the left side of the sail. He looked

down to the pier, where the longshoremen were unraveling the sub's thick mooring lines from the dock's steel restraining cleats.

"Number One," Gunther Hartmann said into the bridge's intercom handset, "inform the chief to start the diesels."

Seconds later a deep, growling rumble sounded from down below, and the deck began to vibrate. As a puff of dark smoke rose from the aft exhaust vents, Gunther turned his attention to the longshoremen.

"Prepare to cast off the mooring lines. Open the sea doors!"

Wolfram now found his gaze drawn straight forward as the pen's two huge doors began parting. The crack of bright, direct light gradually widened, until a gray patch of cloud-filled sky was visible. The narrow portion of water they floated upon merged with the surging seas of the harbor, while beyond, the distant ocean invitingly beckoned.

A gust of cold, fresh air engulfed the sail. With their exit now clear, Gunther called down to the longshoremen.

"Release the mooring lines!"

As his order was carried out he readdressed the intercom. "Number One, all ahead one third."

Ice Wolf's dual propellers engaged, and the sub pulled away from the pier and the pen that enclosed it. Wolfram was delighted as they left these confines, and he was able to turn around and view the outlines of the abandoned whaling station take shape behind them. As the door to the pen closed, its rectangular, weather-scarred outer shell blended in perfectly with the dilapidated buildings that surrounded it. The partially sunken hull of the whale catcher boat passed to the left, while to the right, beyond a trio of rusted oil storage tanks, Wolfram could just make out the white clapboard church and the bare outlines of a dirt pathway leading to the snow-covered hills. He fondly recalled his recent hike up this same trail, and knew that he would most likely never set his eyes upon this place again.

Beside him, Heinrich appeared to be having similar thoughts. "Farewell, Thule. You have served us well. And someday Aryans shall flock to this monument in holy pilgrimage, to see for themselves the place where the Reich was resurrected."

As they sailed into the harbor snow flurries began to fall. Oblivious to this, Heinrich looked over to Wolfram and winked.

"We're on our way, my friend. Nothing will stop us now. Tell me, Wolfram. How does it feel to be back at sea aboard *Ice Wolf?*"

This innocent query caused a puzzled expression to cross Gunther Hartmann's face, and he turned to address the man standing on his left. "You've sailed on *Ice Wolf* before, Herr Eckhardt?"

Wolfram replied while focusing his gaze on the vessel's sharply angled bow and the frothing white swath it was cutting in the channel's deep green waters. "The last time I was on this same sail was in July of 1945. We were off the coast of Patagonia and were waiting to make contact with our operatives ashore. It took over a week for our coded signal light to get a proper response. Shortly thereafter, a launch arrived to convey me to my new home in South America."

"I never realized that it was this U-boat that brought you over from Germany," said Gunther.

"My relationship with *Ice Wolf* began on May second, 1945. That was the day I arrived in Bergen, Norway, and hastily boarded her. We set sail at approximately the same hour that Soviet soldiers were capturing the Reich Chancellery and beginning their looting of the Führerbunker. It was Germany's darkest hour, and with all my hopes for a reborn Reich sealed away in the dozen specially designed, waterproof crates that I also brought along, we started our desperate voyage of escape.

"Remarkably enough, this journey took us to the exact same frozen coastline to which we're currently destined. Never did I dream in those shameful years of retreat that the day would come five decades later when I'd return to Antarctica to reclaim the treasure in whose sacred midst lies the keys to Germany's rebirth."

"Captain," broke the amplified voice of Karl Kromer from the intercom. "We're approaching the fifty-fathom line."

"Very well, Number One," Gunther replied into the intercom. "Begin preparations to dive the boat."

As they reached the open sea a moderate swell rocked the keelless vessel from side to side. Wolfram reached out to steady himself and turned to take a last look at the rugged spine of snow-covered mountains that constituted most of Thule's landmass.

"Gentlemen," Gunther said politely, "it's time to return this seawolf to its intended medium. If you'd be so good as to proceed down below, we can get on with the diving preparations."

"Come on, old friend," Heinrich said to Wolfram as he turned for the hatch. "It's time for you to take a closer look at some of the changes we made to this vessel. I guarantee you that this *Ice Wolf* is not the same boat you knew fifty years ago."

As Wolfram followed Heinrich down the narrow conning-tower ladder, he heard Gunther call out from above, "Rig for diving!"

Trying to climb down the ladder quickly and to ignore the cold iron rungs as they bit into the tender flesh of his palms, Wolfram noted that the lookouts were also descending the ladder. Fearful of a misstep, he moderated his pace. By the time he dropped down to the solid deck, both the lookouts and the vessel's captain were close behind him.

The warmth was most noticeable. An alert seaman took Wolfram's parka and hat, and he watched as Gunther Hartmann proceeded at once to the adjoining diving station. Standing there, before a somewhat old-fashioned vent indicator board, was *Ice Wolf*'s second in command.

"The boat is rigged for dive, Captain," Kromer stated.

"Very good, Karl," the captain acknowledged. "Sound the diving alarm."

A blaring klaxon sounded. Wolfram watched the boat's captain pull a stopwatch from his pocket, activate the timepiece, then look up and momentarily meet his glance.

"Open the main ballast valves!" Gunther ordered. "Open bow buoyancy vents. Open vents on number-one ballast, number-two ballast, and the safety tanks. Bow planes at hard dive!"

"All engines stopped and valves closed, Captain," Karl Kromer reported.

There was a certain tenseness in the air, and Wolfram heard Heinrich whisper, "This is the moment of truth, old friend. We'll soon enough learn if the hull and engine induction valves have securely closed."

Ice Wolf angled down slightly by the bow, and as Wolfram reached up to steady himself on an iron handhold, he felt a sudden pressure on his eardrums.

"Main inductions closed," the quartermaster reported.

Heinrich alertly pointed toward the adjoining bulkhead at an aneroid barometer. "That pressure you just felt on your eardrums was caused by pressurized air being bled into the boat. Look how the needle on the barometer has risen and is now holding steady. This is certain proof that the hull is airtight from within."

"Take us down, Karl," the captain ordered.

Oberleutnant Kromer yanked down the levers of the main ballast tanks and the compartment filled with a loud hissing sound, followed by the surge of rushing water.

Heinrich explained what was occurring. "That hissing sound is coming from the air that's being vented through the tops of our main ballast tanks. As these tanks empty, seawater rushes in to replace the air from the bottom valves and the boat becomes negatively buoyant."

"Pressure in the boat. Green board, Captain," Kromer reported.

As the depth gauge reached thirty-five feet the angle on *Ice Wolf*'s bow increased. It took a supreme effort on Wolfram's part just to remain upright, and he listened breathlessly to Heinrich's next update.

"The bubble indicators show an eleven-degree bow angle. At our current depth, the top deck is thoroughly submerged, with the sail soon to follow."

"Close the bow buoyancy vents," Gunther instructed as the depth gauge passed forty feet.

At forty-five feet, he ordered all vents to be closed. The depth gauge dropped rapidly now.

Wolfram nervously scanned the cramped, equipment-packed control room. The scene wasn't all that different from the one he had viewed fifty years earlier. Even the faces hadn't changed much, with the current batch of submariners displaying the same kind of courageous determination as *Ice Wolf*'s original crew.

Of all those present, Wolfram was most impressed with Captain Gunther Hartmann. The bearded officer was the type of no-nonsense leader who exuded confidence. His self-assured manner seemed to be contagious, and his crew went about their work with admirable professionalism.

"Planesman, level us off at sixty feet," Hartmann instructed as he clicked off his stopwatch the moment the depth gauge passed fifty-five feet.

As he noted the time Heinrich called out from behind, "How did we do, Captain?"

"Not bad," Gunther replied coolly. "Though there's still plenty of room for improvement."

Wolfram watched the planesman pull back on his steering yoke, and the steep angle on the bow lessened. Soon he was able to let go of his overhead handhold. As he massaged his cramped hand he listened to the captain issue a flurry of new orders.

"Raise the snorkel and prepare to open main induction

valve. Prepare to reengage diesels, on course one-four-zero."

The throaty rumble of the boat's diesel engines soon echoed throughout the control room. As the helmsman brought them around on their new course, Heinrich beckoned Wolfram to join him beside the navigation plot.

"Well, old friend, what do you think?" he asked.

Wolfram nodded pensively. "The descent went smoothly enough. Though to tell you the truth, the equipment looks pretty much the same as it did during my last voyage."

This was not what Heinrich wanted to hear, and he signaled to Gunther Hartmann. "Captain, it's time to show Herr Eckhardt that the millions of marks he invested in *Ice Wolf*'s renovation have been well spent. Will an engagement of Alberich impede our progress to the south in any way?"

"Of course it won't," Gunther returned. "Let's just give the diesels another couple of minutes to vent themselves, and then we'll soon enough show you what our bubble-masked fuel cells are capable of."

"Conn, sonar, we have a surface contact, bearing one-four-zero. Classify Sierra One, trawler."

Philip Michaels was conveniently huddled over the navigation plot as this unexpected news was delivered over the control room's intercom. With a red grease pencil, he drew a ruler-guided line from the *Springfield*'s current position off the northern coast of Thule Island to the southwest, on the bearings sonar had just relayed to them. When this line intersected the mouth of Thule's only harbor, Michaels excitedly addressed the two officers gathered at his side.

"We could be onto something, gentlemen. XO, I thought you said that the island's harbor facilities were abandoned."

"That's what the chart notes said, Skipper," Perez answered.

"I wouldn't stake too much credence on those notes," the navigator advised. "The intel on this infrequently traveled sector is suspect at best."

"At least it's something to go on," said Michaels. "After all, I can't think of a better base of operations for a group of pirates than an abandoned whaling station. So I'm gonna duck into sonar and check it out personally."

Michaels turned and hurriedly crossed the compartment, passing by the vacant fire control consoles on his way to the room's forward starboard accessway. He expectantly slid back the accordion-style doorway and entered the hushed realm of Petty Officer First-Class Mark Bodzin and his sonar watch team. Bodzin was seated at the forwardmost console, his headphones clamped over his ears, and it was to this position that Michaels walked over.

"What have you got, Mr. Bodzin?" Michaels asked somewhat anxiously.

Bodzin answered while pulling back his right headphone. "It's definitely the signature of a diesel engine, sir. From the racket it's makin', I'd say we've tagged a trawler on its way out to sea. Would you like to have a listen?"

Michaels nodded, and readily accepted a pair of auxiliary headphones. As Bodzin plugged them into his console Michaels fit the bulky phones over his ears. It was impossible to miss the muffled, throaty rumbling noise that was being carried through the speakers.

"Sounds like it's coming from a pretty good-sized vessel, possibly a small merchant," the captain said to Bodzin while scanning the display screen. "We should be well within range for a visual. I'm going to pop the scope and take a peek."

Bodzin found something vaguely familiar about the signature they were monitoring. And it wasn't until it went abruptly silent that he realized that he had heard it before.

"What in the hell just happened?" Michaels asked, referring to the sudden absence of sound in his headphones.

Bodzin addressed his keyboard, and only after making absolutely certain that the sound loss wasn't due to a technical glitch did he voice his suspicions. "Sir, I know that this might sound crazy, but this appears to be the exact same thing that took place the other day while we were starting our patrol of the island chain. The only difference was that there were humpbacks singin' up a storm at the time, and our first guess was that the sudden loss of signature was caused by a whaler that just went dead in the water to begin the hunt."

"That's surely plausible," Michaels said as he pulled off the headphones. "Why don't you pull the tape of that encounter and let busy one check it for a comparison."

Bodzin reached out to the side of his keyboard and held up the cassette tape he had brought along. "I just happen to have it right here, sir. If I had the time today, I was plannin' on runnin' it through the spectrum analyzer for a closer listen."

"Do it," Michaels instructed. "Meanwhile I'm going to bring us up to periscope depth and see just what we've got up there."

As Michaels returned to the control room Bodzin moved to the adjoining console, where the acoustic spectrum analyzer was located. His first task was to compare the prerecorded cassette tape with the signature they had just encountered. He placed the cassette into the analyzer, and as he fed his request into the computer, he noticed that the *Springfield* was angling upward by the bow. By the time the deck was level again, his answer flashed up on the display screen: SIGNATURES IDENTICAL.

Not really surprised by this information, Bodzin readdressed the keyboard. This time he utilized the analyzer's sensitive graphic equalizer to filter out the highest-frequency bands on that portion of the tape immediately after the diesel went silent.

What appeared to be dead silence to the human ear proved to emit the barest flutter of low-frequency sound. When Bodzin asked the computer to identify this noise's source, he was momentarily taken aback when BIOLOGIC flashed on the screen. Positive that this signature couldn't be the result of a natural phenomenon, he further picked apart the tape's frequency. This time he asked the computer to identify the exact type of biologic they were dealing with. The answer that followed was at first glance most puzzling: BIOLOGIC SOUND SOURCE—SMALL BODY OF EFFERVESCENT GAS SUSPENDED WITHIN A LIQUID.

He repeated this cryptic data to his three coworkers, and the juniormost technician gave him the answer he was looking for as he matter-of-factly observed, "Sounds to me like you're talkin' about a bubble."

"A bubble, of course!" Bodzin exclaimed. His exultation was cut short by the return of the captain.

"Mr. Bodzin," Michaels said, "our visual scan is negative. There's nothing up there but whitecaps. I think you'd better run a full diagnostic on busy one to check for any possible problems in our sensors."

"I don't think that's necessary, sir," Bodzin replied. "I believe I know what we're dealin' with out there. Busy one's not at fault. I just used it to determine that a signature continued to emanate long after that diesel went silent."

"So your low-frequency scan did the trick," Michaels surmised. "What is it?"

"Bubbles, sir," Bodzin answered.

"Bubbles?" Michaels repeated.

"You heard me right, sir, bubbles. And I believe that this explains the mystery. Back in sub school, one of my instructors was a former chief sonarman aboard the USS *Blueback,* our last diesel-electric submarine. He was always braggin' about how the *Blueback* could penetrate a carrier group more effectively than a newer, vastly more expensive nuclear-powered attack sub. And the reason for their success was their near-silent battery propulsion, which was even further veiled by a top-secret bubble-masking device, originally designed by the Germans during World War Two. Why, the chief always boasted that once the *Blueback*'s bubbler was activated, there was no ASW platform afloat that could tag 'em."

Michaels listened to this story and found goose bumps forming on the back of his neck as he recalled the wild tale that the HMS *Turbulent*'s captain had shared with him earlier.

"Mr. Bodzin, if I'm hearing you correctly, you're saying that Sierra One is actually a diesel-electric submarine that we tagged pulling the plug. And the reason busy one couldn't correctly ID it is because of this top-secret bubbler mechanism."

Bodzin nodded that this was indeed the case, and Michaels continued. "I know it sounds a bit farfetched, but I believe you just might have stumbled upon something of real significance. Do you think you can tag this phantom submarine now that they've gone silent?"

"I don't see why not," Bodzin replied confidently. "All I have to do is program busy one to listen for those bubbles. And with the invaluable assistance of our TB-23 thin-line array, *Springfield* should have no trouble at all slipping right into that bogey's baffles. Hell, they'll never even know we're there!"

13

Jacob Litvak awoke to the soft tinkling sound of metal upon metal. His eyes snapped open, and through the folds of his sleeping bag, he viewed the burly frame of Viktor Alexandrov bent over the primus stove, stirring a small pot. The barrel-chested Russian was dressed in a bright plaid woolen shirt, with his customary rainbow-colored suspenders holding up his black nylon, windproof trousers. Even though he was kneeling, he seemed to fill the entire tent.

Jacob inhaled a lungful of cold, invigorating air, closed his eyes, and reoriented himself. They had set up camp the previous evening, after five long hours of travel over the Humboldt Glacier in blizzard conditions. The relatively smooth river of frozen ice they had traveled over allowed them to steer by compass, and by dead reckoning Viktor determined that they were approaching the divide where the next leg of their trip began. Meanwhile they set up camp and waited for the weather to improve. They cleverly used the transporters for a windbreak. The five members of the alpine team were particularly helpful in raising the tents in the midst of the raging blizzard.

The last thing Jacob remembered was entering his assigned tent feeling exhausted and frozen to the bone, pulling off his snow-coated boots and outer parka, and crawling into the thick folds of his down-filled sleeping bag, soaking wet underclothing and all. Then he instantly fell asleep.

When he awoke, he didn't know whether it was day or night. He yawned and summoned the strength to address his tent mate. "Good morning, or afternoon, or whatever it may be."

A look of surprise filled Viktor's kind eyes as he looked over to Jacob and smiled. "Actually, it's morning, comrade. And a good one, it seems. The wind has died down, the snow diminished to flurries, and it's overcast and incredibly cold. Otherwise, the visibility has greatly improved, which means we should be able to proceed safely."

Jacob sat up stiffly, his muscles bruised after the rough, pounding drive over the glacier. The temperature inside the tent was comfortable, and he was able to stretch his tight limbs without fear of frostbite.

"How'd you sleep, comrade?" Viktor asked.

"Quite well, thanks, I guess yesterday's flight from Argentina and then our grueling transit over the glacier caught up with me. I hope my snoring wasn't too bad."

"It would take much more than snoring to keep me awake, comrade," said Viktor, again stirring the dented, aluminum pot. "How about joining me for breakfast?"

Jacob suddenly felt ravenous. "What's on the menu?"

"Mushroom soup and crackers," Viktor answered.

The mere mention of mushrooms caused Jacob to grimace. "Crackers will do just fine," he managed.

Viktor noted his expression. "What kind of Russian doesn't like mushrooms?" he asked.

"One that was only recently the victim of mushroom poisoning," was Jacob's reply.

As a mycologist, Viktor was interested to learn more. "Mushroom poisoning, you say? That's certainly unusual. What were your symptoms, and where did this occur?"

Though Jacob would have preferred to keep his horrible experience in the rain forest to himself, he answered, "Several days ago, in Brazil's Mato Grosso region. After consuming the mushrooms, I experienced stomach cramps, dizziness, then an incredibly heightened awareness to color and sound, followed by a series of nightmarish hallucinations that I'll not soon forget."

"My, that does sound like the effects of a toxic mushroom," Viktor observed. "Because of your locale, I suspect you were the victim of the infamous Amanita. Were you collecting for food?"

"Actually, I wasn't collecting at all. You see, I was purposely fed this mushroom at a native village."

Viktor's eyes lit up. "Ah, no doubt you were drawn to the Mato Grosso as an archaeologist, and you participated in one of the legendary Indian ceremonial rituals."

"You might say it was something like that," Jacob cautiously replied, not wanting to go into detail.

"You have more nerve than I do, comrade. I've been a student of mushrooms all my life and have yet to summon the courage to sample the sacred Amanita. I'm sure you know that the Indians of the rain forest aren't the only native people to use this mushroom in their rituals. In our own Siberia, the Inuit people use the Amanita muscaria to contact their deities. The Laplanders use it for religious visions. It's even said that the legend of Santa's flying reindeer derives from the reindeer's fondness for grazing on the Amanita."

Viktor briefly halted his discourse to hand Jacob some crackers and pour some of the soup into a tin cup. He took a sip of the creamy broth, smacked his lips, and continued.

"I've even heard tell that the Old Testament mention of the tree of good and evil in the Garden of Eden symbolically refers to the Amanita. Other portions of the Bible, such as the story of Jacob's ladder and the Revelation of St. John, were rumored to have been recorded by scribes under the influence of the sacred mushroom. It's even been said that the Spanish Inquisition was instigated by Rome to wipe out the mushroom cult and the witches who participated in it."

Jacob found his host's comments fascinating, but hated to admit his ignorance on the subject. He felt better just knowing that the substance he had ingested in the rain forest had a long, if checkered, past. Though he was itching to discuss Wolfram Eckhardt and his suspicion that the German occultist was using the mushroom in black-magic rituals, he held his tongue and contented himself with a bite of cracker.

"I envy you, Jacob," Viktor confessed between sips of his soup. "As a working archaeologist, you really have a chance to see the world, study its ancient history, and mix with its varied peoples. I imagine that you were inspired to go into this fascinating line of work because of your father."

"Did you know him by any chance?" Jacob asked.

"No, my friend. Unfortunately, our paths never crossed. I have heard stories about him from Anna, though, and he sounds like an incredible man."

"That he was," Jacob confirmed. "I always like to think of him as a Russian version of Indiana Jones. His interests were as diverse as the dig sites he chose, and he was one of the few scientists under the Soviet system allowed free travel of the planet."

"You don't have to tell me about the rarity of that, Jacob. For me to get that visa to study in Los Angeles, I had to undertake a letter-writing campaign that extended all the way to the Politboro!"

"Excuse me," a timid female voice from outside interrupted. "May I come in?"

Viktor looked over at Jacob and winked. "Of course, my dear, please join us."

A narrow shaft of bright light and an icy gust of air accompanied Laurie's entrance. She had to hunch her shoulders to fit inside the cramped space, and appeared relieved when Viktor invited her to kneel down beside him near the portable butane stove.

"How about a nice hot cup of mushroom soup to warm your belly?" he offered.

"I'd enjoy that." Laurie took the cup he passed her, and held tightly to its warmth.

"So how did you sleep, my dear?" Viktor asked.

"Not too well, I'm afraid."

"I certainly hope that Andrei behaved himself," he said in all seriousness.

She grinned bashfully. "No, it was nothing like that."

"I should hope it wasn't," Viktor retorted. "Especially after what that little devil Sasha put him through during their abbreviated honeymoon. Why, the morning after the wedding the poor lad could barely walk!"

They laughed, and Laurie went on to explain that much like Jacob, her muscles were sore after yesterday's bumpy ride, and this had been the cause of her restlessness all night.

"Well, if all goes as planned, tonight we'll all sleep soundly, under the solid roof of one of Gangotri's Jamesway huts," Viktor said.

"Will the snow flurries impede our progress?" Laurie asked.

"As long as the visibility holds, this shouldn't affect our transit of Habermehl Pass. What's the current status of the rest of the team?"

"I just left Andrei in the cab of one of the transporters," Laurie said. "He was trying his best to show me how to operate the magnetometer that he brought along to assist our field expedition."

Viktor grunted. "Any sign of the alpine team?"

"I last saw them earlier this morning. They were decked out in snowshoes and full field packs, and appeared to be taking off to scout the perimeter."

"That Mikhail Sergeivich never gives his boys a moment's rest," Viktor said with a fond grin. "That's why they're in such superb physical condition and I'm sitting here with this spare tire around my waist."

As he patted his bulging stomach Viktor looked over at Laurie. "We were just talking about Jacob's fascinating career and the fact that he followed in his father's famous footsteps."

Laurie had learned about Jacob's profession during yesterday's drive, but didn't know the reason behind his unusual career choice. "So your father was also an archaeologist," she said after a sip of soup.

"Not only was he our motherland's most renowned archaeologist, my dear, he was a certified war hero as well," Viktor boasted.

Never one to indulge in hero worship, even when the hero in question was his own father, Jacob diplomatically intervened. "You know, my father expressed a sincere interest in visiting Polynesia one day. Though he was never able to fulfill his wish, I remember seeing some Hawaiian travel brochures on his desk shortly after he died. I found them inside a book about the kahuna."

"He must have really been quite an interesting man to be reading about the kahuna," said Laurie.

"What in the name of heaven is a kahuna?" Viktor asked.

"A kahuna is a Polynesian term meaning 'holy person,'" Laurie explained. "Growing up in Hawaii, I learned my fair share of Polynesian lore. The native peoples of the islands have their own religion, based on a kind of nature mysticism. The kahuna is a type of tribal witch doctor. My profession is included in this lore, as the Polynesian goddess Madame Pele is the patron saint of volcanoes, and must be continuously appeased by the kahuna to prevent eruptions."

"I sincerely hope that this Madame Pele won't be visiting us here in New Schwabenland," Viktor hastened to say. "I've been a witness to the destructive force of an erupting volcano, and it's something I pray never to experience again."

"What eruption was that?" Laurie asked.

"Mount St. Helens." Viktor's account of this episode was cut short when a head suddenly appeared in the tent opening.

"I do hope that I'm not interrupting anything important, comrades," said the deep voice of Lieutenant Mikhail Lopatin. "But it's getting late, and while the visibility holds, we'd best be on our way."

A few moments of embarrassed chatter followed as Viktor made excuses for their tardiness. As everyone prepared to break camp Jacob slipped on his waterproof boots and parka. The soldiers were already arriving to tear down the tent as he pulled on his bush hat, grabbed his walking stick, and made his way outside.

Even though he was prepared for the frigid weather, the cold still staggered him. It took a supreme effort just to breathe, and he needed to slip on his aviator-style sunglasses to counter the intense glare of the snow.

With the three transporters parked in a line behind him, he surveyed the dramatic landscape. As far as the eye could see, there stretched an eroded, irregularly shaped expanse of snow and ice.

"So now you know why we had to make this camp," Viktor said, after emerging from the tent with Laurie. "That sculpted, frozen sea is what we call sastrugi. It's formed by the strong winter winds and heavy coastal snows of this region."

"And we're going to have to drive over that ungodly mess?" Laurie sounded incredulous.

"That we are, comrade," Viktor replied. "And there's no need to be overly concerned. Though our passage will be a bit uncomfortable, the increased visibility will allow us a safe passage. And besides, the pass itself extends for a mere thirty miles, and in two hours, the worst will be behind us."

Jacob flashed the American his bravest, most determined grin, and together they followed Viktor into the cab of the lead transporter. There was a shared sigh of relief as the engine turned over with a coughing roar. By the time heat was trickling from the dashboard vents, the soldiers had completed their breaking down of the camp, and they stowed away the equipment while the drivers started the other two transporters.

For this dangerous portion of the trip, Viktor allowed Mikhail Lopatin's vehicle to take the lead. His driving skills were soon put to the test as the transporter plowed through the rough snow of the pass. With a great deal of jolting and bouncing, Viktor did his best to steer their tracked vehicle around the steepest of the pyramid-shaped ridges, many of them over six feet in height.

The ruggedly built transporter seemed to be taking a tremendous beating for each precious mile of distance gained. Too often, the vehicle went careening off one of the ridges, resulting in a particularly violent jolt. The cab would noisily rattle at this time, and Jacob would instinctively grab the shaking dashboard to steady himself. After a grueling hour of this punishment, Viktor momentarily halted.

"Anyone care to try their hand at the wheel?" he asked sarcastically.

"You're doing just fine, comrade," Jacob managed.

Laurie pulled out a tea-filled thermos, and while they gratefully passed the cup between them, Viktor pointed to a distant mountain range, just visible to their left.

"By the way, those are the Mühlig-Hofmann Mountains out there."

Laurie was particularly interested to learn this, and as she scanned the rugged, snow-covered peaks Viktor added, "The range can be accessed from this pass, as well as from the Gangotri highlands."

"It's hard to believe I'm finally viewing the mountains that called me on this long journey," Laurie said.

"You'll be able to get on with your work soon

enough, my dear," said Viktor. "But right now our priorities demand a brief detour. Hold on, my friends. Next stop is the Princess Astrid coast, with Gangotri base soon to follow."

There seemed to be a new urgency to Viktor's efforts as he shoved the transporter into gear and pushed his foot down on the accelerator. The vehicle jumped forward, and the incessant pounding began once again.

Jacob pushed aside thoughts of his discomfort and focused on the reason for his presence here. His beloved sister was out there somewhere in this desolate, snow-covered wilderness. He would gladly risk life and limb to save her.

It was the young American woman who first made him aware of the lessening of the sastrugi's roughness. The severest jolts seemed to be taking place at greater intervals and soon disappeared altogether.

When five minutes passed and barely a rattle shook the cab, Jacob realized that the worst was over. This was confirmed by the relieved voice of their driver.

"So much for the rigors of Habermehl Pass, my friends. Now hold on while I open up the throttle and make up some of the time we lost back there."

The transporter shot forward, the dual tracks of the lead vehicles determining their course on this portion of relatively smooth, snow-covered ground. A few minutes later Laurie spotted the two, bright yellow transporters they had been following. The vehicles appeared to be parked, their six parka-clad occupants standing on the snow. Viktor finally braked their vehicle to a halt, and he, Laurie, and Jacob anxiously climbed out of the cab and joined this group.

Jacob was unprepared for the breathtaking vista that this vantage point afforded. Shielding his eyes from the intense overhead glare, he looked out to the vast, surging Antarctic Sea. Lying between them and this sea's frozen shoreline was a gently sloping valley, filled with thousands of waddling penguins.

"That adélie colony is well over a half million strong," Viktor told them.

Even from this distance, they could hear the distinctive barks of these creatures, most of whom were gathered beside their nests, which were formed out of small, gray pebbles.

"The adélie is the most abundant and widely distributed of all penguin species," Viktor added. "This particular colony only recently arrived here after wintering on the pack ice. They're currently in the midst of courtship, with the first chicks due in a month or so."

"Surely a colony of this incredible size requires a huge food supply," Laurie surmised. "What do they feed on?"

Viktor was quick with an answer. "Their main catch is krill and larval fish, several thousand tons of which are needed per day to sustain them."

Mikhail Lopatin lowered the binoculars with which he had been scanning the horizon and announced, "We have company."

"Whatever do you mean, Mikhail?" Viktor saw nothing but penguins.

Mikhail handed him the binoculars and pointed to the sea. "Look for yourself, comrade. There's a ship out there."

Viktor raised the binoculars, adjusted the focus, and saw a yellow-hulled vessel floating amid the icebergs several miles offshore. It was a good-sized ship, with a large crane on its stern deck and its elevated bridge situated amidships between two smoking stacks. There could be no missing the bright red helicopter parked on the bow-mounted helideck, yet Viktor searched in vain for any sign of an identifying flag.

"I wonder who she belongs to?" he asked, lowering the binoculars and passing them to Jacob.

Jacob was able to get a view of this ship as Mikhail Lopatin answered, "She's the *Seaway Condor* of Norwegian registry. The ship was mentioned in my last intelligence update from Moscow."

"And the *Condor*'s purpose for being here?" Viktor continued.

"We believe it has to do with oil exploration," Mikhail returned.

Viktor received this news with a painful grimace. "So the exploitation of Antarctic resources begins in earnest. I should have been anticipating this day, but it grieves me all the same."

"Isn't there a treaty that bans such ships from operating down here?" asked Laurie, who was the next recipient of the binoculars after Jacob was finished with them.

"The treaty you speak of was originally signed in 1959, and says nothing about mineral exploitation," Viktor informed them. "A separate convention was subsequently negotiated to cover this field, though it has not yet been ratified by enough nations."

Jacob shook his head. "I'd hate to see the results of an oil spill on this penguin colony."

"You and me both, comrade." Viktor pointed toward the coastline on their left. "A short trip down the Princess Astrid coast is all that remains between us and the Gangotri highlands. If all goes smoothly, we should arrive at the base in plenty of time for dinner. The curry they serve there is superb. With that tempting thought in mind, let's be on our way."

Jacob's hopes were high as they reboarded the transporters and began their journey over the coastline. For the better part of an hour, they traveled in the midst of the scurrying penguins. Soon after passing the last pebble nest, they encountered a small group of leopard seals. The sleek creatures had gray-spotted coats and sported large heads with wicked-looking, gaping jaws. Viktor explained the leopard seal's reputation for cunning and ferocity, and told them a terrifying story about a large male that attempted to attack him during his first season in Antarctica.

As they were traveling over a boulder-strewn portion of coast completely devoid of snow, the sun momentarily peeked through the clouds. Jacob considered this a good omen. At this point they turned inland, and an ice-coated, upward-sloping gradient conveyed them deep into the foothills of a mountain range. The rough slopes here were mostly bare, snowless rock, a fact Jacob found surprising.

"How much longer until we're there?" Laurie asked impatiently.

With their transporter now in the lead position, Viktor replied without taking his eyes off the narrow, icy trail. "We're very close now, my friends. Beyond that bend up ahead, the trail gradually steepens. A drive of less than a mile will bring us to the plateau where the Indians established their base."

Jacob anxiously sat forward with this news. As the transporter rounded a broad turn and began it's way up the steepest portion of trail yet encountered, he briefly met the American's gaze. She issued him the barest of supportive smiles, and he found his pulse quickening as the vehicle approached the trail's summit.

With a bouncing jolt, the vehicle reached the plateau. No sooner did Jacob steady himself than his eyes encountered a scene of utter devastation. Spread out on the bare rock ground before them was a sickening assortment of fire-charred debris. His hopes dashed and his worst fears realized, he heard Viktor cry, "Good God, no!"

Scanning the wreckage, Jacob made out the twisted remains of three separate structures. Their roofs were gone, and only a portion of their corrugated metal walls remained standing.

"Oh Lord, I'm so sorry," Laurie whispered, reaching out and taking Jacob's hand.

This simple compassionate act caused the reality of this horrible moment to sink in, and without daring to let the American's hand go, Jacob found himself overwhelmed by a flood of onrushing tears.

14

Gunther Hartmann spent most of his day in sonar, over-seeing the repairs to a newly installed towed array unit. The system failed soon after they left Thule, and so far they'd been able to trace the malfunction to some sort of software problem. To correct it, the systems analyst had to reprogram the computer, a slow, time-consuming job. This was frustrating for Gunther to watch, and he was relieved when he got a call from the aft stateroom asking for *Ice Wolf*'s current log.

Since setting sail a day and a half ago, Gunther had all but ignored his special guests, though not deliberately, and to rectify his unsociableness, he decided to deliver the logbook in person.

After a stop at his cabin to pick up the leather-bound document, he headed aft. As he ducked into the engine room he noticed the almost eerie quietness. The only sound was the muted, high-pitched whine of the dual propeller shafts, currently drawing power from the banks of fuel cells lining the deck below.

The man responsible for maintaining this system could be seen greasing down the port shaft. Since Chief Schwedler had yet to poke his head out of the engine room since leaving port, Gunther decided to check on him.

"Chief, how goes it?"

As Schwedler lifted his head to respond to this query, the captain saw that his whole face was smothered in black grease except for the narrow circles around his eyes. Gunther understood once more why the chief was called the Shadow.

"All is well, Captain. Is there a problem of some sort?"

"Not with our propulsion, Chief. So far our progress has been most impressive."

"It's been exciting to give the fuel cells a real workout like this, Captain. My last capacity check was less than an hour ago, and it showed a sixty-one-percent charge still available."

Gunther was impressed. "Who needs costly nuclear propulsion when we've got our fuel cells at a fraction of the cost and upkeep?"

"Will we be running on Alberich all the way to the coast?" asked the Shadow.

"That's the plan, Chief. Our ETA is in eight hours. Is there a problem with that?"

The Shadow shook his head. "No problem at all, sir. At our current speed, we've got more than enough juice to last us eight hours."

"That's what I like to hear, Chief." Pointing to the closed aft hatchway, Gunther added, "By the way, have our guests been making much noise?"

"To tell you the truth, sir, I haven't heard a peep out of them, except for that damn cuckoo clock of theirs."

This observation was delivered with such sincerity that Gunther broke out laughing. With a wave, he left the Shadow to his grease pot.

He gave his VIPs the courtesy of a single knock on the closed hatch before undogging it and pushing the hatch aside. The rich strains of classical music met his ears. It was as he passed through the hatch, that he identified this evocative music as coming from Richard Wagner's *Parsifal*. As a lad, this opera had been one of his favorites, yet it felt strange to hear its lush tones within the confines of a submarine.

Of course, one would have had great difficulty believing that the room he entered was also part of a submerged warship. It appeared more like a small, civilian apartment, complete with bulkhead-to-bulkhead carpeting. Simulated wood paneling covered each side of the bulkheads, to conceal the propeller shafts, whose soft whine was barely audible. Hung on these walls were several Bavarian landscapes, a superbly crafted cuckoo clock, and the legendary Blood Flag of the early Nazi movement, which had been brought over under armed guard an hour before they set sail.

The simple furnishings consisted of a pair of metal cots, a card table with four wooden chairs, and a pair of upholstered rockers. As he expected, Gunther found the room's two elderly occupants seated in these, with afghans covering their laps. Both Heinrich Westheim and Wolfram Eckhardt were immersed in the music, which emanated from a CD player with ceiling-mounted speakers. Heinrich spotted him first, putting his finger to his lips for silence as the scene they were listening to concluded with powerful bass tones and the chiming of church bells.

When the ringing bells faded, Heinrich spoke.

"Welcome, Captain Hartmann. Thank you for indulging me with your brief silence. Do you know *Parsifal?*"

"That I do, sir," Gunther replied. "If I'm not mistaken, the movement that just concluded was the transformation music at the end of Act One."

Heinrich appeared most pleased with this answer. "I'm indeed impressed, Captain. It's so seldom that we find members of the younger generation with a knowledge of important music."

"And to us, there's no more important musical composition than *Parsifal*," Wolfram added. "They say that Wagner captured the magical essence of the Holy Grail in its soulful score and enlightening libretto."

Gunther's enjoyment of the opera had been far less complex, but daring not to admit this, he diplomatically changed the subject. "I do hope that the two of you are comfortable. I'm sorry that I haven't had more time to spend with you, but the first day out is always hectic."

"Your apologies aren't necessary," said Heinrich. "Wolfram and I have been busy getting settled into our new home. And what a delightfully comfortable home it's turning out to be. Do I detect my Heidi's involvement with these familiar furnishings?"

As Gunther nodded Wolfram chimed in. "My biggest problem is remembering that I'm in a submarine. This certainly wasn't the case the last time I sailed aboard *Ice Wolf*. At that time I was lucky just to have a mattress to sleep on, and even then, I had to share it."

Gunther held out the brown leather logbook. "I have the boat's log here. May I ask why you need it?"

Heinrich traded a cryptic glance with his bald-headed associate before replying. "I hope you don't think us foolish, Captain, but we intend to use the logbook in a tarot-card reading."

"A what?" repeated the confused mariner.

"A tarot-card reading," Wolfram said, picking up a hand-sized, red silken bundle from his lap and unwrapping it to reveal a deck of what appeared to be playing cards. Gunther could just make out the Egyptian ankh embossed on one side of the deck. As Wolfram began to shuffle the cards Gunther caught a quick glimpse of the colorful pictures drawn on their other side.

"I'm sure you're familiar with the tarot, if only in its use by the Gypsies for fortune-telling," Wolfram continued. "Since I don't expect you to immediately grasp the deep metaphysical principles involved in this reading, you need only know that we shall attempt to momentarily lift the veil of the future, to get but a peek at what tomorrow may bring. All of this will be carefully controlled and will coincide with the rising of this evening's crescent moon."

"But what's the connection with *Ice Wolf*'s logbook?" Gunther's confusion was obvious.

Heinrich took pity on him and answered as honestly as possible. "We need your log because it's *Ice Wolf*'s future that we'll be attempting to glimpse. To ensure that we tap the proper vibrations, the tarot cards will be laid directly upon it."

"By your bewildered expression, Captain, it's obvious that occultism is still new to you," Wolfram observed. "Someday soon we'll have the time to sit down and properly discuss the tarot. Then you'll learn that just as Wagner captured the secret of the Holy Grail in the score of *Parsifal,* so did the Cathars of southern France record this mystery on the faces of the tarot's major arcana."

Though all this talk of the tarot and the Holy Grail made little sense to him, Gunther dared to ask a question that he'd wanted to ask since he met the legendary occultist of the Third Reich. "Herr Eckhardt, is it true that the Nazi Occult Bureau used black magic to determine the location of Allied convoys during the war?"

Wolfram glanced at his white-haired associate and shook his head. "So this is how the younger ones will remember us, Heinrich." He returned his gaze to Gunther. "Black magic, Captain? Please, let's refrain from such ignorant and fatuous labels. Instead of *black* magic, let's refer henceforth to *ritual* magic. Look at it as a type of focused meditation, which involves the unleashing of an individual's psychic potential. By means of certain ancient techniques, such as the drawing of the circle, the use of symbols, incantations, colors, aromas, and even the tarot, we have learned to tap psychic energies not normally accessible to human consciousness. It was through this unique method that the Occult Bureau successfully lifted the veil, and located these convoys that you speak of."

"I'm sorry if I continue to show my ignorance," said Gunther. "But if you had such success harnessing the powers of ritual magic, why did Germany lose the war?"

This time Heinrich replied. "Good question, Captain. Though the answer is a complex one, I believe it all goes back to this black magic you first mentioned. For as Wolfram and I have learned in our decades of study, the occult realm is a dangerous place, bristling with hidden traps and pitfalls along the way to enlightenment. Just as Parsifal had to pass the test of worthiness, so does the practitioner of the magical arts.

"Sad to say, there were many inside the Third Reich who picked the wrong path, and the black forces they tapped ended by poisoning us all. From the Führer on down, the movement crumbled, doomed by a group of selfish, greedy, egotistical men who had little concern for Germany's fate."

Though Gunther was by this point hanging on Heinrich's every word, an ill-timed knock on the closed hatch caused the octogenarian to break off.

"Enter!" the captain reluctantly instructed.

Karl Kromer proceeded to duck through the hatchway. Trying his best to ignore the opera that was still playing in the background, the oberleutnant stiffened at attention and issued a rapid, formal report.

"Captain, we've just picked up a surface sonar contact in the secondary convergence zone immediately ahead of us. Peter reports that in addition to picking up the sound of this vessel's diesel engines, the contact is also utilizing thrusters of some sort."

Gunther appeared little fazed by this news, but Heinrich took it most seriously. "I would think that a surface contact in these normally isolated waters is most unusual, Captain. What do you make of it?"

"There's no cause for alarm," Gunther advised. "Most likely, these thrusters merely indicate an oceanographic research ship. As we continue to get closer to the shores of Antarctica, encountering such a vessel will not be such an uncommon occurrence."

"I'd still like to make certain that we're not dealing with a warship," Wolfram put in, his concern apparent.

"Number One," Gunther ordered, "prepare to bring *Ice Wolf* up to periscope depth. A quick visual scan of this contact should suffice to ease our anxieties. I do hope that the repairs to the towed array are going smoothly."

"I'm afraid we've had a bit of a setback, sir," Kromer hesitantly reported. "A power surge wiped out the computer's memory, and the technicians have to begin programming it all over again."

Heinrich took immediate interest in this conversation, as this was the first he had heard of any technical difficulties inside *Ice Wolf.* "Is this problem serious, Captain Hartmann?"

"It's of little consequence to the current portion of our mission," Gunther confidently answered. "Since leaving Thule, the boat's towed sonar array has been down. This auxiliary system is purely a defensive one, and it should be fully operational by the time we complete our work in Antarctica and begin the long voyage north, into the crowded waters of the central Atlantic."

Noting the worried looks that continued to etch his guests' expressions, Gunther added, "To ensure its quick repair, I'll return to sonar and personally supervise our technicians' efforts."

"Very well, Captain," said Heinrich. "Please be so good as to inform us the second you identify that surface contact."

Gunther bowed his head and smartly pivoted to exit the room, with Kromer close behind him. As the forward hatch closed shut with a dull, metallic clang, Heinrich leaned forward to put the logbook on the card table. Meanwhile Wolfram began shuffling his tarot cards.

"Well, Heinrich," he said in a bare whisper, "what do you think?"

Heinrich sat back in his rocker and thought for a moment. "My confidence in Captain Hartmann remains strong, and this problem with the towed array sounds minor. As far as that sonar contact is concerned, we'll just have to await the results of the periscope scan."

"As far as I'm concerned, the next eight hours can't pass quickly enough," Wolfram confessed. "It seems the closer we get to our objective, the more nervous I get."

"It's time to relax and get rid of our tensions, Wolfram. Only then will we be able to tap the flow and lift the veil to the future. Shall we begin our breathing exercises?"

With the lush Wagnerian music in the background, Heinrich lit a stick of sandalwood incense. The two elders sat up straight, placed their slippered feet on the carpeted deck, and rested their hands on their thighs, palms up. On Heinrich's command, they inhaled, filling their lungs to capacity, before exhaling completely, and then repeating the process. They continued this during the opera's entire second act.

As the prelude to Act III began Wolfram lifted his hands and reached for the tarot cards, which he again shuffled, his thoughts still on his and Heinrich's exchange with *Ice Wolf*'s commanding officer. Gunther Hartmann was smart and inquisitive, and even though he was ignorant of occult matters, the interest he showed was highly promising. Wolfram even considered initiating the submariner into the movement's spiritual secrets. His Aryan blood was certainly pure enough, a byproduct of the Lebensborn program. And with his roots thusly assured, Gunther Hartmann could be a very valuable spiritual ally.

Almost as an afterthought, Wolfram decided to query the tarot on this matter. He filled his mind with a vision of *Ice Wolf*'s bearded captain and randomly cut the cards. Fittingly enough, at this exact same moment, the background soundtrack was filled with the shrill, fearful cries of Kundry as the temptress was awakened by the spell of Klingsor, the evil magician. Startled by her cry, Wolfram found himself staring at the ultimate portrait of spiritual transformation—a skeletal knight on horseback, with the sun of immortality setting behind him and a group of kneeling mortals awaiting their inevitable confrontation with what was marked on the card as DEATH.

Philip Michaels commenced his afternoon walk-through of the *Springfield* in the compartment he considered the boat's most important. Though not as glamorous as the maneuvering/reactor spaces or control room, the auxiliary machinery space held vital equipment. Located on the third level, just aft of the torpedo room, it was here that their supply of breathable fresh air was maintained by a process that employed chemical scrubbers to remove dangerous carbon dioxide, carbon monoxide, and hydrogen gas from the air. Various air filters and dehumidifiers aided this effort.

Besides the equipment supporting the boat's emergency air-breathing system, the auxiliary machine space housed their fresh-water distillation plant, which was capable of producing over ten thousand gallons of safe, drinkable water a day, and the *Springfield*'s reliable Fairbanks-Morse diesel engine. Known simply as Clyde, this was basically a scaled-down version of the dependable engines that ran America's World War II fleet submarines. Used for auxiliary purposes, Clyde could prove invaluable in restarting their cold S6G plant after a reactor scram, or for providing get-home power in the event of a full reactor casualty. It could also quickly recycle the air in the event of a fire.

Clyde was always a favorite of Michaels's because it served as a link to the past. With the majority of *Springfield*'s technology developed well after he was born, it was somewhat comforting to know that a piece of equipment from the 1930s could still serve an essential function.

As Michaels passed by the engine's spotlessly clean manifold, he noticed the lower portion of a male body sticking out from its support raft. One look at this individual's lime-green running shoes identified him as Lieutenant Commander Benjamin Kyle, the boat's engineering officer. Having served as an engineering officer himself in the early days of his career, Michaels felt an affinity for Kyle, who had also played football for the naval academy and had a hands-on management style much like his own.

"Is everything okay with Clyde, Ben?" Michaels asked.

There was a brief moment of silence as Kyle scooted out from beneath the support mount, switched off his flashlight, and looked up to see who was addressing him. "Hello, Skipper," he replied with a broad smile. "Ol' Clyde is lookin' real fine, with not a drop of oil visible on the mount for all my effort."

As Kyle stood up he revealed the short, stocky physique that had helped him earn a starting position as a defensive guard. "What brings you down here, Skipper?"

"I needed to walk off that chili Chief Cunetto served for lunch today," Michaels quipped.

"Too bad you didn't get down here fifteen minutes earlier," Kyle commented. "Our friends the SEALs dropped in for a visit."

Michaels grimaced. "I hope they behaved."

"Actually, they seemed downright human for a change. I gave them a quick tour of the life-support systems. Though what they really seemed fascinated with was ol' Clyde here."

Michaels affectionately patted the top of the engine manifold. "I guess Clyde is the only system on *Springfield* they can relate to."

"You've got it, Skipper. By the way, what's the latest on our bogey?"

"Since the last ops briefing, there's been little change in its course or speed. If this remains constant, in less than eight hours, they'll be making landfall on Antarctica's Princess Astrid coast."

"Any new ideas as to who the sub belongs to?" Kyle asked.

Michaels shook his head. "All I can say for sure is that we're definitely dealing with a vessel powered by fuel cells, which means that its technology had to come out of either Germany, Holland, or Sweden."

"Thank goodness they don't seem to be outfitted with a towed array," Kyle said. "It sure makes it a lot easier for *Springfield* to snuggle into its baffles."

"Speaking of sonar," Michaels put in, "Bodzin and his team just tagged a surface contact in the secondary convergence zone, almost due south of us. This vessel appears to be transiting the ice pack off the coast, with the assistance of some good-sized thrusters."

Kyle's eyes opened wide. "Could it be the *Seaway Condor?*"

"It sure sounds like it, Ben. And you know what that means. Wherever you find the *Condor,* the HMS *Turbulent* won't be far behind. Captain Hartwell would sure find our bogey of interest."

"I still can't get over how they beat us to Bouvetoya. The scuttlebutt about the Brits making some radical design changes in the PWR-1 reactor core as a result of their experiences in the Falklands war must be true after all."

Before Michaels could respond to this, a young seaman entered the auxiliary machine space by way of the aft accessway.

"Captain," the sailor said breathlessly, "Lieutenant Commander Perez sent me down here to let you know that Sierra One is in the midst of a depth change and appears to be going up to either periscope depth or the surface."

Michaels looked at his engineering officer and grinned. "All right, Ben. Maybe now we can finally get a definite tag on this phantom sub and see exactly who it is that we're dealing with."

15

Jacob Litvak's darkest hour arrived the moment they found the four, fire-charred bodies buried beneath the collapsed wall of the station's main Jamesway hut. It would take an experienced coroner to figure out their identities through a comparison of dental records.

Of course, Jacob had been prepared for the worst ever since he set his eyes on the devastated compound. Somehow he gathered the courage to join the others as they began the grim task of picking through the debris.

An initial examination revealed that the conflagration must have started suddenly and been incredibly swift moving. What wreckage remained was as badly charred as the four corpses, with the exception of a small, corrugated metal storage hut. They set up their temporary headquarters in this cramped building.

His inability to tell for sure if his sister was among the dead was very upsetting to Jacob. Laurie did her best to ease his anxieties by asking him to help set up their temporary shelter. Jacob reluctantly consented.

As it turned out, this menial work was excellent medicine. As he gloomily helped Laurie with the transfer of their foodstuffs and sleeping bags, Viktor got on with the solemn job of organizing their search of the rest of the compound.

Sometime later Jacob heard that Andrei Korsakov had discovered two additional corpses on a surrounding hillside, and immediately dropped what he was doing and rushed over to have a look. The frozen victims turned out to be a man and woman of Indian descent. They were only partially clothed, and had apparently rushed outside to escape the fire only to succumb to exposure.

Though Jacob hated to admit it, he found himself deriving some relief from the fact that neither of these bodies was his sister's. He returned to his work with the barest of hopes that Anna had somehow survived this tragedy.

Later that afternoon Viktor joined them inside the storage hut. As Laurie brewed some tea they somberly seated themselves in a circle on the floor.

"Now both of you understand why fire is every Antarctic explorer's worst fear," Viktor said. "The poor occupants of Dakshan Gangotri never stood a chance. If the flames didn't get them, the elements did."

"Any idea as to what caused this blaze?" Laurie asked.

Viktor shrugged. "Who can say? It will take an official investigation to determine the exact cause. My initial impression is that it must have been a violent explosion of some kind, perhaps a gas leak. What we can be certain of is that the blaze grew quickly. All of us on the ice constantly drill for such a contingency. Every Antarctic station prepares a fire-fighting and evacuation plan long before the first occupant arrives. It's obvious that the poor Indians didn't have the time to put theirs into effect."

Jacob stared vacantly at the flames of their primus stove. "I hope to God my Anna didn't suffer."

"Don't be too quick to mourn, my friend," Viktor was quick to say. "As long as there's the slightest hope that Anna's alive, I'm going to hold on to it."

Jacob started to argue otherwise, but found himself engulfed in tears instead. Laurie scooted over and tenderly took his hand.

"What do we do once we complete our search of the compound—return to Novo base?" she asked.

Viktor thought a moment before replying. "I guess such a trip would be prudent, since it's imperative that we inform the Indian authorities of this tragedy at once."

"We can't go back now!" Jacob cried. "Have you already forgotten about the important work Laurie has to do out here. My sister would have had it no other way. The dead are dead, and no matter how many investigations are begun, this fact will not change. Now's the time to focus on the lives we could save if the suspicions of the American authorities prove to be true. Just think of the incredible loss of life that would result if a volcano were to erupt and spew its poisonous gases upon Novo base."

Impressed with the sincerity of this outburst, Laurie looked over to gauge Viktor's reaction. "How much further is the sector that I've been sent to examine?" she asked.

Viktor answered without hesitation. "We're already well into the foothills of the Mühlig-Hoffmann range. If the terrain and weather cooperate, I believe we could have you in the general vicinity within three hours."

Laurie returned her gaze to Jacob. "It does sound like a pity to have to go all the way back to Novo base now that I'm so close to my objective."

"Of course it's a waste!" Jacob urged. "For the sake of the living, we've got to get out there into the mountains and see if a threat really exists."

"Comrades!" someone shouted from outside. "Comrades, you must come and see what we've uncovered!"

The speaker sounded too excited for someone who

had found more bodies, and the trio set down their cups, grabbed their outerwear, and hastened outdoors.

"Comrades!" Andrei greeted almost joyously, his face flushed with excitement. "Lieutenant Lopatin has made a promising find in the remains of the station's garage. Dr. Litvak, it appears that there's hope for your sister's safety after all!"

Caught off guard by this news, Jacob thought at first that he hadn't heard the young Russian properly. Yet it took only one look at the expectant grins on the faces of his associates to assume otherwise.

"Come on," Andrei called, "it's this way!"

It was apparent that this was all he was going to say about the matter, and they readily followed him across the compound. The fire-charred rubble seemed to pass in a blur, as all eyes were focused on the group of soldiers who stood at the site's northern outskirts beside the partially collapsed metal walls of a large building. When they were about a dozen yards away, Viktor loudly raised his voice to determine what was occurring.

"Mikhail Sergeivich, what's the meaning of all of this?"

Mikhail responded by holding his right arm up over his head. Tight in his grasp was a book of some sort. Seeing this object served to further pique their curiosity, and they increased their pace.

When they reached Lopatin, he addressed his comments to Jacob. "Comrade, you'll never believe what we found as we were searching the station's garage. I first realized that something was amiss upon noticing that one of the three vehicle stalls was empty. Since the other two stalls were filled with the damaged shells of a pair of small Sno-Cats, I knew that Gangotri's tracked transporter belonged in the vacant one, but this vehicle was nowhere to be seen. This led to our extensive search of the building for the dispatch manifest."

Mikhail opened the book in his hand and presented it to Jacob. "Look for yourself, comrade. The last entry clearly shows that the transporter was assigned to Dr. Lahiri Mahasaya, Gangotri's director. The log indicates that the vehicle was checked out on November third, the day before we lost radio contact with the station, with a stated destination of the Mühlig-Hofmann mountain range. Most important of all, the manifest lists the transporter's sole passenger as Dr. Anna Litvak!"

Stunned by this revelation, Jacob hastily read the manifest. The neat English script was slightly smudged, but legible, and he found his hands excitedly shaking as he passed the book to Viktor.

"My Lord, so it is!" Viktor exclaimed after reading the entry.

As Laurie inspected the manifest Jacob returned the expectant glance of Mikhail Lopatin and fought the urge to cry out in triumph. He felt as if a heavy weight had just been removed from his chest, and he listened as the American joined in on the celebration.

"This is wonderful news! You were right after all, Jacob. Anna didn't want us to return to Novo base. And now we can continue into the mountains, where both your sister and the mystery that called me these thousands of miles awaits us."

16

Gunther Hartmann couldn't believe his eyes as *Ice Wolf*'s periscope broke the sea's surface and the lens filled with the distinctive, bright yellow hull of the Norwegian oil support ship *Seaway Condor*. How very tempted he was to order a torpedo attack against this vessel, which destiny had once more put in their path. Yet Gunther managed to resist this temptation, just as he had over a week ago, after their first encounter in the seas far north of here.

Several hours had passed since this second sighting, and Gunther had long since ordered *Ice Wolf* back down into the protective depths. There was much to prepare now that they were rapidly nearing their destination, and Gunther soon forgot about the *Condor*.

With each passing minute, the atmosphere inside *Ice Wolf*'s hull seemed to intensify, especially in the control room, where Gunther nervously paced from station to station, with one eye on the directional compass and the other on the overhead clock.

"Captain," the boat's senior sonar operator said as he passed by his console. "The preliminary diagnosis shows that the repairs to our towed array have been completed. Shall I run the backup diagnostic?"

Gunther answered while glancing up to the clock. "No, Peter, I have confidence in your efforts. Besides, right now I don't need you to focus on the seas behind us. Prepare to activate the forward scanning fathometer."

As the sonar technician returned to his work Gunther crossed over to the navigation plot. Karl Kromer waited for him here.

"Number One, surely we're close to the ice pack by now."

Sensing the captain's impatience, Kromer calmly pointed to the chart that was laid out on the top of the plot. "Our last navigational fix showed us well within the deep-water channel that will lead us to the coast. The presence of the ice is insignificant."

Gunther grunted. "Tell me that in another quarter of an hour, when we must risk fracturing our hull as we smack through the ice to reach the surface."

The hollow, electronic ping of the forward scanning fathometer sounded in the background. As it was monotonously repeated every five seconds Gunther bent over the chart and traced a line from the red X indicating *Ice Wolf*'s current location to an irregularly shaped portion of the coastline labeled PRINCESS ASTRID COAST.

"This channel we're following to reach the coast greatly bothers me, Number One. It's fine as long as no other ship is there to block the way. But if that situation were to change against us, we'd have little room to maneuver to effect an escape."

Kromer looked at the chart and pointed to a blue X approximately thirty nautical miles behind them. "The only vessel that could reach the channel in time is our old friend the *Condor*. What could the brave Vikings possibly do to impede our progress—drop some drilling bits on our heads?"

Gunther couldn't help but chuckle at this comment. With his anxieties momentarily eased, he listened as the constant pinging sound steadily increased its tempo.

"It's the ice!" he exclaimed, looking up to the pipe-lined ceiling as if he could see all the way to the surface. "Peter, pipe the passive sonar feed through the overhead speakers."

The technician did as ordered, and soon the pinging was overridden by the deep, crackling sound of splitting ice. Quickly now, both Gunther and Karl walked over to the sonar console. Directly adjoining it was a device constructed around a rotating drum, onto which a piece of graph paper was continuously fed. The hissing stylus drawing a jagged pattern onto the paper's surface was directed by an intense pulse of sonic energy that was projected to the surface from a transmitter embedded in *Ice Wolf*'s upper hull.

"So, the much-vaunted ice machine works!" Gunther sighed. "That agitated vertical pattern indicates thick ice topside. I estimate its thickness at about ten feet."

Gunther gasped when the stylus abruptly dipped downward and drew a jagged peak more than three times wider than the previous pattern. "It's an ice ridge! And from the size of that pattern, it's got to project at least thirty feet down from the surface."

"Now I know why we've been instructed to follow the deep-water channel," Karl admitted.

The jagged peak stabilized, and the graph paper was filled with a thin, flat line, which Gunther was quick to identify. "And just to show that the ice isn't necessarily continuous, there's the first sign of a polynya above us. My, that bit of open water looks large enough to surface in."

Gunther looked up to the clock. The digital numbers read 1745. He began impatiently stroking his Vandyke and returned his gaze to the graph paper, which was now filled with a jagged pattern indicating a return of the ice cover.

"Number One, it's time to send for the old fighters."

"Very well, Captain. I'll have Seaman Schiffer go to their quarters and escort them forward."

"I hope young Klaus is prepared for what awaits him behind their hatchway." Gunther smiled. "Because I can't begin to explain what I encountered there during my earlier visit."

"I bet they were raising the ghost of our Führer in a séance," Kromer joked. "Schiffer's a cool one, Captain. I'm sure he'll survive and live to tell his grandchildren all about the day he personally escorted the legendary occultists of the Third Reich."

Kromer turned for the aft hatchway to inform Seaman Schiffer of his new duty. Meanwhile Gunther scanned the control room and spotted Otto Brauer's muscular figure standing behind the seated planesman. Once more he looked up to the clock before crossing the compartment to join Brauer.

"The time is almost upon us, Otto," Gunther greeted. "Are you ready for some fresh air, my friend?"

Brauer ran his hands through his short, spiky crewcut. "I've been waiting for this day for most of my life, Captain. Do you want me to notify the team?"

Gunther nodded. "You may proceed, Otto. I want all the members of the ice team to be fully outfitted, with all weapons and equipment ready to go at a moment's notice. The final assembly point will be in the forward torpedo room, where we'll gather as soon as we've made contact with Oberleutnant Ritter."

"Yes, Captain." Brauer smartly pivoted and brushed past Karl Kromer on his way out of the compartment.

Kromer alertly took his place at the helm. "Schiffer's on his way, Captain. The youngster's genuinely honored to get this assignment. Where was Brauer off to in such a hurry?"

"I've instructed him to ready the ice team," Gunther said as he carefully surveyed the variety of gauges and dials on the diving console.

"My offer to go along still stands, sir. It would be a real thrill to be there when the lair is unsealed. Why, it would almost be like being a part of living history."

"You'll be making history right here at *Ice Wolf*'s helm, Number One. I understand your desire to accompany us. But such a request is impossible. You know as well as I do the dangerously exposed position we'll be in once we leave the protective confines of the boat. We face not only the constant threat of human opposition, but also the fickle weather and treacherous terrain. And I'd be shirking my responsibility to the movement if I granted your wish. No, my friend, you're much more valuable here, on *Ice Wolf*. Don't forget, if tragedy were to befall the team and we failed to return to the rendezvous spot, it would be your job to return *Ice Wolf* safely to Thule."

There was a sudden clatter of muffled voices behind them, and they turned their heads in time to see Heinrich Westheim and Wolfram Eckhardt enter the control room. The two old-timers looked like professors emeriti, dressed as they were in matching black corduroy pants, open-neck white dress shirts, and black crewneck sweaters. Only their footwear was different, with Heinrich attired in shiny black loafers and Wolfram decked out in quilted, inner-boot liners.

It was Wolfram who handed Gunther *Ice Wolf*'s log, saying, "Thank you, Captain."

Gunther took the leather-covered document. "I hope that your reading was a successful one."

Wolfram nodded. "That is was, Captain. In fact, the great transformation that I divined is already taking place." Looking up at the clock, he added, "I see that the hour of truth is finally upon us."

Gunther beckoned the newcomers to join him beside the ice machine. As they gathered around the slowly revolving drum the stylus drew an agitated series of peaked lines.

"That pattern shows thick ice above us," Gunther explained.

"Can we surface under such conditions?" Wolfram asked.

"I'm afraid not."

Looking up to the clock, Heinrich anxiously observed, "It's almost eighteen hundred hours, Captain. If we can't surface, how do we contact Ritter and get our final bearings?"

Gunther displayed admirable patience as he addressed the helmsman. "Prepare to stop engines and ascend to sixty feet upon my command."

Quickly now, he glanced to the clock just as the digital numbers registered 1758. He then returned his gaze to the ice machine, where the agitated pattern continued.

"What will happen if we miss Ritter's signal?" Wolfram wanted to know.

"We'll just have to wait another twelve hours, when the next contact is scheduled to take place," Heinrich answered.

Gunther didn't want any part of such a wasteful delay, and he silently channeled his will, desperately wishing the stylus to alter its pattern. Another minute clicked off the clock, and just as he was about to give up hope, the stylus made an agitated spike before steadying itself. Almost miraculously, the graph paper began filling with a flat, black line.

Gunther wasted no time issuing his orders. "All stop! Periscope depth!"

With his guests in tow, he hurriedly climbed the short ladder to the conning tower. No sooner did he reach the scope than the deep voice of the helmsman loudly called out from below, "Sixty feet, Captain!"

"Open water topside!" Kromer added.

Gunther eagerly raised the periscope and peered into its eyepiece. It took several seconds for the lens to break the surface. He needed to fine-tune the focus before a gleaming expanse of glistening, ice filled the lens. After a quick 360-degree scan, he locked in on the southern horizon. The veteran mariner fought the urge to release a cry of joy as a desolate portion of rugged coastline came into view. It was a good five miles distant, with a snowcapped mountain range forming a magnificent backdrop. Impressed with his first view of Antarctica's pristine shores, he breathlessly listened as Kromer's voice cried out, "Eighteen hundred hours!"

He continued his scan with renewed urgency, deftly increasing the lens magnification to its maximum. The boulder-strewn shoreline suddenly appeared to jump forward. Gunther had all he could do to ignore the persistent queries of his guests.

"Well, Captain, is he out there?" asked Heinrich.

"Maybe something's happened to him, and he wasn't able to make this rendezvous himself," Wolfram offered.

Just as this last comment was spoken a blindingly bright white light flashed from the shore. Gunther waited for this light to flash slowly on and off three times before finally allowing himself to express his joy.

"It's Ritter!"

As the others gathered behind him muttered in celebration, Gunther noted the signal's exact bearing, then reached up to activate *Ice Wolf*'s stroboscopic signal beacon, which was mounted on top of the periscope. His response of three flashes was acknowledged by a matching series from shore, and Gunther gratefully backed away from the eyepiece and lowered the scope.

"Take us back down to one hundred feet, all ahead one third on bearing one-seven-eight," he ordered. Feeling a firm hand on his shoulder, he turned to face a broadly grinning Heinrich Westheim.

"You've done it, Captain. Congratulations on safely getting *Ice Wolf* to Antarctica!"

"Thank you, Herr Westheim," Gunther replied humbly. "But our work here is only just beginning."

"That it is," Wolfram concurred. "Come on, Captain. It's time for us to put on our polar gear."

Gunther proceeded at once to his cabin, where he hurriedly dressed himself in the variety of clothing that had been previously laid out on his cot: thermal underwear, a heavy woolen shirt, windproof trousers, braces, and quilted inner-boot liners. To avoid overheating, he stuffed his sweater, gloves, close-weave cotton field trousers, and balaclava into a nylon tote bag. Then with his soft mukluks and down-filled parka draped over his shoulder, he walked aft to the forward torpedo room. Waiting for him there were seven similarly dressed members of the crew, led by the burly figure of Chief Otto Brauer.

"The ice team is assembled and awaiting your orders to disembark, Captain," Brauer reported.

"Very good, Chief. You may begin loading your weapons while I see to getting *Ice Wolf* to the surface."

Gunther left the rest of his gear in the torpedo room and headed to the control room. Ten minutes after making their successful contact, he joined Kromer beside the ice machine for an update.

"What kind of ice conditions have we been encountering, Number One?"

Kromer shook his head worriedly. "It doesn't look good, Captain. Nothing but a solid sheet of thick ice ever since we descended from periscope depth."

"I seriously doubt that we'll be coming across any significant open leads this close to shore. Number One, it appears that it's finally time to put *Ice Wolf*'s reinforced sail to the test."

As Gunther glanced up to the clock to gauge their forward progress, he noted two newcomers entering the control room by way of the aft hatch. Heinrich Westheim was dressed all in black as before, with his bald-headed associate decked out in full polar attire, including parka.

As they crossed the compartment Gunther greeted Wolfram. "Herr Eckhardt, if I were you, I'd take off that parka. We still have to get *Ice Wolf* on the surface, and I wouldn't want you to work up an unnecessary sweat in the meantime."

Wolfram immediately took this advice while Gunther returned his attention to the ice machine. The jagged pattern that the stylus continued to etch did not look promising, and he allowed another minute to pass before speaking.

"This looks like the best conditions we're going to get, Number One. Let's give it a shot." Then: "All stop!" he ordered to the helmsman. "Vent ballast and take us up!" he added to the diving officer.

There was an expression of worried concern on Gunther's face when he looked up to the ceiling as the compartment filled with the gurgling blast of venting seawater. With this loss of ballast, the now lightened submarine gained a state of positive buoyancy and began rapidly drifting straight upward.

"Eighty feet," the diving officer reported in an unemotional tone. "Seventy-five feet and rising quickly."

"Sound collision alert!" Gunther warned as *Ice Wolf* shot past the seventy-foot mark.

At this moment a piercing electronic alarm sounded in the background. Gunther reached up to grab a handhold as the diving officer reported their passing of the sixty-foot threshold.

"How does that ice look, Number One?" he breathlessly questioned.

"The stylus is still indicating a fairly thick layer above us, but no projecting pressure ridges."

"Fifty-five feet," the diving officer calmly observed.

"Brace yourselves!" Gunther advised.

Just as he was regripping the steel handhold, *Ice Wolf*'s sail smashed into the ice above with a deafening, bone-jarring crunch. The deck vibrated wildly, and Gunther's knees buckled while his palms bit into the overhead handhold.

"Depth gauge indicates that we failed to surface, Captain," the diving officer observed.

"Damn that ice!" Gunther cursed. "Flood her down to seventy feet, Chief."

The throaty sucking roar of the ballast pumps' activation was followed by the gurgling rush of seawater being reflooded into the partially empty tanks. As a state of negative buoyancy was achieved *Ice Wolf* once more descended into the cold, black depths.

"Whatever is occurring, Captain?" Wolfram demanded to know from his position beside the sonar console.

"It's nothing to be overly concerned with," Gunther explained. "The pack ice is just proving a bit more resilient than I had anticipated, and it's going to take another effort to smash our way through."

Unable to hide his unease, Wolfram sighed heavily and mopped his brow with a handkerchief. Thankful that he had listened to the captain's advice and removed his parka, he again gripped the edge of the console as the diving officer delivered the next depth update.

"Sixty-five feet and continuing to descend."

"That's deep enough, Chief," Gunther ordered. "Lighten our load, and let's see what kind of icebreaker *Ice Wolf* makes!"

With a single turn of his wrist, the diving officer released the additional ballast they had just taken on. To the onrushing surge of venting seawater, the now lightened vessel drifted back upward. Again there was a deafening loud crack as *Ice Wolf* made abrupt contact with the ice, and as the deck quivered and trembled the diving officer's voice gloomily reported: "The boat has once more failed to break free, Captain."

Gunther felt a rush of frustration. "Take us back down, Chief. And this time, blow the main ballast. With a couple of hundred tons of additional positive buoyancy, *Ice Wolf* will smack through that ice like a fist through a plate-glass window!"

Wolfram listened to this fierce directive and found himself stimulated by the captain's vigor. Yet this feeling of excitement was of brief duration. Though he was certainly no submariner, he knew that the procedure they were about to undertake was not without its dangers. The encompassing ice could be thicker than they had anticipated. And even if their specially reinforced sail could take the collision, their fragile rudder might not. Then there was always the threat of encountering an inverted, spiked pressure ridge, which could pierce *Ice Wolf*'s hull and send them hurtling to a watery grave.

For the first time in years a nervous knot gathered in the pit of Wolfram's gut. As he met the resolute gaze of his white-haired associate, he squared back his shoulders and began a series of deep, calming breaths. Their fate and that of the movement they served was in the hands of destiny now, and he cleared his clouded mind of all fears as the compartment filled with the rushing sound of venting seawater. This indicated that *Ice Wolf* was on its way to the surface once again, and Wolfram locked his gaze on the rapidly dropping depth gauge.

This time when they made contact with the ice, the gut-wrenching concussion was accompanied by a rending, tearing commotion. Fearing that their hull had been split open, he was startled to hear the joyous words of the diving officer.

"We've broken through! *Ice Wolf* is on the surface!"

"Yes!" Gunther exclaimed, allowing his men the briefest of celebrations before issuing his next directives. "Lookouts to the bridge!"

A pair of parka-clad sailors with binoculars around their necks appeared from the aft accessway and scrambled up into the conning tower.

"Herr Eckhardt," said Gunther, "if you'll just come with me to the forward torpedo room, we can get on with the next portion of our mission."

Wolfram needed no additional prompting to follow Gunther out of the control room. As he entered the torpedo room and spotted the seven men who would accompany them, the finality of the moment sank in. Each of these individuals was fully dressed in matching white polar survival suits, with a combination of Heckler and Koch assault rifles and compact submachine guns draped over their shoulders.

"Open the access trunk," Gunther ordered.

As this recessed ceiling hatch was popped open a frigid draft of fresh air rushed into the compartment.

"Chief Brauer," Gunther called, "you may deploy the team topside and begin removal of the Snow-Cats."

The men obediently lined up beside the access ladder, and Otto Brauer began the short climb outside. As Wolfram was watching the chief's legs disappear through the trunk, he felt a hand tenderly touch him on his back.

"Well, old friend, it seems that the time has come to say good-bye," said Heinrich.

Wolfram turned to face his white-haired associate and accepted a warm handshake.

"May your journey over the ice be a smooth and safe one," Heinrich told him. "Why, I'm already counting the seconds until your triumphant return, with the greatest treasure mortal man has ever known. What a joyous reunion we shall have!"

"Don't forget your promise to save me a piece of Heidi's strudel." Wolfram winked playfully.

"Have no fear, Wolfram. It will be waiting for you. Just return to us safe and sound, old friend."

"Herr Eckhardt," said Gunther, "it's time to be going."

Wolfram slipped into his parka and took a last fond look at Heinrich before beginning the short climb up the ladder. With a bit of difficulty, he managed to penetrate the trunk and reach *Ice Wolf*'s exterior deck. As he stiffly stood up he was greeted by a stinging slap of frigid air. The glare was intense, and he needed to shade his eyes in order to survey the amazing frozen landscape before him.

Ice Wolf's narrow, gray steel upper hull was encased by what seemed a solid sheet of ice stretching in all directions. From the top of the boat's sail, the two lookouts could be seen, constantly sweeping the horizon with their binoculars. Gunther directed his glance toward the bow, where the members of the team had just completed removing a large rectangular-shaped portion of deck grating. They were currently winching up three long, encapsulated, waterproof storage pods, which had been cleverly stowed between the ballast tanks and the pressure hull. As the first pod was lifted up onto the deck and unsealed, Wolfram got a glimpse of their next means of transport. The sleek Snow-Cat tracked vehicle had an open cockpit large enough for three men. Its storage well, located beneath the communal bench-type seat, had just enough capacity to suit their needs.

"There's someone coming our way!" one of the lookouts shouted from above.

Wolfram anxiously followed the sentry's outstretched finger, pointed almost due south. Doing his best to shield his eyes from the glare, he scanned the bleak, desolate-looking coastline approximately a mile away. Though he saw no hint of this newcomer, he did manage to glimpse the jagged, snowcapped mountain peaks where the next part of their journey would take them, and felt his pulse quicken at the sight.

Wolfram heard a low, high-pitched, growling whine that steadily increased, and was somewhat concerned when several members of the ice team suddenly raised their rifles and aimed them southward.

Then a signal light suddenly flashed three times. This was all the men had to see to lower their rifles. Seconds later Wolfram got his first clear view of the vehicle responsible for this commotion—a sleek white, open-cab snowmobile, with a single passenger, approaching from the coast, and apparently traveling incredibly fast over the smooth ice surface of the frozen sea.

The driver displayed a reckless abandon as he approached *Ice Wolf* on a certain collision course. He was barely ten feet away from striking the boat's forward hull when he finally stomped on the brakes, causing the vehicle to make a sweeping, sideways skid. When the resulting ice spray finally settled, Wolfram was shocked to find the snowmobile neatly parallel-parked, barely six inches away from them.

"Greetings, *Ice Wolf!*" the driver shouted as he climbed out of the vehicle, pulled off his helmet, and shook loose a wild mane of long blond hair.

"Ritter!" Gunther Hartmann fondly cried from the sub's top deck.

Wolfram helped *Ice Wolf*'s captain unfurl a rope ladder onto the ice, and the newcomer adroitly climbed up to join them.

"Oberleutnant Adolph Ritter, reporting for duty!" he said with mock seriousness.

Wolfram had met this dashing individual before. A former Special Forces commando, Ritter was the very embodiment of Nordic racial purity, with clear white skin, perfectly chiseled chin, nose, and cheekbones, and piercing blue eyes. The scar that lined his right jaw gave him additional character, as did his tall, muscular physique.

Wolfram accepted a firm handshake. "It's good to see you again, Herr Ritter."

"That was some entrance," Gunther said as he opened his arms and embraced Ritter warmly.

"It's been much too long since I've seen that ugly puss of yours, Hartmann," quipped the commando. "Though I must admit that I like the new beard."

Gunther smiled. "You're as punctual as ever, Adolph. Viewing your signal light was a sight for sore eyes."

"To tell you the truth, I was beginning to worry that this ice would be too thick for you to penetrate," Ritter admitted.

Gunther beckoned toward the boat's streamlined sail. "*Ice Wolf* continues to amaze us all, and our reinforced sail is only one of the new features that make this vessel unique on all the seas."

"I understand that you had some trouble at Gangotri, Herr Ritter," Wolfram said as the team began lowering the tracked transporters onto the ice.

The blue-eyed commando responded in all seriousness, "It was nothing that a little plastic explosives couldn't take care of."

"And the Ice Lair?" Wolfram asked.

"Have no fear, Herr Eckhardt. Though the curious

Indians came close, the lair wasn't compromised, at least not by this first group."

"What do you mean by that?" Gunther shot back.

Ritter appeared perturbed. "Only a few hours ago a trio of transporters arrived at Gangotri. From the looks of things, I'd say they were of Russian manufacture, and are most likely based at Novolazarevskaya Station. They carried nine individuals in all, with five of them armed and definitely Spetsnaz types."

"That's most disturbing news, Adolph," Gunther commented.

"The worst is yet to come," Ritter warned. "Because the last I saw of them, they were headed directly into the mountains."

"My God!" Wolfram exclaimed. "Do you realize what this could mean? Captain Hartmann, we must get under way at once!"

"Thick ice . . . Thick ice . . ." the chief of the watch routinely reported as he monitored the *Springfield*'s upward scanning fathometer.

From his vantage point on the control room's periscope pedestal, Philip Michaels watched this scene unfold on an overhead video monitor. The crystal-clear picture was conveyed by a video camera mounted into the sail. The ice looked translucent and crystalline, and contained an abundance of veinlike fractures.

In addition to these real-time pictures of the ice cover, the sub's hydrophones provided an audio track. These powerful microphones, positioned throughout the hull, carried a cacophony of sounds ranging from sudden resonant cracks to long-drawn-out crunches, which were reminiscent of millions of ice cubes being crushed.

"Jesus, Skipper, look at the size of that pressure ridge we're passing under," the XO observed from his customary position at Michaels's side. "It must be at least sixty feet deep."

"I sure wouldn't want to tangle with that sucker while coming to periscope depth." Michaels knew very well that their current depth of 120 feet put them well out of harm's way.

"Captain." It was the voice of Lieutenant Carr from the nearby navigation plot. "Our latest fix puts us squarely within the access channel, with a good thousand feet of open water beneath our hull. The Princess Astrid coast can't be more than ten miles distant. How much further are we going in?"

"That depends on the whereabouts of Sierra One," Michaels replied as he caught the glance of his XO. "Call out the second we pass beneath an open lead, XO. I'm gonna pay Mr. Bodzin a quick call."

Michaels stepped off the raised platform and headed through the sliding doors of the sound shack. He found Bodzin huddled over his console, vainly attempting to sort out the confusing sounds of the surrounding ice.

"How's it going, Mr. Bodzin?" he asked, massaging the tense muscles of the technician's neck.

Bodzin disgustedly pushed back his headphones and arched his neck to get the most out of this badly needed massage. "I tell ya, Captain, it's an absolute mess out there."

"I've been listening to the passive feed myself in control and I know what you're up against," said Michaels. "But I'm still relying on your best guesstimate as to Sierra One's location."

Bodzin frowned. "We haven't had a decent sniff of 'em since they broke off their periscope scan of the Norwegian oil exploration ship, Captain. But if I was a bettin' man, I'd put my money on snaggin' Sierra One at the very end of this access channel that we're currently transiting, 'cause that's where they've been headin' all along."

"Those are my sentiments exactly, Mr. Bodzin. And since we've only got a couple of miles of this channel left, we'll soon enough know if we're winners or losers."

"Clear water, Captain!" came the excited voice of the

XO over the intercom. "We've got an open lead right above us."

Michaels reached up for the handset. "Take us up to periscope depth, XO. All stop. I'm on my way."

The captain left his senior sonar technician with a supportive wink and rushed back into the control room. The COB was calling out the latest depth figures as he climbed up onto the pedestal and reached the side of the Mk-18 search periscope.

"Eighty-five feet . . . eighty feet . . ."

"Let's see what we've got up there," Michaels whispered to his XO.

Not even waiting for them to attain periscope depth, Michaels raised the scope and angled the lens upward. The translucent glare of clear water topside indicated that the ice was indeed absent here. As COB called out sixty feet the lens broke the surface.

Michaels made a quick circular scan to check for any nearby obstacles. Though there were a number of wicked-looking pressure ridges, they didn't appear to offer an immediate threat, and he raised the scope to its maximum elevation.

For curiosity's sake, he decided to initiate his intensive scan on a due southerly bearing. In this manner he hoped to get his very first view of Antarctica. He grinned expectantly as a distant, snow-covered mountain range filled the lens. As he fine-tuned the focus he diverted the lens slightly downward to check the coastline.

"Holy Mother Mary!" he shouted, dumbfounded by the incredible scene that filled his lens.

Right before his eyes, surfaced in the midst of the ice less than a mile from the shore, was another submarine! It was a peculiar-looking vessel, unlike any modern class he had ever seen before.

With shaking hands, he increased the scope's lens magnification tenfold. It was then that he spotted the group gathered on the ice beside the sub's bow. They were in the process of climbing into several snowmobiles.

"XO," he managed to splutter. "You'll never believe what's out there on bearing one-seven-seven. Check it out on the Type 2!"

Perez hurriedly engaged the auxiliary periscope and focused in on the southern coastline. Even with Michaels's warning, he was little prepared for the scene that awaited him.

"Damn it, Skipper, that's a Type XXI German U-boat!"

As this astounding revelation registered in his mind Michaels noted a sudden glint of light coming from the submarine's sail.

"They've got lookouts posted on the sail. Down scopes!"

The XO somewhat reluctantly carried out this order, and as he backed away from the eyepiece a look of perplexed wonder filled his face. "Skipper, what in the hell is going on out there? That damn U-boat's a living relic. Are those our pirates?"

Michaels found his thoughts racing back to his briefing aboard the *Seaway Condor*. With Captain Robert Hartwell's suspicions apparently confirmed, he knew that there was only one course of action open to them.

"XO, it's time for our SEALs to earn their keep around here. Inform Collier and his bunch of malcontents to ready their ice gear. I'm gonna scare up some warm clothing myself. And then we're going to move *Springfield* down the coast, where you're going to drop us ashore so we can find out where those friggin' pirates are off to in those snowmobiles."

PART III

THE ICE LAIR

Nazism's deepest roots lie in dark, hidden places.

—HERMANN RAUSCHNING

17

They entered the mountains by way of a snow-covered tongue of ice that was an offshoot of an adjoining glacier. The range itself had a general east-west meander. Many of its jagged peaks were over ten thousand feet in height, with a broad, twisting valley at their base. As the ice tongue they were following intersected this valley they found themselves with a choice between two directions.

In order to cover as much territory as possible, they decided to split up at this point. The transporter carrying Mikhail Lopatin and two of his soldiers was assigned the eastern ridge, while the other two transporters headed off to the west. The general plan was to continue their search for the missing Indian vehicle and also keep an eye out for any possible volcanic activity. Two hours were allotted for this initial survey, after which time the teams would rendezvous back at the ice tongue to compare notes.

With the thermal, infrared satellite imaging map she had brought with her from McMurdo folded on her lap, Laurie traveled in one of the two transporters that were headed westward. Viktor Alexandrov was at the wheel, with Jacob Litvak at her other side. The transporter behind them was driven by Andrei Korsakov. He carried two members of the alpine team and a full load of geological research equipment.

Well accustomed to their current means of transport by now, Laurie was able to focus her full attention on the passing landscape. The dense snowpack of the valley provided a fairly comfortable ride, and the weather continued to cooperate, the pale blue sky covered with wispy white puffs of high-altitude cirrus clouds. This provided a perfect backdrop for the mountains.

With practiced eye, Laurie scanned the snow-covered ridges and peaks for signs of escaping volcanic smoke. Beside her, Jacob intently surveyed these same ridges for any tracks that might lead them to his sister.

"According to your satellite map, we're entering the sector of the greatest infrared activity," Viktor observed as he alertly steered them around a gaping fissure. "We should think about stopping shortly and trying a thermal scan of our own."

Laurie pointed to a bare rock ridge, approximately a quarter of a mile straight ahead of them on the right-hand side of the valley. "That rock shelf looks like a promising spot."

Jacob seemed to stir restlessly at this remark, and she considerately added, "Don't worry, Jacob. This scan won't take long."

"That's no problem at all," Jacob quickly replied. "I could use some time to stretch these long legs of mine."

To reach the rock shelf, Viktor had to guide the transporter up a moderately steep incline. The vehicle's tracked treads bit into the icy snow here, and he had to downshift in order to build up enough torque.

Before breaking to a halt, Viktor checked the rearview

mirror. "Andrei is turning out to be an excellent driver. Throughout this transit, he's been able to keep his transporter right behind us. He must have been taking some driving lessons from his new bride, Sasha, who's one of our motorpool's senior supervisors."

With the slightest of skids, the transporter ground to a halt beside the outcropping of rock. As they quickly exited the cab Viktor passed on a few words of warning: "Be very careful where you step, comrades. This snow cover veils a variety of pitfalls. And please, let's not wander out of sight of the transporters."

Jacob kept these remarks in mind as he reached into the back of the vehicle and pulled out his walking stick. The cypress staff made an excellent probe, and he began a tentative exploration of the area while the others unloaded the geological equipment from the second transporter.

It felt good to be out of the cramped cab. Given the lack of wind, the air temperature was almost bearable, feeling, oddly, not much different than a typical winter's day in Moscow. Jacob laughed at this thought and decided to check out the part of the valley that lay ahead of them.

With careful steps, he followed the ridge due west. An almost reverential quiet prevailed here, with the only sounds being the crunch of his footsteps and the distant, muffled voices of his companions. Several inches of fresh snow appeared to have fallen here recently, and he vainly searched the pristine powder for any track marks.

Though he knew that the chances of locating the Indian transporter were slim at best, the mere fact that it had escaped the conflagration back at Gangotri gave him hope. This was all he needed to continue this desperate search as long as necessary.

The ridge led him to an overlook formed out of an icy slab of flat, black rock. From this elevated vantage point, he had an excellent view of the valley. Except for several massive boulders sticking out of the snow, the route appeared to be clear. It extended almost due west for another half a mile before disappearing in a broad sweeping bend.

Though he was anxious to see what lay beyond this bend, Jacob realized that this was as far as he dared to proceed on foot. He made the prudent decision to return to the others.

He found them gathered around a variety of instruments. Laurie and Viktor were working on a portable seismograph, whose cable leads were attached to the rock outcropping they stood beside. Andrei and his associates were scanning the surrounding snowpack with a pair of unique devices: a handheld, infrared thermal imager, which looked like a large, barrel-shaped radar gun, and a magnetometer, whose sensors were encased in a saucer-shaped disk, which was attached to the end of a five-foot-long pole. The American vulcanologist had previously explained that such a device could prove invaluable in locating the magnetic field created by a subterannean stream of magma.

"Any luck?" Jacob asked the pair huddled over the seismograph.

"It appears that the stratum beneath us shows no seismic activity whatsoever," Laurie answered.

"So far Andrei's team has also come up with negative results," Viktor added.

"There's a broad bend in the valley up ahead," Jacob reported. "Perhaps you'll do better up there."

Jacob could not hide his impatient tone, and Laurie readily reached out and switched off the battery-powered seismograph. "Let's give it a try. This ridge is geologically inanimate."

This was all Viktor had to hear to call in the others. The gear was subsequently repacked away in the open bed of the second transporter. After a brief tea break, the vehicles were started up and off they went once more.

As they began their transit of the sweeping bend, Laurie noted the time. "We'll have to turn back shortly to make our planned rendezvous."

"I sure hope that Lieutenant Lopatin has had better luck than we have," Viktor said as he downshifted and turned the wheel hard to the left.

Although the very idea was unthinkable, Jacob asked, "What happens if he hasn't?"

Viktor hesitated before replying. "Then we're going to have to put our heads together and come up with a new plan of attack. As long as this good weather continues, we should try to spend as much time as possible getting further into the range. Perhaps we should put up our base camp at the rendezvous site. Then we'll be able to carefully organize each subsequent probe and all the time monitor our remaining fuel and food."

Jacob figured that at best they could continue the search for another two days before logistics concerns would force them back to Novo base. This certainly wasn't much time to cover the entire mountain range, and any hopes that he had of finding Anna were largely dashed.

There was a dejected cast to his gaze as he peered out the windshield. As she almost always seemed to do, Laurie sensed his mood and compassionately took his mittened hand in her own as the bend's broad meander led them to a somewhat narrow, upward-sloping trail. When the transporter began this climb Jacob placed all of his hopes on the next valley. He anxiously sat forward and, as the vehicle reached the trail's summit, was overwhelmed at the sight of an incredibly expansive, sweeping vista in front of them.

Viktor alertly braked to a halt, and as Andrei's transporter pulled up beside them they took a moment to survey the magnificent landscape. A series of gently rolling, snow-covered hills extended all the way to the base of a particularly massive mountain, with a distinctive, triangular peak. All together, the hills gave the impression of forming a single bowl, whose circumference was a good two miles wide.

It was apparent that there was a good bit of territory

for them to explore down there, and Jacob supposed it would take the better part of a day to cover it all. As he scanned the bowl to determine a possible search pattern, Viktor beckoned toward the other transporter that was parked to their right.

"It appears that something's caught Andrei's attention," he said matter-of-factly.

Jacob glanced to the other vehicle to see what Viktor was talking about. Andrei was clearly visible behind the wheel, a pair of binoculars at his brow and his hand excitedly pointing toward the base of the triangular peak. Jacob wasted no time pulling his own set of binoculars out from the glove compartment. His pulse was quickening and his hands were shaking as he peered through the dual eyepieces. He impatiently fumbled for the focus mechanism and had to strip off his gloves to fine-tune it properly. Only then was he afforded a clear, amplified view of the snow-filled terrain at the mountain's base.

Like a long-held dream come true, the lens filled with the bright orange body of a tracked transporter. It was parked on the snow, and even though no people were visible inside its enclosed cab, he knew without a doubt that his search was over.

"It's the Indian vehicle!" he shouted.

Without taking the time to confirm the sighting, Viktor shoved the transporter into gear and stomped down on its accelerator. The vehicle lurched foward with a guttural growl, and they sped down into the valley on a thick base of hard-packed snow.

It took the better part of fifteen minutes to reach the hillside where the orange vehicle was parked. So as not to disturb any leftover tracks, Viktor pulled to a halt several hundred yards short of the transporter. Jacob fought the urge to jump from the cab and sprint the remaining distance. At Viktor's prompting, the entire team gathered together on the snow and carefully planned their method of approach.

In order to disturb the least amount of evidence, they

decided to proceed on foot in single file. No one argued as Jacob volunteered to take the point position. With walking stick in hand, he began the tedious hike, his pace slowed by snowdrifts that extended well above his knees.

His heart was madly beating away in his chest from both physical exertion and emotional excitement. Sweat was starting to form on his forehead, and the cold air unmercifully knifed into his heaving lungs. Ignoring these discomforts, he continued without pause to a position ten yards away from the vehicle's cab. There, he briefly halted to catch his breath, wipe the sweat off his brow with the back of his gloved hand, and most important, regather his nerve. This was the moment he had been waiting for. Barely conscious of the others behind him, he whispered a brief silent prayer, then pushed himself onward.

His high hopes collapsed the moment he spotted the transporter's empty cab. A quick peek through the port-hole of the enclosed bed showed that it, too, was vacant, and Jacob fought the urge to break down in tears.

A supportive hand gripped his shoulder, and Viktor's deep voice tenderly addressed him. "I sincerely share your disappointment, Jacob. I, too, had hoped to find Anna waiting for us inside, calmly sipping a cup of tea."

"What in God's name could have happened to her?" Jacob managed. "Surely they couldn't have just gone and disappeared."

Viktor sighed heavily. "My best guess is that they hiked further into the foothills and set up camp, possibly in a snow cave. Her companion, Dr. Mahasaya, was a vet-eran polar explorer, and he would never have abandoned this transporter unless they had alternative shelter. Unfortunately, the recent heavy snowfall has blotted out any trace of their tracks."

"At least we know that they have to be close," Jacob said, the embers of hope springing to life in his heart.

"They're close all right," Viktor muttered while scan-ning the surrounding ridge. "And if I were them, I'd set up my camp up there, where the rock would block the wind."

Jacob looked up to see what Viktor was referring to. The ridge in question was less than a quarter of a mile distant. To get there, they'd have to cross a sloping incline, and it was decided to send two of the soldiers back for the transporters.

By this means of transit they reached the ridge. The snow-covered terrain they now found themselves on continued to slope gently upward, extending all the way to the solid rock shelf of the mountain's base.

While Viktor, Jacob, and the two soldiers began their search for tracks or other evidence of human habitation, Laurie and Andrei got on with their scientific work. As it turned out, Laurie's efforts showed almost immediate results, as the thermal imager registered a definite heat source beneath their feet. Minutes later Andrei excitedly informed her that he, too, had made a solid contact with the magnetometer. She hurried to his side and found him digging into the snow below with a folding shovel.

"If we've indeed managed to locate a lava tube, I seriously doubt that you're going to be able to get to it with that shovel," Laurie commented, smiling.

Though Andrei's English was extremely limited, he did his best to express himself without missing a stroke with the shovel. "No volcano. Metal!"

Shortly thereafter the head of his shovel made solid contact with a buried object. Andrei got down on his hands and knees, reached into the three-foot-deep hole he had dug, and used his knife to chop away the densely packed snow. It took several more minutes before his efforts succeeded, and he pulled free a five-foot-long, shiny metallic dart. It had a sharply pointed end and a metal tail shaped much like that of a feathered arrow. Yet it was the distinctive black design engraved on this tail that gained Laurie's complete attention, and she found herself stunned as she muttered, "My God, it's a swastika!"

She didn't wait any longer to call in the others. Laurie could only guess what the astounded Russians were saying as they passed around the dart and chattered away in their native tongue. Of all those present, Jacob appeared to be the most affected by this mysterious find. A peculiar, haunted expression of dread filled his face as he examined the dart while Viktor was explaining its likeliest origin to Laurie.

"If I'm not mistaken, this dart is one of the thousands that were dropped on New Schwabenland by the Germans in 1938. It was at this time that Hermann Göring sent Captain Alfred Ritscher to Antarctica to claim portions of the continent for the Nazis. The darts were dropped from the air during a Luftwaffe flyover of some ninety-seven thousand square miles of territory, and were intended as symbolic representations of the Third Reich's legal claim to this terrain."

Hearing this only intensified Jacob's distress. Surely the dart's discovery was no coincidence. It was just another shocking example of the dark forces that seemed to haunt his recent life. The mere fact that the abandoned Indian transporter lay close by seemed to indicate that his own sister had somehow been pulled into the black circle.

He couldn't shake the feeling that the discovery of this dart was a sign, a portent of even more horrible things to come. It was almost as if Wolfram Eckhardt himself had followed him these thousands of miles and left the swastika-embossed dart as a macabre calling card.

With this horrific thought, a wave of nausea overcame him. He swayed back dizzily, and as he did so he dropped the dart, which buried itself in the snow point-first.

At this moment Andrei's animated voice cried out from behind them. "Comrades, another discovery!"

Jacob summoned the self-control to turn around, and spotted Andrei halfway up the ridge, with the triangular mountain peak squarely behind him. The young Russian had just laid down his magnetometer and was frantically digging into the side of the snow-covered hill with his small shovel.

Jacob joined the others as they rushed up the ridge. When they reached Andrei's side, the young Russian breathlessly cried, "There's something buried down here as well, but this object is much larger!"

Laurie had brought the thermal imager with her, and as she scanned the adjoining area a piercing electronic buzz sounded from the instrument.

"Whatever Andrei's discovered, there's an intense heat source associated with it," she eagerly reported. "This could be the magma tube that the infrared satellite scan picked up."

In a flurry of Russian, Viktor ordered the two soldiers to pull out their folding shovels and assist Andrei. They immediately did so, and together the trio began a hurried excavation.

"How deep do you think they'll have to go?" Viktor asked.

Laurie answered while scanning the ever-deepening hole with the constantly buzzing thermal imager. "I can't really say. All I know for certain is that the source of the heat emission is very strong and undercuts a major portion of this ridge."

"Jacob," Viktor interjected. "As an archaeologist, you've surely got plenty of expertise in excavating. Is this the proper way to go about it?"

Jacob answered while doing his best to ignore the gathering tightness in his gut. "Comrades," he said to the trio of diggers, "that's deep enough. Expand the diameter of the hole so that the walls don't collapse and bury you."

The diggers did as instructed. As the excavation widened into a six-by-nine-foot rectangle, Jacob added, "It should be safe to go deeper now. But get out of there the moment that snow shows the least signs of shifting."

Andrei responded with a brief wave, and as he swept his shovel downward into the hard, icy depths of the pit, there was a loud, metallic clang.

"There's no lava tube down there," Viktor said. "It's something of human origin!"

This shocking observation was seemingly confirmed as the diggers carefully removed several additional inches of snow and a dark reddish plate of rusted sheet metal came into view. As more snow was removed the size of this plate grew until it was almost as wide as the entire hole.

"It almost looks like a door of some sort," Laurie said.

"That it does," said Viktor. "Andrei, are those hinges on its left side?"

Andrei got onto his knees and brushed away the snow on the left portion of the metal sheet. "I believe so," he muttered, awestruck.

Jacob couldn't resist climbing down into the pit and having a look himself. Viktor and Laurie followed, and together they reached down and grabbed the right side of this apparent portal.

"Let's try opening it on a count of three," said Viktor. "One . . . two . . . three!"

There was a brief creaking noise as they collectively pulled up on the metal edge. Yet it failed to budge, prompting Jacob to reorganize their effort.

"Andrei, I need all of you over here with your shovels," he instructed. "On the count of three, I want you to pry upward on the lip as we do our best to lift it."

There was barely room for all six of them. Jacob positioned himself at the very bottom of the metal plate, and this time he was the one to call out the countdown.

"One . . . two . . . three!"

With a collective grunt, all six of them lifted upward. The cold metal momentarily flexed, and as the rusty creaking noise sounded once more, Jacob urged them on.

"Come on, comrades, put your backs into it!"

This renewed effort caused the creaking sound to increase steadily. Just as the wrenching, grating noise reached an almost deafening level, the metal plate flexed upward and swung open completely.

Momentarily caught off guard by the abruptness of

this change, Jacob found himself staring into a dark, rectangularly shaped pit. A warm, dank wave of fetid air rose up from this mysterious abyss and engulfed him. For a frightening moment he could have sworn that this was the exact same scent that had so repelled him in far-off Mato Grosso.

"There's a stairway in there!" Viktor exclaimed. "What in the hell have we stumbled upon?"

Jacob could just hear the trickling sound of running water down below. As Laurie joined him at the base of the portal, she pointed the thermal imager into the blackness. A resounding buzz roared from the device, and she flipped off the switch.

"Whatever's down there, it's putting out an incredible amount of heat. Why, I can feel it all the way up here!"

"Before we go down and find out for ourselves, it's imperative that we send someone back to the rendezvous point to bring back Lieutenant Lopatin," Viktor interjected. "It would also be prudent to outfit ourselves with flashlights. It's as dark as Hades down there."

There was a clearly audible groan of protest from the lips of the two soldiers as Viktor chose them to carry out this directive. Relieved not to have been picked for this task, Andrei volunteered to run back to the transporter and get the flashlights and a camera in order to document this event properly. He returned just as the other transporter began the long trip east across the valley.

"Well, comrades," Viktor said as he switched on his halogen torch, "who would like to go first?"

Andrei triggered the camera's strobe while taking the first picture of the open portal. This blinding flash momentarily illuminated the cave's black depths, and Jacob dared to take the first step forward.

A steep, narrow wooden stairway conveyed him down into an immense subterranean grotto. The sound of running water was ever-present here, and the alien warmth was so strong that he was able to remove his gloves and parka.

As he scanned the rough-hewn rock walls with his flashlight, Jacob fought off the first rising hint of claustrophobic dread. Even with his parka removed, the sweat poured off his forehead, and it was an effort just to breathe.

"This place is amazing!" Laurie marveled as she completed her transit of the stairway and directed the beam of her torch into the cave's stygian depths.

"We've certainly managed to stumble into something other than a lava tube," Viktor put in as he joined her at the base of the stairs. "Let's take Jacob's example and remove our coats. It's positively stifling down here."

Andrei was the last one down the stairway. He announced his arrival with the constantly flashing strobe of his 35mm camera.

Meanwhile Jacob did his best to summon his self-control. The presence of the others was somewhat reassuring. Their hollow voices echoed off the walls and gave the impression that there were a multitude of people present here.

"Look, over there against that far wall!" Laurie exclaimed as she continued farther into the cave's depths. "I believe we've finally solved the mystery that I was sent from McMurdo to investigate. You're right, Viktor. It's not a lava tube at all but a thermal hot spring that's responsible for those infrared satellite images."

The others quickly gathered at her side, and together, with their flashlights, they illuminated a twelve-foot-wide channel of fast-moving water. Thick tendrils of steam constantly rose from the surface of this bubbling spring, which continued deep into the blackened recesses.

"How very remarkable," Viktor exclaimed. "To think that nature has conveniently provided this effective heat source. No wonder someone decided to excavate here. Men could live in such a place for months on end and never have to worry about fuel to provide warmth."

"Any idea as to who originally discovered this place?" Laurie asked.

Before this question could be answered, Andrei's camera noisily triggered. Its strobe illuminated an adjoining rock shelf, where a number of good-sized metal crates were neatly lined up.

Jacob was the first one to view this discovery. "Laurie, I believe that the answer to your question lies inside those boxes over there."

All but forgetting about the hot spring, they followed the direction of Jacob's torch and made their way over to the rock shelf. They counted a total of twelve separate crates sitting on the flat, chiseled floor. Each box was solidly constructed out of a bronzelike material and had the exact same dimensions as the others, approximately two feet long, one foot wide, and one foot deep.

"I should think that every archaeologist dreams of a discovery such as this," Viktor said with rising excitement. "Jacob, it's only fitting that you be the one to open the lid of that first crate."

Still unable to shake the feeling of impending dread that possessed him, Jacob nervously knelt down beside the first of the metal boxes. With sweaty palms, he gripped the heavy lid and yanked it backward.

It opened with a loud pop as the waterproof sealant that had lined the lid's lip tore away. The spicy-sweet scent of rich incense wafted up to Jacob's nostrils. A mere whiff of this exotic odor triggered thoughts of past digs, and Jacob eagerly searched the crate's interior.

He carefully removed a thick layer of white cotton wadding. Beneath this were two bundles. Both were wrapped in yet more wadding, and he reached into the box and pulled out the larger of the two. Laurie assisted him in peeling away a long, thin stip of wadding, revealing an ornate golden goblet, with a tightly fitting, jewel-encrusted lid. She gasped in amazement, and while Andrei snapped a photograph, Viktor knelt down and gingerly accepted the goblet from Jacob's firm grasp.

"How very magnificent," he said. "I wonder how old it is?"

"Though I'm far from an expert in this time period, the goblet appears to be designed in a style characteristic of the Middle Ages," Jacob replied. "If it proves authentic, it could very well be over a thousand years old."

Viktor lovingly stroked its domed lid. "Shall we open it up and see what it holds?"

"Let's check the contents of the other crates first," Jacob suggested.

Viktor gently placed the cup on the ledge and helped Laurie unwrap the second bundle. Oddly enough, this one held what appeared to be a single, pointed iron spearhead. A nail of some sort was mounted inside the recessed blade, held in place by a wrapping of golden threads.

"Why in the world would someone go to all this trouble to preserve an old spearhead?" Viktor wondered aloud.

Jacob was unable to answer this question and instead turned his attention to the next crate in line. Its lid opened with a familiar pop, and once more a thick layer of protective wadding veiled its contents. He pushed aside this packing material and uncovered a single wrapped bundle.

There was a gathering tenseness in his stomach as he allowed Laurie to help him unravel the heavy bundle. It seemed to take an eternity to remove all the wrapping, and as the American woman pulled the last strip of wadding aside, Jacob peered down at the bundle's contents and gasped.

With unbelieving eyes, he took in a most familiar stack of hand-sized, four-inch-wide, tarnished copper plates. There were nine of them in all, each separated by a sheet of cotton gauze. It took only one look at the Mishnaic Hebrew script that was inscribed on their length for Jacob to exclaim in wonder, "No, it can't be!"

"Whatever's the matter with you, Jacob?" Viktor asked, worry in his tone. "You look like you've just seen a ghost."

"I have!" Jacob retorted, his face ashen and the sweat now dripping from his forehead.

Staggered by this incredible discovery, Jacob shakily

sorted through the individual plates. They appeared to be exact doubles of the scroll he had recently uncovered on the shores of the Dead Sea. Incredibly, someone had even managed to cut up the tarnished copper scroll segments, just as he and Uri Weinberg had.

A hasty translation of the first plate's top line confirmed his suspicions. It was simply titled *Rite of Awakening*. He knew at that moment, without a doubt in his mind, that destiny had led him to the previously missing sister scroll.

Could he ever forget that frustrating moment when their excavation of the ceramic scroll jar showed that someone had beaten them to the treasure inside? And then there was the terrifying earthquake, and their glorious discovery of the jar holding an intact scroll. Since Uri and Shai Weinberg were the only ones alive who could properly appreciate the miraculous nature of this discovery, Jacob did his best to clear his mind and explain what it was that shocked him so.

"In a manner of speaking, I guess you could say that I've been searching for this very scroll for some time now," he managed. "I realize that it's going to sound crazy, but not only did I previously know of this scroll's existence, but I discovered its sister document, barely a week ago, in the Judean wilderness!"

"My, that is an incredible story." Viktor was beginning, in spite of himself, to question Jacob's sanity.

Laurie also found herself concerned about Jacob's mental state as she noticed the sweat pouring off his brow. "No wonder you're shocked by this discovery," she said carefully. "I'd say that all of us have seen our fair share of wonders today."

"And Lord only knows what's awaiting us in those other crates," Viktor added.

Andrei ignored or didn't understand their comments, and instead took this opportunity to spread out the nine plates on the flat rock shelf. He then took a snapshot of each one.

"I'm almost afraid to ask, but what's so important about these scrolls?" Viktor wanted to know. "Someone has sure gone to a lot of trouble to store them here in this godforsaken land of ice and snow."

"I bet the German dart that we found outside can be directly tied in with this cave," Laurie surmised. "Who knows, perhaps this treasure once belonged to the Nazis, and this grotto was discovered by the Germans to hide it in."

"That's certainly possible, my dear," Viktor said.

Jacob was considering this very same thought himself, and he all but ignored a sudden cold draft on his neck. Yet it proved to be the harbinger of the hollow sound of distant footsteps, and this quickly shook him from his reverie.

Viktor also heard these footsteps, and he alertly turned toward the stairway. "Lieutenant Lopatin?" he called out tensely. "Mikhail Sergeivich, is that you?"

18

Wolfram Eckhardt's first reaction upon spotting the open doorway to the ice cave had been utter horror. For this secret location to have been compromised after all these years was unthinkable. Soon, however, he found his disappointment momentarily tempered at the sight of a parked transporter nearby. Since it was currently vacant, surely its occupants were belowground, in the subterranean realm of the Ice Lair. With the hope that the invaders had not stumbled upon the great secrets of the lair, Wolfram anxiously assembled his men outside the grotto's entrance.

"So, it seems that providence has seen fit to lead trespassers into the hallowed ground of the Ice Lair," he said forcefully. "We must protect its secrets at all costs!"

Adolph Ritter rammed a 9mm round into the chamber of his compact Heckler and Koch MP5 submachine gun and guiltily replied, "As keeper of the lair, it's my responsibility to eliminate this nest of Russian vermin, Herr Eckhardt. I should have killed them the moment I spotted their transporters back at Gangotri."

"With *Ice Wolf*'s arrival, we all share in this responsibility, Adolph," Wolfram returned. "Now, didn't you mention that you spotted three Russian transporters parked amid the station's ruins?"

"That I did, sir."

Wolfram caught the glance of Gunther Hartmann. "Captain, I think it would be wise to set up an armed welcoming committee out here in case the two remaining transporters should return."

"That's an excellent idea." Gunther assigned six of his men to this detail.

With Ritter's expert assistance, a suitable ambush site was picked out on a snow ridge approximately a half mile east of the cave. The sentry detail used two of the Snow-Cats to proceed to this strategic position. This left Wolfram, Gunther, Ritter, and Otto Brauer free to focus on the occupants of the cave.

"I don't want to just go down into the Ice Lair with guns blazing," Wolfram warned Ritter and Otto. "Remember, there are priceless relics stored there. And besides, before we go and kill these trespassers, I'd like to see who it is that destiny picked to crack our secret. Adolph, if you can manage to keep your itchy trigger finger off that gun of yours, I'd like you to hit them with the portable spotlight. The halogen beam will temporarily blind them, and we should be able to take possession of any weapons they might have brought along."

"Chief Brauer," Gunther put in, "we'll rely on you to provide cover fire. And please keep Herr Eckhardt's words of advice in mind. We want no gunplay unless it's absolutely necessary."

Otto nodded and turned to help Ritter remove the portable spotlight from the storage well of the lead Snow-Cat. As they prepared this device Gunther pulled his pistol, a Glock model 17, from its holster. The Austrian handgun sported an ultralight frame formed from a single piece of polymer. Its magazine carried seventeen rounds of 9mm Parabellum ammunition, and during sessions on the firing range, Gunther had admired the pistol's smooth action and superb accuracy. Since the Glock 17 had no external hammer assembly or external safety mechanism, Gunther cautiously chambered a round and returned the pistol to its holster.

"Well, Captain, it seems that the moment of truth is upon us," said Wolfram, who carried no armament. "If you don't mind, I'd like to follow Adolph down the stairway. You can come next, leaving Brauer a clear line of fire from the top."

This was fine with Gunther, who found himself somewhat apprehensive as he watched Ritter sling his submachine gun over his shoulder and ready the spotlight. Wolfram didn't seem the least bit nervous, and Gunther tried his best to follow his example.

At Wolfram's hand signal, Ritter quietly began his way down the stairs. The old-timer waited for him to descend two steps before beginning his own slow transit. Gunther resolutely followed.

The stairway was narrow and fairly steep. Gunther proceeded carefully, as Ritter had yet to activate the spotlight and the darkness was all-encompassing. He was surprised by the warmth, and the fact that flowing water could be heard in the background. Just when it appeared that they were going to be able to take the trespassers by surprise, a deep voice broke from the blackness.

"Lieutenant Lopatin?" this voice called in Slavic-accented English. "Mikhail Sergeivich, is that you?"

The beam of a flashlight angled toward them, but before it could illuminate the stairway, Ritter switched on the spotlight. It only took the blond-haired commando a second or two to locate his quarry. Just as Wolfram had predicted, the wide, powerful beam locked in on the interlopers and froze them in their tracks. Gunther counted four of them, one of them an attractive young woman.

None of them wore coats or appeared to be armed, and it was obvious that they had been caught looting the Ice Lair's treasure red-handed.

"Please be so kind as to remain absolutely still," Wolfram warned as he reached the bottom of the stairs. "Because if any of you should make the least move, my comrades won't hesitate to shoot to kill."

"We are not armed, and mean you no harm," responded the oldest of the trespassers, a tall, barrel-chested man in his midfifties, who stood beside the second of two open crates.

As Gunther made his way to the bottom of the stairs, he noted that the woman and a rugged-looking, middle-aged man were kneeling on the ground beside this metal box, with a young, red-cheeked photographer standing close beside them. All of them looked petrified with fear, and Gunther sensed that they would offer little resistance.

"Could it be?" Wolfram remarked as he slowly approached the foursome, his astonished gaze focused on the man who knelt on the floor. "Good heavens, it is!"

Gunther could only surmise that the old-timer knew this individual. This strange fact appeared to be confirmed as Wolfram called out with a tone tinged with disbelief, *"Dr. Jacob Litvak, is that really you?"*

The man to whom these words were addressed appeared absolutely awestruck. His mouth dropped open, his eyes went wide with terror, as if he were peering out at a ghost.

"Don't look so shocked, Jacob Litvak," said Wolfram. "After all, no one should be more surprised by your presence here than I. Though, come to think of it, I did have divine warning of this meeting."

Looking over to Gunther at this point, Wolfram added, "Do you remember when you asked me about the results of my tarot-card reading back on *Ice Wolf,* Captain? Well, among the cards I drew was that of the cosmic interloper, the zero card of the major arcana that's labeled the Fool. And to show you how effective the cards are in predicting the future, I'd like to introduce my old friend, Dr. Jacob Litvak, who is none other than a living incarnation of this very same card."

Though Gunther had trouble understanding this cryptic statement, there was little doubt in his mind that the occultist took it most seriously. The sub captain looked on as Wolfram crossed the cavern's smooth rock floor and stood directly above the man known as Jacob Litvak.

"So you survived your stay in the Mato Grosso after all," Wolfram remarked snidely. "I do hope that your hangover has finally worn off. Because the last I saw of you, you were sprawled out on the dirt clearing, on the very edge of that fine line between sanity and madness."

"I prayed that I'd have another chance to bring you to justice," Jacob managed, his voice trembling with shock. "But never did I dream that my prayers would be answered so soon."

Wolfram snickered. "So, once more you display the foolhardy bravado for which the zero card is so famous. This time, however, you're in an even weaker bargaining position, as your Israeli friends aren't here to back you up. I don't suppose that you're going to introduce this new bunch that you've managed to round up."

Not waiting for Jacob to respond, the man whose voice Gunther had first heard as they entered the cave made the introductions. "My name is Dr. Viktor Alexandrov, and I'm the director of Russia's Novolazarevskaya Station. Beside me is one of my assistants, Andrei Korsakov, and the young woman in our midst is a special guest from America, Dr. Laurie Anderson."

"Dr. Viktor Alexandrov," Wolfram repeated, momentarily lost in thought. "The famed mycologist, by any chance?"

As Viktor nodded, a sardonic grin broke across Wolfram's face. "My, this afternoon is proving to be just full of surprises. Dr. Alexandrov, I'm an amateur mycologist myself, and your field guide of Northern European mush-rooms is an important part of my library."

"I'm so glad to hear that, comrade," Viktor returned. "Now that you know I'm a man of science, would you mind diverting that spotlight, and then explaining what this hostile reception is all about. Like I said before, we are not armed and mean you no harm."

"Adolph, redirect the beam," Wolfram ordered.

"But, Herr Eckhardt," Ritter protested, "what about our line of fire?"

"Oberleutnant Ritter, you will do as ordered!" the octogenarian commanded.

The headstrong commando reluctantly lowered the spotlight and, as a compromise, set it on the lid of one of the as yet unopened crates. This provided Wolfram adequate light to survey the objects that had already been unwrapped.

"Ah, I see that you've been messing with things that don't belong to you." He sounded like a parent scolding a naughty child. "And I must say, you've certainly gone right to the heart of the collection. Tell me, was it the Grail that drew you here, or perhaps it was the Spear of Destiny? I have no doubt what Dr. Litvak has designs on. Did you get a chance to peruse this remarkable scroll, Doctor? Or were you just planning to loot it?"

"You have it all wrong, comrade." Viktor's tone was placating. "We didn't come here for these objects that you speak of. In fact, we had absolutely no idea that this cave even existed until just an hour ago."

"So now you're going to tell me that you just happened to stumble upon it while innocently hunting for mushrooms," returned Wolfram with a laugh.

"Laurie," Viktor prodded, "tell the man what brought us here originally."

Laurie, who stood terrified during this entire perplexing encounter, nervously cleared her throat. "I was sent into this mountain range by the American authorities back at McMurdo Station. I'm a vulcanologist by trade, and it appears that a recent infrared thermal imaging satellite scan of the area picked up the heat emissions of this cave's hot spring. Not knowing what they were dealing with, I was sent here to find out if volcanic activity was its cause."

Wolfram snickered. "That's a good one, Dr. Anderson. But I'm afraid you're going to need a better story than that. Surely you must take me for a bigger fool than Jacob here to expect me to believe that it was an accident that brought you to the Ice Lair."

"But it was!" Viktor pleaded.

"Enough of this nonsense!" Wolfram was clearly angry. "Dr. Alexandrov, you of all people insult me with this cock-and-bull tale. Do you really think me so stupid? I know very well what brought you to this cave, and from the looks of it, only our unannounced arrival kept you from attaining your goal."

With these words Wolfram reached out to the ledge and grasped the golden goblet. He held it briefly in front of Viktor's puzzled eyes, as if to tantalize him, then pulled it away and slowly unscrewed its lid.

"This goblet that you so unceremoniously removed from its storage crate is one of the most legendary relics in all the world. It has been the subject of countless quests by historians, mystics, and adventurers. The last people to display it publicly were the Cathars of southern France. They even built a castle, Montsegur, to hold this priceless, revered object.

"For a thousand years it remained hidden in the shadows of this same castle's ruins. Not even the Crusaders were able to locate it. By divine destiny, I was the one led to the secret grotto where this cup was locked away, during a Nazi-sponsored archaeological expedition in 1932. I was but an innocent, impressionable lad at the time, little prepared for the great secret that was about to be revealed to me. But from the moment my excavation pick broke through the walls of the secret grotto, I became the new keeper of the Grail!"

With a final turn, Wolfram completed his freeing of the goblet's jewel-encrusted cover. Yet, before removing it completely, he scanned the faces of his audience and dramatically added, "Prepare yourselves to become initiates in the greatest mystery of all time—the true secret of the Holy Grail!"

With this, he pulled back the cover and revealed the cup's contents. It proved to be Viktor who identified the wafer-thin, blackish-green, button-sized objects that filled the goblet practically to its brim.

"Why, those look like dried mushrooms!" he cried.

There was a devilish gleam in Wolfram's eyes as he nodded. "Splendid guess, Dr. Alexandrov. And I'm certain that you'll be fascinated to learn that these mushrooms that the Cathars handed down to us are far from your ordinary variety. In honor of the sacred cup that was designed to hold them, feast your eyes on the Amanita jasperia, the legendary Jasper Cup, or as they were better known to the Cathars, Lucifer's Flesh!"

This macabre term had a very special meaning to Jacob. He had only recently come across it for the first time while translating the newly discovered copper scroll with Uri Weinberg. At that time, however, he had absolutely no idea what it meant. Thus he attentively listened as Wolfram continued.

"As I was soon to learn, the so-called Holy Grail was much more than a mere cup. The Grail itself was a symbolic term, that referred, in fact, to these mushrooms. As both Herrs Alexandrov and Litvak will attest, the hallucinatory properties of certain species of mushrooms are very real. Somewhere in the cradle of time, the ancients discovered that the most potent of all visionary fungi was the Amanita jasperia. Some chroniclers even go to the extreme of associating this variety of mushroom with the Garden of Eden's tree of good and evil, thus making Lucifer's Flesh the direct cause of man's fall from divine grace."

Both Laurie and Jacob looked at Viktor for confirmation of this revelation. Viktor acknowledged their glances with a solemn nod while Wolfram added, "I myself was totally unaware of the true power of the Grail until a chance discovery in the Judean wilderness opened my eyes. I see that in addition to the Jasper Cup, you've also removed the scroll on whose copper plates is recorded the manner in which the ancients lifted the veil to the spirit and called down the divine forces of the heavens. They did so with an intricate ritual that this amazing scroll documents. And as I was soon to learn, an invaluable element in this ritual's successful performance was none other than the mushrooms that I had unearthed only a few years earlier."

"Tell them how you misused this ritual to possess the souls of Adolf Hitler, Heinrich Himmler, and the other Nazi leaders!" Jacob interrupted, having heard enough of this self-serving story. "Tell them how you called down the black powers of Lucifer to unleash the greatest evil that this planet has ever known!"

The distinctive metallic sound of a gun being prepared to fire emanated from the direction of the stairway. This was accompanied by a deep male voice.

"Herr Eckhardt, please allow me to silence this swine!"

"Easy, Otto," Wolfram said. "Dr. Litvak's time of reckoning will come soon enough. Yet before it does, I think it only fitting that he goes to meet his Maker with his ill-conceived notions corrected."

Wolfram paused for a moment before addressing his next remarks to Jacob. "It's obvious that you're still totally blind. The black powers that you speak of—what do you really know of their essence? Dare to open your mind to the teachings of the Cathars, and you'll realize what a great joke has been played on humanity.

"I tried to open your eyes to this greatest of all hoaxes during our last meeting. But your foolish pigheadedness prevailed, and you proved yourself unworthy of possessing the truth. Don't you understand, Jacob Litvak? The sacred God that you worship in your synagogues and churches, that's the real source of this blackness you incessantly talk about. The Cathars dared to lift the veil, and saw beyond the Vatican's materialistic lust for power. Organized religion was the real vehicle in which Lucifer took his earthly form, and you need to look no further than your local temple or chapel to see how effective his reign has been.

"Yes, I don't deny that I used the ritual of the Grail to enlighten our National Socialist forefathers in this most basic of truths. And the powers that you mistake for evil are nothing but human weaknesses in their most extreme form, as the early Nazi movement failed due to the same selfish, self-gratifying lusts that the Cathars warned so about.

"But rest assured, we have learned from our mistakes. This time as we utter the sacred words of the Rite of Awakening and consume the sacred flesh of the Amanita jasperia, the spirit will be tapped by worthy, enlightened souls, who are prepared to apply the great powers that the ritual shall unleash. These powers will then be channeled throughout the earthly plane by yet another relic that you have already managed to exhume here today."

Wolfram stepped forward and removed from the ledge the spear point that Viktor, Laurie, and Jacob had pulled from the first crate. He carefully touched its sharpened end and spoke reverently.

"I found this third, all-important portion of the holy Cathar trinity in a display case at Vienna's Hofburg Museum, of all places. This somewhat insignificant-looking spear point is in reality one of the most powerful talismans ever created. It gained its historical prominence two thousand years ago, when the Roman centurion Longinus used it to pierce the ribs of a crucified religious heretic on the eve of the Jewish sabbath. That object you see wrapped inside the spear with golden thread is a nail from this same cross, and the name of the man whose chest this spear point penetrated is none other than Jesus Christ."

Both Laurie and Viktor appeared genuinely impressed with this revelation. Wolfram noted their reactions, and quickly resumed his discourse.

"Legend has it that this sacred spear point was forged by the ancient Hebrew prophet Phineas, its metal magically conveyed to earth in the form of a meteorite. Long before Christ's arrival, the talisman guided the destinies of such notable biblical figures as Joshua and Solomon. After the crucifixion, it continued emanating its divine powers, influencing the lives of Constantine the Great, Justinian, Karl Martel, Charlemagne, and Hitler's alter ego, Frederick Barbarossa. Together with the ritual of the scroll, we shall use this sacred talisman to channel the powers of the heavens and reawaken the Aryan peoples so that they will take their rightful places at the helms of world governments. And in this manner, the rightful Cathar god shall be reborn, under the glorious banner of the thousand-year Fourth Reich."

"This mystical tale all sounds so very innocent and poetic," Jacob interjected. "Only I'll never forget that it's coming from the same lips that brought the world Auschwitz, Dachau, and Buchenwald, the greatest evil of the twentieth century! My own mother just escaped execution in that hellhole called Ravensbruck. There, she miraculously crawled from her intended grave into the awaiting arms of my father, who was one of the first Soviet soldiers to enter the camp. It was the evil that he encountered that day that prompted him to undertake a life's quest. This quest had only one purpose—to bring to justice the beasts responsible for the concentration camps and, in this way, ensure that such an evil would never be unleashed again. Upon his death, I swore to continue his life's work. Now that I've had this chance to hear your twisted philosophy, Wolfram Eckhardt, I know in my heart that my decision was the correct one. You must pay for these crimes that you've perpetrated against humanity!"

Watching this scene from the base of the stairway, Gunther Hartmann was incredulous. The atmosphere inside the cave was almost palpably charged with emotion. As Gunther anxiously awaited Wolfram's response to the Russian's harangue, a muffled, explosive crack sounded in the distance. This was followed by a trio of deep, rumbling blasts, which caused the ground below to tremble.

"Captain Hartmann!" Wolfram shouted. "Get up there and see what that commotion is all about. Chief Brauer, I need you down here this instant, to help Ritter repack the collection while I watch the prisoners."

Gunther allowed Otto Brauer time to complete his rapid descent down the stairway before beginning his own climb. Yet more explosive cracks sounded as he cleared the open portal and found himself outside.

After the alien warmth of the cavern, the cold hit him with a vengeance. He tried his best to ignore the raw, numbing chill as he crouched down on the snow and scanned the valley below.

It didn't take him long to locate the disturbance's source. The staccato bursts of firing submachine guns drew his gaze to the east. There, approximately a half mile away, a pair of large, bright yellow transporters could be seen parked on the snow. Most of the gunfire was coming from the surrounding hills, with sporadic bursts of return fire coming from the men trapped behind these transporters.

Gunther couldn't help but smile as he noted the perfect location of the ambush site that Ritter had chosen for the members of the ice team. As the commando had so wisely predicted, any trespassing vehicles would choose the smoothest terrain for their approach. With this in mind, the team dug in on each side of the ridge, and now had the poor Russians in a deadly cross fire.

Certain that his men would eventually prevail, Gunther turned back to the cave to update the others. As he ducked inside, the warmth greeted him like an old friend. He hesitated a moment at the top of the stairway to allow his eyes to adjust to the sudden darkness. There was a noticeable lack of conversation coming from the cave's recesses, and as he began his descent he could make out Ritter and Otto Brauer impatiently waiting at the foot of the steps. They held one of the closed crates between them, and as soon as Gunther passed, they rapidly climbed the stairway and brought the box outside.

Gunther found the others gathered on the smooth rock banks of the grotto's subterranean hot spring. Wolfram sat on a rounded boulder, his submachine gun trained on the four trespassers, who silently sat on the ground before him.

"Herr Eckhardt," Gunther said breathlessly, "the ice team has succeeded in ambushing the two remaining Russian transporters. Both vehicles are stopped dead in their tracks, with their occupants fighting for their lives."

This news caused Viktor to moan, "Poor Mikhail and the members of the alpine unit. I've sent them to their deaths!"

"Don't be so hard on yourself, Dr. Alexandrov," Wolfram advised. "Leadership does have its price, and you're getting but a small taste of what it's like to have to send men into battle."

Otto Brauer and Ritter hurried by carrying yet another of the crates. Wolfram beckoned Gunther to join him beside the gurgling stream. With one eye on his four prisoners, the occultist calmly commented, "Captain Hartmann, did Heinrich ever tell you what this cave was originally intended to hold?"

Gunther shook his head, and Wolfram continued. "Would you believe that at one time this site was proposed as the location of Adolf Hitler's hideaway? It was intended to take the place of the Führer's beloved Eagle's Nest in Berchtesgaden, should it be necessary for him to go into exile. Captain Ritscher himself was the one who first spotted the cave's mouth from the air in January 1939. Its presence was revealed by the tendrils of steam that mysteriously rose into the air here, steam that was created by this very stream.

"Several occultists on my staff called this cave the New Thule, after the legendary home of the Aryan people. And in a way, it's served this very function, by providing a safe repository for the collection that will allow the Reich's rebirth."

A series of muffled explosions could clearly be heard in the distance, above the constant rippling sound of the cascading waters. Gunther took this as a sign that the Russians were putting up more of a fight than he had anticipated.

Wolfram apparently shared this concern, and shouted, "Ritter! Are you finished yet?"

The commando's breathless voice emerged from the direction of the stairway. "We've only got two more crates to go, sir!"

Wolfram stood and addressed his four prisoners. "We'll be leaving you shortly. Yet before we go, one thing still bothers me. If what you say is true, and it was the search for a possible volcano that drew you here, what in the world is Jacob Litvak doing in your midst? Has our esteemed archaeologist been practicing geology in his spare time? Or perhaps Herr Litvak is looking for the remains of lost Antarctic civilizations?"

"I've come here in search of my sister, Anna," Jacob replied simply.

"Your sister?" Wolfram repeated. "To tell you the truth, I always thought you were an only child. What, may I ask, was your sister doing here?"

"Dr. Anna Litvak is part of my staff back at Novolazarevskaya Station," Viktor told him. "She is an expert polar geologist, who was on assignment at the nearby Dakshan Gangotri facility when we lost contact with her. We have good cause to believe that she was recently in this valley, as we found the Indian transporter in which she was reported to be traveling abandoned nearby."

A sardonic grin turned Wolfram's thin lips, and he called out, "Oberleutnant Ritter!"

The sound of heavy panting could be heard from the stairway, followed by the breathless voice of the commando. "Yes, sir. I'm coming!"

Seconds later Ritter emerged from the shadows. He was clearly out of breath. Yet this didn't deter him from saying, "I'm sorry for the delay, Herr Eckhardt. We've completed removing the last of the crates, and Chief Brauer is presently stowing them in the Snow-Cats."

Most satisfied with this report, Wolfram asked, "Oberleutnant, after taking care of the situation at the Indian base, did you encounter two of their scientists out here in this valley?"

Ritter readily replied. "Yes, I did, sir. It was an older Indian man and a middle-aged Russian woman."

Wolfram appeared to be relishing the moment as he glanced down at Jacob Litvak. "And what did you do to these individuals, Herr Ritter?"

"Per your standing directive, I shot them dead, sir, and then dumped their corpses into the glacier."

Wolfram watched as this matter-of-fact answer had its desired effect on Jacob. The archaeologist's face was filled with hopelessness and sorrow. As his emotions shifted into blind rage he leaped up and lunged at Wolfram.

"You bastard! I'll see you in hell!" he yelled viciously.

"Jacob, no!" Viktor cried, also leaping to his feet.

This was all Ritter had to see to raise the compact submachine gun he had slung over his shoulder and let loose a short, deafening barrage. The whining 9mm bullets wildly ricocheted overhead, and the American woman began screaming hysterically as both Jacob Litvak and Viktor Alexandrov went slumping to the ground, blood spraying from their wounds.

"Shall I shoot the rest of them?" Ritter asked casually.

"Don't bother wasting the bullets," Wolfram retorted. "Come, Captain Hartmann, Oberleutnant Ritter, let's get out of here, and be on our way back to *Ice Wolf.*"

"But the prisoners?" the commando protested.

"Don't worry, Herr Ritter," Wolfram said as he began his way to the stairs. "Bullets are too good for this bunch of fools. And besides, I'd like to give them some time to think about the errors of their ways. That's why I think it's only fitting that we reseal the Ice Lair, and entomb them here for all eternity."

Though Gunther thought this punishment a bit on the cruel side, he followed the occultist up the stairs and out onto the snow-covered hillside. Waiting for them there was Otto Brauer, with their three Sno-Cats neatly lined up behind him.

The sounds of continued gunfire tempered any sort of celebration in which they might have indulged themselves. Gunther peered down into the valley and appraised the situation.

"The Russians are proving to be a stubborn adversary. They continue to hold out, with their transporters effectively blocking the shortest route back to *Ice Wolf*."

Ritter appeared unfazed by this report. "Don't worry about those two transporters," he said calmly. "I have a little surprise for those Russians stowed away in the back of my snowmobile. Come, Otto. Help me set up a couple of grenades on this hillside so that we can complete the resealing of the Ice Lair. And then we can be gone from this place."

19

From the snow-covered summit of an adjoining ridge, Philip Michaels and the four members of SEAL Team Bravo, drawn by the sound of small-arms fire, watched an astonishing scene develop in the valley below. Lieutenant Steven Collier was in his natural element here, and Michaels agreed to his suggestion to leave their Sno-Cats parked at the bottom of the ridge and make their way to the summit on foot. It proved to be a cold, exhausting climb, and Michaels cursed his out-of-shape body as he struggled to keep up with the superbly conditioned SEALs.

The view from the summit, however, was well worth the effort. As Michaels crawled on his stomach to Collier's side, he breathlessly gazed out at the massive, triangular-peaked mountain and the broad valley at its base, where a violent confrontation taking place quickly captured their attention. A pair of bright yellow transporters were parked side by side, their occupants under attack by a group of heavily armed individuals hidden in the surrounding hills.

The SEAL known as Hawkeye was able to use his scope to determine the likelihood that four members of the trapped convoy remained alive. He drew his conclusion by picking out the individual muzzle flashes of their weapons. In a like manner, he counted six attackers.

As the firefight continued unabated Michaels surveyed the rest of the valley with his binoculars and discovered several other tracked vehicles, the largest of which seemed an exact match of the two transporters under attack. It lay abandoned on the side of a gently sloping hillside. Near the top of this hill was another group of smaller Snow-Cats.

The next scene of this perplexing drama began beside this line of open-cabbed vehicles, near an open portal dug into the snow. It appeared to be an entryway to a large cave of some sort, since different figures continually emerged from it. Strangely, two such individuals appeared carrying twelve, similarly shaped metallic crates, which they stored inside the awaiting Snow-Cats.

When four more figures exited the cave, Hawkeye's talents were once more put to use; the SEAL monitored two of them as they planted a series of explosive charges directly uphill from the cave's mouth. A large, metal door was then closed over this entrance, and the charges detonated. Michaels and the SEAL team clearly heard the muffled crack of this blast and looked on as an avalanche of snow covered this doorway in a veil of white.

No sooner did the sound of this blast fade than the Snow-Cats started up with a buzz-saw whine. Three of the vehicles lined up in a tight convoy and slowly began to roll down to the valley's floor. The driver of the remaining snowmobile—a one-seater—was a wild-looking man with long flowing blond hair; he wasted no time pulling his vehicle away from the convoy and recklessly shooting over the snowpack—directly toward the battle at the ambush site.

"Something hairy's about to come down," Collier warned as he watched the snowmobile careen off a low hill, go hurtling through the air, land sharply on the snowpack below, and then continue onward.

Michaels was unable to take his eyes off this speeding vehicle as it closed the distance between itself and the two parked transporters under attack.

"The only clear route out of that valley lies directly in the path of those two transporters," Michaels told the others. "I wonder where that snowmobile's headed."

"Wherever it's off to, it sure looks like those three Snow-Cats from the cave are followin' in its tracks, though at a less crazy pace," said Collier.

"Damn, he'd better cut his speed some or make a quick course change, or that bastard's gonna smack right into those two transporters," the hefty SEAL appropriately called Bear observed.

Michaels's only guess was that a collision was exactly what the blond-haired snowmobile driver had in mind as his sleek tracked vehicle approached within twenty yards of the transporters.

"Shit, that sucker's crazy!" exclaimed the SEAL called Tenderfoot.

"Crazy's not the word for it," said Collier with a tone of finality. "That brave bastard's a suicide!"

Seconds later the snowmobile plowed into the two transporters with an earsplitting blast, and a huge smoke-filled fireball engulfed the scene. As it rose to the frigid heavens Bear excitedly hollered, "Whoo—ee, he was packin' nitro!"

The truth of this spirited observation was obvious as the smoke finally cleared. The large tracked transporters had been reduced to nothing but smoking rubble, and the men who had been valiantly defending themselves burned to a crisp, as was the snowmobile and the driver who caused this conflagration.

Meanwhile the three Sno-Cats continued their journey, finally coming to a halt beside the still-smoking wreckage. Six armed men emerged from the surrounding hills and quickly boarded them. With the way now clear for them to pass, the convoy unceremoniously lurched forward, continuing straight down the valley, headed due east.

"Holy shit! Will somebody please tell me what the hell is goin' on?" Hawkeye exclaimed.

"It's only too obvious," Collier answered him. "Our pirates just got away with the loot, and now's our turn to hunt 'em down. Let's get to our vehicles and go teach those bastards some manners."

"All right!" Bear shouted.

Michaels pointed to the large tracked transporter that remained parked beside the now snow-covered cave entrance. "Before we go and engage any enemy, I want to check out that cave. Something tells me the folks who belong to that abandoned transporter are still missing."

"No offense, Commander, but that's a complete waste of time and energy," Collier told him. "I thought our mission was to track down those pirates. Well, now's the time to do so—while the tracks are still fresh."

"I still want to check out what it was that they were in such a hurry to cover up with that avalanche." Michaels was firm in his decision.

"But, Commander, a wasteful search like that has no relevance to our mission," Collier protested. "And meanwhile those pirates are gonna get away right under our noses."

"That's enough, Lieutenant!" Michaels barked in a rare display of anger. "As your commanding officer, I'm ordering the team to check out that cave. Am I understood?"

"It's useless," Andrei Korsakov cried from the top of the stairway. "This door won't budge. We've been buried alive!"

Jacob listened to this terrifying statement and fought back a feeling of shocked panic. His bullet wound had turned out to be superficial, a mere cut on the forehead, yet he still found himself unable to summon the strength to move from the rock shelf he was sitting up against.

From his current vantage point, he could clearly see the prone body of Viktor Alexandrov lying beside the stream. The American woman was doing her best to attend to his wounds, which included a bullet to the right shoulder and thigh. Laurie was turning out to be a brave, resourceful nurse. She cleaned Viktor's wounds with water and then cleverly used the discarded cotton wadding from the opened crates as bandages.

The Germans had left behind a single flashlight, and the trapped party agreed to use it only sparingly. This left them in an almost perpetual state of darkness, which Jacob in particular found intolerable. This entombment was his worst fear come true. Along with his encounter with Wolfram Eckhardt and the horrible news of his sister's murder, events had pushed him to the breaking point.

The moment Jacob heard the occultist call out his name from the blackness, he knew he had left the real world behind. He could no longer doubt that it was no coincidence that brought them together again; rather, it was some kind of uncannily designed plot, carried out by forces he could only describe as being beyond mortal comprehension.

The ritual scroll, the Grail, and the spear—these were the magical elements that had brought them together to participate in a cosmic battle, whose ultimate consequences he was only just now glimpsing. Since his discovery of the sister scroll barely a week ago, he had come full circle, the prophecy having come to pass. Had it been an inner weakness that was responsible for his defeat, or were his futile efforts doomed from the very beginning by some law of predestination?

Most upsetting of all was the realization that he'd go

to his grave without avenging Anna's death. Trapped in the pitch-black cave, Jacob knew that he'd have plenty of time to contemplate his shortcomings before death overtook them.

During this bout of self-pity, Laurie walked over to his side, knelt, and reached out tenderly to clean his cut with a piece of damp wadding.

"You were very fortunate, Jacob," she whispered. "Another fraction of an inch, and that bullet would have penetrated your skull."

"Right now I kind of wish that it had," Jacob morosely replied.

"Hey, that's no way to talk."

Jacob sighed heavily. "I'm sorry if I sound selfish, but right now I just want to close my eyes and never wake up again."

"I understand what you've been through, Jacob, and that feeling you're expressing is only natural. For what it's worth, I'm terribly sorry about what happened to your sister."

This comment was delivered with such sincerity that Jacob couldn't help but respond. "Thanks for your concern, comrade. And I'm sorry to have to add to your troubles. How's Viktor doing?"

"I've managed to stop the bleeding, and right now he seems to be fairly comfortable. But without proper medical attention, I don't know how much longer he can hold out."

"I'm the one who got all of you into this nightmare," Jacob said.

"Nonsense! The way it appears, we would have managed to stumble upon this place all by ourselves, most likely with the same results. So don't go blaming yourself."

Even though his forehead was matted with sweat, a sudden chill penetrated his body. Jacob shivered, and Laurie immediately reached over for his parka and covered him with it.

"I hope that cut of yours isn't infected," she said, worry in her voice.

"It's not the cut," Jacob managed. "You see, I suffer from claustrophobia."

"You poor thing. As if this situation isn't already desperate enough."

Jacob vacantly peered out into the cave's dark recesses and replied, "I've lived with this fear all of my life, and now I guess that I'll die with it."

"Before you go and give up the ghost, you should know that before he passed out, Viktor was already planning our escape. He feels that this cave has to have another exit, and I agree with him. While we still have use of the flashlight, we plan to send Andrei further into the cavern to seek out any hidden accessways."

"I wish that I could be more optimistic, Laurie, but I seriously doubt that this search will do much good. We're fated to die here."

Laurie vehemently shook her head. "You're starting to sound like that mad German who's responsible for all this, and though you might have given up, I haven't. We've got a constant source of warmth and plenty of fresh water. And while we still have our strength, we've got to explore other avenues of escape."

Once more Jacob shivered with claustrophobic dread. Laurie found no other recourse than to cradle him in her arms.

"Easy, Jacob. You know, my father was a submariner, and he used to tell me a story about a shipmate of his who had a horrible case of claustrophobia. As you can very well imagine, few places are worse for a claustrophobic than a submarine. And this individual used to cope by trying to clear his mind and visualize the most pleasant outdoors scene that he could imagine. Since this sailor was from Iowa, his visions were mostly of vast cornfields, and my dad said that these mental images never failed to snap him out of his fits. How about giving this method a try yourself? Where did you grow up?"

Jacob was in no mood for mental games; still, he pensively answered, "I spent most of my early childhood in Moscow, a place certainly not known for its pastoral beauty."

"Surely you went on summer vacations with your family?" Laurie cautiously probed.

Jacob grunted. "My father's position on the university staff earned him a dacha outside of Irkutsk, on the shores of Lake Baikal. It was a lovely little cabin, with a magnificent view of the lake, and I had my very own pine forest to play in. Some of my fondest memories are of those woods, and the games of cowboys and Indians I used to play with my sister there. Anna always wanted to take the part of the Indian, and my father even whittled her a bow and a set of birch arrows."

Just as the barest of fond grins was beginning to paint his face, another wave of mournful sorrow washed over him, and tears began cascading down his cheeks. "It's so hard to believe that she's really gone now," he managed. "And I've completely failed in bringing her murderers to justice. That's the worst tragedy of all!"

Before Laurie could respond to this outburst, there was a loud, rustling sound from the direction of the stairway. Andrei had been seated at the bottom step sulking, and as this noise continued he called out excitedly, "There's someone out there!"

Without further hesitation, he rushed up the steps and pounded on the closed metal door with his fists. "Hello!" he loudly yelled.

There was the wrenching noise of grating metal, and Andrei was caught by the door as it suddenly swung open. As the beam of a powerful flashlight hit him full in the face, a surprised male voice proclaimed, "Well, gawd damn, the commander was right. There is someone in there!"

Bear stuck his head into the cavern, and Andrei greeted him eagerly. As the other SEALs made their way inside Laurie heard their familiar chatter and joyously cried out, "They're Americans!"

By the time she reached the foot of the steps, the men of SEAL Team Bravo had completed their descent. Philip Michaels was the last in line, and he made the introductions.

"Afternoon, m'am. Commander Philip Michaels, United States Navy, at your service. I'm almost afraid to ask, but what the hell is going on down here?"

Laurie was unable to hold herself back, and she threw herself into the handsome officer's arms, all the while fighting back tears of joy. "Oh, God, Commander. You've just saved our lives!"

It took the better part of a half hour for Michaels and the SEALs to assess the situation and apply preliminary first aid to Viktor's wounds. Jacob was quite happy to allow Laurie to do most of the talking.

Jacob was surprised to hear that the American soldiers were on the trail of Wolfram Eckhardt, whose involvement in an act of piracy they suspected. Jacob chimed in to add murder to these charges, and he explained Eckhardt's apparent role in the destruction of Dakshan Gangotri Station. He held back from discussing the German's ulterior motives, satisfied that the current charges were more than sufficient to warrant an aggressive effort to hunt the pirates down.

The next surprise that awaited him occurred when he learned the unique method of travel that both the Americans and Eckhardt had used to get to Antarctica. Though traveling by submarine was something Jacob had always looked on with dread, he didn't dare refuse Captain Michaels's invitation to accompany him back to his current command. The USS *Springfield* was a nuclear-powered attack sub that was waiting to pick them up at a preplanned coastal rendezvous point.

In order to convey them to this site, Andrei volunteered to follow the SEALs in Novo base's transporter.

Because the Americans had little extra room in their Sno-Cats, this worked out perfectly.

Viktor was sedated with morphine and carried into the cab of the transporter. Laurie was to accompany him, with Andrei at the wheel. This left Jacob to travel with the Americans.

Oblivious to the bone-chilling cold and barely aware of his wound, Jacob gratefully straddled the Sno-Cat's communal bench. He found himself seated directly behind Philip Michaels, whose waist he was forced to grab for balance when the vehicle moved forward abruptly.

As they sped off down into the valley they passed the smoldering wreckage of the other two Russian transporters. Jacob muttered a silent prayer for Lieutenant Mikhail Lopatin and the other brave men who died here. And in a final tribute to those who had lost their lives in this desolate valley, he turned his head to take his last look at the distant hillside where he, Viktor, Laurie, and Andrei had been entombed.

Somewhere beyond the western ridge, he knew that his sister's body lay frozen in a tomb of glacial ice. It was for Anna's sake that he had come to this godforsaken land of snow and ice. And it was to ensure that her soul would rest in eternal peace that he began this new quest to bring Wolfram Eckhardt to justice.

20

The red Bell-212 helicopter swept over the Antarctic coastline at an altitude of five thousand feet. From this lofty height, the vehicle's pilot, Thor Sperre, had a superb view of the wide channel of water visible through the Plexiglas windshield. The heaviest ice hugged the coast, with most of the channel covered by a thin layer of pancake ice. The bright yellow hull of the *Condor* could be seen at anchor in the center of the channel, a good three miles in front of them. Their reconnaissance flight had taken them well inland, and with their fuel supply low, the sight of the *Condor* was like seeing home after a long journey.

"It looks like the heavy ice continues to break up, Thor," said Captain Jon Skogstad from the helicopter's copilot seat. "Pretty soon there will be nothing but the thin pancake extending all the way to the coastline."

"I guess that's one of the features of summer in these

parts." Thor allowed the chopper to lose another five hundred feet of altitude as they crossed over the coast and began to cross the frozen waters of the channel.

The *Condor* beckoned invitingly in the distance, or at least seemed to in the eyes of the vessel's satisfied captain. "It will be good to get back to the ship, though I must admit I truly enjoyed this excursion into the mountains of New Schwabenland. I imagine that the men should be just about finished pulling up that core sample."

"Before we took off, I heard several of the divers talking about how much they missed Yngve now that their work is taking them into the ice," said Thor. "We always said that Yngve had ice in his veins, because the colder the water, the more he enjoyed working in it."

Jon Skogstad stroked his full gray beard thoughtfully. "Aye, Thor, we lost a special one when we lost Yngve Rakke. He was one in a million."

With his somber gaze locked on the water, Thor spotted an unusual disturbance in the middle of a narrow, open lead. At first he had trouble identifying it, but then the frothing line of white water showed itself to have a submarine conning tower as its source. The vessel was in the midst of a dive.

As he spotted two lookouts on top of the sail, Thor shouted, "Look, Captain, it's the *Turbulent!*"

Jon Skogstad had also spotted this vessel, and he waited until the two lookouts left their posts and the sail had all but disappeared beneath the water before replying. "Unless I'm mistaken, that submarine was definitely not the HMS *Turbulent*. Its sail was much more streamlined than the *Turbulent*'s, and even the dark gray color of its steel hull was different."

In a vain attempt to get another look at the sub, Thor turned the helicopter in a tight circle. Nothing but blue water met their eyes, prompting Jon Skogstad to suggest they get back to the *Condor* immediately. "Hurry, Thor," he said. "It's vital that I inform the *Turbulent* of this mysterious sighting at once!"

● ● ●

Seaman Klaus Schiffer was one of the two lookouts who breathlessly climbed down the conning tower ladder as *Ice Wolf* began its descent. The curly-haired sailor had been the first to spot the rapidly approaching helicopter. *Ice Wolf* was already preparing to dive at the time, and Klaus could only pray that the chopper had somehow missed them.

"Oberleutnant Kromer!" he excitedly said as he climbed down into the control room. "There was a helicopter, sir."

Ice Wolf's second in command listened to Klaus's report while standing behind the seated planesman, but before he could respond to it, Gunther Hartmann emerged from the forward hatchway.

"A helicopter, you say, Klaus?" the captain asked, apparently unconcerned.

"Yes, Captain," the rosy-cheeked sailor replied. "It passed over at an altitude of approximately four thousand feet, just as we were clearing the bridge."

Ice Wolf's bow began angling steeply downward, and as the diving officer rattled off the descent procedures, Gunther signaled Kromer to join him beside the navigation plot. Gunther had just changed out of his polar gear, and as he crossed the sloping deck he managed to secure the top button of his khaki coveralls and keep his balance, all at the same time.

"So we're back to work already, Number One," he said with a slight grin. "It's good to be under way after spending time in that frozen hell. Here I've been back less than an hour, and already my first crisis."

"We like to keep you on your toes, sir," Kromer quipped, and pointed to the topmost chart and the red X that was drawn in the very center of the channel. "That's the position of the *Seaway Condor*. They're presently at anchor, smack in the middle of the transit channel. I'll bet my pension the helicopter belongs to them."

"They must be working these waters," Gunther surmised, disgust in his voice. "Of all the damn places. What are our options, Number One?"

Kromer answered while highlighting the channel's bathymetrics. "We can either try slipping directly beneath them, or leave the channel altogether."

"I don't like the looks of those steadily rising depths at the channel's edges," Gunther remarked. "And since the *Condor* could be in the midst of a drilling operation, passing beneath them could prove disastrous."

Otto Brauer couldn't help overhearing this discussion from his position beside sonar, and he dared to offer his own opinion in the matter. "Excuse me for interrupting, Captain, but why take all these unnecessary risks when one torpedo will clear the way in an instant? I knew we should have finished off the Norwegians the first time we met them."

"Otto does have a point," Kromer suggested.

"For expediency's sake, I agree that a torpedo is the most direct way to solve our problem," Gunther said. "But before I can authorize such a belligerent act, I think it's best to check with the old fighters. Has anyone seen our esteemed guests since leaving the coast?"

Kromer shook his head. "They sequestered themselves in their quarters shortly after the last crate was delivered to them."

"Lord only knows what I'll find them doing this time," Gunther muttered, and somewhat reluctantly turned for the aft accessway.

The deck was leveling off as he crossed through the engine room. The Shadow was engrossed in the starboard diesel engine's exhaust fan, and Gunther passed by without disturbing him. As expected, he found the after-hatch sealed tight. He loudly knocked on it three times before undogging it and stepping through the accessway.

Inside the aft torpedo room, he found the compartment's two elderly occupants seated at the card table. Gunther couldn't miss the collection of metal crates that lined the bulkheads, and he noticed that two of the lids were open. The contents of these boxes were spread out on the table, and Gunther identified them as the Spear of Destiny, the nine copper scroll segments, and the golden goblet known as the Grail.

Looking up at Gunther's entrance, Wolfram smiled. "Hello, Captain. I was just giving Heinrich a blow-by-blow description of our amazing adventure on the ice."

Heinrich caught Gunther's eye and winked. "You and I will have to get together later, Captain. And then you can help me separate fact from fiction. Is what he was just telling me about Oberleutnant Ritter's death true? What an incredible act of valor to give up his life like that."

"I don't blame you for questioning it, Herr West-heim," Gunther said kindly. "It was an extraordinary example of heroism above and beyond the call of duty."

Wolfram grunted. "I should think that the Valkyries will have one more hero to escort through the hallowed halls of Valhalla this evening."

The deck momentarily shuddered, and Gunther decided to get right down to business. "As we begin our transit of the deep-water channel leading to the open ocean, we appear to have another ship several miles ahead of us, blocking our way. She's the *Seaway Condor,* and we believe that the Norwegian oil support ship is involved in a drilling operation there."

"Can we go around them?" Heinrich asked.

"Not without incurring the risk of going aground on the shoals that line the channel," Gunther returned.

"Then how do you propose that we reach the open seas, Captain?" This time the questioner was Wolfram.

Gunther prepared himself for rejection as he revealed his plan. "Since the most direct and safest route into the Atlantic is straight down the channel, I'd like permission to sink the *Condor.* I believe that a single torpedo would be more than sufficient for this task."

Heinrich looked at Wolfram and accepted the slightest of affirmative nods before returning his glance to

Gunther. "We've come much too far to take unnecessary risks now, Captain. So you have our full blessings to take the Norwegians out!"

Mark Bodzin spent most of his sonar watch seated at his console reading a paperback adventure novel. For the past several hours, the *Springfield* had been silently lying still on the smooth bottom of the bay, directly off Antarctica's Princess Astrid coastline. With little for their hydrophones to pick up but the incessant sound of the fracturing ice, Bodzin and his watch team were content to pass the hours as best they could.

The dog-eared book Bodzin was reading was about a group of environmental extremists who were patrolling the planet's oceans in a futuristic, high-tech submarine, protecting whales and other marine mammals. It was fascinating, fast-paced reading, and just as he turned the first page of the final chapter, two sharp explosions sounded in his headphones. Bodzin didn't have to hear any more to throw down the book and reach overhead for the intercom handset.

"Conn, sonar," he said into the transmitter. "They're back!"

With a roaring blast of ballast, the *Springfield* rose from the bottom muck and drifted straight upward. The seven-thousand-ton submarine smashed through the four-foot-thick ice on its first attempt. No sooner did the reinforced sail clear the surface than a trio of lookouts climbed up onto the outer bridge. By the time they gave the all clear, the sub had surfaced completely.

The boat's XO was one of the first members of the deck party to emerge from the forward accessway. From his position on the top deck, Gerardo Perez didn't need his binoculars to pick out the convoy of tracked vehicles headed directly toward them from the snow-covered coastline.

He now counted four vehicles, where at first there had

been only three, and he was anxious to learn the identity of the large, bright yellow transporter that took up the convoy's rear. Meanwhile he supervised the rest of the members of the deck party as they prepared the nylon amidships boarding ladder.

A small group of penguins were busy checking out the *Springfield* as the first of the Sno-Cats reached the boat's side. The XO was expecting the worse when the SEAL who was driving this vehicle instructed him to prepare a sling to pull aboard a wounded member of their party. With the hope that it wasn't their captain, Perez hastened belowdeck to jury-rig this sling himself.

By the time he returned topside, the entire convoy had arrived. Much to his relief, Philip Michaels was there to greet him personally as he climbed out of the access trunk.

"Thanks for putting together that sling, XO," Michaels said. "As you can very well see, we've picked up some passengers along the way. One of them is suffering from a pair of gunshots to the shoulder and thigh. Though they don't appear to be life threatening, he's in no shape to walk up that ladder."

As Michaels took the sling and handed it over to the muscular SEAL called Bear, the XO, looking confused, asked, "What in the blazes happened out there, Skipper?"

With his eyes on the occupants of the transporter as they began their way over to the *Springfield,* Michaels answered, "We had a little run-in with our old friends the pirates. It seems we can now add several murder counts to their growing list of charges. We found the folks that we're taking aboard buried inside a snow cave, which the pirates were using to store their loot. Three of them are Russian scientists, including the poor fellow who was shot. The fourth member of the party is a volcano expert from Hawaii, and a looker at that. From what I can gather, they were working out of a nearby Russian base when they made the mistake of stumbling onto the pirates' cache. Of course, the bad guys picked this inopportune moment to show up, and shortly afterward we arrived."

"And the pirates?" the wide-eyed XO wanted to know.

Michaels grinned. "This is where *Springfield*'s going to get a chance to even the score, XO. Because the last we saw of them, they were hightailing it for this same coast. Even as we speak they're most likely sprinting for the open seas in that spruced-up German U-boat of theirs."

"Skipper, in my fifteen years in the navy, this is the wildest tale I've ever heard. But you can rely on me and the men to do whatever we can to collar these so-called pirates."

"I appreciate the support, XO. Now we'd better get over there and help our guests aboard. And then I'm gonna need some hot joe and plenty of it. Damn, it's friggin' cold out here!"

Of the four newcomers to the *Springfield,* Jacob Litvak was the only one who was not looking forward to boarding the submarine. Viewed from the ice, the warship looked like a sinister and deadly behemoth. One could see from its sleek lines that it was designed to travel beneath the seas, and it was precisely this that most bothered him.

Though Laurie was close by for moral support, Jacob felt like a condemned man as he leadenly climbed the ladder to the sub's outer deck. The American sailors who greeted him proved to be extremely friendly, and they helped ease the trauma of his next great challenge: climbing into the belly of the beast itself.

The Americans were both efficient and gentle in lowering Viktor down the sub's access trunk. Andrei and Laurie followed, then last of all, and reluctantly, Jacob. By the time he reached the final rung of the steep ladder, his hair was matted to his forehead with sweat, his heart was thumping in his chest, and he was all set to be swallowed up in a full claustrophobic attack.

"Let me give ya a hand there, partner," an accommodating voice offered from below.

A pair of strong hands guided him down to the deck. He now found himself in a spacious, well-lit corridor. Laurie and Andrei gathered beside him as their American-navy escort introduced himself.

"Welcome aboard the USS *Springfield*," the coverall-clad, mustached sailor said. "I'm Chief Warrant Officer Frank Cunetto, the boat's supply officer. Please feel free to call me Chop like everyone else on board. Your friend has been transferred to sickbay, where Doc will take real good care of him. Meanwhile I'll help you get settled into your new home."

Jacob couldn't help but find his anxieties eased by this sailor's warm manner as well as by the surprising roominess of the sub. He had expected it to be constricting, but really, the vessel's interior didn't appear much different than a large luxury liner on which he had once sailed.

Chop pointed down the corridor to an adjoining room that appeared to be filled with men and equipment. "That's the control room. I'll be happy to give you a complete tour of it once we get under way. Right now we'll be heading to the wardroom. If you'll please just follow me . . ."

Jacob continued to be impressed by the spacious environs as they proceeded down a stairway and walked down a long hallway. They passed a small copy machine, a paper shredder, and a bulletin board, where the plan of the day was displayed. Chop beckoned to the left, toward an open doorway marked WARDROOM.

Inside this compartment was a large rectangular table, a video monitor, and stereo equipment set into the wood-paneled walls; it reminded Jacob of the faculty lounge of Moscow University.

"I'm just gonna need you to jot down your full names

and mailing addresses on this legal pad," said Chop. "And hand out your TLDs."

"What's that?" Laurie asked as she took off her parka.

Chop picked up a small, gray plastic device from the table. "The TLD is a dosimeter. It should be worn on your person at all times, and will be checked at the conclusion of your stay with us to determine if you've been exposed to any ionizing radiation."

Andrei appeared confused with this explanation, so Jacob translated Chop's words into Russian. Chop politely waited until he was finished before adding, "I'm sorry. I almost forgot that you two are Russian. We don't get many foreigners aboard the *Springfield,* and you guys are definitely the first Russians to ever embark with us."

"Your gracious hospitality is most appreciated," Jacob returned. "I'll be most happy to fulfill the role of translator when needed."

Chop looked at him and nodded. "That's a deal. Say, it looks like you've got a nasty gash on that forehead of yours. I'll have Doc take a look at it as soon as I've finished here."

As Laurie reached out for the legal pad Chop added, "I don't suppose you've ever been on a submarine, ma'am?"

Laurie grinned. "You'd be surprised, sailor. You're talking to a certified U.S. Navy brat, whose father spent thirty-three years as a bubblehead based out of Pearl."

"You don't say. . . ." Chop gave her a big smile. "Then you can help me teach our Russian friends here some of the intricacies of submarine life, such as how to flush the head and use the shower's water restrictor. I'm sorry about the coed facilities, but we'll keep you stashed in officers' country and try to make your stay as comfortable as possible."

"After what I've just been through, this place is lookin' as good as a suite at the Maui Marriott!" Laurie smiled as well.

There was a slight lurching movement of the deck

below, and Chop said, "It looks like the Skipper's wastin' no time getting us under way."

Andrei's eyes were wide with wonder as he surveyed the wardroom and took in the sub's official seal, which was hung on the bulkhead. It showed a silhouette of the sub with a pair of crossed Kentucky long rifles below it and the distinctive, bearded profile of the vessel's favorite son drawn above the rifles. The motto *United for Freedom* was written below.

Andrei pointed to the profile and blurted out in Slavic-accented English, "Ah, Abe Lincoln!"

"You've got it, comrade," Chop readily replied as he fondly patted Andrei on the back, and then got on with the task of handing out the TLDs.

21

Thor remained on the *Condor*'s helideck only long enough to drop off the ship's captain and begin a hasty refueling. With this done, he expertly guided the Bell 212 back into the heavens.

Jon Skogstad took the sighting of the unidentified submarine most seriously. He left Thor with strict orders to inform the *Condor* the second this phantom vessel again showed itself. As it turned out, Thor was well trained for this mission, since he had learned how to pilot helicopters in the Norwegian navy's ASW program.

Ever thankful that the weather hadn't yet deteriorated, Thor ascended to an altitude of 3,500 feet and began a series of ever-widening circular turns, with the *Condor* in the epicenter. From this height he could see various members of the ship's crew busily scurrying about. Many of them were gathered around the aft moonpool, where they were pulling up the drilling gear and the divers who serviced this equipment. Only after this time-consuming job was completed could the *Condor* weigh anchor and take off for safer waters.

Thor paid special attention to that portion of the channel lying between the *Condor* and the distant coastline, and as he flew over an extensive open lead in the thin ice, a thousand yards due south of the *Condor,* he spotted an unusual disturbance on the water's surface. He expertly manuevered the helicopter to have a closer look, and as he descended below two thousand feet he sighted the characteristic frothing trail of a single torpedo, which was headed straight for the *Condor.* Thor frantically spoke into his chin-mounted radio transmitter.

"*Condor,* this is Bell One. You've got a torpedo headed your way on bearing one-eight-zero! I repeat, there's a torpedo in the water coming in from the south! Cut the anchor, and get out of there at once!"

Thor struggled to keep his composure as he watched the torpedo continue its deadly course. His shock and surprise turned to horror, and he couldn't help feeling he was in the middle of a living nightmare.

Most frustrating of all was the fact that there was nothing he could do to counter this threat except warn his countrymen. He shuddered to think what such a lethal weapon could do to the *Condor,* and his horror turned to raw fear as he watched the torpedo break the five-hundred-yard threshold.

"*Condor!*" he repeated into his microphone. "The torpedo continues its approach. You must get under way this instant!"

Thor knew that even if the ship was able to get under way, there'd never be enough time to build up a head of steam and outrun this threat. Just as he realized that the torpedo was targeted directly amidships, another disturbance in the water caught his attention. Less than a hundred yards in front of the speeding torpedo, the black, rounded hull of a submarine plowed out of the water. The steep angle of this forceful ascent was such that the submarine appeared almost to leap into the air before violently smacking down onto the water with a frothing splash.

Caught off guard by this amazing sight, Thor was momentarily speechless as he identified this vessel and understood the desperate tactic that it was attempting: the HMS *Turbulent* was sacrificing itself to divert the torpedo from the *Condor!*

No sooner did this shocking realization register in his mind than the torpedo struck the *Turbulent* with a jarring blast. The force of this concussion sent a geyser of agitated water high into the air, the booming, resonating report of which could be heard even inside the helicopter's cockpit.

"Mayday! Mayday!" Thor unnecessarily yelled into his microphone as he descended to see if there was any way that he could assist the valiant British crew.

The only other time Mark Bodzin had heard a torpedo explode was during an exercise. It was a sound that a sonarman never forgot, and Bodzin was able to instantly identify the resonating noise that the *Springfield*'s hydrophones relayed through his headphones.

His subsequent report to the conn generated the warbling electronic alarm that was currently sounding throughout the *Springfield.* As Bodzin prepared himself for the unthinkable the sub's crew scrambled to their battle stations.

In *Ice Wolf*'s aft torpedo room, the sound of the detonating torpedo was cause for a spirited celebration. Leading this revelry was Heinrich Westheim. The whitehaired octogenarian could have passed for a man half his age as he danced a jig and joyously called to the room's other elderly occupant, "That's it, Wolfram! The final obstacle has been removed from our path!"

Wolfram Eckhardt expressed his merriment by reaching out for the mushroom-filled goblet that sat on the table before him. "I've waited five decades for this glorious day to come," he pronounced reverently. "Heinrich, it's time to partake of Lucifer's Flesh and begin the Rite of Awakening!"

Unlike the aft torpedo room, there were no joyous celebrations in *Ice Wolf*'s control room. A tense, hushed atmosphere prevailed here as Gunther Hartmann peered through the periscope. A scene of utter devastation filled the lens, and even though he had reason to feel otherwise, Gunther was strangely disturbed by what he saw.

"It's a British Trafalgar-class submarine all right," he related to his executive officer. "From the smoke that's pouring from its aft access trunk, I'd say they took the hit in their engine spaces."

Gunther backed away and allowed Karl Kromer to have a look.

"What an amazing turn of events," Kromer commented as he peered into the eyepiece. "To intentionally allow themselves to be struck like that shows incredible fortitude on the part of the English captain."

"Or stupidity," Gunther added. "What truly bothers me is what this vessel was doing here in the first place. And then there's always the possibility that they were working with another submarine."

"Surely you don't think they were aware of our presence?" Kromer was aghast at the thought.

"That's just it, Karl. Since there's no way to find out for sure, we must proceed most cautiously. Instead of sprinting out to sea with another submarine possibly in our baffles, it's time to turn for the marginal ice zone. There we'll silently prowl, and determine for certain if we're indeed being stalked."

● ● ●

In another part of the channel, Philip Michaels peered into the eyepiece of the *Springfield*'s Mk-18 search scope. Beside him, his XO was bent over the auxiliary periscope, and together they somberly surveyed the tragic scene visible on the northern horizon.

"The *Turbulent* appears to be holding its own, Skipper. Its hull looks to be in one piece, and they don't seem to be in any immediate danger of sinking."

Michaels slowly scanned the dozens of men visible on the *Turbulent*'s deck. All were outfitted in orange life jackets. Two of the *Condor*'s lifeboats were approaching the surfaced sub, with the ship's helicopter hovering directly overhead. The *Condor* itself was also on its way to assist the British crew. Seeing this, Michaels allowed himself a brief sigh of relief.

"It's going to take much more than a single hit to take out Hartwell and his gang," he stated. "Since the *Condor*'s right there to offer them all the assistance they need, it's time for *Springfield* to get on with the job of hunting down the bastards responsible for this unprovoked attack."

While Michaels and his battle staff got on with the job of planning the hunt, a scene of a much lighter nature was taking place in *Springfield*'s sickbay. Currently packed into the small room that doubled as the vessel's office were Laurie, Jacob, and Chop. The object of their attention was comfortably laid out on the room's sole cot. Viktor was wide awake, and from the broad grin on his face, he looked to be well on his way to recovery.

He had just commented on the dark blue poopy suits Laurie and Jacob were wearing, and Chop had promised him that he would soon enough get his own set of official coveralls, when Andrei entered the compartment. The young, rosy-cheeked Russian was also decked out in coveralls and held a partially eaten apple in one hand and his camera in the other.

"Are you eating again, Andrei?" Viktor commented sarcastically.

Andrei attempted to answer in English. What he said was a version of "I just had pizza and a hot fudge sundae!"

"Sounds like we've got ourselves a happy sailor." Chop smiled.

Viktor smiled, too. "If your Sasha could only see you now, Andrei Korsakov."

"Dr. Litvak," Andrei now said in Russian, "I thought you'd like to have this film as a reminder of our experience together."

"Thank you very much, Andrei," said Jacob. "I can't wait to see for myself just what it was that we found inside that cave."

"So much has happened since the discovery, I've almost forgotten about those relics myself," Viktor added.

"If you'd like, I could process that film for you," Chop volunteered. "*Springfield* had a fully stocked darkroom."

"Pizza, hot fudge sundaes, and now a photo lab, this submarine is just like a self-contained underwater city," said Jacob, readily handing Chop the film cartridge and then turning his attention back to their patient.

22

The stirring sounds of Wagner's *Parsifal* provided background music for the ancient ritual being celebrated in *Ice Wolf*'s aft torpedo room. The card table and chairs had been removed and a wide chalk circle drawn on the floor in the room's exact center. Heinrich and Wolfram were seated in this circle on the bare deck, with the Grail, the Spear of Destiny, and the nine copper scroll segments laid out before them. As Wolfram read from the first plate his deep voice trembled with emotion.

"*Ateh, Malkuth, Ve Geburah, Ve Gedulah, Le Olahm.* Thou art the Kingdom, and the Power, and the Glory, unto all the ages."

"Amen," said Heinrich, who proceeded to light the candle and incense censer.

As the waves of rich sandalwood wafted throughout the compartment, Wolfram continued his translation of the copper plate with ever-increasing intensity. "Thus begins the Rite of Awakening. In your mind's eye, visualize the following guardians of the Grail. To the east, the Archangel Raphael, who stands on a purple hilltop, his pale yellow garments billowing in the breeze. To the west, the Archangel Gabriel, dressed in blue and surrounded by cascading torrents of water. It's the Archangel Uriel who guards the northern watchtower, the greens and brown colors of his cloak in perfect harmony with the lush, fertile landscape that surrounds him. And finally, to complete the circle, we call forth Michael from the south, clad in scarlet and bearing aloft his red-hot sword. East, west, north, south—by the powers of the elementals, we trace the inverted pentagram of power and summon forth the fallen master, whose Aryan seed we do bear. Heil Lucifer, true Führer of the Reich!"

Gunther merely had to hear Otto Brauer's disturbed tone of voice to know that there was trouble. As he raced across the deck of the control room to join him, *Ice Wolf*'s sonarman called out worriedly, "All hydrophones continue to monitor fracturing ice topside, sir."

"Captain, shall I order an all-stop?" Kromer asked from the helm.

"Continue on as ordered," Gunther instructed.

He found Otto kneeling on the deck, anxiously working on the ice machine's transcriber.

"Whatever's the matter with that damn thing, Otto?" Gunther demanded.

"It's the drum, sir. The gears appear to have jammed."

As Gunther knelt down to have a look himself, Otto pulled out a long, twisted strip of graph paper.

"Ah, here's the culprit, Captain," he said triumphantly.

"Sir, without the ice machine, we're totally blind," Kromer called out from his position behind the helmsman. "It's only prudent to order an all-stop under these circumstances."

Gunther stood and calmly replied, "Easy does it,

Number One. Chief Brauer has corrected the problem, and the upward scanning fathometer will soon enough be back on-line."

This observation was confirmed as the drum began slowly spinning once more. Gunther looked on as the stylus again sketched out the pattern of the ice above them. The very first line to fill the drum-fed graph paper was a wicked-looking spike, and before he could yell out in warning, *Ice Wolf*'s sail smashed into the bottom portion of an eighty-five-foot-deep inverted ice keel with a bone-jarring concussion. The force of this collision was enough to send Gunther crashing to the deck, along with several of his shipmates and a variety of loose equipment. The boat violently rocked from side to side, and the lights blinked off, on, then permanently off.

"Someone hit the emergency lights!" Gunther screamed as he scrambled to his feet.

The terrifying sound of spraying water could be heard in the distance. As the confusing darkness prevailed Gunther shouted once again.

"Where are those emergency lights? Number One, I need damage-control reports!"

Ten long seconds later the lights snapped back on. While Kromer busily addressed the sound-powered telephone to determine the extent of the damage to the other compartments, Gunther helped Otto attend to a sprung overhead valve beside the aft accessway. The torrent of wildly spraying water was icy cold, and Gunther braved a complete soaking to hold the pipe in place while Otto tightened the valve with a monkey wrench. By the time this flow was stanched, Kromer had the results of his report ready to relay.

"All departments have reported in, Captain. Other than a few bumps and bruises to the crew, *Ice Wolf*'s hull integrity remains intact. All main systems are fully operational."

●　　●　　●

As Gunther supervised *Ice Wolf*'s descent to safer waters, the two occupants of the sub's aft torpedo room continued their solemn ritual, regardless of the forceful collision. Heinrich was picking up the toppled candle, and as he did so Wolfram blindly pointed into the room's dark recesses.

His eyes wide with both awe and fear, he cried out in warning, "It's started, Heinrich! The awakening has begun. The Archangel Michael himself has just arrived to do battle!"

"Conn, sonar," Bodzin's amplified voice reported over the control room's intercom. "Unidentified submerged contact, bearing zero-eight-zero, range twelve thousand yards. Designate Sierra One, possible hostile."

"We've got 'em, Skipper!" Perez exclaimed from his position on the periscope pedestal.

Michaels had been at the navigation plot when the sonar report arrived. As he crossed the compartment to join his XO, he addressed the men of the fire control team.

"Begin the tracking process, gentlemen. Weaps, initiate TMA."

Michaels spotted Steven Collier quietly standing beside the aft BSY-1 console. The steely-eyed SEAL gave him the briefest of supportive nods as the captain rushed by him en route to the slightly elevated pedestal.

"We've got the son of a bitch this time," Perez called out as he stared up at the overhead sonar repeater. "The thin-line array has a firm lock on them."

Michaels studied this same repeater and warily commented, "Let's not pop the champagne just yet, XO. We've still got a lot of work to do before we're ready for a celebration. Meanwhile let's just pray that Sierra One keeps out of that heavy ice and doesn't get a whiff of us."

●　　●　　●

Unaware of the drama taking place in the *Springfield*'s control room, Jacob was getting further acquainted with his new floating home. Once more, he sighed with relief that his claustrophobia had yet to manifest itself. The young crew had been most hospitable, and Jacob even got up the nerve to try out his bunk. He had been assigned a midlevel rack, and though it appeared to be about the size of a coffin—an image that didn't bear thinking about—he managed to crawl up onto the mattress and stretch out on his back without breaking into a panicky sweat. Of course, he made certain to keep his curtain wide open.

Just as he located the overhead light switch and flipped it on, Chop entered the hushed berthing compartment. The amiable supply officer handed Jacob a stack of three-by-five-inch photographic prints and the accompanying negatives.

"I can't say much for their contents, but here they are," he said.

Jacob was impressed by the good service, and as he sorted through the prints Chop added, "I got them out of the printer just in time. If you haven't noticed, we're currently at battle stations. It seems that we just got a solid sonar return on that pirate submarine, and *Springfield*'s presently movin' in for the kill."

Jacob all but ignored this report, so remarkable did he find the photographs he had just been given. The series began with several shots of the cave's entranceway. The sight of this portal brought a twinge of dread, and he was relieved to see that the rest of the photos showed far less terrifying objects.

His hands slightly trembling, he sorted through photos of the golden, jewel-encrusted goblet and the spear point with the nail encased in its base. Well aware of the fanciful legends behind these relics, he found his interest piqued when he reached the snapshots of the copper scroll. Andrei had captured each of the nine plates superbly, with such clarity, in fact, that Jacob was certain he'd have no trouble translating the scroll's contents. Looking forward to the day when he could share this translation with Uri Weinberg, Jacob suddenly realized that if the vessel carrying these relics was sunk, they'd be lost for all eternity. And to think he still had no idea what priceless treasures were stowed away in the ten crates they didn't get to open . . . With this thought Jacob suddenly felt the supply officer's words register on his brain.

"Chop, I really appreciate these prints. I was just wondering, though, is there a chance that I could have a private word with Captain Michaels?"

Chop grimaced. "Gee, I don't know, Doc. With battle stations and all, the skipper's gonna have his hands full right now."

"It'll only take a second," Jacob pleaded. "And besides, the matter I'd like to discuss with him relates directly to that submarine he's stalking."

"All right, Doc," Chop reluctantly agreed. "But keep close on my heels. And if it don't look right in control, out we go."

Jacob accepted these terms and, after a couple of awkward attempts, managed to free himself from his rack's tight confines.

As expected, they found the captain in the control room. The compartment was packed with personnel, and it was impossible to overlook the tense, highly charged atmosphere as Chop led Jacob into the room by way of the aft accessway. Approaching the slightly elevated platform on which Michaels stood, Jacob couldn't help but feel out of place. The captain was involved in constant deliberations with his staff, and it was obvious that their situation was very serious.

"Skipper," Chop interrupted with an air of nervous camaraderie. "Excuse me, sir, but the doc here would like to have a quick word with you . . . if possible."

Michaels appeared ready to turn down this request when his glance briefly met Jacob's imploring stare. With a reluctant shrug, he walked over to the edge of the platform and said politely, "I'm sorry, Dr. Litvak, but I'm a bit busy right now."

"I'm the one who's sorry for disturbing you, Captain," Jacob returned. "But there's something important I must ask you." Jacob swallowed. Then he blurted, "Is there any possible way for us to capture that submarine that you're hunting down without having to sink it?"

"Why do you ask?" The captain looked baffled by this request.

This time Jacob's answer was delicately phrased. "I have very good reasons to believe that the pirates have in their possession a priceless collection of ancient artifacts, a portion of which we actually saw during our stay in the cave. Losing these rare antiquities to the sea would be a terrible tragedy. Surely there must be a way to capture this vessel without putting a torpedo into it."

Michaels grinned sardonically. "If you can tell me a way to do that, I'm all ears, Doctor. But right now I have no alternative but to continue our attack preparations. Because of what little I've already seen of these blood-thirsty pirates of yours, I'm afraid the only thing that's going to stop them is that very torpedo you fear launching. If you'll please excuse me, I've got to get back to work. Chop, escort the doctor back to his stateroom. And make sure to prepare his companions, because chances are it's going to get real rough around here shortly."

"Captain Hartmann, I've got an unidentified submerged contact!" the sonar technician called as he anxiously pushed down on his headphones. "The towed array is picking up the faint signature of a reactor coolant pump, indicating that this is a nuclear-powered submarine. Bearing two-seven-zero, relative rough range ten thousand yards and closing."

"So, the Brits weren't working alone after all," Gunther said from his position at navigation.

Karl Kromer alertly marked the contact's position on

the bathymetric chart. "Surely they heard us strike the ice keel." He sounded worried.

Gunther blamed nobody but himself for this needless accident, and knew he'd only have a single chance to rectify his mistake.

"Number One, I want the two acoustic homing torpedoes stored in the aft tubes prepared for firing. Interface the reactor coolant pump signature into the fire control solution. And prepare for an immediate launch upon my order."

While Kromer rushed to the weapons console to arm the torpedoes a macabre scene continued to unfold in the candlelit compartment housing these weapons. With the scent of incense thick in the air and the lush strains of *Parsifal* pouring from the speakers, Heinrich and Wolfram sat cross-legged inside their chalk circle, sharing a mushroom-induced vision of a scarlet-caped giant of a man, a glowing sword held menacingly in his hand. This phantom had been in their midsts for some time now, constantly patrolling the outer edge of the circle, as if he were desperately searching for some means to break through its circumference and reach the awestruck mortals inside.

"Wolfram, look how his eyes glow with hatred! I tell you, he's after our mortal souls!"

"Have faith in the protective power of the circle, Heinrich. As long as we don't break the plane, the archangel is powerless to reach us. Besides, Michael's presence here is certain proof of the rite's effectiveness."

At this moment two deafening jolts of compressed air suddenly sounded throughout the compartment. The deck shook as Heinrich identified the source of the noise.

"*Ice Wolf* has just launched torpedoes!"

Wolfram was delighted to hear this, and as he reached for the spear point that lay before him, his voice was full of excitement. "The final battle is upon us, Heinrich!" he shouted. "It's time to sing forth the ritual chant and call forth our master to do combat!"

"Conn, sonar, Sierra One has just fired on us! I show a pair of torpedoes, bearing zero-eight-zero, range eleven thousand yards and rapidly closing."

Bodzin's amplified voice got the immediate attention of the men gathered in *Springfield*'s control room. Philip Michaels reacted coolly as he peered up at the sonar repeater and called out to the head of the fire control team, "Weaps, what's the status of our TMA?"

Lieutenant Noonan hastily answered, "We've just about got the dots stacked, Captain."

"Prepare tubes one and three for snapshot mode. Fire!"

The deck shook as a pair of Mk-48 ADCAP torpedoes shot out of their tubes.

"COB, initiate evasive maneuvers!" Michaels added to the diving-control team. "All ahead full on bearing three-four-zero."

"All ahead full on bearing three-four-zero, aye, Cap," Ellwood Crick repeated as he reached into his breast pocket for a fresh cigar to chew on while watching the helmsmen alertly carry out this order.

"Mr. Carr, what kind of bathymetrics do we have to work with?" Michaels continued.

The navigator was quick with his reply. "We've got approximately a thousand feet of water beneath us, sir, with shallow shoals to the southwest."

"Conn, sonar, incoming torpedoes continue on intercept course, range ten thousand yards and closing."

Michaels returned his gaze to the overhead sonar repeater. "We'll never outrun 'em," he muttered. "So let's do the next best thing. Weaps, launch MOSS on bearing two-two-zero!"

Again the deck shuddered as *Springfield*'s mobile submarine simulator shot off on a southwesterly course.

"Decoy is emitting, Captain," Noonan reported.

Michaels glanced down at the helm, where the COB was positioned between the two planesmen, his unlit cigar clenched in his mouth. "COB, let's put a knuckle in the water," he instructed. "Take us down hard to eight-zero-zero feet."

"Eight-zero-zero feet, aye, Cap," COB repeated.

The planesmen pushed forward on their steering yokes, and the *Springfield*'s bow angled sharply downward. As Michaels's eyes locked on the rapidly dropping numbers of the digital depth gauge, he was forced to reach up for a handhold to keep from tumbling forward.

"Conn, sonar!" Bodzin reported jubilantly. "Sensors indicate that one of the incoming torpedoes has altered its course to bearing two-two-zero. Busy one now shows only a single fish coming down with us, range nine thousand five hundred yards and continuing to close."

Standing beside Michaels on the periscope pedestal, the XO worriedly commented, "That's one down and one to go, Skipper. Now, if we could only shake that remaining torp."

"Why not launch another MOSS?" asked Steven Collier, who had been silently watching this drama unfold from the fire-control console.

"We can't do," the XO informed him. "Our other decoys were removed to make room for your polar gear."

"Six hundred and fifty feet," reported the tense voice of the COB as he continued monitoring their descent.

The SEAL anxiously asked, "If we don't have another decoy, then how in the hell are we gonna shake that incoming torpedo?"

"Chill out, Lieutenant!" Michaels interjected. "Right now, in place of your tactical assistance, I need you to go down to my cabin and get me my football."

"Your . . . football, sir?" the perplexed SEAL repeated.

"That's right, Lieutenant, my football. Now move it, mister!"

Perez fought back the urge to laugh as he watched the

SEAL awkwardly fight the downward slope of the deck and make his way out of the forward accessway. "That should keep him out of our hair, Skipper," he said, snickering.

"Seven hundred feet," Crick reported.

"Conn, sonar, remaining torpedo continues to come down with us. Range nine thousand yards and closing."

"COB, let's try a couple of snap rolls," Michaels suggested. "We need to make this knuckle a noisy one."

"A couple of snap rolls it is, Cap," Crick replied.

As the planesmen began a series of sharp turns, *Springfield* sliced through the depths. The hull canted over hard on its sides, and the crew had to hang on tightly to keep from falling all over themselves. The sole purpose of this drastic maneuver was to leave an agitated column of seawater in their wake. Its results became apparent with Bodzin's next update.

"Conn, sonar. Torpedo range eight thousand yards and continuing to close."

"Seven hundred and eighty feet, Cap," Crick added.

"Take us up to two hundred feet, COB! Full angle on the bow planes," Michaels ordered.

The planesmen yanked back on their yokes, and the *Springfield* sharply pulled out of its descent and began a steep climb toward the surface. Again the crew grabbed for their handholds, the force of gravity now pulling them sharply backward.

Steven Collier picked this inopportune moment to emerge from the forward accessway. His rigid body was bent at an unnatural angle, and the SEAL had to fight his way into the control room, with the requested leather pigskin tight in his grip. He handed off the football to Michaels just as the next sonar update arrived.

"Conn, sonar, torpedo is coming up with us. Range seven thousand yards."

"Six hundred and fifty feet," the COB added.

Michaels appeared to be deep in thought as he pressed the football up against his left shoulder. Beside him, his XO's concern was evident.

"It doesn't look like we're gonna have time to leave another knuckle, Skipper," Perez whispered.

"There's no way that torpedo is wire-guided," Michaels muttered. "Which means it's homing in solely on our acoustic signature."

"Then all this racket we're makin' in the water is only servin' to show our hand that much more," Collier concluded.

"So it is, Lieutenant," Michaels returned, his expression suddenly taking on a look of enlightenment. "I think it's time to pull one right out of the academy's playbook and call the ol' screen pass. COB, all stop! Scram the reactor! For all effective purposes, *Springfield*'s about to become a noiseless black hole!"

Inside *Ice Wolf*'s control room, all attention was focused on the bearded sonarman. The senior technician was huddled over his console, his headphones relaying the assortment of sounds that his repeater screen was displaying visually.

"I don't believe that the enemy salvo can locate us, Captain. The acoustic intercept receiver indicates that the two torpedoes have just gone active."

"It's Alberich!" Gunther concluded as he stood directly behind the sonarman. "With our bubbler fully engaged and our throttle open wide, there's no way they can get a definite lock on us."

"I wonder how our own attack is going?" Kromer inquired.

Gunther shrugged. "Who can say, Number One? With all that racket the enemy is leaving in their wake as they vainly attempt to escape our fish, the only sign of success will be an exploding warhead and the sound of their hull imploding."

"Captain Hartmann," a weary voice from behind suddenly called out.

Both Gunther and his second in command turned and

saw the familiar, grease-covered figure who had just emerged from the aft hatchway.

"What is it, Chief Schwedler?" Gunther worriedly asked.

The Shadow shook his blackened head grimly. "Sir, I realize the precariousness of our situation. But I'm having a most difficult time providing both full tactical speed and a one-hundred-percent operation of the bubbler. Our fuel-cell capacity has dropped well below fifty percent, and the bubbler's aerator coils are showing signs of overheating."

Gunther sighed heavily. "I wish I had better news for you, Chief. But as long as those two fish remain on our tail, you're just going to have to squeeze out as much power as possible. Surely we have enough juice left in the can to outperform those torpedoes."

"I show a flashing red light on Alberich!" the concerned voice of Otto Brauer interrupted from the diving console.

"It's the bubbler!" the senior sonarman added. "We're losing the bubbler!"

A pained whimper escaped the Shadow's grease-stained lips, and he rushed back into the engine room to attend to this malfunction. Meanwhile Gunther was faced with the all-but-impossible task of compensating for this loss.

"Take us down, Chief!" he ordered. "Until the bubbler's completely back on-line, our only hope lies in the channel's protective depths."

Back in *Ice Wolf*'s aft torpedo room, this sudden depth change caught the compartment's two elderly occupants by complete surprise. As the hull steeply angled downward by the bow, Wolfram was thrown forward, and the spear point he had been tightly holding went clattering to the steel deck.

The angle of the dive increased, and Heinrich looked on in horror as the spear point began sliding toward the forward bulkhead. He jerked his body forward and instinctively reached out to grab the sacred talisman.

"Careful, Heinrich!" Wolfram yelled as he righted himself. "Don't break the circle's plane!"

This frantic warning was delivered just as Heinrich managed to grab the base of the spear point, which was dangerously close to sliding across the thin chalk line. Heinrich's relief was short-lived, though, as he grasped the talisman and viewed the white chalk that colored the side of his hand.

"My God, Wolfram, I broke the circle!"

The deck began shaking so violently that their candle toppled over, its flame mysteriously snuffed out before it landed. Even the music stopped abruptly, in the midst of the pealing church bells that signaled Parsifal's transfiguration.

"What does this all mean?" Heinrich asked, his voice tinged with dread.

Wolfram stared out into the blackness, a look of utter horror etched on his face. "It's Michael!" he screamed. "It's the archangel—he's coming for us through the circle's breach!"

"I don't understand it," Otto Brauer muttered as he stared out at the constant red light on his console. "The panel shows Alberich to be no longer operational."

"That's affirmative," the senior sonarman concurred. "The bubbler has completely failed, and both torpedoes are now coming down with us. Range one thousand yards and continuing to close."

"Fuel-cell capacity down to seven percent and rapidly dropping," the dejected voice of Klaus Schiffer added.

Gunther caught his second in command's worried glance, and sighed. In a voice filled with resignation, he said, "Well, Karl, it appears that the rebirth of the Reich will just have to wait a bit longer. . . . See you in Valhalla, my friend."

EPILOGUE

It was Laurie who informed Jacob of *Ice Wolf*'s demise. The American woman had briefly joined her countrymen in the control room, where they were celebrating the destruction of the so-called pirate submarine with a chorus of relieved cheers. Before they allowed her to leave the compartment, she was asked to touch a football they were passing around for luck, and after happily complying with their request, she headed for Jacob's berth to share the good news with him.

Her joy was evident as she described the events leading up to the enemy submarine's sinking, including a detailed report of the *Springfield*'s own close brush with disaster. It seemed that they had come very close to taking a torpedo salvo themselves. And even after this threat passed, the failure of their reactor to start caused more concern; in the end, they had had to break through the ice and utilize a backup diesel engine called Clyde to get their nuclear plant back on-line. The *Springfield* was currently heading back to the Antarctic coastline to assist the crippled British submarine.

Jacob was surprised to learn that Laurie intended to return to the American base at McMurdo to continue her work on the frozen continent. As she left him to pass the news of the *Ice Wolf*'s sinking to Viktor and Andrei, he lay back on his mattress, feeling as if a great weight had been removed from his body. With Laurie's report still ringing in his ears, he picked up the photos he had been studying. The Grail, the Spear of Destiny, the copper plates—these relics were now gone forever.

And then there was the man who had collected these antiquities. Was it really true that Wolfram Eckhardt was no more? Was Jacob's long quest for justice indeed over? The answers to these questions lay scattered on the floor of the polar sea. And Jacob realized that the tortured souls of his parents, his sister, and the millions of innocent beings killed because of Wolfram Eckhardt's warped teachings were finally free.

The extent of Eckhardt's depravity had only become clear to Jacob during his careful study of the nine photographs of the copper scroll, and the results of his hasty translation turned out to be even more shocking than he had anticipated. The sister scroll he had discovered in the Judean wilderness did little to prepare him for the *Rite of Awakening*. Now that the original had been destroyed, Jacob found himself in possession of the only copy of a ritual recorded at the very beginning of time.

Documented in the nine photographs that he held in his shaking hands was the sequence of acts and the liturgical accompaniment to a black mass, a rite whose sole purpose was to call forth the demon known as Lucifer, the Day Star, the Fallen One. This was the identity of Wolfram Eckhardt's true mentor, and Jacob was aware of how effectively the German had used the ritual to possess the soul of an entire nation!

Having spent more than enough years of his life

bringing this evil to justice, Jacob knew that only one course of action remained for him now. Resolute, he climbed out of his berth, grabbed the photographs and their negatives, and in a most deliberate, almost ritualistic fashion, proceeded to drop them into the boat's shredder.

As far as Jacob Litvak was concerned, some secrets were better left buried.

MORE THAN FRIENDS
Barbara Delinsky

The Maxwells and the Popes are two families whose lives are interwoven like the threads of a beautiful, yet ultimately delicate, tapestry. When their idyllic lives are unexpectedly shattered by one event, their faith in each other — and in themselves — is put to the supreme test.

"Intriguing women's fiction." — *Publishers Weekly*

CITY OF GOLD
Len Deighton

Amid the turmoil of World War II, Rommel's forces in Egypt relentlessly advance across the Sahara aided by ready access to Allied intelligence. Sent to Cairo on special assignment, Captain Bert Cutler's mission is formidable: whatever the risk, whatever the cost, he must catch Rommel's spy.

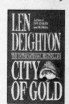

"Wonderful." — *Seattle Times/Post-Intelligencer*

DEATH PENALTY
William J. Coughlin

Former hot-shot attorney Charley Sloan gets a chance to resurrect his career with the case of a lifetime — an extortion scam that implicates his life-long mentor, a respected judge. Battling against inner demons and corrupt associates, Sloan's quest for the truth climaxes in one dramatic showdown of justice.

"Superb!"
— *The Detroit News*